City of Night

NIGHTFALL - BOOK 2

October K Santerelli

To Venessa.
You have been a huge force for good and community in the writing world.
Especially for me.

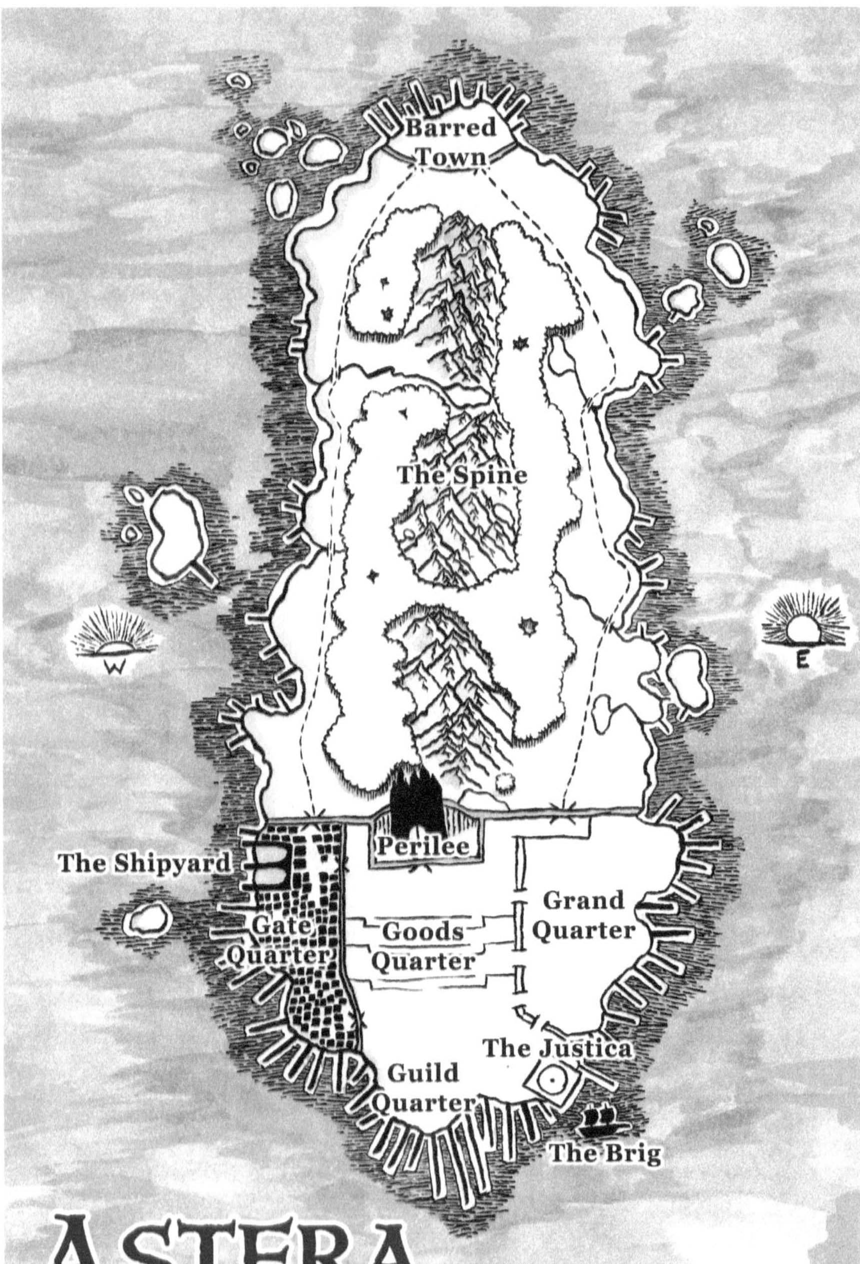

Barred Town
The Spine
W
E
The Shipyard
Perilee
Gate Quarter
Goods Quarter
Grand Quarter
Guild Quarter
The Justica
The Brig
ASTERA

1

P*ap. Pap. Pap.*

Water dripped off Thislen's dampened black hair, sliding down the coiled wet waves to land on the back of his hand. Each breath came in a ragged gasp. His head lolled. Beads of water coalesced and ran races down his bare chest, trailing around a mottled mess of bruises. His fingers, curled around the seat's arms, tightened until they ached. His wrists chafed beneath the thick leather straps that held him fast.

Pap. Pap. Pap.

Lord Soren, Thislen's captor, sighed heavily from where he leaned against the wall of the ship's small cabin. His doublet, embroidered in silver thread, glittered in the low light of a single lantern overhead.

"I'm running out of patience, Garridan. Make him talk."

Garridan Artaith dried his hands with a cloth, studying the heavy iron implements spread on his workbench. "I'm working on it."

"If you go into another lecture on how torture is an art, I swear—"

"Soren, will you let me work?" Exasperation crept into the edges of Garridan's words.

Soren lifted his hands with a shrug. He didn't say another word.

They had argued before. In fact, they argued every night Soren came to watch his friend work. The esteemed Lord Bestant, high-ranking member of the Ruling Council, wanted answers from his cousin. He wanted to know Thislen's lineage, how much he knew about the Bestants, their secrets, and the Vaim. He was most curious about what the pendants he'd stolen from Thislen and his friends were for. Therefore, wresting answers from the thief was Garridan's priority.

Thislen hadn't given them any.

"Now, don't get me wrong, Thislen," Garridan said. "I'm impressed you've lasted so long. Most people don't."

Twenty-seven days, Thislen thought. Nearly a moon passed in captivity in the bowels of *Ship Artaith*. Every night, the guards dragged him from his cell and Garridan 'questioned' him. It started with fists. Once his body was littered with bruises and he remained silent, Garridan stepped it up. He'd burned Thislen with hot irons, the black and red scabs of which cracked and bled on his side. Now, they were on to worse. Over and over, Garridan put clinging cloth over Thislen's face, holding it tight and pouring water over it until he couldn't breathe, until he was choking, until his lungs burned. He was drowning on land.

Thislen lived an unending nightmare—and not just of the flesh.

"Hold on, Thislen," whispered a voice in his ear.

A shudder coursed down his spine. He lifted his dark gaze to the tortures of his mind. In the shadows, made darker by the swinging glow of the single lantern overhead, he could make out the half-formed figures of his personal ghosts. He couldn't remember when they appeared, but now he saw them all the time.

Percivan Coppermund offered a sympathetic look, his black skin covered in dark red blood that still glittered as if it were wet. A bloom of crimson spread across his chest, staining his finely fitted doublet. More was smeared over his throat.

You died. I watched you die.

The long, claw-like fingers of the Vaim flashed in his memory. Percivan's hands over the shadowy spirit's, fingers interlaced like lovers a moment before they sank into his skin. Thislen remembered his eyes, staring sightlessly at the sky the next morning.

You died, so you can't be here.

"I am."

Percivan wasn't alone, either. Vern, the sailor from the *Bestant Belle*, stood in the corner. He dripped water, soaked through, his hair plastered to his face. His lips and fingertips were blue. His gaze never faltered, accusing and quiet.

Thislen could almost hear his pleading, agonized question. *Why?*

Why are you even here? Anger warmed his shivering body as he scowled at the ghosts, dropping his head. Neither of them was the spirit he expected to see, the one he waited for.

Mila.

What happened to Mila?

His gaze drifted to his hand. He watched each drop of water burst apart against his skin. It was easier to hold on if he didn't look at the affable round face of the nobleman before him, easier to stay quiet.

Breathe. Just breathe.

The scent of stale water and wet wood filled the air. The half full barrel beside the table sloshed, the bucket floating inside clunking against the edge; the cloth draped over its lip dripping.

"Garridan," Soren said, drawing out the word.

"I know, I know." Garridan closed his eyes and took a deep breath.

Seems his patience for his friend is running low. Not that it would help Thislen.

Garridan sighed heavily. "I thought you might be like this, Thislen." He turned to his table.

"Use the pliers," Soren suggested, leaning in.

"Not yet."

"I don't want to waste much more time on this. I have better things to do." Soren tossed his golden curls.

"Leave me to it, then. I'll let you know when he's feeling talkative. I know what I'm doing, Soren."

Soren folded his arms over his chest and made no move to leave. "Fine. Do it, then."

Thislen fought a bitter smile. They'd take it the wrong way and redouble their efforts. He learned early the more miserable he looked, the slower things escalated. Every part of him ached or throbbed in time with his racing pulse.

Garridan took his time. The slow rise of panic in Thislen's chest made the walls lean in, threatening to fall and crush him. His ragged breath caught in his chest, stuck beneath his sternum.

"Breathe, Thislen. Just breathe," Percivan's spirit urged softly.

Thislen forced himself to inhale.

"You're leaving me no choice, you know. I've done my best to be kind, but clearly Soren's patience is running out. Not just for you, either. For both of us." The torturer held a pair of heavy iron pliers up to the light, inspecting them.

Soren's eyes gleamed, an eager grin twisting his face into a mad mask.

"As much as I regret it, I'll have to move on to other methods."

"What, fists and water not working?" Thislen croaked, the words a hoarse but brazen challenge, "What a surprise. Maybe there's nothing to learn."

It was bravado, a desperate bluff—*and we both know it.* Thislen had precious little left inside him. Little hope. Little strength. He felt he might snap with the slightest push, as if he were a rope breaking one frayed fiber at a time. Another thread gave way with every blow, and he didn't know how many were left. All it would take was a push in the right place and—

And there was no end in sight. The ship creaked around them, loud in the silence. Garridan savored each tool in his kit, running his fingers over them fondly. Spiked wheels, mallets, pliers, knives, irons in a bowl of coals.

Thislen's heart pounded, as trapped beneath his ribs as he was in his chair. It was effective, the way Garridan wielded fear as another tool in his arsenal. The waiting, guessing, and anticipation were agonizing.

"At least you found Soren?" The ghost of Percivan crossed the room to study his murderer, who was oblivious to his presence.

He killed you, now he's killing me. Thislen's chest was aflame. How much water had he coughed up?

"You can survive. I believe in you." Percivan forced a weak, worried smile.

Garridan chose his words delicately as he selected a small, round-headed hammer. He hefted it and held it up to the light. "You are being very brave—but it's time for answers. I'll ask you one last time before we get...serious."

Thislen lifted his head. It took monumental effort, but he put on a show as he stuck out his chin and steadied his gaze.

How much longer can I hold out? The question had haunted him for days as he was pushed ever closer to that looming breaking point. He could feel it like a yawning precipice at his feet. How far would he fall?

Garridan sat on the table, foot swinging idly. He toyed with the hammer, spinning it, hefting it, testing his grip. "Did you truly steal a fishing boat with our guests?"

Tamsa and Aften are 'guests' the way I'm 'family.' The pair were prisoners, locked away, and the only reason they hadn't been subjected to the same treatment as Thislen was because he hadn't broken yet. They weren't fisherfolk, as Tamsa claimed. They were the children of Rendyn Sivivan, head of the Night Council. That Night Council shouldn't exist, because everyone knew no one could survive on the island of Astera at night. The Vaim would murder anyone left on land after the sun set—or so the stories went.

Thislen couldn't break. The siblings sharing his cell would be as good as dead. He'd expose the existence of the Nattfolk, and they'd been kind to him and Mila. He couldn't betray them. He couldn't fail them.

Garridan leaned forward. "What were you and Mila Ominir trying to steal?"

Thislen stared at his hand. He pulled as much strength from this brief respite as he could. Whatever came next, it would hurt.

The vial. We were trying to steal the vial. A tiny bottle of a plague-like poison concocted by the court mage who created the Vaim hundreds of years ago.

"Your mother was Elena Bestant, my father's second wife and Soren's aunt, but I don't know anything about your father. Tell me about him. What was his name?"

Thislen gritted his teeth. Not a word fell from his lips.

"He and Elena were in love?"

Silence.

"How did they meet?"

Like I'd tell you.

Garridan sighed heavily. "I really hate to do this."

No, you don't.

Soren smirked over Garridan's shoulder as the torturer slid off the table, boots thudding on the wooden floor of the ship. He circled the chair, a thoughtful look on his face. Thislen squirmed.

The first blow came from behind. The round head of the hammer hit Thislen's hip with a sickening crunch. A hoarse cry rent the air a moment before a wave of agony rolled over him and left him reeling in his seat. His head spun. His ears rang. His chest burned.

His hip was a blaze of pain radiating all the way through him.

"Tell me *something*, Thislen. At least confirm the story your friends told me. No? I'm sure they'll be much easier to talk to than you are. Should I ask them?"

No! Cold dread in his stomach warred with the heat of spreading pain up his side and down his leg. *Not Tamsa, not Aften. Don't hurt them, please don't hurt them.*

Thislen failed to save Percivan Coppermund. He murdered Vern. He was helpless when they dragged Mila away. He wouldn't, he *couldn't* fail Tamsa and Aften. The lies Tamsa told when they were captured were the only thing protecting them. Soren Bestant and his two cronies believed they were useless nobodies.

If they were tortured, eventually they'd break and the Nattfolk would suffer. The Nattfolk were innocent and blissfully unaware of the curse of the Vaim, the ghost of Ninian Ominir, the vial, and the plan to steal it. They weren't part of this. There were children in their underground city. There were elders.

Tamsa lied to protect her people, throwing him and Mila to the wolves in nobles' clothing. Though Thislen fought not to care, he did.

I care about them because my friends care about them.

Little over a month ago, he didn't have friends. Now, he would do anything for them. Including enduring weeks of torture.

The hammer came down again, and this time he saw it coming. His knee crackled beneath the metal. Sparks of pain arced through his body like lightning. He shouted hoarsely, leg spasming and only making it worse.

"Anything to say?" Garridan yanked Thislen's head up by the hair.

The pain made him nauseous. Thislen knew he couldn't take another blow. Not just for his bones, but for his sanity.

His tormentor let go and lifted the hammer again.

"Wait. Wait!" Thislen clutched at the arms of the chair until the wood bit into his fingers.

Garridan paused, a brow lifting. Without a word, he lowered the hammer and leaned against the table, arms folded. He looked for all the world like he was about to discuss the weather or what to have for tea. Soren, in contrast, leaned forward like a hound on a tether that caught a scent.

Thislen let the silence hang, his mind racing. He had to give something away—but whatever it was, it had to be good enough. Good enough to end this for the night. Good enough to save him.

Soren's brow furrowed. He was running out of patience. Garridan glanced at his friend. It was perverse how soft and sympathetic his expression could be, as if the torturer actually had a heart. Garridan's hand rested on the table beside the hammer, fingers stretching toward it in a silent threat.

"Linden. My father's name was Linden."

Thislen didn't know why he chose that. Perhaps because it seemed safest. It was meaningless. Linden was dead, and the Ruling Council couldn't hurt him. Lord Soren Bestant, Lord Judge Avasten Barnweir, and young Lord Garridan Artaith couldn't reach him.

"Linden?" Soren scoffed.

"Linden what? What is your surname?" The table creaked as Garridan leaned forward.

The lantern light swung gently back and forth, back and forth with the waves. The ghosts stared intently from the shifting shadows, eyes boring into him. They waited.

Say it, a voice inside him urged.

Thislen's name hovered on his lips—but that would give away too much of himself. He couldn't do it.

"I don't know his surname," he lied. "My father gave me Elena's so I could have a better future. He called me Thislen Bestant."

"He can't do that," Soren snapped.

"He did it anyway. What does it matter? I don't use it. I don't use any surname."

"Did he know?" Soren pushed away from the wall, pacing in front of Thislen. "When he met my aunt, did he know who she was?"

Thislen clenched his jaw, hollow gaze following the nobleman's path. He couldn't see why it mattered. He weighed his options, eyes fixed on the hammer as Garridan's fingers played along the handle.

"Yes. He knew."

Soren's pacing stopped. He crossed the room and planted his hands over Thislen's wrists, leaning in until his cloying perfume threatened to choke him. "How did they meet?"

"He never told me."

Garridan dragged the metal head of the hammer across the table as he picked it up. Soren gave him room.

A spike of icy panic lanced through Thislen like a blow. "I swear, he never told me!"

Garridan tapped the head of the hammer on his palm thoughtfully, then nodded. "I believe him, Soren."

Soren waved a hand dismissively. "Fine, then. Where is Linden now?"

This isn't fair. He shifted in his seat, regretting it immediately as his hip and knee made their agony known again. He could still picture his father's back as the man walked away, never to be seen again. He heard his own thin, reedy voice as a child calling after him. He didn't want to tell these people about his pain, his loss.

He didn't have a choice.

"Dead." The word was empty and faint.

At least I still have the ring. He felt it, tucked into the heel of his boot, pressing into his skin. It was his treasure, the only thing his father left him. He'd been lucky they hadn't taken off his shoes—yet. *I should give it to Tamsa before they do.*

"That seems like enough for one night, hm?" Garridan dropped the hammer among his tools with a clatter and a heavy *clunk*.

"I have more questions," Soren said.

"You said if I told you something, we would stop. I told you plenty. This isn't what you promised!" Thislen hated the desperate, pleading edge to his words. His stomach twisted in knots. *I can't take any more. I can't do this.*

Garridan shrugged, picking up a small knife. "Go ahead, Soren. Try something gentle now that he's talking. One little question at a time, yes?"

Thislen's breathing grew unsteady, a shudder running through him. After everything Garridan did with a cloth and a hammer, he didn't want that knife anywhere near him.

Soren looked imperiously down his nose at his cousin, a brow raised. "Who told you about Percivan Coppermund?"

Percivan's head shot up, staring at Soren's back in surprise. The question summoned forth a sliver of memory. Thislen knew the nobleman for mere minutes. He lifted the other end of a rowboat, standing sweat-drenched in his fine clothes. "*It's getting dark, and I've missed my boat,*" Percivan whispered in the back of Thislen's mind.

Another memory—his hand wrapped around Thislen's like a vice, hard enough to bruise. They stood at the water's edge, one foot on the lip of the tiny vessel that would save them. The ghosts rose from the ground, boiling to life, and they knew. They knew it was too late.

Dark hands pressed into Percivan's chest and throat while the black malformed shadow with its glowing red eyes cradled him close. Blood flowed dark and fast.

"*Find Soren, he—*" The words echoed in Thislen's head.

Percivan's ghost reached out, resting his hand on Thislen's arm. It weighed nothing. He couldn't feel it.

Thislen jerked away from the phantom, turning his gaze to the wall. He was trembling. *You wanted me to find him, and I did. That's how I got into this mess. What did you want? Did you think I could bring him to justice? Look how well that turned out.*

"I'm sorry," Percivan whispered. His presence didn't diminish.

What else can I do?

Pressure drew along his side, followed by the sensation of warm, sticky liquid running down his skin. The searing pain came after. Thislen shouted, twisting in his bonds as much as they allowed.

Garridan held up the knife, the edge now stained with blood. "Who told you about Percivan Coppermund?" he repeated.

"Percivan," Thislen gasped. "Percivan told me himself, before the Vaim killed him. He told me about Soren."

It wasn't a lie, but it wasn't the whole truth. A pang of guilt ran through him. The truth was, he had snuck aboard Soren's ship, the *Bestant Belle*, in the night and listened as he bragged about the murder with his co-conspirators.

"There, that wasn't so hard, was it?" Garridan smiled, leaning in to pat his prisoner's cheek.

Thislen's chest heaved. He turned and vomited water and bile. *No more, please. Ancestors, save me.*

His silent prayer was answered by a knock at the door. Garridan frowned, setting the knife down to open it.

"Are you two done yet?" Thislen recognized the oil-slick voice of Avasten Barnweir. He hadn't come to watch the proceedings often, but he always came to end them.

It was over.

For tonight.

"We were just getting somewhere, Avasten. Go away," Soren said over his shoulder, never once taking his gaze off Thislen.

"It's late, Soren, late enough that it will soon be early. I want to go back to my own ship and sleep," Avasten said sharply.

"Fine. Garridan, handle this." Soren swept from the room, off to the rowboat that would ferry him and Avasten back to their beautiful, grand ships.

"What did he say?" Avasten asked as the door swung closed.

Garridan studied Thislen. His thick brows furrowed over dark brown eyes. The tormentor's face was inscrutable—or did Thislen see a flicker of concern?

Does he know how close I am to breaking? What does he see?

Thislen tried to glare, but he was so exhausted he wasn't sure it worked.

Garridan leaned into the corridor. "You there, dress him and take him to his cell."

"Yes, sir." A guard stepped into view, dressed in the livery of House Artaith.

"Get someone to clean this up." Garridan waved a hand at the table.

"Yes, sir."

With that, the nobleman left.

Thislen sagged, his relief nearly as nauseating as the pain. His torment was over—for tonight. He fought down the lump in his throat and the sting in his eyes.

The guard wrestled with the wet leather of the belts around Thislen's wrists and ankles. Another appeared, grasping Thislen by the shoulders to restrain him. He needn't have bothered.

When his limbs were free, Thislen didn't move. He couldn't. He didn't lift his arms until they shoved his dark gray shirt over his head. When they hauled him to his feet, his leg buckled and a lance of agony ran up his entire left side. He shouted, crumpling.

They caught him under either arm, dragging him unceremoniously into the narrow corridor.

Something's wrong. It hurts, Ancestors it hurts! He couldn't walk. White hot knives stabbed through him with every step. Something must have broken.

Outside, a roll of thunder shook the heavens. The ship's swaying grew stronger. A storm was coming that matched Thislen's own black despair. Every step the guards took jostled his leg, a new torture all its own. The agony left him shivering. His stomach churned and bile coated the back of his throat; not that there was anything left to throw up.

How much worse would tomorrow be? How much worse could it get?

No more, please. I can't survive another night in that room. The secrets he held behind his teeth would be pulled out, one by one, and he would be relieved to tell.

The all-too familiar belly of *Ship Artaith* slid past as Thislen sank into an exhausted stupor. Doorways lined either side of the corridor with their locks on the outside. A set of steep stairs capped one end, and a heavy door on the other. It was through there the guards hauled Thislen.

The cabin beyond ran the width of the ship, the walls curving up to the ceiling and heavy wooden beams lining it in ribs. Half the cabin held a few tables and chairs with straps, all fastened to the floor and stained with rust-colored reds in unnatural mottled patterns. The second half was a cell—*the* cell. It was one massive set of bars and three wooden walls, as it was set against the stern.

Inside were two huddled lumps.

Thislen looked the worst of all of them, but Aften and Tamsa Sivivan were in poor shape. They were fed and watered every day, but only a little. Thislen was fed and watered just enough to stay alive. None of them had bathed. The room was rank with the stench of urine and sweat.

Tamsa's curly dark hair was a tangle. Aften's had grown long enough to cover his ear tips. Both of them bore pinched masks of misery tinged with overwhelming, unending fear. Each of them huddled beneath a thin blanket, a luxury that wasn't extended to Thislen.

True to their word, the noblemen who captured them hadn't harmed either of his friends. Yet.

The guards opened the cell door with a rattle of keys and unceremoniously swung Thislen inside. He fell with a hoarse shout, his hip and knee pulsing with sharp, jagged pain. He clenched his teeth and curled his hands into fists, but he didn't move.

The barred door clanged shut behind him, and the wooden one after that. The three of them were alone again. The quiet was painful. It dragged on, broken only by the groans of the ship in the rising storm and Thislen's ragged breath.

"Thislen?" Aften asked softly.

He didn't have the strength to answer.

The ghost of Vern the Sailor lowered itself to the deck, laying beside him. "You should sleep."

It had been twenty-seven days.

No one was coming for them.

Thislen's only hope was to spare Tamsa and Aften the same fate. *I have to save them. I have to help them escape. I can't fail them.*

I can't fail again.

He closed his eyes.

2

Aften looked from the prone, starved, and battered form of Thislen to his sister, whose face was frozen with worry and fear. Her eyes glistened in the moonlight coming through one of the portholes.

"Is he—?"

"No, he's alive. He's breathing," Tamsa said quickly.

"They're killing him."

"I know."

"But he hasn't said a word about us." Aften slumped against the wall, all the fight and strength drained out of him. For a moon, he worried the thief they brought underground to the Nattfolk would have no choice but to betray them. Every night, he was proven wrong.

No torture came for Aften and his sister.

This wasn't how things were supposed to go.

When he, Mila, and Darran went to Perilee, the castle that crowned Astera's capital city, they learned of the Vaim and their curse. They made a plan to break it, and all it would take was one measly vial. It seemed so easy.

Then Tamsa came along. She always needed to be right, always knew best; the tiny perfect copy of their father. It was her interference with their plan that led to their capture. It had been working, too. They were opening the safe, and then—

Caught like fish in a net. Their capture led to Tamsa lying, weaving a story about how they were just fisherfolk, poor and stupid. She did it to save Aften's life, but that didn't make it better.

Aften shuddered, remembering being wrestled into the chair in the middle of the room, the roll of tools unfurled beside him. His gaze slid to Thislen. The thief knew how that felt better than anyone.

Tamsa rustled beside him, and he frowned. No, Tamsa's stories led to Darran and Mila being hauled away and left on the island for the ghosts to rend limb from limb. Her story took away their talismans, ancient magical pendants that hid them from the Vaim. It took Darran's, and he needed it to protect himself from the curse, from the Coppermund blood that ran in his veins.

Darran was dead.

It was a simple fact, one that struck Aften far harder than he ever thought possible. He was dead, and they would never see each other again.

I loved him, and now he's gone.

And Aften never told the scout captain how he felt.

For weeks, he said nothing to his sister. Resentment and grief warred inside him, and neither side won. The worse things got with Thislen, however, the more the siblings spoke, worrying in whispers. They were both Nattfolk, after all. Their way of life was at risk.

Aften hadn't forgiven her by any stretch of the imagination, and he wasn't sure he ever would.

It's only until we're free of here, however that looks, he told himself repeatedly.

It would be more believable if they had a plan to escape. They plotted when Thislen was taken, hunting for any chance—but their wrists and ankles were bound in heavy iron cuffs, and they weren't fed enough to keep strong. Aften was exhausted. He couldn't imagine how Thislen felt. How would they get the thief to safety, too? He could hardly move.

I wonder what they're doing to him.

Three nights in a row now, Thislen slipped out of consciousness when he was brought back to the cell. His breath rasped in a way Aften didn't like, as though he were falling ill. And now, tonight, his gray shirt was stained with blood in a long, splotchy line down one side.

Understandably, Thislen didn't talk about his torture. That didn't make Aften any less curious. If he knew, maybe he could help more. If Thislen felt like he could share, maybe the thief would never break. It wouldn't be Thislen's fault. The noblemen were tearing the secrets from his skin. Slow outrage built up inside Aften day after day, watching what the power-mad Ruling Council of the Solfolk did to their people.

What sort of world is it if those in power can torture those who have none, and get away with it? Who takes pleasure in these methods, in holding people hostage, starving them, beating them, and whatever else?

Monsters. That's who.

In the back of his mind, another thought took root. He tried to ignore it, but its creeping tendrils wove ever further through his consciousness.

Will we ever get out of here? Is this where we die?

Aften shuddered, squeezing his eyes shut.

He clung to the thinnest thread of hope like a lifeline. Even if his father forbade it, he believed someone would come for them. Anyone. They had to. He wrung the fraying thread in his heart, knowing...

Knowing what? Look how long it's been. No one is coming. You're on your own.

It snapped. Aften huddled miserably against the ship wall, fighting overwhelming waves of despair.

Outside, thunder tore the sky in two.

Thislen woke to a crack of thunder and a rolling sway of the ship that threatened to slide him into a wall. How long had it been? The last of his strength ran out, and he'd sunk into the black oblivion of unconsciousness. He couldn't fight it.

Just woke up, and I'm already exhausted.

He wished he could roll over and sleep, but he didn't dare. These days, he was plagued by nightmares every time he closed his eyes. The ghosts, his father, and Perilee swirled in his mind in a tangle, bound with angry red eyes and licking flames.

Thislen sluggishly lifted his head.

Through the small portholes set high in the sides of the ship, he could see the dark velvet sky of night, turned silver when lightning lit up the heavy clouds. The storm grew. The wood shuddered around them, their vessel battered by the sea.

Aften huddled against the wall, eyes closed and breathing deep and even. *Asleep, then.*

Tamsa sat, pushing the edge of her rough blanket through her fingers, her gaze on the tiny sliver of sky.

Slowly, Thislen rolled over and dragged his arms underneath his chest. He gritted his teeth as he hauled himself the few feet to Tamsa's side. Moving set every bruise throbbing and cracked the congealed blood on his side. Worse, it sent stabbing knives of pain through his knee and hip. He choked back a groan, regretting he moved at all.

Her hazel eyes never left him, though her expression didn't change. The crease between her brows might have become permanent.

Thislen slumped beside her, using the last of his strength to roll onto his back. He couldn't move another inch for all the freedom in the world.

Percivan's ghost stared down at him.

Go away, he begged, draping his arm over his eyes.

Tamsa shed her blanket, wrestling her cuffs to drape it over him. The rattle of the chains was louder and more jarring than the violent crash of thunder overhead.

Thislen could barely manage a grateful nod. A chill settled in the cabin, or maybe just in him. It sank deep into his bones like creeping frost.

"Are you alright?" Tamsa asked. "I mean, I know you aren't, but..."

"I know what you mean." Thislen's voice was barely audible over the creaking timbers that surrounded them. They were on the lowest deck of *Ship Artaith*. He prayed it was sound, with no holes or rotted wood, so he wouldn't drown.

But wouldn't that be a relief?

"Are you?" she repeated, softer than before.

He grunted, gaze roaming over the ceiling. Flickering lightning made it flash before his eyes. "Is he still upset with you?"

"Aften? I don't know if he'll ever forgive me." Tamsa's studied the huddled shape of her brother. "I don't blame him. We don't know what happened to Darran and Mila, but they aren't here. Aften says...Aften says the ghost in Perilee said Darran would die without his pendant?"

The ghost was Ninian Ominir, court magician to the last king of Astera. The mage died hundreds of years ago, placing a curse on the island. The twisted, malformed monsters that killed residents of the kingdom were his creation. The Vaim were souls of those long dead, tethered to his magic and his revenge. The spell kept his spirit alive so long as the curse was intact.

"I wouldn't know what he said. I was asleep."

Thislen had been bespelled by Ninian after the Vaim dragged him into the castle, waking a day later when Mila pleaded for his release.

"Aften and I are talking, barely. When we need to." Tamsa pulled her battered tin cup away from the wall and held it out. "Here, I saved you some water."

"He thinks Darran is dead," Thislen said, propping himself on an elbow with monumental effort. His lungs burned from his torture, but his mouth was dry. The stagnant water tasted of tin. He drank every drop.

"He might be."

Thislen nodded. It was true; Darran was likely dead.

Like Mila.

"You don't look so good."

Thislen tried to laugh, but all that came out was a half-hearted scoff as he sank back to the floor. Tamsa took the cup.

"I don't feel so good," he admitted.

"Are they...are you..."

"I haven't told them anything."

"That wasn't what I was going to say."

Thislen closed his eyes. "I don't want to talk about what they're doing. Please."

Tamsa fell silent. After a few minutes she spoke again, the words a whisper. "Thank you. Thank you for protecting my people. You're so much stronger than I thought. When we first met, I assumed you were the worst kind of Solfolk. I thought, 'look at him, so soft and full of his own cleverness.'"

The day Thislen and Mila faced their execution felt like a thousand years ago, the terror faded away to almost nothing in the wake of all that followed. It was all just one more part of Before. Before this ship, before this cell, before this unending, terrible dream. He hardly remembered the desperate flight through the city, the confusion as the Vaim simply stared, the stunning shock of discovering the Nattfolk. Tamsa's waspish remarks were just a dim memory.

"To be fair, I'm very clever." The joke fell flat. *I'm too tired.*

Or it was another frayed fragment of himself that he could never put back together, a shred of sanity lost to another night in this place, another day.

"You grow on people. You're a good person, Thislen."

He hoped that was true. He ran his tongue over cracked lips. "Have you and Aften come up with anything?"

"What?"

"For your plan to escape."

"How did you know—?"

"It's what I would do, knowing they'd be too busy to overhear me when they were...working."

Aften and Tamsa were plotting their escape. He didn't believe they would figure anything out, but it gave them something to do. It gave them a reason to speak. He couldn't begrudge them that slim hope. Someone had to have some, and his was gone.

"We're working out how to pick the locks." Tamsa turned her wrists, studying the keyholes on the iron manacles. "Aften thinks you could help us, if you can grab a knife or something, something small and metal."

From the table, she meant. It flashed through his mind like a blow. The table full of gleaming instruments, waiting to cause pain no matter what their purpose had been before. He saw the glint of the hammer as it swung toward his knee, a ripple of agony racing up his leg. His nails pressed into his palms. Bound, helpless, as hammers, knives, and pliers pranced before him, each promising more pain than the last. His chest felt tight, as if he were caught beneath a boulder, crushing him until he couldn't breathe. He choked, staring at the ceiling, willing the images to disappear.

Lightning flashed. The world went silver, then black.

She doesn't know what she's asking. I don't want to go back in there. I can't. I can't risk worse, either. If they catch me trying to break them out, Soren will suspect there's more to Tamsa and Aften's story, and he might...

No, it wasn't a matter of wanting to protect them. It was a matter of need. He needed them to be safe. It was the only thing that kept him from shattering and spilling every thought that crossed his mind.

More than that, he needed this to come to an end, one way or another.

Another thread snapped, fraying away into nothing.

Thislen huddled under the blanket. "I can't promise anything."

"But you'll try?"

No. His heart sank. "I'll keep an eye out," he hedged, hating himself for it. They wanted his help, but he wasn't strong enough. Not on his own. There were too many secrets behind his teeth. If he told the Ruling Council one, the others might come tumbling after.

Silence hung between them. Thislen drifted into a half doze where the pain he suffered was muted and distant, as though it belonged to someone else.

"Thislen?"

Tamsa's voice wasn't enough to pull him from that comfortable, floating place, but he grunted. *What is it?*

"Your mother, Elena Bestant. Did you know her?"

That was enough to make him stir, cracking an eye open. He traced the beams of the ceiling while he mulled over his answer. "Sometimes I think I remember what she smelled like, when I catch a whiff of the right perfume. That's all, though. My father said she left when I was small, not long after I was weaned."

"Why?"

"To get money from her family. She thought if she were married with a child, they couldn't take us away from her. She was wrong." *Horribly wrong. They married her off again and locked her in a tower, and she went mad and died.*

Tamsa was quiet, angling her head to stare out the porthole. The ship lurched softly beneath them. The thunder rumbled in the distance as the storm moved away. A bell clanged somewhere nearby. It was nearly dawn. Soon, all the ships would return to the docks of Astera after their long night out at sea. Fall was well on its way out, winter was creeping in, and the time between sunset and sunrise felt like an age.

"Aften and I lost our mother when he was small," Tamsa said. "I still remember her. I remember her hands in my hair, braiding it. I remember how her hugs felt. And, same as you, how she smelled. Like cedar chips, the kind she put in with our clothes so they wouldn't get musty."

"I remember things like that about my father." Thislen closed his eyes, picturing Linden. His big hand, planted in the middle of Thislen's back as he steered him through a crowd. His booming laugh and his broad smile. His infectious desire to make the most of every moment.

"Come on, Thislen, or we'll be late."

"Late to what? We aren't going anywhere."

"All the more reason to be on time for our next adventure. Don't want to miss it."

"But we're just going to the market to get breakfast!" Thislen tugged on his father's hand, and the man turned a smile down to him.

He took after his father, sharing the same dark wavy hair and dark eyes and tanned skin. Linden scooped Thislen up, planting him firmly on his shoulders. Both of them were grinning then.

"Whether to the market or the unknown, we have to be three things, right? Do you remember what they are?"

"We have to be careful." Thislen held up one finger.

"Right." Linden lifted a finger as well.

"We have to be wise." Up went a second.

"That's two."

"And we have to be strong!" He held three fingers in the air, laughing as his father gave enthusiastic, exaggerated nods of his head that threatened to topple Thislen from his perch.

"Exactly. Everybody should have these traits, but us most of all. Everything we do will affect another life. Even a trip to the market is important, for the merchants and our stomachs both!"

Thislen laughed again, hugging Linden's head with both arms. "So we should buy extra breakfast."

"That sounds like an excellent plan." As they walked, Linden's smile faded and his expression grew solemn. Thislen quieted. Every time his father got like this, it

was important. "We're going to be alright, Thislen. No matter what happens in the future, we'll make it through. Remember that. We have to make it through."

Thislen failed to be careful when he helped Mila escape the marriage proposal of Lord Soren Bestant, drawing the attention of the Ruling Council. Wise he had abandoned when Mila asked him to rob the *Bestant Belle* of the vial that could break the curse, and he agreed.

Strong, he was losing now.

We have to make it through, Linden's voice repeated.

I'm trying, I swear.

"Thislen?" Tamsa's hand appeared, reaching toward him.

He flinched, breath catching in his chest.

Tamsa froze. "I'm sorry," she breathed. "I'm so sorry. I just wanted to see if you have a fever. You really don't look good."

Thislen shuddered. "It's fine."

It wasn't. He thought she meant to grab his hair, to hurt him. How deep did the damage go beyond his body? How much had he changed in twenty-seven days? When he began this journey, he was confident and lonely. Now there was so much to protect, and more people added themselves to that list with alarming frequency. Soon, he wouldn't be able to ignore who he was, what he could do. Soon he might—

"Distract me," he blurted.

"What?"

"Distract me. Just start talking. Please."

"I can't stop thinking about my father," Tamsa said quickly. "I was so proud of how much he liked me, how much responsibility he was willing to give me. I was ready to push Aften away to keep his affection all to myself. But it was all a trick."

"Because he was playing you against one another?"

"Yes, and the way he did it...I wanted so badly not to be in Aften's shoes that I forced myself into the mold he wanted for me. But I don't want to lead."

I know how that feels. Thislen spent his life avoiding being noticed, avoiding other people, so he wouldn't have to make decisions that affected anyone but himself. With Mila, he stepped into the role easily—and failed her so terribly, he never wanted to do it again.

I've learned my lessons. When my father left me, when they dragged Mila away. Every action has a consequence, and it's best if those consequences affect me and only me.

"I don't want to be in charge, either. It's never turned out well for me," he said aloud.

Tamsa tentatively rested her hand on his shoulder. He closed his eyes, savoring the gentle touch.

"I used to love it," she laughed. "Giving orders and watching people jump to follow them. I was drunk on it, and it was stupid. They only listened because of the unspoken threat of my father's wrath, not because they wanted to or trusted me. He twisted me up until all that mattered was being just like him, where everything I said was absolute. If I hadn't been so concerned with being his heir, I wouldn't have been caught up in being right. I never would have come after all of you like I did. You might have gotten whatever it was you wanted to steal, with no one the wiser."

"A vial."

"That's it? A single vial?"

"According to Ninian, yes."

"What's so special about one vial?"

Thislen opened his eyes. It got harder every time. "Inside that vial is a magical toxin created by an alchemist. It replicates a plague. After someone contracts it, they can pass it like one, too. Ninian wants the vial back so it can never happen again. Then he'll break the curse."

There were only three ways to shatter the spell that summoned the specters—one unthinkable, one impossible, and the vial. There was no doubt in anyone's mind that letting the ghosts enact Ninian's revenge was not an option. Over the centuries, the bloodlines of the Ruling Council spread from their illegitimate children, second and third sons, and runaway daughters until they couldn't even guess how many would die. The second option was to crown the descendent of King Barleyn, last king of Astera, whose son Yewen escaped during the coup.

The vial was the easiest choice.

"I wanted to say...I'm sorry, Thislen."

He looked up at Tamsa, brows raised. He hadn't expected her to apologize, but just let things fade. She surprised him. Her gaze was fixed on the porthole, her hand resting on his shoulder, warm and soothing.

I could come to like this version of her, the one that knows who she is.

But did he forgive her?

If Tamsa hadn't shouted, they might not have been caught. If they hadn't gotten caught, he wouldn't be facing torture again tomorrow night, the night after, and the night after that.

He didn't know if he could forgive her, not now. Not when his hip and knee were swollen and throbbing, not when his body was scarred by hot irons, not when his chest burned from inhaling water.

I understand her, though. She wanted to protect those who mattered to her—and that was every Nattfolk in Astera, and not him. Not Mila. Something changed between them over their time in captivity. He won her respect without meaning to, and now she wanted to protect him, too.

Too bad she can't.

No one could.

He closed his eyes, resting his hand over hers. "Keep talking."

Tamsa smiled. He could hear it in her voice. "Did I ever tell you about the time Aften and I convinced half the kids in the Commons to stage a siege of the tavern until they gave us all the pies?"

She set off on a tale about wooden practice swords and indulgent, amused adults, about sweet pastries dripping with honey, overfull stomachs, and laughter. Thislen's lips curved into a smile as he pictured it. He couldn't remember the last time he'd smiled. It was a time when everything was innocent, a time when everything was safe.

He surrendered to his nightmares, hoping against hope that tomorrow he would wake up to something better. He wanted to wake up to pies.

He wanted to wake up safe.

Ancestors, save me. Please, save me.

3

Mila tied her hair up with a gray and black mottled scarf, though tendrils of honey brown hair immediately slipped loose to hang around her face and ears. The stone edge of her bunk in the Barracks leeched heat from her, but the air was the same temperature as it always was underground: a little cool. The sound of conversation echoed off the hewn walls and ceiling of the sleeping cavern. People moved all around her. Somewhere above the Nattfolks' underground city, the sun was setting. It was time for their day—well, their night—to begin.

Carved niches ran up the walls, each given the illusion of privacy by a curtain strung along the top, and shelves along the back to store belongings. Carved ladders between the bunks allowed people to climb to the second, third, and fourth rows. The wall curved slightly, giving Mila a full view of people conversing with their neighbors and friends, sitting in their little stone cubicles high above the floor. Her own bunk was on the ground.

She sighed, scooting back and folding her legs. The stuffed pallet of straw and wool rustled beneath her. This space wasn't intended as a room for living, merely for sleeping, the same way the Solfolk above slept on their ships and not in their homes. The Commons was where Nattfolk worked and mingled.

At least there are no children in here.

The Barracks were for young couples or single persons, a way of granting them freedom in the enclosed, secret community. Families, their children, and the elderly occupied caverns similar to houses, which lined the sides of three other tunnels.

The noise here was all a comfortable sort of chatter instead of the cacophonous din there would be in the Commons. Mila preferred it.

Slowly, the crowd moved. People filtered out in twos and threes. They were off to work—there were no idle hands among the Nattfolk. Some of them were craftworkers ready for a day of sewing, weaving, or working leather that had already been cured by a Nattfolk agent above. Some would work at the stalls, alone or with their families. Money wasn't much use down here, but they would trade and barter with their friends and neighbors all night.

Many in this room, however, were scouts. It was the best job for restless youths and allowed them the freedom to run the streets and rooftops of Astera between sunset and sunrise. They were easily distinguished from the rest by their clothing. Scouts wore mottled blacks, grays, and browns that would turn them into little more than shadows in the night.

Through the sluggishly milling crowd, a familiar face appeared, vanished, and appeared again. Her eyes narrowed.

Ah, here he comes. My warden.

Scout Captain Trevon wove his way across the cavern, pausing every few steps. Everyone stopped him for a chat, and he was more than willing to indulge if the smile on his face was any indication. Among the crowd of scouts, he hardly stood out. Like many of the Nattfolk, he had brown hair—though his was closer to the amber-brown of honey than the color of walnut shells. His skin was covered in freckles. His eyes were a particularly uninteresting shade of green. She didn't like him.

After Darran and Mila's rescue from the stocks outside the Justica, Trevon brought them both back to the Nattfolk's hidden city and straight to the Night Council. Rendyn Sivivan, the head of that council, was also Aften and Tamsa's father. Mila clearly remembered the vein pulsing on Rendyn's forehead, his red face, and his dark scowl as he listened to what transpired. When they got to the part where his children were stuck on a ship, held by members of the Ruling Council, and at risk of being tortured, Mila thought he was going to have her and Darran executed.

The rest of the Night Council intervened. The Nattfolk weren't the sort to execute anyone, after all. Mila couldn't forget a word.

"Rendyn, we are not monsters like the Solfolk rulers, and you are not our king. You aren't even the only person leading our people," Councilman Grayson said, standing toe to toe with the raging father.

"Then I want her banished! I want her on the next ship away from this island, without a coin to her name, and may she never come back." Every word was clipped short and spat out with vehemence. He glared at Mila over Grayson's shoulder, his hazel eyes fixed on her like a hunting cat waiting for its prey to move.

Well, she wasn't about to be sentenced to banishment for a second time, not after she escaped execution twice. Her hands balled into fists.

"You need me," she said, voice cutting through the Night Council's chatter like a whip. Silence fell, quick and heavy. Every eye turned to her. Darran eased a step away from her side.

"Excuse me?" Rendyn asked.

"Why?" Councilwoman Ami sat down in her seat, folding her hands before her on the polished surface of the table.

Mila's heart was pounding, but she had made up her mind. She was a Nattfolk now, whether they wanted her or not. "I know more about Lord Soren Bestant, Master Garridan Artaith, and Lord Judge Avasten Barnweir than any of you. I know more about the curse than any of you. I know more about the Solfolk than many of you, except maybe your recent acquisitions and your agents above."

"The Solwalkers," Helena murmured.

"The Solwalkers still aren't Solfolk, and I was."

"Was?" Ami's brows rose toward the elegant pile of curls on top of her head.

"Was. I am Nattfolk, now, and I am your resource. You might condemn Aften and Tamsa without my help."

Rendyn's face twisted, his lips pressed thin and his hands clenched into fists so tight his knuckles were white. Mila knew she was right—and so did he. With a disgusted noise, he slammed his hands on the table.

"Fine! If you are Nattfolk, as you say, then you won't mind accepting whatever punishments I see fit to set."

Mila lifted her chin defiantly. "I don't mind at all."

He scowled, baring his teeth. She didn't doubt he was on the verge of snapping. Then again, he just found out his children were captives of his people's sworn enemy. He cared about them—at least one of them, anyway.

"You will not move from the Barracks without the accompaniment of your scout captain, and you will not leave his sight above ground. Any failure to follow these rules, and you shall be locked away in these caverns and taught a useful trade. You will dedicate your spare time to rescuing my children. Should they not return or should someone else rescue them first, I, and I alone, will determine your fate. Are we agreed?"

He wasn't asking her; he was asking the Night Council. Half the faces there bore deep frowns, but two nodded. When Rendyn's gaze slid to her, Mila nodded as well.

"I agree. I'll stay with Darran—"

"Darran is no longer a scout captain."

Beside her, Darran started, his eyes widening. "Sir?"

"For going along with this...scheme, you are demoted back to a simple scout. You will share in Mila's punishment. Scout Captain Trevon." Rendyn crooked two fingers, beckoning Trevon forward.

Trevon, who had tucked himself against the wall near the door, stepped up to Mila's right. "Councilman?"

"These two are your responsibility now. Do not let them out of your sight."

Even now, it left her furious. They were right; they did what was *right*, and they were punished for it.

Mila sighed, dropping her head back against the stone. She wrestled with the rising heat of simmering fury inside her chest. The scent of smoke hung faintly in the air. None of this was precisely Trevon's fault, after all. Her patience was wearing thin, and so was Rendyn's. Nearly a moon slipped past with no progress. Her fate hung on Aften and Tamsa's, and no one even cared about Thislen besides her and Darran.

At least I convinced them I was necessary. After all, who knew Lord Soren Bestant, their jailer, better than the woman he wanted to marry? Nevermind that Mila didn't want to marry *him*. And not just Soren, but the torturer Garridan Artaith and the lurking spider of Avasten Barnweir—his partners in his crimes. She knew them all.

That argument proved effective enough to spare her, and landed her in a dozen meetings with the Night Council, going over everything she remembered about the three noblemen in excruciating detail.

When she wasn't stuck in the Council Chamber, she was under the constant watchful eye of Trevon, a scout captain well known for sticking to the rules. He was two years Darran's senior and had been a captain for five.

Speaking of...

Darran popped around the corner of her bunk with a grin. He was dressed in plain scout leathers. He looked strange without the bandolier with its crest of the moon, and the pouch on his hip stuffed full of pendants that protected people from the Vaim. Mila knew he was wracked with anxiety about Aften's fate. Despite that, he always showed up in good spirits.

"Hey," he said.

"Hey." She took her boots from the shelf at the foot of her bed and tugged them on.

"It's been almost a moon. We have a plan. We should tell him."

Mila's brow furrowed. "I don't know if we're ready. He's going to tell Rendyn."

Darran leaned against the stone wall with a soft scoff. "Try him. He's not as much of a stick in the mud as he seems."

"How would you know?"

"We used to talk, back when I was a captain." His expression grew distant. It chafed at him, not being able to run his own patrols. He had too much idle time he was used to filling with duties he no longer had.

"Alright, but not until after training."

She still had doubts, but they were out of time to discuss them. Mila lapsed into silence as Trevon finally came within earshot, lifting her hand in greeting.

"Hey, you two. Ready to wrap yourselves around some breakfast? After that, I booked us time on the archery targets." Trevon jerked his thumb toward the tunnel that led to the Nattfolk Commons. "Training grounds are ours for at least a bell."

Thank the Ancestors; he chose bows, the one weapon I'm decent at. Mila surprised herself as much as the Nattfolk by having a natural aptitude for several types of weapon, but the bow was by far her favorite. She'd only been using it for a short while, but she always hit the center of the target these days.

She slid off her bunk. Darran fell in at her side, and the two of them followed Trevon. Her days now passed in one blur after another, filled from sunset to sunrise. She was sure the enforced schedule was created by Rendyn to keep her out of any further trouble.

I only snuck off to Perilee once. Well, twice. Still, it isn't like I plan to do it again. Not until Thislen and Aften were safe, at least.

First came breakfast at 'the tavern' in the center of the Commons. The tavern was built around one of the great stone pillars that supported the cavern's ceiling. The long, round counter was surrounded by tables, chairs, benches, and stools, and served up food from a single massive oven built right into the support behind them. How they got a chimney in a pillar big enough around that four men could barely touch fingertips, Mila would never know.

Weapons training followed. An entire chamber had been set aside for the purpose, littered with wooden pells, straw targets, and racks packed with practice tools. They fired arrows until Mila's arms were numb and her fingertips throbbed beneath her two-fingered glove. When she could hardly draw the bowstring, Trevon called for them to move on.

Her next lesson was the one Mila dreaded. Trevon and Darran sat on either side at a worn table in a quiet alcove. They were surrounded by common objects and a dozen locks, keyholes, and latches. She struggled as she prodded a heavy padlock with a small metal file; the sort used by blacksmiths.

"It's not working."

"Here, try the hairpin."

"Can't I go back to the lock picks?"

"You're already good at the lock pick." Trevon pressed the hairpin into her hand. "Try this instead."

"Ha, got mine!" Darran crowed, holding up the lock he picked with nothing more than a bit of wire.

Mila sighed, jabbing the hairpin into the keyhole with a frown.

After an hour of toiling through her lessons on lock picking, which were admittedly an improvement on the lessons for hiding her movement in the shadows, Trevon called a halt. He escorted her and Darran back to the bustling heart of the Commons and left them to get their midnight lunch.

Two stories high, with a distant painted ceiling and murals on every inch of available wall, the Commons still took Mila's breath away. The second level was a gallery walkway of stone around the edge, connected to the pillars throughout the room by wooden platforms and rope bridges that linked them like a spider's web. Caverns lined the walls, with bright heavy curtains or wooden doors hung over their entrances. Signs painted above them told everyone what lay beyond. There, a tailor who needed the privacy for measurements. There, one of the two midwives. There, a healer of the mind and soul. Each trade required privacy. Every craft that didn't had a stall somewhere on the cavern floor, with wood or stone walls and brightly colored awnings made of heavy cloth.

It was lit by lanterns hung on the walls and from the ceiling, and kept warm by large braziers. There was remarkably little smoke, and a remarkable amount of noise. Streamers of fabric hung from the ceiling helped to dampen any echoes, but the blacksmith's clanging hammer was impossible to muffle.

A cluster of children watched the crowd from one of the bridges, giggling over something they saw below. Several others were playing a game of tag that appeared to have a very complex set of rules. An elderly woman was playing a game of Hunter's Hounds against an old man who held her hand and smiled fondly while she soundly beat him. People were everywhere, dressed in bright colors and swirling from one cluster to the next. Everyone knew everyone down here, after all.

It's like a palace holding an indoor festival. It was rich, and vibrant, and somehow more beautiful than all the pomp and fanfare around the balls and feasts thrown by the Ruling Council. *It might be because no one is left out.*

Not even she and Darran, and their stars could not fall any further. They were greeted half a dozen times as they threaded their way through the tables to the tavern's counter. Kellan, the cook who presided over the kingdom of the kitchens, nodded at them as he carried a tray of risen bread loaves around to the oven.

The pair of them joined the line of people, grabbing plates and picking food off platters. Mila piled hers high with sizzling meat, crispy shelled rolls, and soft white cheese. There was no alcohol available, despite being called 'the tavern.' Ale and mead were rare down here, often reserved for special occasions. Instead, there was cool, sweet water, syrupy cordials, and a dozen sorts of tea. Hot or cold, all drinks were served in large clay mugs. Mila got water.

Once she and Darran were suitably laden with food, they wandered among the tables, looking for empty seats. By this point, everyone was swinging by for a meal. If Mila had a choice, she would have waited half a bell for the crowd to clear out. Scouts, however, were due for their patrols not long after midnight.

Darran slid onto a stool at the end of a long table. There were several seats between him and the next occupant. Mila sat across from him and dug in, ravenous from training.

"Will you tell him now?" Darran asked, spearing a few cooked carrots.

Mila frowned at her roll as she tore it in half and spread the soft cheese in the middle. "You really think we can trust him?"

"I think he listened to you the first time, when you were in the stocks. He risked his position as much as I risked mine, bringing you back down here. That means there's at least a chance he'll listen to you again, right?"

Am I willing to risk the lives of our friends on a mere chance?

"Maybe when we're on patrol," she said with a shrug.

Telling anyone is my decision. It's my plan, and my life on the line. I'm the one in charge if we bring him on board, and Trevon won't like that.

Mila trusted Darran, though. She relied on his opinions and ideas more than she wanted to admit.

"We don't have a list today. They gave them both to the early patrols." Darran grinned.

No list means no stealing from the Solfolk tonight, and that means Trevon will split us up. At full strength, a group of scouts numbered six. Five regular scouts and one captain. There were half-size groups, too; Darran's had been one of those until Mila and Thislen joined it. When the Nattfolk needed things from the surface they couldn't get or make themselves, it was the scouts who took bits and pieces from a dozen houses and shops to hide their presence.

With nothing to fetch, Trevon would divide his scouts into two sets of three. Thanks to Rendyn's instructions, she and Darran would remain with Trevon while the other three scouts—Ophelia, Agathe, and Harlon—split off.

Not that we usually get lists. Being part of the second shift, there's never anything to do. First shift got all the excitement, all the work, and all the glory.

Trevon's patrol had been demoted from that coveted first shift when Mila and Darran were added. The other three scouts didn't like them. Mila's punishment was boredom, monotony, and constant supervision—with just a dash of distaste and judgment on the side.

"You trust me, right?" Darran ducked his head to catch her eye, his grin bright in his dark-skinned face.

Mila rolled her eyes, a smile tugging at the corners of her lips. "I trust you, Darran."

"Then trust me."

Beyond Darran's head, she saw Trevon. He let them have their space, but he always sat where he could keep watch while he ate his own food. He looked up and caught her staring. The scout captain smiled and lifted a hand briefly.

Mila went back to her food with a faint frown.

I really hope we can trust him.

"Eat faster, Mila, we're almost out of time." Beneath the table, Darran kicked the toe of her boot.

He was right; their turn for patrol was coming up fast. She scarfed the last of her lunch.

Mila was out of options, and she knew it. Every plan she'd offered the Night Council was rejected, and this was her last, best bet. It would work—if she didn't tell them what she planned. Otherwise, they'd say no. Again.

Thislen was running out of time. Aften was running out of time. Even Tamsa, who Mila hated for her lies, was running out of time.

She had to do something tonight, or she would go mad.

Darran was right. Again. She had to tell Trevon.

Tonight.

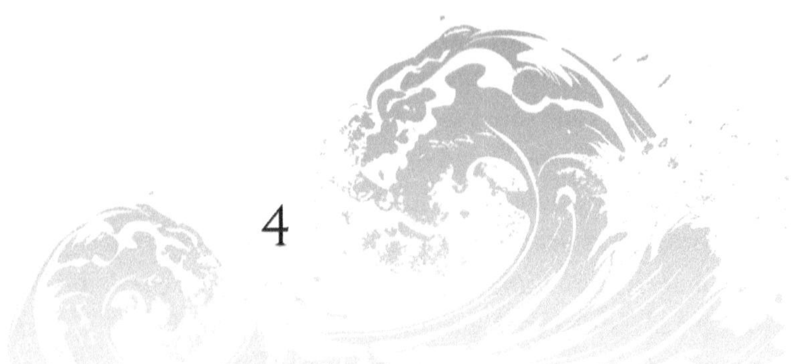

4

Several pathways led out of the Commons and up to the surface of Astera. The first was the tunnel Mila was most familiar with, the long set of worn stairs in the dark. The entrance of that tunnel let out into the Sivivan mausoleum. Set in a row of similar crypts with noble names over the doors, it didn't stand out at all. The graveyard it was in wasn't far from the Ominir Apothecary where Mila grew up, and was right in the shadow of the castle itself. The stairway's entrance was marked with a beautiful painting of Astera crowned by Perilee in all its glory.

Trevon rarely used that route. Mila couldn't figure out if it was personal preference, or if there were orders from Rendyn Sivivan to keep her as far away from the castle and more trouble as possible. When all six scouts gathered in the Commons, it was next to a tunnel entrance marked by a painted winding pathway, a lake, and a simple wooden door.

Trevon led them down the tunnel. As soon as they were out of the Commons, there were no lights on the walls, no torches, and no braziers.

Not that it matters very much. Trevon always brings—aha.

Trevon lit a lantern, turning it up until a golden globe pushed back the darkness surrounding them. Every step tossed wavering shadows over the walls as the flame flickered and danced. Mila missed Aften's magical orb, a rare and valuable family heirloom. Its light was steady and bright, only affected by fingers wrapped around it. The lantern's deep shadows grew and shrank. Mila shuddered. The movement reminded her of when the Vaim appeared each night, dragging themselves out of the smallest piece of darkness.

Wordlessly, she stepped forward and held out her hand. Trevon passed her the lantern. She held it much steadier. The start of a headache faded, as did the knot in her stomach.. Now the shadows felt less alive.

We'll get Aften back, and with any luck, we'll find his orb. A thin hope, she knew. The orb ought to be long gone into the pocket of Soren Bestant or one of his friends.

No one could cast magic anymore, not since her many-times-great grandfather tied every drop of magic in the kingdom to his curse. That power summoned the Vaim every night when the sun set. Now the only magic left resided in objects enchanted before the curse existed.

Hence, a lantern.

The tunnel they traveled in silence was slightly sloped, switching back and forth. It was part of a living cave, with undulating walls that looked like melted candle wax and dark little holes that wound off into who knew where. It dripped water constantly, a soft, muffled sound that never seemed close until a droplet hit someone's head. Slow as it was, this tunnel was changing, and had been for centuries.

The twisting path widened to a low-ceilinged cavern festooned with stalagmites and stalactites like some strange subterranean forest—except where a lake of crystalline water lay. It was a natural spring, cool and clear, that came from somewhere below. This was how the Nattfolk got their supply of water, though it always tasted faintly of minerals.

The path curved around the edge of the lake before narrowing back into a slender tunnel. The gentle slope gave way to large, shallow steps, worn away in the middle until they nearly formed a ramp again. Mila turned the lantern down. They were near the entrance now.

The Nattfolk never used light above ground. The Solfolk, the day-to-day residents of the island kingdom, spent their nights safely tucked away on ships berthed just offshore. This kept them safe from the Vaim. It was in everyone's best interest to keep up the facade of Astera being too dangerous to live on at night. No one else knew why the Vaim killed the people they did, and Mila didn't know how many would die.

The ghosts were hunting the descendents of an ancient Ruling Council.

Lights bobbing around a shore that was supposed to be empty would attract the wrong sort of attention. It would only take one or two watchful sailors to spread a rumor that could endanger countless lives. The bloodlines of that long ago Council were now diluted. There was no telling who was related—however distantly—to whom. The Vaim might never stop hunting to sate Ninian's revenge.

Unless I break the curse.

Ninian Ominir was her great-grandfather, several generations distant. Her bloodline was tied to this curse, and that made it her responsibility to break it.

Thislen, Aften, and Tamsa first, she reminded herself. *Once I get them back, I'll be allowed to stay. Then I'll have all the time I need.*

Breaking the curse would release the Vaim, spirits of poor and unfortunate residents of the kingdom murdered by the Ruling Council in an effort to cull the population. Astera's resources had been on the verge of drying up. The nobility split into factions over the possible solutions, and the ones who ruled today were the progeny of ruthless murderers who staged a coup to get their way.

The actual story of how they got their power is one secret they don't want to get out. Mila was determined to break the curse *and* spread the story. The truth would change everything, and she wouldn't hold back. She just had to make sure everyone was safe from retaliation first. The Ruling Council might take measures to quell such 'rumors' otherwise.

Mila traced her fingers over the rough, cool wall. The closer she, Trevon, Darran, and the others got to the surface, the more she felt the weight of the world pressing down on her shoulders. So many things needed to happen for everything to turn out all right. Anything could go wrong at any moment. How was she going to do it?

Not alone, I hope. Thislen would know what to say. He'd know how to help.

She missed him. She missed him almost more than she missed her family, left behind when she was sentenced to execution for rejecting Soren Bestant. Their friendship hadn't been very long, and she wasn't even sure Thislen would call it that. Mila spent more time with Darran over the past moon than she had spent with Thislen, but it wasn't the same. The thief saw things others didn't. He just *knew* things about her she never had to tell. He saw right through her, understood her, and trusted her all in an instant.

Mila missed that. Her family saw her as a child. The Nattfolk saw her as new, unknowing, or foolish, if not downright dangerous. Even Darran, her only friend right now, didn't understand why her plans were too important to trust to chance. Thislen would.

Thislen is my best friend, and I want him back. She couldn't even think about breaking the curse when her mind was full of inventive nightmares about what Soren was doing to him. Thumbscrews, racks, iron brands—who knew what was happening on *Ship Artaith*?

I need help. Damn, I hate when Darran is right. I have to tell Trevon the plan. We can't carry this out on our own. It would be too dangerous. The last thing she wanted was to end up imprisoned again. When she and the others were caught on the docks by Soren and his men, Mila had been sentenced to execution on the island, with the promise of beheading if she survived. She and Darran had been chained up as the sun set.

As far as the Ruling Council knew, the ghosts killed her that night. She shuddered at the thought of coming face to face with Soren Bestant for a third time after her second death.

Trevon reached the top of the shallow staircase first. It ended in a simple stone landing, surrounded by four wooden walls. The space was tiny, like a closet. Mila turned the lantern down to the barest glimmer of blue flame and set it on the stairs.

Only one wall had a door, difficult to see. It was little more than a latch set amongst the boards, but when the scout captain unfastened it and pushed, the hidden exit was revealed. Stone ground against stone. While the interior was made of wood, the exterior had to match the surrounding buildings. Outside of the poor Gate Quarter, every building in Astera was made of the same pale stone. A single wooden wall would stand out—so the hidden entrance was covered with a thin layer of stone bricks. The door was heavy, but well hidden.

The sky was dark. Ink black clouds spread as far as the eye could see. The air tingled with the promise of a storm, but the stones were already wet. The air was thick with the earthy scent of petrichor. They'd just missed it; the rumble of thunder overhead was the faint farewell of a storm moving away.

Mila stepped into the alleyway, tipping her head back and taking a deep breath. *I wanted moonlight,* she thought with a sinking heart. Fresh air was fine, but bright silver moonlight was better. It was as close to the light of the sun as she could get. She committed to being a Nattfolk, and that meant this was her world now—darkness and ghosts.

A Vaim lurched across the mouth of the alley, a twisted black shadow that resembled a human only in that it had four limbs. Its hands ended in spidery fingers that came to a talon-like point, as sharp and real as knives. Its back was curved in an animalistic hunch. Thin, knotty shoulders pulled up toward its head. It had a long neck, so slim it seemed it might snap when the creature whipped around as quickly as it did, but Mila had seen the spirits snap to attention more than once. Their heads were completely featureless but for their eyes—no ears, nose, or mouth. Beneath the barest hint of a brow, they had sunken holes with a red-yellow gaze like a glowing ember.

Mila met the glare of the Vaim as it slowed to a stop, looking right at her. She didn't wear one of the magical pendants, bespelled hundreds of years ago by her many-times-great grandmother, Willa Ominir, the daughter of Ninian. She didn't need to. Because of who she was, the Vaim wouldn't harm her.

They could see her, though.

Her heart always raced beneath their stares, but she didn't recoil or look away. Once, that spirit, now trapped in unending fury spurred by a ghost bent on revenge, had been a person. They had been Asteran.

The twisted black shadow turned away, staggering out of sight on legs that barely seemed to support it, moving with twitching, jerking movements.

Mila exhaled.

I never imagined that the nightmares of my childhood would one day be something I pitied. They were harmless to anyone without the blood of the Ruling Council in their veins. For the Nattfolk, they were inconveniences, difficult to steer around during their nightly patrols. The Vaim filled Astera's streets in hundreds, if not thousands, every night. They stumbled through the motions of lives long since passed, clogging the streets and markets.

A grinding sound filled the air again as Trevon pushed the hidden door closed. He stretched his arms over his head. "Alright. Assignments. Harlon, Ophelia, Agathe, you run the inland half. I'll take the new arrivals and run the shore. Agathe, you're in charge."

"Alright, Trevon." Agathe cast a glance at Mila that would sting like acid if given form, then led the other scouts into the night. They scaled a stack of crates outside a tannery to reach the nearest rooftops—and vanished a moment later, slipping into the shadows with practiced ease.

Mila sighed. She'd never be as good as they were.

Darran fiddled with the chain around his neck, adjusting the pendant beneath his clothes with a slight tug. The magic of the pendants only worked when it was against the skin. Mila supposed it drew energy from the bearer. Darran, a descendant of the Coppermund line of the Ruling Council, needed to wear a talisman at all times to stay alive.

"Are you alright?" she asked softly.

"Fine. It just digs in sometimes. I guess when it's working hard, it gets heavier." Darran shrugged.

Trevon came between them. "Ready?"

Mila waved a hand dismissively. "Sure. Are we starting near the Gate Quarter or the Grand Quarter?"

They stood near the heart of the Guild Quarter, where various craftworkers made raw materials into supplies the island needed. Tanners, leatherworkers, weavers, metalsmiths, jewelers—all of them had workshops or compounds here in which they made products for the Goods Quarter's shops. The Grand Quarter to the east housed the wealthy and powerful in large estates. The Gate Quarter, the only one surrounded by a wall, was where the poor lived. It stood to the west.

"I thought we'd start with whatever you two have been whispering about the past few weeks."

Mila's stomach plummeted. Her mouth went dry, and her palms grew slick. Her heart skipped uncomfortably inside her chest. *How did he—*

"What?" she said numbly.

"We haven't been—" Darran began.

"You have. I've been keeping an eye on you, remember? I was waiting for you to be ready to bring me in on it. You've spent half the night looking at me out of the corners of your eyes or avoiding me entirely, so I take it you're working up the courage." Trevon gestured at the street below. "I know a smithy where we can sit and talk."

It wasn't a suggestion; it was an order. Mila felt as though she were walking on the swaying deck of a ship instead of perfectly solid cobblestones as she followed Trevon. *Is he going to tell Rendyn? Even if he does, this is what Rendyn told me to do—find a way to save his children. They can't be cross if I was following orders.*

Except Rendyn Sivivan would detest this plan, start to finish. He'd forbid it.

The smithy stood on the corner of a round crossroads. A wooden awning was built over an outdoor forge. A sturdy oak counter made a decent seat for her and Darran, and Trevon leaned against the massive anvil nearby. He folded his arms over his chest.

"What's going on, then?"

Trevon's words were calm, tinged with curiosity, and not angry at all. This wasn't what Mila expected. She thought he would be demanding; that he would press them for answers, interrogating them until they told him everything. She thought he would threaten to take them to Rendyn and tell the Councilman their plan. She thought...

I guess I thought wrong, didn't I? Maybe he will surprise me.

She glanced at Darran. Darran flashed her a grin and a shrug. She understood his silent message: it was up to her to decide.

Mila took a deep breath, the words tripping over themselves in a rush as she spoke, afraid he would interrupt. "We have a plan to rescue our friends, and before you tell us we can't, we truly believe this will work, and we know the Night Council is also looking for a way to do this, but they're just going to keep trying to solve the problem with a perfect solution, and by the time they figure it out it will be too late. They're all talk and no action, and we need to *do* something. Darran and I think we can have them rescued by tomorrow night. We just need help."

She stopped, breathless.

A corner of Trevon's mouth turned up in a faint, crooked smirk, and he nodded. "It's true, they're throwing away dozens of ideas as they try to puzzle out how to help Tamsa and Aften. Your friend, Thislen, too."

"I know, but—"

"And it's true that none of them are even close to a plan they can act on. I'm interested. Breathe, Mila. Tell me what you have planned."

"Then you'll help us?" Mila's head was swimming. She forgot to breathe.

"I hope so. Tell me, and I'll decide if I'm in or out."

"If you're out, you won't tell the Council, will you?" Darran asked.

Trevon tipped his head back, mulling over his answer. "No, I don't think so. There's plenty of things I was told to report to Councilman Rendyn, but plots and schemes weren't one of them. He didn't think you'd come up with anything."

A sudden surge of heat flared through her, and it felt like a static shock. She jumped. It came so quickly, accompanied with the scent of smoke. Mila dropped her gaze to the counter beneath her hands. It was singed. Soot coated her fingers. The feeling faded as she studied the black smudges on her skin. Her anger was another matter.

Rendyn Sivivan was planning to trap me underground all along, as soon as he could make it look reasonable. As soon as I failed. He could do as he liked with me, even banish me forever. He believed so firmly that I wouldn't help his children that he didn't even bother to have his spy report to him. That manipulative monster!

Mila wouldn't have argued with the decision, the way he set up all the pieces. She'd believe she deserved it, that she failed. Rendyn wanted her to pack her own bag and walk away from Astera, meek as a mouse.

Focus, Mila, she told herself, taking a deep breath.

"We're going to steal a rowboat from a ferryman just before sunset, paddle around to the Grand Quarter, and find Garridan Artaith's ship. Then, we'll climb on board and sneak them out. We paddle back to the dock where we found the ferry and leave it there."

Simple, and hopefully effective.

The ferrymen were a craft all their own, with a large common house in the Guild Quarter and entire docks dedicated to their rowboats. If one were wealthy enough, they could pay to be rowed close to their destination without having to walk. Some high-end shops and guilds paid the ferrymen to take goods to the Grand Quarter and deliver them. At night, the ferries ran between the ships, mostly among the nobility. Some would row up the sides of the island between the fishing and farming settlements and Barred Town, the only other large settlement in the kingdom. Each boat was a carefully guarded commodity, but it wouldn't be impossible to take one. Probably.

Trevon's brows pulled in. Once more, that intent and thoughtful look stole over his features.

Mila held her breath.

Darran swung one foot idly back and forth, head tipped to the side while he waited, the picture of calm.

"Allow me to poke a few holes in this plan of yours."

Her heart sank. *He won't help us?*

"You plan to paddle around from ship to ship, at night, looking for one specific one out there on the open ocean?"

Heat began to prickle up Mila's cheeks. "Well, yes."

"We'll find it eventually," Darran added cheerfully. "Might take us a while, though."

"Then you're going to climb onto the nobleman's ship. At night. When it is full of sailors, his personal guards, his servants, and possibly the noble himself?"

Now even the dark couldn't hide the flush that crept across her face and climbed toward her ears. "We said we needed help. It won't work at all with just the two of us."

"It won't work at all, period."

The heat in her cheeks went from embarrassment to anger between one heartbeat and the next. It felt like molten rock was bubbling inside her, filling her until she couldn't hold it any longer. She tamped it down with effort, hands balled into fists while she took slow, steady breaths.

How dare he just throw the whole thing out? It was the best plan we had. It took us this long to come up with it, and just like that, it's gone? We'll never get to them in time.

Trevon circled the anvil, planting his hands on it and leaning forward with a gleam in his eye. "Let's figure out a new plan together. You have something in part of it. Using the ferries is inspired. We haven't got them at night, so we Nattfolk wouldn't have thought of it."

"I *am* a Nattfolk," Mila said flatly.

"I know. But your Solfolk experience can come in handy, that's all I'm saying."

"Well...thank you."

"You're welcome. Now, when are the Solfolk ships emptiest?"

Mila hesitated.

I want to be a good Nattfolk scout. I want to show them I can handle this, that I meant what I said when I decided not to be a Solfolk anymore. If I'm being honest, though, the best time for all this is...

"During the day, early afternoon, most likely. The ships are restocked, the sailors are sleeping, the servants are at the estates. Garridan himself will be at his estate or handling his duties. His father will be attending the Ruling Council. The most we'd have to contend with would be a few guards, I think. Maybe one or two servants."

"Perfect. That gives us the time." Trevon clapped his hands together. His palms were covered with fingerless leather gloves, so the sound was only a muffled *plap.*

"During the day?" Mila's brows rose.

Darran grinned at Trevon. "I told her as much before, when she first thought of it."

"And I'll tell you now what I told you then—I'm not a Solfolk anymore. Besides, I didn't want to tempt myself," she blurted.

Mila's fingers flew to her lips. Her defense had the bite of too much truth to it. The temptation would always be there, a deep longing for the sunlight. She'd never completely get over losing her family or the life she knew before. Even throwing herself into the life of a Nattfolk scout with the utmost dedication hadn't kept her distracted enough to avoid feeling homesick.

Even if I went back, it wouldn't be the same. She wasn't the same person. Once, she was a girl who never left home until she was fleeing a marriage proposal she didn't want. This new version of her didn't fear the Vaim, shot bows, picked locks, and planned rescues. Twice. *I don't know if I have a home anymore. The Nattfolk aren't home, not yet. Going back isn't home.*

Mila was trapped between two lives. She was on her own.

"Darran and I will be with you," Trevon said, startling her out of her thoughts. "You'll be fine. Now, do the Solfolk ships dock in the same place every day?"

Mila straightened. She wasn't alone anymore. Maybe being stuck between the night and day could be helpful. "Yes, they do. It makes it faster and easier to get on and off the ships every day."

Trevon nodded, tapping his fingers on the anvil. "We get a ferry and row around to the Grand Quarter in the middle of the day. No one will look at us twice, right?"

"Not at all."

"Then we climb aboard, handle any guards, and get our friends onto the boat. Then what?"

Darran leaned forward. "Then we take them to the Gate Quarter door. It's a long row around the island, but that one is our best bet."

Trevon snapped his fingers, grinning. "Perfect."

Mila looked between them, brows raised, waiting for an explanation.

"The Gate Quarter door to the Commons is inside a warehouse down by the docks. Our Solwalker sailors unload cargo into the building, and we can take it below without anyone the wiser. No matter what state they're in, we can carry them right through the door without attracting much attention." Trevon's broad grin widened even more, somehow, and Darran smiled in return.

Their optimism was infectious, and the realization they had a plan they agreed on, a plan that might actually work, made Mila lightheaded. She laughed breathlessly, putting a hand to her temple. "You're probably right."

Trevon smacked a fist into his palm. "This plan, I like. I'm in."

"You are?"

This went much better than Mila anticipated. She wasn't being hauled up before Rendyn, she'd found an ally, and the plan was much improved by the scout captain's thinking. Her heart rose in her chest.

"Darran, are you in?" Trevon asked, turning to him.

"Oh, I've been in since the start." Darran dismissively waved a hand through the air.

Trevon's smile faltered, and he nodded. "Right. I should have guessed that, what with you and Aften."

Mila knew Darran loved Aften. The night she became a Nattfolk, she and her fellow scout stood on a pier, staring over the water. *"I never told him how I feel,"* Darran said.

Darran's easy-going mask slipped and his smile grew taut and worried.

Mila's gaze wandered, giving him a moment to compose himself. *He's as worried—no,* more *worried about Aften than I am about Thislen.* A pang of guilt sat in her stomach like a stone. The two of them avoided talking about how they felt over the past moon. The first few days, they'd been wrapped up in the whirlwind of the Night Council. Then she dove into her lessons. She didn't want to think about what was happening with Thislen if she could avoid it. Maybe Darran wanted to share his fears, and she didn't notice with her head buried in the sand. She owed Darran an apology. She made a mental note to take him aside later to talk.

"Well, I don't see any reason to put this off. We can get started today, after everyone else is asleep." Trevon strolled out of the smithy. "After our patrol, of course."

"Today?" Mila skipped after him, lighter than air.

"Did you want to wait?"

"Did I say that? No, today is perfect."

"Today," Darran echoed, grinning again as he caught up to them. "I like the sound of that."

Mila watched Trevon's back as he led the way up a small garden wall and onto the nearest rooftop, though he was hard to see in the moonless night. She'd misjudged him as a stuck-up rule follower, but he was something different. He was someone she might, perhaps, be able to trust. He hadn't turned her in, and he danced around his orders as if he'd done it a thousand times. To the letter of the law, not the spirit.

She liked him.

Once she stood atop the roof ridge, a salt-brine breeze tugging coils of hair from her scarf, she turned toward the Grand Quarter. Beyond the mansion rooftops of all sizes and shapes sat the black glass of the sea, dotted with distant, glittering lights. The ships were nearly invisible, the clouds and ocean conspiring to hide them from sight. One of them was *Ship Artaith*. Mila's eyes swept over them all.

Hold on, Thislen. We're coming.

5

A stera was beautiful during the day. Mila never appreciated it before, but being trapped so long gave her a new perspective. Night after night, she saw the hollow shells of the city she loved, as ghostly as the Vaim themselves. Most of her time was spent beneath the heavy press of miles of stone, as far from the sun as one could get. She drank in every ray of sunlight, every noise, every open door like a person dying of thirst in a desert.

The cobbled streets and many of the houses were made of pale stone, and the wooden ones were whitewashed to match. Their shutters were brightly painted, and their tile rooftops were all shades of rust-colored red. In the sunlight, they were almost too much for her eyes. She squinted at everything, even beneath the shade of her hood.

The people moved so fast compared to a Nattfolk scout. Mila reminded herself not to stoop and slink; she'd attract too much attention that way. She was already strangely dressed, wrapped in a brown Ravan cloak so dark it was nearly black. Everyone around her wore the bright, loose clothing Asterans favored, decorated with embroidery at the cuffs, hems, and collars, accented with tied sashes at the waist or around the hair. And they were loud! Mila nearly forgot that the city bustled and hummed, sunup to sundown.

Shouting, the clatter of cart wheels, a snatch of a song. Here, a pie man bawling his prices, there, a mother scolding her child for running under the nose of a whickering horse. She could hear a clanging bell in the distance, could see the girl dancing on the corner rattling her tambourine. A gaggle of teenagers walked past, chattering louder than an entire flock of chickens. Everywhere she looked were faces of all ages, heights, and builds. Everywhere she looked was life.

Mila watched people pass the mouth of the alleyway she and Darran were waiting in, listening to snatches of perfectly mundane conversation.

Two girls swung around the corner arm in arm, skirts swirling.

"Did you see him mooning over her?" one said, giggling beneath her hand.

"And she hasn't caught on! If he just told her, then maybe they'd…"

Their conversation was swallowed by the crowd.

Three children darted past, a slightly older girl and boy trailed by a younger boy running as fast as he could.

"If you don't give me my horse back, I'll tell on you," the little boy shouted.

"Come and get it, Julian, come and get it," sang the girl.

"You won't tattle or we'll dunk you in the washtub."

"I will too. Uncle Benjin carved that for me, not you!"

And they were gone.

Outside a shop, a woman folded her arms over her chest, brows climbing closer and closer to the embroidered headscarf she'd tied around her dark hair. Before her was a burly young man, swaggering about.

"They basically said I'm going to be an officer within a six-moon," he said casually.

"The City Guard." The woman was unimpressed.

"Are you worried for me, Lacie?"

"What for? We both know you aren't really joining the guard."

The man deflated. "Well, I might," he said sullenly.

Lacie scoffed and disappeared inside, and the man followed her, his next words too faint to hear, cut off when the door closed behind them.

Even the air smelled different. The salt-brine scent of the sea was always there, even now, but it mingled with wafts of various scented oils on the wrists and necks of men and women, of fresh bread and sizzling meat pies, and the less savory smells of sweat, horse dung, and something burnt. Every few steps, it changed. She breathed deep, as if she could store each one away for later, even the bad ones.

Because *this* was Astera alive. This was how the world should be.

This is what breaking the curse will give the Nattfolk, and the quiet night will be what the Solfolk get in turn. She could turn her focus to that soon. Very soon.

Tomorrow.

"Alright, I got another one," Trevon said behind her, tearing her attention away.

"Perfect." Darran took the Ravan cloak and pulled it on.

The Ravans were Astera's closest neighbors. Even then, they were days of sailing to the south. A full week, the sailors said. The people of Rava thought the island kingdom of Astera was full of heathens and drowning in wealth. Healthy trade in the gemstones from the Spine mountains, blue pearls from the Asteran shallows, and ships made by the most skilled shipwrights in existence lured the

Ravans back again and again. They didn't like to come, the superstitious visitors were terrified of the Vaim. They hated the weather in the fall and were miserable in the winter, when the island became far too cold for the southerners. But Rava was the only port of trade for Asteran goods and made them both a lot of coin.

The cloaks the Ravans used on the island were dark and heavy, a sharp contrast to the Asteran love of colors. Their deep hoods were perfect for hiding faces, and the long, bell-like sleeves easily swallowed Mila's hands. The top was made of two scarves worn tossed over the shoulders, hiding one's build and gender. No one would notice two Ravans with an Asteran guiding them, either. Foreigners often needed help to navigate the city. Most merchants were wealthy enough to take the ferries, too.

They made a perfect disguise for two people who were supposed to be dead. Mila suggested it. Trevon and Darran were fascinated. Being Nattfolk by birth, they had never seen nor heard of the Ravan people.

How much of my life I've taken for granted. I never imagined I'd meet someone who doesn't know the same things I do.

They joined the trickle of residents moving through the city streets. As the trio made their way through the Guild Quarter toward the distant dome of the Justica by the shore, Mila explained. "The Ravans think Astera is cursed by the gods they worship because we worship our Ancestors instead. They think the Vaim are the soldiers of Hitolome, their god of death, come to chase us away from the stars for our false belief."

"They're not too far off," Darran said, only his grin visible beneath the cowl of his cloak.

"They're not right, though, either. Why do they come here if they think Astera's cursed?" Trevon stepped around a small cluster of children playing pickup-sticks on one side of the street.

"Money," Mila answered simply. "We're small, but we're rich. It keeps everyone coming back."

They strode into the massive courtyard before the Justica. The building was tall, topped with a glittering glass dome. The walls were carved with figures of the Asteran people, all reaching up to lift their fellows until they could reach the carved statue of King Aldan Asteran himself, founder of the kingdom and their first king.

The sight of it made Mila shiver. When they brought her to trial, she saw the carvings on the back. They were different, with every eye and every hand pointed down in accusation, stone faces twisted in disgust. She watched the carved figures as she trailed behind Trevon, waiting for them to change from happy to angry, to cruel, to fearful. They walked in the shadows of the shops on the edge of the courtyard. Maybe that was all that prevented the sightless stone eyes from seeing her now.

Would they believe me or Avasten?

The first time she had been here, she was sentenced to execution, to the mercy of the Vaim, for rebuffing Lord Soren Bestant and his marriage proposal. The lies were outrageous. They blamed her for seducing him, for using spells, for trying to worm her way into a better position. Lord Judge Avasten Barnweir, Soren's close friend, turned every word she said into a lie. She never had a chance. The judges unanimously found her guilty. Worse, her father watched, crying out for his daughter, desperate to be by her side. They never got to say goodbye.

The second time she came here, City Guardsmen fastened her and Darran to wooden stocks with chains and wooden cuffs, then left them to the mercy of the Vaim yet again. They believed she and Thislen snuck off the island the first time and found refuge on a fishing boat, thanks to Tamsa's lies.

That second time was why she was here now, staging an ill-advised rescue without permission from Rendyn or the Night Council. Not that she cared what Rendyn thought. She was here, and Thislen was there, and someone had to do something before it was too late.

I'm still alive, and Thislen had better be.

Mila lifted her chin and huffed, tearing her gaze from the Justica. What good was it to be afraid of a heap of stone, anyway? The building didn't do anything to her. The Ruling Council did. Soren did.

The Justica's courtyard was flanked by cook shops and drink stalls. Many people came to view the trials of friends or foes, or to petition cases. Often after their cases, and sometimes before, if they weren't too anxious, people would get something to eat.

There was a single tavern that stood alone, twice the size of the rest, resting at the shoreline to the Justica's right. The sign above the door depicted a man in a boat, tipping overboard as he drank from a tankard. A short pier floated on the sea beyond it, fixed to the quay by strong ropes. Lines of rowboats bobbed there, clunking together as the waves grew choppy where they met the shore.

This was the Ferryman's Mead, the most popular hub for the people who rowed others around the island. Where other cookshops and drink stalls were plying a modest trade, the Ferryman's Mead was overflowing. People who could find no space inside sat on benches or stood leaning against the walls. It was early afternoon, a time when many of the ferryfolk ate their lunch.

Trevon dressed in the clothes favored by the seafaring workers. A thick coat with an oil-cloth top layer, a hooded cowl, and a pair of fingerless gloves with rough leather palms made a perfect disguise. Apart from paler skin that wasn't weather-worn by the sea, he looked much the same as every other ferryman.

Mila's confidence rose with every step. She'd done well in choosing their clothes. This scheme of hers might actually work.

No, not might. This time it has *to work.* She set her jaw, following Trevon past the crowds at the tavern, dodging a pair of drunk sailors singing bawdy songs at the top of their lungs. As they circled past the Ferryman's Mead, the rowboats came into clear view.

Oh no.

Mila's heart sank at the sight of several ferryfolk sitting in their rowboats with lunch pails open at their feet. The plan hinged on taking a rowboat without no one the wiser, with no alarms raised. How could they do that with eyes on them? Her steps slowed. She was ready to turn around and leave, but Trevon—

Trevon hesitated only a moment. Between one step and the next, his gait changed. His steps wobbled, he swayed. A foolish smile grew on his face. Mila's eyes widened beneath the cowl of her hood.

Is he...is he playing the drunk? This wasn't part of my plan, none of this was part of my plan!

Mila hunched her shoulders and ducked her head as she followed, hoping against hope that the scout captain knew what he was doing. Not for the first time, she wished she knew him better, knew if she could trust him.

They came to the edge of the shore, where cobblestones turned to wood. Trevon stumbled as he stepped onto the bobbing platforms of the pier, laughing softly and shaking his head as if to clear it. Then, with no hesitation at all, he veered toward one of the mooring ropes.

"Oi," a ferrywoman called, lowering her hand pie. "So far in your cups you can't find your own boat? That one isn't yours, it's Herron's."

Trevon paused, looking from the rope to the rowboat and back. "Well, damn. So it is! This is absolutely not my boat. So sorry, honored guests." He turned to Mila and Darran and bobbed his head apologetically.

The ferrywoman stood on her boat, planting a hand on her hip. The other swept down the line of bobbing vessels. "Fool. I think you came in on that one, three ropes down."

Trevon stared at her, expression blank—and then a broad, bright smile bloomed on his face. "You are a lifesaver."

Mila's heart pounded as she followed Trevon down the dock, Darran at her elbow, to the place the woman directed them to. Trevon made a show of examining the skiff, hands on his hips, before nodding.

"This is definitely it. This is where I moored." With practiced ease, he put one foot onto the boat and held it steady, offering Darran and Mila a hand down into its belly.

Mila shot him a silent look of grudging admiration as she took her seat. *He's clever, acting drunk to excuse any mistakes.*

He flashed her a grin and a wink. Her cheeks heated. *I keep underestimating him.*

As she and Darran waited, perched on the benches, Trevon fumbled the mooring rope loose, dropping it into the bottom of the bow. Trevon sat heavily on the middle-most bench, setting the whole vessel bobbing in the water. He fumbled an oar into the oarlock; the other he used to push them off the pier and into open water. He locked that one into place, too, rubbing his hands together with a grin before he began to pull. His ruse covered any missteps he made in getting them away from shore, not that he made many.

I could almost believe he actually is a ferryman, if I didn't know any better. Mila fought a smile. She made a mental note to ask him later how he knew what to do. *And how he knows how to act as if he's had several cups of ale.*

The oars dug smoothly into the water as Trevon rowed them slowly around the back of the Justica and into the Grand Quarter. The docks of the noble and wealthy stretched just as far into the sea as those in other quarters, though less than a quarter of the population used them. Small ships lined the ones nearest the Justica. These were the vessels of the merely wealthy, who could afford their own quarters and quarters for their families, but nothing ornate or oversized.

"I thought you said you hadn't been out during the daylight hours," Mila said, arching a brow.

Trevon laughed. "I haven't, but I remembered Pollon. He's a good man, though he'll slip away for a nap or a drink if you look away for two minutes. Kellan gave him a job in the tavern after he came down to us. You've seen him. He cleans the tables and picks up the dishes."

"Pollon pretended to be drunk for a moon just to get out of doing too much. Grieving his past life, he said." Darran snorted.

"Kellan let him get away with it," Trevon pointed out. "More importantly, Pollon pushed a ferry. He had a nobleman fall asleep drunk in his boat, and he took the man's purse. Got caught red-handed."

Mila's eyes widened. "So you—"

"I went and asked Pollon about ferrying. I may have given him some mead I found up here to oil the wheels." Trevon grinned.

Darran and Trevon fell into a conversation about Pollon and his antics, and Mila felt a small twinge of jealousy.

These two grew up together. They know the same people. They have the same stories. I had that once, with Ivan. She usually avoided thinking about her family. It still ached. Every night, she watched the Nattfolk. There was a familiarity among every single one of them, they all knew each other's names and families. They gossiped, played, and visited. They had their families and friends.

She lost hers the moment she was sentenced to her execution. All but Thislen had been torn away, and eventually even him. She didn't fit in. Would she ever, without those stories and ties? Would anyone want to hear about her time as a Solfolk, about her childhood?

Looking out over the water, Mila indulged herself. She closed her eyes and let thoughts of her family float to the surface of her mind.

Mila's earliest memory of Evelie, Olen, and Ivan, was when she was young and small. Her mother had passed within a week of Ivan's father—both struck by a fever that swept across Astera. Evelie held her on her lap, her arms around her waist, while Ivan told her a story about a delivery of too many flowers, and how their entire home had been crowded with them. He was small, then, and pudgy.

As they grew up, Ivan grew tall and burly, and Mila stayed small, though she was stocky in build. They played games together, making up stories. They went on adventures to slay dragons, climb mountains, and rescue entire wagonloads of orphans from any number of imagined perils. They fenced with wooden sticks, used them as walking canes, and rode them as if they were horses.

They got into the same mischief. When Ivan knocked over an entire vase of flowers, he and Mila stood among the shards and refused to say who had done it. Mila once led the charge against the tailor's dummy when it was dressed in a fancy doublet, and they had knocked it into the mud. The moment she made up the story about moths trying to eat it, Ivan backed her up.

As they got older, Mila and Ivan grew busy with work, helping their parents with their shops. Every evening, however, they ate the same food. The four of them shared dinner together on the ships, or luncheons in one shop or the other.

All of it was overseen by the constant presence of Evelie and Olen. The two were fond of one another, and respectful of the loyalty each bore to their departed spouse. Evelie wasn't her mother, but it was she who taught Mila to cook and mend. It was she who told her what growing up would entail for a woman. It was she who teased her about boys and gave her advice, even when Mila didn't show much interest in courtship.

And Olen, there would never be enough words to describe what Olen meant to her. Her father was once her sun and moon, the guiding force of her life. Now that she was on her own, what he taught her was the armor she wore to face the world. How many days had been spent learning the names of flowers and herbs at his elbow? How many afternoons did they sing while they worked, the air full of the sharp scent of crushed herbs and off-tune lyrics?

As cobbled together as their little family was, it was still hers. And it was gone.

Will I ever have those kinds of stories again? How long will it take before I feel like I belong?

Except she felt she belonged in a different way—and that frightened her. When she had been a Solfolk, her life was steered by her family. Olen expected her to learn his trade of healing and do apothecary work. Eventually, he said more than once, he wanted her to take over the shop. Ivan grew strange as they got older, changing from her closest friend and brother to someone who wanted more. He wanted something Mila couldn't give, because she didn't want to lose what they had. He was her brother in all but blood. Evelie fussed over every potential husband and talked about the children Mila would have and the family she would raise, never once asking if that was something Mila wanted.

The Nattfolk were different. They didn't know her past, and they didn't care. They asked her what she wanted to do. When she accepted the position with the scouts a second time, they helped her dive into it with both feet. Mila chose adventure for herself, chose weapons work and running along the rooftops. Among the Nattfolk, she made her own choices. She chose freedom.

And I like who I am as a Nattfolk. This, this is me.

Or was she fooling herself? Was she playing a part that wasn't real? How could two such separate ideas—that she was happy where she was and she missed what she had before—coexist?

Mila shook her head, pushing the thoughts from her mind. They were too painful. She had a job to do. She would locate *Ship Artaith*. That was what mattered right now.

Trevon rowed through a forest of silent ships, their masts reaching toward the sun. Every pier held a miniature army of carracks, the modest vessels the wealthy favored, and galleons, immense vessels passed down for generations. Each one belonged to a single family of merchants, esteemed artisans, or nobility. Not one was unadorned, all of them decorated with painted carvings, gilt scrollwork, and large glittering glass windows. They were a disgusting show of wealth. Mila wondered whose idea it was to house a single family and the odd servant or five while others crammed onto ships like fish in a barrel to survive.

Mila lifted the front of her hood, scanning the ships as they passed and the shoreline beyond. The *Bestant Belle*, Lord Soren's ornate vessel, always docked just behind the Bestant Estate, a distinctive mansion three stories tall and decorated from top to bottom. *Ship Artaith* was moored a few spots down the same pier.

All she had to do was find— "There," she breathed, pointing.

A large, sweeping expanse of lawn dotted with hedgerows and fountains surrounded the miniature palace. Garish towers stood at all four corners, their peaked roofs a feeble mirror of the glittering spires of the castle Perilee in the distance.

"Which one is it?" Darran asked, leaning in beside her.

"That's Soren's estate, which means that ship there is the *Bestant Belle*, and that means…" she trailed off, counting the ships along the dock.

The galleon stood three down from the *Belle*, swaying sedately. Just above the waterline was a row of portholes. The level above that bore regular windows, and a cabin built in the center of the deck seemed made of nothing else. The vessel's carvings were beautiful, but unpainted. No gilding glinted in the weak light. The entire ship had the air of making itself invisible among its ornate peers.

Probably because of what goes on in its depths, Mila thought bitterly.

"I see it," she said aloud, voice tight as she fought the urge to shout. They were so close now. Thislen was *so close.*

Darran squinted. "Strange. It's the only one that hasn't got a name on the side."

Trevon slowed the rowboat, glancing over his shoulder toward the shore. "Before we go storming a ship in broad daylight, I have to ask. Mila, are you sure this is the right one?" His brow furrowed. His jaw was taut, a muscle jumping at the corner of his lips. 'Nervous' was an understatement.

A surge of admiration bloomed within Mila. She understood. Her own stomach was tying itself in knots and her palms were sweaty. *He's afraid, too, and he still broke every rule and law his people have to help me carry out this insane plan.*

"Take us in, I'll make sure," she said as softly as she could above the waves.

The closer they got to *Ship Artaith*, the more insane Mila felt. She clutched the handle of her borrowed short sword beneath her cloak. Her heart hammered like a drum against her ribs.

All she had to do was confirm this was the right ship. If she did, Trevon and Darran would be right beside her. They'd board, they'd fight, and then they'd...what? Die? Get hurt? It was far-fetched to believe this would work without a hitch.

What if Thislen, Aften, and Tamsa are already hurt? What if one of them is already dead? No Nattfolk spies could get near enough to learn anything about the three captives, and they tried for weeks.

That put steel in her spine. This was the moment. There might not be another. She made it further than others, with a little help, and now there were mere moments between her and a successful rescue.

Mila straightened. "That's it. That's *Ship Artaith*."

"Get ready, then," Trevon murmured, digging the oars into the water.

They rounded the end of the dock and pulled toward the shore. Darran kept his head low, his hood pulled close over his face, but Mila scanned their target as they neared.

She counted three guards. One stood near the prow, glancing down at them briefly before dismissing them. One stood at the stern, pacing back and forth along the broad railing, turning on his heel, and pacing out of sight again. The third she couldn't see, but she could hear. Their boots thunked on the wooden deck overhead with every step.

Three guards. One for each of them.

Trevon thought along the same lines. He pulled up to the ship's stern, gesturing for Darran to climb the carved side toward the deck. Once the scout was moving, his cloak dangling from his back, Trevon rowed on. At mid-ship, he gestured for Mila to go.

She could hardly breathe from the anxiety—or was it a thrill?—as she climbed. This was her first fight. As soon as she was free of the rowboat and in no danger of falling into the water, Trevon rowed to the prow.

Mila constantly wrestled her cloak's billowing sleeves away from her hands as she felt for one painstaking handhold at a time. She considered letting the ocean have it, but decided against it. Wearing the cloak, there was no danger of her face being revealed, especially if she were spotted climbing the side of the ship.

The nearby vessels stood empty. In the morning, the Grand Quarter bustled as servants and sailors loaded supplies, and in the evenings the merchants would set out the purchases to be loaded up the next day, hours before the nobles left the island—but in the early afternoon, it was dead quiet. Sailors were sleeping. Servants were at the massive houses, attending to a thousand different tasks. The families themselves were off doing whatever it was the wealthy did to fill their time. Walking in parks, eating fine food, and shopping, no doubt.

There was no one to see her. She, Darran, and Trevon all scaled the gently curving sides of the ship until they hung just below the railing. Mila's heart fluttered. She sucked in a quiet breath and held it.

She peered cautiously between the spindles of the railing. The guard before her paced, then let out a great sigh. He sat on a stool in the middle of the deck, facing the gangplank before him.

The gangplank on the *other* side of the ship. Her target was facing away from her. She lowered herself back down and glanced toward the prow.

Trevon nodded, his jaw set. She turned and passed the nod along to Darran, and they began.

Easy, now. Slow and steady, Mila coached herself. She grasped the railing above, arms straining as she used them and a meager foothold to haul herself up. She swung over the railing, twisting so her target was in sight. The man hadn't spotted her.

The ship's rigging creaked softly. Something metal rattled. The faintest scuff of her boot went entirely unnoticed. She glanced to either side. No sounds of fighting reached her ears. Darran and Trevon either weren't in place or were waiting for the perfect opportunity to strike. Perhaps with the way their guards were placed, they couldn't get over the railing.

A small, grim smile crossed her lips. All they needed was a moment to get aboard the galleon, and for that, they needed a diversion.

Mila eased her sword free, turning the blade as she raised it over her head—and brought it down hilt-first in a swing at the side of the man's head.

The shadow of her arm, sprawled across the deck, gave her away.

"What the—" The guard whirled on his seat.

The pommel caught him and sent him reeling, but it didn't hit the right spot. He was still conscious. Mila felt adrenaline course through her, sending sparks along every vein in her body. Her fingers and toes tingled. Every breath she took she could feel fill her chest. She pursued the man, even as she heard a soft shout from one side and a rattle from the other.

Darran and Trevon are in the fight. I did it.

"Help, someone, the alarm," her target gasped, lurching to his feet and staggering toward the gangplank.

Oh no, that won't do at all.

Savage determination drove her forward. This was too important. This time, she would succeed, damn it all! Mila darted around the man, putting herself between him and his exit.

He drew his sword. It was a proper blade with much longer reach.

Mila's heart thudded somewhere behind her ears. *You trained for this,* she reassured herself, even as her palms became clammy. Her blood roared through her body with all the force of a massive waterfall, making every nerve come alive. Sparring in the training cavern with the other Nattfolk scouts never felt like this. Then again, those controlled bouts could never be as dangerous, either.

She was in an actual fight.

Her breath caught. The guard lunged. Mila spun to the side on pure instinct, watching the blade catch the light as it passed through the empty air where she had stood. She stuck her foot out, trusting Trevon and his advice.

"When an opponent commits to a big action, they can't easily change direction. Big actions fail without following through. Either it's a feint or the perfect opportunity to use their own momentum against them."

Mila nodded, brow furrowed, nervously adjusting her grip on the hilt of her sword. The scout captain lunged, swinging down at her with a big overhead strike. He slowed it down dramatically as soon as her eyes lifted to follow it, giving her ample time to dodge to one side.

"Good. Now again, but this time push me as I pass."

Over and over they practiced the move, until Trevon was doing it at speed. His practice blade was made of wood. Mila would have bruises for days—but in the end, she sent him tumbling to the ground more often than he landed a blow.

It was difficult to change direction once sword and body were already in motion. Mila brought up her elbow, driving it into the guardsman's shoulder.

He sprawled face-first toward the deck. She didn't hesitate to scramble after him. It wasn't graceful, but she pounced on his back, locking an arm around his neck. He struggled, tossing an elbow back that struck her side. She bit back a yelp, lifting her sword again.

No killing. No murder. I'm not like my enemies.

She thwacked him upside the head with her hilt, and this time the blow struck true. He went limp.

Mila waited. What if it was a trick? What if he was just waiting for her to loosen her grip before he turned on her to attack again? Slowly, she relaxed her grip, easing the man to the deck.

Darran and Trevon hurried toward her. Trevon bore a bruise on his cheek, but the boys appeared otherwise unharmed. Relief flooded through her.

"Mila, are you hurt?" Trevon asked, kneeling beside her and her fallen foe.

"No." As she stood, her ankle throbbed from where the guard had tripped over it. Her side protested any movement. Come tomorrow, she would have new bruises. "Well, not badly," she amended.

Her pulse slowed, her heart back where it belonged. She should have been terrified. This was her first fight, her first actual battle with someone who wanted to do her harm. She could have died. She could have killed him!

Instead, she felt as though she had swallowed lightning, as if it coursed through every inch of her body. Arcs of crackling levin could burst out of her fingers and she wouldn't be surprised. She wanted to move. She wanted another fight.

This isn't like me. Or was it? Could she be so different from the gentle healer she was raised to be and still be herself? Was this who she always was deep down?

"Your eyes are enormous." Darran clapped her on the shoulder, grinning.

Trevon laughed. "You fought well. If you start to shake, let me know. Now, didn't we come here for a reason?"

Mila adjusted her grip on her sword and squared her shoulders. "Right. We have a job to do. Let's go get our friends."

6

Outside the meager sliver of the porthole window, the midday sun painted the sky a brilliant, vivid blue. Aften stared at it, unmoving. His hands were weighed down by the heavy chains around his wrists. It was hard to move them. They ached, and the skin was chafed and raw. His stomach growled. It was loud in the quiet, the only sound beside the soft creak of wood around him and a slow drip of water somewhere. His mouth was dry, and his throat burned. Every *plip, plip, plip* made it worse.

I've never gone with so little food and water before. Not that his captors cared. His wrists were thinner than before, the bones jutting out.

Strange how little the guards' and Garridan's actions affected their lives, and how they had consumed his. His mind was brimming with dreams of food and freedom, both equally impossible to attain.

Part of it might be his fault. Aften always wanted to see the sun, to walk among the Solfolk, to see what the world was like outside of his monotonous night to night. Like in some twisted fairy story of old, his wish came true in the worst possible way.

See what you get for stepping out of bounds?

He dropped his head against the wooden wall behind him, closing his eyes. His father, Rendyn Sivivan, head of the Night Council and unofficial king to the Nattfolk, never hesitated to tell him how much trouble he was. He was always in the way, always a nuisance, always useless. Now, his eagerness to charge into the sun landed him in real trouble.

For all their plotting, Aften and Tamsa couldn't find a way out. Litanies of his own shortcomings echoed through his mind in his father's voice. He'd heard the same words often enough over meals and delivered in lectures. Everything he did to fix it always fell short. He was just too carefree, irresponsible, lazy, foolish...

I kept my thoughts to myself. I knew he'd hate every single one. He knew exactly what Rendyn would say if he ever asked to be a Solwalker agent.

"We are Nattfolk, and you in particular. You are my son. Our family has a reputation to uphold. What would people say if you ran off to the Solfolk? What would they think of me, of your sister?"

He'd heard it before, when he asked to move out to the Barracks.

Tamsa, of course, could do wrong. She was the shining example of a Nattfolk and Sivivan both. She was the heir their father always wanted, and she lorded it over Aften every chance she got. Tamsa always knew what was best. Tamsa always made the best plans. Tamsa knew what everyone needed and when, and there was no point in arguing with her about it.

Except now the tables had turned. Tamsa ruined everything in one fell swoop. She refused to listen to him, as usual, because she was always right. They were caught. Once they were captives, Tamsa lied through her teeth—because, again, only *she* could handle the situation. The only part that truly surprised Aften was that she lied to protect him. He didn't realize she cared.

Lord Soren Bestant ordered Aften dragged out of the cell and fastened to a chair in full view of his friends to be tortured. Tamsa stopped them. She bargained for his safety in return for answers, and then she lied so masterfully they got away with it. She convinced the noblemen that they were simple fisherfolk, convinced by bad people to do bad things. All she had to do was betray Mila and Thislen, the first people outside of Darran that seemed to like Aften just as he was.

Her lies led to Darran being sent to Astera to die. She never intended it, but it still happened. For the first time, she knew she had done wrong. She'd *apologized*.

A kernel of anger still festered in Aften's chest. Even now, after weeks of trying to sort through his complicated feelings around her, around the changes he saw in her, he couldn't forgive her entirely.

Maybe it's time to really try. We might not have much time left.

Thislen couldn't withstand the torture forever. When he broke, it would be Aften's turn, or Tamsa's. Rendyn drilled one thing into his children's skull above all others. The secret must remain so. Every possible horrible consequence ran through Aften's mind.

The Nattfolk would be captured, their home destroyed, their lives uprooted. If they were lucky, they would be split up. Sound men and women would be sent to the mines as slaves, everyone else would be sold off-island. If they were unlucky, every single Nattfolk would be executed. Maybe no one but the Ruling Council would learn of their existence. Maybe word would get out. If that happened, the Solfolk would be in danger, too. Not knowing what would happen, they might stay on the island, Vaim or no Vaim. How many would die? How many would the Ruling Council punish for surviving? The entire balance of power in Astera would be thrown off-kilter, and it was all teetering on a knife's edge as it was.

The secret must remain hidden. Their sole responsibility now was to deny anything Thislen said, say nothing, and die as quickly as they could.

Aften shouldn't go to his Ancestors angry at his sister. The pieces of his heart seemed impossible to glue back together, but time was running out. Hope was all but gone, a hollow platitude that did nothing to ease his grief or fury.

Tamsa slept, curled in a ball that faced the prone figure of Thislen. The thief lay wrapped in her blanket. She twitched, her eyelids flickering and her hand stealing across the wood toward the man beside her as she suffered a fitful dream.

I'll regret hating her if we never make it off this ship.

Darran often told Aften he was too easily taken advantage of because he wanted to be kind. Was his sister playing on that, on the situation they were in? What would Darran say about forgiving Tamsa?

I'll never find out.

A pit in his chest yawned into a chasm, sucking up everything inside of him but pain. He closed his eyes. A deep breath eased the empty ache. He opened them again.

Things might never get better, but they could get worse. Time was running out. Aften's gaze drifted to Thislen, whose face was pale. Wavy locks of dark hair clung to his forehead. His breathing was ragged and uneven. Despite the horrible situation they found themselves in, Aften couldn't help but admire him. It was truly impressive to last nearly a moon through daily—well, nightly—torture. No one could expect him to last much longer.

How long before he talks? How much longer do we have? As meager as their safety was, it was still protection of a sort. How long before the end?

Over and over, his mind circled these thoughts, picking at them until they ached before moving on to the next. Tamsa, Thislen, Darran, the end of his life. Tamsa, Thislen, Darran...

I'm exhausted. I'm hungry. I'm...scared. He wasn't as strong as the thief. If they tortured him, he might break. He might betray his people.

He'd probably last less than a single bell.

Maybe I should ask Tamsa to kill me. Maybe that's all I can do for the Nattfolk now.

He closed his eyes, fighting the lump in his throat. His father was right. He wasn't good enough. He'd stumbled into a way to hurt them all. He didn't fit amongst his own people. He wasn't wanted there, and now it was time to do what was necessary. This last, ultimate act was all he could do to help the Nattfolk and honor his family legacy.

He licked his lips, trying to work up the courage to wake his sister. If only the lump in his throat weren't choking him!

I can't let it be my fault that the Nattfolk fall. I can't let Father be right. Why did I have to be born a Sivivan? If I hadn't been, maybe I could have fit somewhere. Maybe I could have done something useful. Maybe I could have helped more.

At least he wouldn't have to face his father again. Their last meeting, before Aften and Mila escaped with Darran's help, was when Rendyn Sivivan took away the surface entirely because Aften told the entire Night Council long-held family secrets. He told them about the Vaim and the curse.

Maybe after we're gone, someone will do something about it. Mila couldn't. She'd been banished before they ran away. After what happened, she undoubtedly was bundled onto the next ship off the island and was long gone. The only people left who knew that the Vaim weren't what they seemed were the Night Council themselves. One of them *had* to step up.

Aften knew they wouldn't.

Everything lay in shambles. Chains clinked as he dropped his head into his hands.

More than one set of boots thudded down the stairs at the end of the corridor. Aften's head snapped up, his breath catching. A tight, cold band of steel formed around his head and chest. Both ached with anticipation and nerves.

It isn't time for food. It wasn't evening. It wasn't even that far past noon. Garridan Artaith had responsibilities during the day, didn't he? What were the chances it was the torturer, coming for Thislen at a strange time to make everything worse? His heart pounded so fast and so wildly, Aften was sure it would beat its way right out of his ribs.

I should wake Tamsa. I should warn Thislen. I should say something.

Aften couldn't move. Why couldn't he move? His mouth was dry, his throat closed. He couldn't force a single word out. His hands curled around the chains below his wrists until the cold metal warmed, until it bit into his skin.

A strangled sound caught in the back of his throat as the door rattled. *They're coming for us. They figured out that me and Tamsa have secrets, and they're coming for us, not Thislen.* He opened his mouth to shout. Nothing happened.

The sound of metal sliding into the lock was clear in the silence. Aften's lips worked as a cold sweat broke out across his body.

Clunk.

The door swung open.

Aften reeled. The first thing that greeted him was a ghost. A dark shrouded figure, black from head to toe, stared at him across the room—and it had Darran's face. He fell back against the wall, hardly able to breathe.

I've snapped. I've lost my mind. Or worse, it's Darran come down from the stars to take me with him. Am I dying?

Wasn't that what he wanted? Here he was, reuniting with Darran at last. No more hunger, or thirst, or pain. The threat of torture wouldn't be able to reach him now. He would never betray the Nattfolk.

Yet now that his end was standing before him, he wasn't so sure death was the answer.

His eyes burned. His chest ached for air he couldn't pull into his lungs.

"Aften," the spirit breathed, crossing the room in great bounding strides. "Aften, breathe. Please breathe." Darran shoved lock picks into the cell's barred door, wrestling with them. A grimace twisted his face.

It sounded just like him. And the ghost wasn't alone. Behind it came another cloaked figure, the hood shadowing much of their face—and Scout Captain Trevon.

Why would Trevon come to take me to the stars?

Darran couldn't keep his eyes on his work. They kept darting up to Aften's stunned face. Tamsa woke as the second ghost hit the barred door, rattling it.

"Thislen! Is he alright? Tamsa—" That was Mila's voice. She pushed the hood back impatiently, stretching an arm through the bars toward the prone bundle that was her dearest friend.

Tamsa stared, as stunned as Aften was, her jaw hanging open.

Trevon gently took the picks from Darran's hands and shouldered him aside. He prodded, twisted, and the lock clicked open. Aften shook his head. He couldn't be dreaming. He would never summon Trevon to his fantasies or death throes or...whatever this was.

The moment the barred door swung open, Darran pushed past Trevon, falling to his knees at Aften's side and gathering him into his arms.

"You're so thin. Ancestors, Aften, I'm so sorry. We wanted to come sooner, I swear."

Numbly, Aften curled his fingers into the mottled shirt beneath the cloak. The arms that encircled him, the chest he was pressed against—they were warm.

"Are you real?" Aften croaked, eyes burning.

"Of course I'm real." Darran pulled back, yanking the blanket away and checking Aften for injuries. His jaw was taut, his lips pressed thin.

He's afraid.

"I'm not hurt," Aften blurted. Not like Thislen was.

"Aften and I are fine," Tamsa managed. "We're hungry, and thirsty, and our wrists and ankles are a mess, but we...we weren't tortured." Her eyes darted between their rescuers as if she couldn't quite trust what she was seeing, either.

Mila woodenly crossed the cell toward Thislen, her face a mask of fear and concern.

Aften's attention was recaptured as Darran cupped his cheek with a hand and pressed their foreheads together. His breath caught.

"I was so worried. I was so afraid of what we'd find." Darran let out an explosive sigh of relief and pulled Aften close again, squeezing him tight.

Aften clung to the cloak at Darran's back as heat climbed up his cheeks and toward his ears. He'd dreamed of reuniting with Darran by some miracle or other, imagined what he would say, what he'd do. He'd never imagined it quite so...intimate.

It was better than he could have hoped. The words he meant to say a hundred times and never managed sat on the tip of his tongue. Was now the time to confess? No, he was just glad to have his best friend in his arms.

They only parted when Trevon put a hand on Darran's shoulder, holding up the lock picks. "Let me get him loose."

Darran sat back, holding Aften's hands as the locks were picked. It felt strange to lift and move his arms with such ease. Now that his hands were in Darran's, it was easy to see how dirty he was, how much grime and dried blood crusted his skin. He shuddered, letting the scout pull him to his feet.

Aften's knees buckled, and he staggered into Darran's chest. Without a word, Darran caught him and held him steady until he found his balance. The room spun, and he wasn't sure how much of it was from the blood rushing to his cheeks and how much was from hunger, thirst, and pain.

Oh, the pain! He hadn't realized his knees, ankles, and wrists would hurt this much. They ached from disuse, from being trapped in the same uncomfortable positions for days.

"Are you alright?" Darran asked.

"I will be. Can we leave?"

"Thislen won't wake up," Mila said, turning to face them.

The thief hadn't stirred, not even to a gentle shake of his shoulders. Tamsa, also freed, had two fingers on Thislen's wrist. "He's weak. He's been through a lot."

Mila snapped a glare onto Tamsa. "I can see that. He looks awful."

Tamsa frowned. "He's feverish and hurt. You'll need to carry him."

"Darran and I can do that," Trevon assured, passing Aften his sword. It felt impossibly heavy, far more than it ever had before. He held it up anyway, a determined grimace on his face.

With a blade in his hand, Aften felt much better.

Let them try to trap me again, I dare them. I dare all of them.

He closed his eyes, breathing deep. There was too much going on. Darran was alive, not dead. He stood so close Aften could feel his warmth. He and Tamsa survived and might live to see many more days—so he could be angry with her if he wanted to. Mila was. Thislen was hurt. They were escaping. There would be no chains tomorrow. There would be food, and a bath.

There would be his father.

So much good mingled with so much bad that he couldn't sort out what he was feeling. For the moment, he chose not to try. Instead, he crammed all those emotions deep down for another time. Aften opened his eyes and started toward the door.

Only then did Darran pull one of Thislen's arms over his shoulder.

"It's daylight, we can't carry him through the city like this," Tamsa said, hovering nearby. Mila hovered as well, casting a seething glare at Aften's sister.

"Good thing we have a boat," Trevon said with a grin, ducking beneath Thislen's other arm. "Now, let's get out of here."

The first thing Thislen became aware of was pain. His feet were dragging, and his knee and hip throbbed with agony with every step the people carrying him took. He struggled feebly, breath catching.

They're taking me back there. No, I can't. I can't do it!

"Thislen! Thislen, stop, it's us," Mila said. A cool hand pressed to his cheek.

It took enormous effort for him to open his eyes, as though his eyelids were made of lead.

Mila's face swam into view, her concerned eyes fixed on his. Behind her, the ghosts of Percivan and Vern leaned in. Their expressions mirrored hers. Had Mila died? Did her ghost now haunt him, too?

No, please no.

"Mila," Thislen breathed, his tongue heavy in his mouth. "I'm sorry. I'm so sorry."

Mila shot a worried look to one side.

"He didn't break," Tamsa said firmly.

"Don't be sorry, then. Everything will be alright." Mila smiled as she turned back to him, though it was tense and small.

I must look awful. Even the dead are worried.

"Come on, we have to get out of here," Aften said from somewhere ahead.

It took a few more miserable, painful steps for him to realize that Tamsa and Aften had spoken to Mila's ghost. His head jerked up. "Wait, Mila? What's happening?"

"I'm here. Don't worry, Thislen, we're taking you home."

But I haven't got a home.

His head was spinning. Regardless of where, they were *going*. Thislen did not have to face that room tonight. They were free. He was *free*. The thought made his ears ring.

They were in the corridor, he realized. A Nattfolk he didn't know was under one of his arms, and a cloak-shrouded Darran was under the other. The hall was quiet and empty, a single door swinging gently back and forth with the slight sway of the ship. As they passed, Thislen glimpsed the table inside the cabin. It was littered with tools. Beside it stood a chair with straps all over, and rust-red stains.

Thislen retched. Nothing came up. His stomach heaved and turned, but it couldn't even wring out bile. His bearers moved faster. Someone, he didn't see who, slammed the door shut behind them.

Up the steps they went, Thislen grimacing, his head floating in a fog that enveloped him and passed through him, as if he weren't quite real. He shivered, struggling to help Darran and the stranger haul him along. He was probably more of a hindrance than a help, but it seemed wrong not to try, now that he was awake. Adrenaline and adrenaline alone kept him that way. He could feel exhaustion pulling at the back of his mind like an army of the Vaim wanting to drag him down into still, quiet darkness.

The transition from belowdecks to the open air was abrupt. The rush of fresh air cleared his head and flooded his lungs, making his dizziness all the worse. The thin light of a late autumn sun stabbed into his eyes until they watered, even though he wasn't looking up. Every step jarred his leg, and the warm fire of pain crawled along his skin. The combination of it all hit him like a blow. He sagged, his head lolling.

Too much, it's too much.

Darran and the stranger staggered, but neither fell. As they crossed the deck, he tried again and again to open his watering eyes. He gave up as they approached the railing.

Wait. This is the wrong side. The gangplank is...

Mila swung over the railing and vanished, her cloak snapping briefly behind her as she fell. Thislen couldn't even muster a cry of alarm, though his heart raced. There *was* a splash below, but a small one, and a *thunk* that went with it.

"I've got it. I'll hold it steady. Drop down a line." Mila called.

There was plenty of rope on the deck for Tamsa to choose from. She quickly tied off a knot on the railing and dropped the rest over the side, gesturing Aften to go down first.

Thislen watched Aften vanish over the railing, their eyes meeting briefly. The stranger beside him was now holding a sword, which he sheathed by balancing most of Thislen's weight against Darran for a moment. Strange. Where did he get a sword from?

Tamsa vanished from view next, her gaze sweeping the deck and whatever else lay behind them. A dock, Thislen presumed. A quiet, empty dock because no one raised an alarm.

Darran held Thislen up while the stranger loosened the rope. Instead of tying it, he wrapped it around the railing twice and offered Darran the end before leaning over to pull up the other side.

Darran looped and knotted the rope around Thislen's waist.

"Gah," Thislen gasped, grimacing as the coils pressed on battered ribs, two of the burns, and the long cut down his side.

"I'm sorry. We have to do this. You're in no shape to climb down."

"I know. I don't care." He was lying. The pain intimidated him, after experiencing so much of it for so long. It didn't matter nearly as much as escape, though.

When Darran carried him to the railing, the rope shortened with them. Thislen turned his head to see the stranger, the other end of the rope slung around himself, backing across the deck. He planned to serve as a counterweight to their rudimentary pulley.

Ah, that will work.

Thislen helped Darran as much as he could to lever himself over the side. He curled both hands around the rope, clinging with all the strength he had left.

"Do it quick, please." Thislen looked into Darran's eyes.

"Hold on," was all Darran said in return, gesturing over his shoulder.

Darran let go. Fire spread along Thislen's ribs. He could hardly breathe, even with the rope knotted so it couldn't cut in. It still squeezed. They let him down in short, jerky bursts of movement. His world narrowed to the rope in front of his face and a single thought: Don't let go.

Hands caught him, too many of them, all sharing his weight. Five on his back and one on the rope over his head, guiding him down. They untied him quickly, but his vision swam too much to tell who did what. All he knew was when it all stopped, when he was lowered to the bottom of the rowboat, bobbing like a cork in the sea. Every beat of his heart throbbed in his bruises, his cuts, his burns, his knee, and his hip. Every breath ached. He half expected to be sick, the pain wracking him with nausea.

Thislen was dimly aware of the thunk of feet on either side of his head, of the clunk of wood on wood, and the sudden swaying movement as their vessel began to move. He felt a hand in his own, a hand with thin fingers. Someone lay on either side of him, also nestled in the boat's bottom. Tamsa, he guessed, and Aften. Tamsa, who was holding his hand.

One of the pair above them shed their Ravan cloak and draped it over them. Darkness fell, pierced in little pinpricks by light leaking through the woven cloth. The air became stuffy and close.

"We did it," Mila said outside their makeshift shelter, a smile in her voice.

The stranger laughed breathlessly. "We did. Now, we just have to get home. Easy."

They were free.

It was over.

With a weak smile and a sigh, Thislen let himself fall to the abyss in the back of his mind.

7

Mila couldn't reconcile her relief and her concern. They warred inside her with every step, mixing until she couldn't tell what she felt between one moment and the next. She held the lantern aloft as they made their way down the gentle slope that bordered the underground lake, glancing back every few seconds.

Trevon and Darran were sweating with the effort of carrying Thislen. He'd fallen unconscious in the boat, and they hadn't been able to rouse him. His head lolled as they walked, swinging back and forth with every staggered step.

"We're almost there," she said, her voice whispering softly from the walls.

They had covered him and Darran both in a Ravan cloak to get through the city. Even then, they'd attracted more attention than Mila felt comfortable with. She'd held her breath until they reached the safety of the stone corridors beneath Astera. Her hands still trembled, she couldn't quite shake her nerves.

Thislen's injuries worried her. They had no time to stop and look him over on their way down. Aften and Tamsa weren't in good shape either, if their appearances were anything to judge by. They'd changed so much in such a short amount of time.

It must have felt like years to them.

The siblings were thinner, with hollows in their cheeks that hadn't been there before and bones jutting out of their wrists. Their clothes and skin were filthy. Their curly hair was in snarls. Worse, their expressions were different. It unsettled her to look at Aften and see him without that sparkle in his eye or a grin on his face. Something dark and sad set into the way he held his jaw. Tamsa, in contrast, had softened. Her eyes were no longer agate-hard, but vulnerable and frail—and fixed on Thislen.

Thislen had changed the most.

Mila remembered their first meeting. He'd been injured then, with the same ashen pallor to his skin and the same high spots of color on his cheeks from a fever. He'd been thin then, too. Food must have been scarce for a thief on Astera's streets, after all. Still, he'd been strong, made of muscle more than anything else.

Now, he was so starved his skin hung loose on his bones. She feared a good push might snap one of those bones in half. When they found the captives on the ship, Thislen's face had been a picture of anguish and misery that went all the way through him. When he'd looked at her, he hadn't seen her. He'd looked beyond her.

Somehow, he gained more secrets on that ship.

Mila could see them in the depths of his dark eyes, like the flicker of a distant candle in the night. He hid them away, using silence as armor. How many more did he have? Every single one pierced him like a thorn in the side. Mila could *see* it, but he refused to trust her, refused to trust anyone enough to let them out. Maybe he didn't even trust himself.

He's carrying more than he can bear, though, and I'm right here. I just have to let him know. I'm here.

All that worry washed over her like a wave onto the shore, and when it went out, the relief came in its wake. The rescue worked. Aften, Tamsa, and Thislen were back with the Nattfolk, safely tucked beneath the ground once more. They'd spirited them away with no one the wiser.

The massive lake cavern narrowed back down to a tunnel. Their shuffling footsteps echoed airily off the walls, fading away a moment later. Mila glanced back again.

She caught Darran doing the same. Behind him, Aften walked sluggishly at the rear of the group. His head and shoulders were slumped with exhaustion, and his feet scuffed the floor. Darran looked forward again, hefting Thislen's weight. His eyes met Mila's, and he gave a small smile. His own relief was writ large on his features—and a hint of longing.

He wants to talk to Aften, but not with us listening in. Mila felt her cheeks heat as she turned back, and a smile of her own formed. About time they had the chance.

Ahead of them, light bled into the tunnel from the lanterns and braziers of the Commons. Three figures stood at the mouth of the path, black silhouettes Mila couldn't identify at a glance.

"I see them. And they have—Ancestors, is that—Someone go get Councilman Rendyn, go, hurry!" The voice echoed toward them. Mila recognized it as Penni, one of the other scouts.

One figure took off, vanishing from sight. The other two ran toward them.

Well, we're in for it now. Mila grimaced.

Harlon and Penni replaced Trevon and Darran, giving them a much-needed break the last length of their journey. They carried Thislen carefully, exchanging worried looks.

"Trevon, what did you do?" Harlon asked.

"Rescued a few of our own. Someone had to do it." Trevon gave his scout a tired smile.

Penni looked dubiously between the scout captain and Mila. "The Councilman isn't happy."

The wrath of Rendyn Sivivan was something to be feared, so Mila understood the reluctance to celebrate. When someone was in trouble with Rendyn Sivivan, the punishment was swift and harsh. He never injured anyone—but he rarely gave them second chances, either. Mila was one of those few exceptions, and she was pushing her luck.

He may be the most stubborn man who ever lived, but there's no way he can stay angry when we've saved his children. At least, I hope.

She couldn't decide who was worse: Rendyn Sivivan or Lord Soren Bestant. Soren wore his ego on his sleeve, strutting about with cocky confidence, demanding whatever he wanted and expecting it to be delivered. Rendyn hid his demands in layers of suggestion and questions. His iron will and heated retaliation for those who failed his expectations was unforgiving. With a quiet word, he could guide the Night Council to do exactly what he wanted. Soren wasn't subtle. His maneuvers were a showy display, enacted by guards and the Ruling Council alike. And where Rendyn bore grudges without relent, Soren could be persuaded to forgive—if the price was right.

Then again, Soren tried to kill her more than once. Rendyn had never gone *that* far.

Yet.

The Commons were empty apart from a small cluster of scouts. Ophelia and Agathe stood to one side, watching the tired rescue party stream into the cavern. Others, too. It seemed a guard had been set at every entrance to the underground city, waiting for them to return. It struck Mila that Rendyn might have assumed they'd made a run for it and weren't planning to come back at all. A flash of irritation raced up the back of her head and down into her cheeks, and she frowned. She did what she said she would, damn him, and she wouldn't let him ruin her triumph.

"Ophelia, Agathe, get soap and fresh clothes to the baths. Aften and Tamsa are going to want to wash up," Mila snapped, taking charge. She held out the lantern until a scout took it from her. She didn't know his name.

Aften and Tamsa looked up at the mention of their names. Relief washed over Tamsa's face, and she self-consciously tugged the sleeves of her shirt down over her wrists. The raw patches of chafed skin disappeared.

"You," Mila said, pointing to another cluster of scouts. "Get bandages and salve to the baths as well. You two, get food and take it to the Barracks. Wake Kellan if you have to, but make sure it's hot. Broth, too. You two, go set up ground level bunks near mine—I know they're empty. Blankets, pillows, sleeping pads, the works."

Her miniature army set to their tasks, scattering. The bathing cavern was made of three modest hot springs and one cool pool. She didn't know where the water came from, or how it left, but it was always crystalline clear when she went to wash up. Darran split off from her, leading Aften and Tamsa away.

"Don't worry, I'll stay with them," he assured Mila as he passed.

"Thank you."

That left her free to turn to Harlon and Penni. Thislen stirred, semi-conscious at best. His lips moved, but she couldn't make out what he was saying. Her brows drew down. She grew up learning how the body worked, and a fever that caused muttering and drifting in and out of consciousness meant the thief had an infection somewhere. Mila hadn't even seen the full extent of his injuries, but now she knew there was at least one open wound. It needed to be cleaned.

How much of her past did she want to reveal? How much of the apothecary's apprentice did she want to show the Nattfolk if it meant helping Thislen?

"We have to get him into a bunk," Mila said. Only once Harlon and Penni moved did she realize she said it aloud.

Trevon appeared at her elbow, steering her along in their wake. "Are you alright?"

"I'm fine," she snapped.

Trevon's brows jumped. "Really?"

Mila felt a flush creep up her cheeks.

No. I'm furious. How could Soren do something like this to another person? How could anyone justify torture? And what about me, what about my past? There's only so much I can do without revealing my hand. If I let anyone know I'm a healer, I'll be chained to these caves forever. No more moon, no more air. And there's a fight yet to come, when Rendyn arrives, and, and, and...

She didn't dignify Trevon's question with an answer, hurrying a few steps ahead of the captain. She hadn't meant to snap at him, and she couldn't trust that she wouldn't do it again. Not when so much anger was simmering beneath her skin.

They came into the cavern that housed the Barracks at last. Sounds whispered over the stones, endlessly repeating as the Nattfolk sleeping behind their curtains rustled or snored. After living here for a moon, Mila was used to the noise. In fact, she felt every ounce of her exhaustion as the thrill of the rescue faded away. Her bunk sat open, calling to her, and the scouts Mila sent prepared the bunks on either side of hers with all the industriousness of ants.

Once the mattresses were set, the blankets laid out, and the pillows propped, they prudently slipped into the crowd of their fellows. All the scouts had trailed after them like the Vaim, silent specters that wanted to see what was happening, and what would happen next.

It was easy enough for her and Trevon to help maneuver Thislen into a stone cubicle and tuck him in. Mila perched on the lip of the bunk beside him. "Can someone get water and a cloth? I want to clean him up."

She didn't bother to look over her shoulder. She heard footsteps as someone leapt to do what she asked. Instead, she reached out and tucked Thislen's hair behind one of his ears.

His eyes opened. His breath caught. He ran a hand over the stone wall beside him, over the blanket across his chest. Then Thislen looked at her.

"We...we made it?"

"We made it." Mila offered him her hand.

He took it, his grip weak. Slowly, his eyes sank closed again. This time, however, he slept.

I have to look him over. I have to do what I can to help him.

Only that held its own dangers. Mila grew up in her family's apothecary, learning the trade of a healer since she was small. She could mix a potion or a salve, wrap a bandage, or stitch a wound as well as her father could.

When she came below-ground with the Nattfolk, she told them she had no special skills to speak of. Thislen was the only person who knew any different, and he kept her secret. In her time among her new people, she learned they made do with what medicines they could steal from above-ground and the barest of basics. The Nattfolk didn't have a proper healer. The midwives did their best. It was never enough.

The moment I reveal what I know, what I can do, they'll make *me do it or* threaten *to send me away again. Rendyn will finally have his excuse to trap me in these caves forever.*

Mila frowned. So she could grow herbs, harvest every part of countless plants, identify and treat many ailments and injuries—so what? She didn't want to, and that ought to be that. Part of why she leapt at the chance to leave home in the first place, before she was sentenced to execution for seduction and witchcraft, was to avoid the future her father had so neatly laid before her feet.

Olen never asked if she wanted any of it. There was no one else to help him with the shop, however, no one else to mix the mixtures or cut the cuttings, no one else to help when he had to make a house call. Mila did what was expected of her, purely to lighten her father's load.

What a nice trap I set for myself. Now what can I do?

Thislen needed healing. She needed her freedom. Now two more emotions warred within her—resentment and sheer, stubborn pride.

The arrival of the water and cloths she asked for spared her the decision for now. She set to cleaning off Thislen's hands and arms. Removing the grime showed how badly his wrists had been rubbed raw. Her heart ached as she cleaned her way up his arms to his face and his neck.

Mila paused, then leaned in. Her brow furrowed. She hadn't imagined it—there was a rasp in his breathing she didn't like.

"What is the meaning of this?"

Mila turned quickly, instinctively bracing herself for the imminent argument, her fingers curled so tight in the damp cloth that it dripped. She set her jaw, squared her shoulders, and faced the Councilman head on.

Rendyn Sivivan hadn't spoken loudly, so as not to wake the sleeping Nattfolk around him. However, each word was laced with seething fury. His hands were balled into fists as he strode across the stone, sending the scouts scattering before him like startled gulls.

The head of the Night Council and leader of the Commons was dressed as he always was—in plain clothes, but of high quality fabrics. He put on the airs of a common man but always held himself separate. Mila didn't know why the Nattfolk couldn't see through his disguise. He was just as bad as the entire Ruling Council, no matter what he wore. He, too, had to have everything go his way, or else.

He wasn't rumpled or mussed, as he would be if he slept. His clothes didn't have a single wrinkle or crease. Had he stayed up, waiting for this to happen?

"I knew I should have sent you away from this island. What foolish, idiotic, irresponsible—" Rendyn froze, catching sight of Thislen in his bunk.

Behind him, Aften and Tamsa came into the room. They shared their father's hazel eyes and tightly curled hair. Both of them froze at the sight of the man. Mila wasn't at all surprised when Tamsa was the first to step forward.

"Father?"

Aften's heart was in two places at once. He didn't know it could do that. It was in his throat, pounding so hard he could feel his own pulse, and at the same time, it had plummeted to his feet.

His father whirled where he stood. His brows went from pulled down and together in a deep scowl to climbing toward his hair as he came to a stop.

His eyes were fixed on one person, and one person only. "Tamsa?"

Aften held his breath, waiting—but Rendyn's eyes didn't move to him at all. He knew they wouldn't, but it still stung.

Tamsa stopped several steps away from their father. "We're home." Exhaustion colored the two simple words.

A flash of resentment ran through Aften, though he tried to smother it. He knew he had failed when Darran came up beside him and gently brushed his shoulder.

"Are you alright?" he whispered.

"I'll be fine." Aften trailed after his sister. His expression chilled until it was as hard as ice. Why should he pretend he was glad to be here? Tamsa had come home, but he hadn't.

How long has it been since I thought of that cave as our home? He couldn't remember.

Still, he thought Tamsa would run to their father, and be swept into his arms and paraded around as the heir returned; the valued daughter on display for everyone to see. He hadn't expected her to keep her distance.

A lot changed on that ship, in that cell. Maybe Tamsa changed for the better.

Aften stopped a step behind her.

For a moment, everything was still. The surrounding scouts, Mila perched on the edge of Thislen's bunk like she might launch into a fight, Trevon with his arms folded, leaning against the wall beside her. Rendyn seemed a statue, chiseled from the same cold stone as his heart.

In three massive steps, Rendyn closed the distance between himself and Tamsa, wrapping her tight in his arms. "Oh, Tamsa!"

She scowled, wrestling her way free and pushing him away. He couldn't have looked more shocked if he tried. For the first time he could remember, Aften saw doubt creep into his father's eyes.

"Tamsa?"

"And Aften," Tamsa said firmly, reaching back to grab her brother's forearm.

Aften jerked, jaw slack and eyes wide. *What? Why is she—*

His sister pulled him to stand beside her, as if they were equals. His shock melted into confusion. Did she think this would mend every hurt between them? It was a start, though, and one he never expected her to make. He didn't know how to react.

Aften didn't want to forgive her. Her lies on the ship, the weeks of grief, how tired and hungry and miserable he was—that was only the beginning of his list of grievances. Ever since they were small, their father only cared about one of them. He only cared about her. Tamsa lorded it over Aften every day for most of their lives. One gesture would not be enough.

His gaze slid from his sister to his father. Rendyn's expression had gone still, an expression Aften knew well even if no one else did. His father was calculating, deciding what to do to get the best results.

The resentment inside of Aften swelled.

We were both taken; we were both held, and the only one he's glad to see is his precious heir. It isn't fair. It isn't right. This man is not my father, and he never wanted to be.

The thought was like a slap in the face. Aften never dared to think it before, but now that he had, he knew it was true. He'd never be able to forget it.

"Aften," Rendyn said at last, holding out a hand with the barest hint of a smile. "I'm glad to see both my children returned to me. Come, we have a lot to discuss. Mila Ominir—report to the Council Chamber at nightfall. For now, I am going home with my family."

Mila's grip on the towel in her hand grew tight enough her knuckles went white, and Aften could have sworn he saw curls of steam rise from the damp cloth. He felt the same anger in his own chest, the heat of it rushing through him, blooming and spreading like wildfire to the top of his head and the ends of his toes.

"I'm not going with you."

Rendyn turned to Aften, his mask of relief vanishing. There was the expression he knew best, the disappointed scowl. The councilman threw his hands up, exasperated. "What do you mean you aren't coming—of course you are. Aften, we are going home. Now."

Aften's fingers curled into fists, and he squared his shoulders. "I said I'm not going back, and you can't make me. I'm moving into the Barracks. I'm staying here."

Every word was a brazen challenge, one he never would have dared before, but the memory of his decision in the cell drove him. He felt like his only use was to die or disappear, which was a set of bars all its own. Beyond every chance of hope, he survived. He wouldn't let anyone take away his choices again. They would *never*. Trap him. Again.

Rendyn's face went ruddy with mounting fury. His eyes swept to either side, taking in their audience of scouts, every single one watching with expressions ranging from confused to disappointed to angry and back again.

He leaned in, every hissed word clipped short. "We have discussed this before. How would it look to the rest of our people if—"

"No, we never discussed it," Aften interrupted. He didn't bother to lower his voice. Let them hear. In fact, with every word he got louder, though he wasn't shouting. Yet. "I asked if I could, and you said no. Then, as always, you wouldn't listen to anything else I had to say."

Rendyn made a sharp gesture with his hand for silence, then put his finger to his lips. He turned to the scouts, his back straight and his customary frown fixed in place. "I believe we have this under control now. You're all dismissed. Get to bed."

No one moved. Aften's nails bit into his palms. How dare he send everyone away to their rooms like unruly children just because he couldn't stand a single ounce of criticism?

"Now!" Rendyn barked.

Everyone scattered. Everyone except Mila, protectively ensconced in front of Thislen, and Trevon, who still leaned against the wall beside her, and Darran. Darran, who came up to Aften's side, shooting him a quiet, encouraging smile. That smile alone filled Aften with a light that couldn't be extinguished by Rendyn Sivivan. Not today. Darran was *alive,* and so was he.

"I believe we should all retire to the Council Chamber. There are plenty of seats in there and we can discuss this without waking every person here. I'll send for refreshments." Rendyn smiled, but it was the fake smile someone wore when they were trying to convince someone to do something unpleasant. It was too wide and stiff.

He doesn't want this to play out in public. Well, I said I wasn't going and I'm not.

He opened his mouth, but Tamsa spoke before he could.

"If Aften isn't going back, I'm not either. We're tired, Father, and this can wait until tonight. We'll come by later for our things."

She whirled to face the open bunks, hands planted on her hips as she scanned the wall. Thislen's old cubicle, the one above Mila's, lay untouched and waiting. His sister climbed into it, rolling onto her back and tugging the curtain across the entrance with an air of finality.

There were other bunks nearby that held pallets, empty and waiting. Aften chose a lower one and tucked himself into the corner. The niche was just tall enough to sit in. He leaned back against the cool stone with his arms crossed. Darran sat on the ledge beside him.

Rendyn couldn't have looked more shocked if Tamsa punched him square in the mouth. For the first time in his life, Aften watched the man flounder. After running through shock, confusion, frustration, and outright fury, Rendyn took a deep breath. He calmed down so quickly it was almost frightening.

"Fine. We can discuss this later."

From his tone, Aften knew that wouldn't be the end of it. *Too bad. I'll never be backed into a corner again, here or anywhere else.*

Mila watched the tense exchange between Rendyn, Tamsa, and Aften with shock and more than a little alarm. As the Councilman turned away, she held her breath. That was all? She'd expected worse. Then again, he'd have them alone in the council room later where he could yell all he wanted with the Nattfolk none the wiser. She frowned.

A groan pulled her from her thoughts as Thislen stirred behind her. He grabbed her arm.

"Mila, please. I...I need help." His dark eyes held hers. He needed healing. They both knew it.

Mila turned to Rendyn's retreating back. She'd kiss his boot if he would let a healer tend to her friend. She owed Thislen everything. Without him, her new life wouldn't exist. She never would have had the courage to reject Soren and brave the island. She wouldn't know about her part to play in the curse, and the power to break it would have fallen into the wrong hands.

"Do the Nattfolk have a healer at all?" she asked.

Rendyn stopped, frowning over his shoulder. "We have one, but she's a day's walk away through the tunnels, in a fishing village outside the walls. No one asks questions there."

"Can you walk that far?" She asked the thief.

Thislen shook his head.

"Do you have a cart or something?" She asked Trevon.

"We do, but it won't fit through that tunnel."

"We need someone closer, then." *And not me.*

Tamsa dropped beside her from the bunk overhead. "What about your father? He's an apothecary, isn't he?"

"From the Solfolk? From above?" Rendyn asked sharply.

A flare of frustration and resentment boiled in Mila's chest, surging all the way to her fingertips. Her grip tightened on the towel she held until the fabric creaked. "Yes, from above. Thislen needs help, and my father's a healer. He'll come down here willingly once he finds out I'm alive."

"And it benefits the Nattfolk to have a healer close by." Tamsa turned to her father, folding her arms over her chest.

"No. It's out of the question."

"You're not king," Tamsa snapped. "Stop acting like you are and learn to listen to other people for once."

Mila's jaw dropped, and she saw Trevon's drop too. Rendyn was turning purple with barely contained rage, his hands flexing at his side like he wanted to strangle someone. He stared at Tamsa with venom, as if he were looking at a stranger that came home to him in his daughter's place. Mila felt the same way. She never expected Tamsa to side against the man, ever.

"They're right," Aften said, scooting to the edge of his bunk. "Thislen protected me and Tamsa every day we were on that ship. He deserves our help, and if it would help all of us, why not? What possible reason do you have to say no?"

"We have rules," Rendyn hissed, eyes scanning the curtained bunks around them.

How many ears are listening right now?

"Change them," Mila said.

"No! We do not go up to Astera during the day, and we don't take Solfolk underground unless they are left here after dark. These rules have been in place for hundreds of years, and I will not be the man who breaks tradition. If you dare go to your family, Mila Ominir, I will have you on the next ship off this island in a heartbeat." Rendyn leveled a look as cold and hard as iron on her.

Oh, because this is all my fault and mine alone?

Her anger grew hotter. She thought she smelled smoke again. Maybe it was coming out of her ears.

"If you banish her, you'll have to banish me, too." Trevon squared his shoulders and shifted in front of her.

"I'm not about to abandon her after she saved me. I'll be going, too," Aften said firmly.

"Well, if he goes, I'm afraid I have to." Darran smiled apologetically at Rendyn.

"I'm going wherever Aften goes from now on," Tamsa added.

If Mila thought Trevon's words surprised her, the way the others stepped in to defend her sent her reeling. The heat inside her faded, washed away by a wave of gratitude. They were her friends, and they proved it now. These were her people.

Go ahead, try to banish all of us. Explain to the Nattfolk why your children are on a boat to Rava.

Mila stood, flinging the dry cloth at Rendyn's feet. The challenge was made.

Rendyn stared them all down in silence, grinding his teeth. No one moved. Mila hardly dared to breathe. She kept her gaze steady, smothering every creeping doubt as it rose so he wouldn't see them on her face.

"No one goes to the surface," Rendyn said. "Trevon, I want a full report at moonrise. You have much to answer for. Tamsa, Aften—you *will* come to the Council Chamber to discuss this sudden desire for space. Your things are staying right where they are." Every word was bitten off, chewed up, and spat out like gristle.

"Why don't we do breakfast first, Father? I think that would be a better place for a discussion. And I told you, we'll send someone for our things," Tamsa said smoothly.

The more Mila watched Tamsa dance around Rendyn, the more she admired her. She knew every way around her father, turning commands into suggestions and dismissing them in the same breath. Tamsa learned from the best, after all. Part of Mila—a very small part—even considered forgiving Tamsa. This new version of her would be an excellent friend, if the changes lasted more than a few days. She was glad the Nattfolk heiress was on *her* side now. She was formidable.

Yes, Mila would consider forgiving her for getting them captured, nearly killing Darran, getting Thislen tortured, causing grief for Aften, and foiling their plan to save the island. Especially if Tamsa planned to continue making her amends this way.

A muscle in Rendyn's jaw worked as he clenched and unclenched his teeth. The mottled red and purple of his face was a sight to behold as he fought and failed to contain his rage. Mila could hear the churning whirr of his calculating mind from where she stood.

"Fine. Breakfast at sundown. And you—" He pointed at Mila. "No Solfolk! Do you hear me?"

"I hear you," Mila said.

I'm just not going to listen.

Rendyn didn't give anyone a chance to argue with him further. He turned on his heel and stormed through the tunnel toward the Commons.

Only then did Mila exhale, a knot of tension in her shoulders fading away. "What in Ancestors' name was that?"

"Long overdue?" Tamsa smiled weakly.

"I'll say," Darran said, smiling at Aften. The Nattfolk scout blushed at the bald pride in Darran's words.

Tamsa caught Mila's arm as she bent to pick up the towel from the ground. "Mila? I just wanted to say...thanks. Thank you for coming for us."

"You came right in the nick of time. Thislen couldn't last much longer, and I was losing hope," Aften said.

Mila looked between them, giving a faint smile that felt stiff and uneven. *That's right. Whatever else happened, I saved three people today. They're much worse for the wear, but they're alive. That's one good thing, right?*

"Let's not make a habit of needing to rescue anyone, alright?" she said aloud. "I'd like to avoid any future near-death experiences, captures, and—" She stopped short of saying 'torture.' Her gaze slid to Thislen, whose eyes were mere slits, glittering black as a beetle in the shadow of his bunk.

He gave her a single nod. "Promise," he croaked.

A lump rose in her throat as his eyes closed and he turned his face toward the stone wall. *Oh, why did I have to say that?*

"Well," Trevon said, stretching his arms over his head. "We're in for it now either way, so do you want to make another plan while we're behind?"

"Another plan?" Mila echoed. "What do you mean?"

"You said you need your father—what's his name?"

"Olen," Rising hope bloomed in her chest, but the lump in her throat only grew. Her eyes stung. Was he saying what she thought he was saying?

"Thislen needs a healer, and so do the Nattfolk. We get a lot more done when we're not asking Rendyn Sivivan's permission. No offense intended." Trevon gave the Sivivan siblings an awkward smile.

"None taken. You're right," Aften said blandly.

"I'm with Trevon on this one. Let's get what we need." Tamsa smacked her fist into her palm.

Darran touched Mila's elbow gently, drawing her attention. "I think I promised you, when we went to rescue Thislen from Perilee, that I would bring you and your family back together. Now is the perfect time to make good on it, don't you think?"

Trevon clapped Darran on the back, grinning. Darran laughed. The excitement between the two was palpable.

Mila rolled her eyes, fighting tears even as she smiled. *Those two have become partners in crime. What have I done?*

She turned to Thislen and his bunk to see Tamsa sit at the thief's feet. She set a hand gently on his ankle. To Mila's surprise, Thislen relaxed. He turned, and their eyes met. Something passed through the silence between them, something no one else could touch.

No one else mattered to Thislen and Tamsa for a moment, not even her. *When did that...no,* what *happened on that ship?*

"If your father's as good as you say he is, Mila, I say we make our move during the day tomorrow," Tamsa said, breaking her gaze at last.

Mila exhaled slowly, pacing back and forth. "We only have one problem, but unless we solve it, my father will never come down here."

"What problem is that?" Aften asked.

"He won't believe you when you tell him I'm alive. We'll have to prove it, but I don't have anything to give you to show him. All I have is me, myself. I have to be there, but I'm..."

"...supposed to be dead," Trevon finished with a grimace. "You can't be seen on the streets around your childhood home. Someone will recognize you."

"Undoubtedly. And all it would take is one rumor for Soren to find out. Who knows what he'll do then, what he'll think." Mila sighed, stopping short.

Nothing can ever be easy, can it?

Mila saw the exact moment Trevon thought of a plan. He lit up and clasped her shoulder, grinning. "Don't worry, I have a plan. You're not going to like it, but it will only take you and I to pull it off."

"What will we do?" Aften asked.

Darran held up a hand. "You and Tamsa can rest, eat, and take some time to recover. The three of us can keep an eye on Thislen and run interference with Rendyn, too. This time, no one can alert him to our scheme before it's done and can't be changed."

"Mila and I will head to the farm tonight before moonfall. In the meantime, we should get some sleep." Trevon turned to leave.

"Is that all you're going to tell me?" Mila asked.

He grinned over his shoulder. "Well, I don't want you to argue."

She rolled her eyes. Despite herself, she smiled. It was impossible not to. *Why do I feel like he knows me better than anyone else?* It made no sense. They only met a month ago.

And I met Thislen only a week before that.

Tamsa closed the curtain to Thislen's bunk and climbed into her own. Aften rolled into his, and Darran perched on the stone ledge, whispering something to Aften and Aften alone before he retreated to his own bed.

Left alone, Mila pulled off her boots and flopped back, staring at the smooth, blank stone above her. Her mind was a welter of thoughts and emotions. She worried about Thislen. She was excited to see her father. Tamsa baffled her. Aften and Darran warmed her heart. Trevon... Trevon was a surprise and puzzle all in one.

Well, now is as good a time as any to sort all this out.

Moments after she finished the thought, exhaustion caught her by surprise.

Surrounded by her friends, *all* of her friends, Mila slept.

8

This was a terrible idea.

Mila pressed her hands to the wood surrounding her. It bit into her palms, threatening to stab her with a dozen splinters if she made one wrong move. That wasn't even the worst part of this jouncing, swaying, rattling ride on the back of the hand cart. No, the worst part was that the air inside the crate was close and stuffy, so warm that sweat dripped down the tip of Mila's nose, and she couldn't even wipe it away without ramming the side of her hiding place with a shoulder.

She closed her eyes, praying for the barest thread of a breeze to weave its way through the little gaps between the slats, even though they were only wide enough to let in tiny slivers of light. Her skin tickled and itched in equal measure as sweat formed, rolled, and cooled, and she felt hair sticking to her cheek.

Mila couldn't tell how long she'd been stuck like this, either. Trevon hammered her into the box before the sun was up and loaded her onto the cart with the help of a Solwalker who didn't ask any questions. First thing in the morning. Then, he towed her off toward Astera.

She knew they were in the city by the sound. Muffled chatter, shouting, laughter, music, the wheels of a cart or carriage clattering past in the other direction. She could only guess at *where* in Astera they were though. Somewhere in the Goods Quarter, she thought, and very near their destination. Not long ago, the crate had tipped backward as they rolled up one of the ramps. Her heart hammered the entire time, picturing the crate falling off and shattering, ruining the plan entirely.

We have to be close, or I will jump out of this box myself. Why did I even agree to this? I should have come up with a different plan, a better one, but no! Trevon asks and I willingly jump into a crate. What does that say about me?

Straw rustled beneath her as she shifted a foot into the corner to help brace herself—and not a moment too soon. The crate dipped forward so fast her stomach flipped and she bit back a startled yelp. Mila pressed her legs into the corners and her back against the wood to keep from sliding.

Pins and needles prickled up and down one of her legs that resented its confinement as much as she did. A moment later, the tingling transformed into a wash of discomfort as blood rushed through her veins. She rolled her eyes toward the top of the crate and bit her lower lip, praying to the Ancestors to let this end quickly.

Trevon, she assumed, knocked on the door. *Someone* knocked.

The familiar sound of jangling bells chimed nearby. She'd heard them every day of her life as the door opened and closed, setting them off again and again. Mila closed her eyes, savoring it.

"What? Yes, hello, how can I help you?"

Father. Mila's heart did a somersault. Her eyes flew open. With her head crooked at an odd angle and braced to keep herself from sliding into a corner of the box, she couldn't even peer out of the cracks to see him. His voice would have to be enough for now.

"I have a delivery for you, but I need help carrying it in. It's a little heavy." Trevon's voice was bright, and she could hear the coy undertone as he relished the coming reveal.

She fought down a smile. She was still annoyed with him! *You get the easy part, and I get to suffocate inside this box. I am never letting you make the plans again,* she vowed.

"I'm sorry, there must be some mistake. I didn't order anything."

Now Mila could hear how tired her father sounded, and sad. He believed, as everyone did, that she died at the hands of the Vaim mere weeks ago. He was grieving.

"This is the address I was given, and I came from all the way outside the walls," Trevon said slowly.

You didn't think about what you'd do if he didn't accept the delivery, did you? Mila scoffed silently, rolling her eyes. Some plan this was. *Not that I thought he'd turn it down, either.*

"From the farm? I...I must have lost track of the days. I thought it was coming next week. Here, I'll help you get it in."

Footsteps approached on either side. The crate's handles, made of knotted rope, pulled taut. Being lifted from the cart was more than disconcerting. It presented an entirely new challenge. The weight inside the crate couldn't wiggle, or Olen would stop in the street to see what was inside, or at least ask questions.

Loudly. Mila pressed every bit she could against the rough wooden walls of her temporary shelter, teeth gritted as she held herself as still as possible. The crate jerked and swung with every step.

I could throttle Trevon right now. She would never, ever, *ever* climb into a crate again.

"What in the Ancestors' name did I send for," Olen panted, "that is so damnably heavy?" His deep voice was tinged with strain and surprise in equal measure.

"If I had to guess, I'd say it might be something valuable." She could tell Trevon was grinning. She muffled a scoff and rolled her eyes. Again.

Those familiar bells rang overhead, and the light vanished abruptly as the crate was carried indoors. The sharp smell of herbs and the light fragrance of flowers reached her nose, mingled with the muted scent of dust. Mila closed her eyes, breathing in deep and slow. It might not be her home any longer, but this would always be what home smelled like in her heart.

"Here, we can set it down here. I don't think we'll get it over the counter," Trevon offered, his own voice starting to sound taut with the effort of carrying her around this way.

The crate hit the ground with a *thunk* that made her teeth rattle, and only then did she relax.

"What are you doing?" Olen asked. His low voice rumbled so close by that he must have been standing beside her.

"Closing the shutters. Are you okay?" Trevon asked.

The shop's lock clicked.

"Me? I'm fine." Olen was baffled. She could picture his thick brows climbing toward his hair, his eyes following Trevon like he was mad. To be fair, the scout captain was a little mad.

At least Father's a little distracted from his grief by Trevon's antics.

"Not you. Are you all right?" Trevon repeated.

Mila groaned softly. "I'd be a lot more all right if someone would open this box."

There was a crash, followed by the sound of paper packets and glass and tin falling onto the wooden floor.

Mila started. "What happened? Trevon, open the box!"

Trevon cursed under his breath, shoving a pry bar into the crate. He wrenched it open with a squeal of nails. "It's fine, he just jumped back so hard he hit the shelf."

Air! Blessed, beautiful, wonderful air rushed into the crate. Mila kicked with both feet to help free herself. Trevon offered her his hand and she took it, scooting out into the open with a heavy sigh of relief. The first thing she did was stretch out every limb. The second was turn to her father.

Their eyes met. Olen stared, as stunned as if he'd been struck over the head. In his arms were a few paper packets of rolled pills and glass jars of dried herbs, no doubt caught instinctively when everything began to tumble. Far more were scattered around his feet.

Mila smiled, crossing the distance between them and cupping his cheek. Her thumb ran over the ruddy, weathered skin. The wrinkles on his forehead and around his mouth were deeper than when she'd left. The streaks of gray in his mane of rust red hair had widened and were joined by a new one in his long, fluffy beard. His thick and bushy eyebrows were wilder than ever, nearly lost in his hair because his eyes were so wide.

"Mila?" He breathed at last, his voice cracking.

"I missed you."

Olen dropped everything with a clatter. His arms folded around her, squeezing her tight the same way they had when she was a girl. She breathed deep of the scent of him as she flung her arms around his neck. It was the same as it always was. Clean soap, sharp herbs, and rich earth.

Olen sobbed. "You've come back to me. Ancestors, all my prayers have been answered, you've come back to me!"

Mila pulled away with a laugh. A tight lump was stuck in her throat and her eyes brimmed, threatening to overflow despite her best efforts not to cry. She gently wiped the tears off his craggy cheeks.

"Yes, I have. But I can't stay, Father."

"I thought you were dead."

"That's what Soren wanted, and we need him to think I am."

Olen grasped her shoulders, holding her at arm's length as he looked her up and down. "Mila, what are you wearing? Where have you been staying? You can't come back here, Bestant still comes for his mother's medicine—"

Her heart skipped a beat. "Not today?" she asked quickly.

"No, not today, but…" He frowned. "You weren't planning to stay."

It wasn't a question. Mila did her best to look apologetic as she nodded. "You're right, I'm not. I've come to ask you to come with me instead. Soren can't find out I'm alive."

"Which is why you packed yourself into a crate." Olen's gaze slid sideways to the wooden container, then up to Trevon who stood behind it, doing his best to blend in with the shelves that filled the front half of the apothecary.

"Oh, Father, this is Trevon. Trevon, this is my father, Olen. The crate was his idea, and loathe as I am to admit it, it worked."

Trevon smirked at her, then stepped forward to shake Olen's hand. "I told you it would. Pleasure, sir."

"The pleasure is all mine, believe me. It isn't every day a young man brings my daughter back from the dead." Olen laughed, mopping his cheeks dry. "Mila, I can't believe this is what it took for you to bring a boy home."

Mila flushed, the heat creeping up her cheeks until she was red as a tomato. Trevon's ears turned pink before his face did.

Olen gasped, grasping her arm. "Boys, speaking of boys—Mila, where's Thislen? What happened to him?"

"That's why I'm here. We need—"

"And where are you staying? Where am I going?"

"If you'd just—"

"And what have you been doing this entire time?"

"Father! If you'd just let me answer one question before you ask another," Mila huffed, exasperation creeping into her voice. "Thislen is hurt, and he needs a healer, which is part of why I need you to come with me. The other part is that he isn't the only one. A whole community of people need you. This might be hard to understand, but Father there's a whole other city here in Astera, a city that's—"

"The Nattfolk? Of course! Why didn't I think of that? You took up with the Nattfolk." Olen laughed breathlessly, smacking the heel of his hand to his forehead.

It was Mila's turn to be surprised. "Wait, how do *you* know about them?"

Trevon cleared his throat. "The Ominir Apothecary is one of our sources for medicines. We've been coming here for a long time."

Olen nodded. "Yes, precisely. It's our family's secret. I was going to tell you when you took over the shop. Didn't Thislen tell you?"

"Thislen knew?" Mila felt a roil of hot frustration roll through her. That night when she thought Darran, Tamsa, and Aften were robbing her father's store, Thislen pointed out they had a key—but he'd never said anything about secrets her father told him. Why did Olen tell the thief and not his own daughter?

"You're a healer?" Trevon asked, brows lifted.

"Yes, she is," Olen said.

"No, I'm not." Mila folded her arms over her chest, a stubborn set to her jaw. "The Nattfolk think all I did was run your register, and that's how I like it. I don't want to be an apothecary, Father."

Oh no. She said it. She just blurted it out. This was not going the way Mila wanted. This conversation was one she hoped to have later, when Trevon was helping move supplies and she and Olen were alone.

Olen paused. He seemed to realize the same thing she did, glancing at Trevon before changing the subject. "Anyway, Thislen knew we had a family secret, and I assumed he would have made the connection once you two took up with the Nattfolk. He's too clever not to. However, yes, I know about the Nattfolk. I know they come for medicines and herbs from time to time. Our family has supplied them for centuries, ever since—"

"My many-times-great-grandmother Willa Ominir?" Mila guessed.

"Precisely. I never thought to ask how they came to exist, I just knew they did. I didn't know they could save someone from the Vaim."

"Not everyone," Trevon offered. "Mila and Thislen were some of the lucky ones."

"And they don't save us from the Vaim so much as pick up the ones who—look, this is a very long story. I promise I'll tell you all of it after we get to the Commons. We've only got this afternoon to get you packed and ready to leave before it gets complicated. Will you please go and pack?"

Olen hugged her tight again. "As you wish, Mila."

His whiskers tickled her cheek as he kissed the top of her head. She smiled and rolled her eyes, nudging him with an elbow to get moving.

He let her go, wandering among the shelves of the shop. "Hm, medicines, I think. Herbs, yes. Clothes, clothes are important."

"If any of it is too much to carry, I've got my cart outside," Trevon said as he pointed a thumb toward the locked shop door. "Anything we don't take in the next few loads, we can send some scouts up to get later."

"Perfect. If you want me to set up shop down there, I'll need a lot. Is there a way to grow my plants?"

The doorknob rattled. They all froze. Mila's heart was gone. It beat so quickly it ran right out of her chest and left her feeling cold all over. It rattled again.

"Upstairs, quickly," Olen whispered, grabbing her by the arm and towing her toward the counter that divided the apothecary in two and the stairs beyond.

Before they'd made it past even one of the worktables, the lock clicked open. The bells jangled. Ivan stood there, outlined by the afternoon sun. "Olen, my mother wanted to know if—" He looked up.

Everyone stood absolutely frozen.

This was a stupid idea. This was a stupid plan! I should have guessed that Evelie and Ivan would catch on. Ivan can never keep his nose out of someone else's business, and—

Trevon reacted first. He stepped forward, pushing Ivan aside and closing the door. The lock slid home.

As if the touch were all he needed to snap out of it, Ivan moved next. He crossed the shop, flinging the counter leaf out of his way with the sharp slap of wood on wood. He swept her into his arms, whirling her around with a stunned laugh. His face turned toward hers. His eyes closed. He leaned in close, and his lips—

No!

She leaned away, hands pushing hard at his chest. "Ivan, stop that! What are you doing? Put me down."

He froze, his face blank. Slowly, Ivan set her back on the floor. His green eyes searched hers intently, and she stared back with a frown. He didn't find even an ounce of affection in her face. He pulled away.

"I thought you'd be glad to see me."

"I am, but I'm not going to kiss you over it. You're my brother, Ivan."

The words were firm, and she meant for them to hurt. Before she'd left, he began to flirt with her and push at that line between friendship and something more, and she wasn't interested. She'd tried to let him down gently and failed, and now she was angry, at him and at herself.

I wanted to be happy to see him again, and he took that away from me. I didn't want to have this conversation now, especially not in front of Trevon and my father.

Yes, it was time to put this infatuation to rest, especially because she'd never expected him to move on it so abruptly.

Ivan's face shifted through several emotions. His brows drew in, his lips turned down. A moment later, his mouth opened. His brows rose toward his hair. His hands clenched, then relaxed. His jaw worked. His eyes gleamed. He cleared his throat.

At last, Ivan settled on a faintly hurt look.

"I did miss you, Ivan," she said gently.

"How are you even here? I thought—we all thought you were dead."

Oh, now he thinks to ask. Mila sighed heavily. "Look, it's a really long story and I don't want to go over it more than I have to. Evelie's involved now that you are, so why don't you go and get her? It will be easier to tell everyone at the same time."

Ivan turned to go, but paused with his hand on the door to look back at her. His eyes ran over her from head to toe and back.

"You're different," he accused.

"Of course I am. I was nearly murdered, Ivan, and even if that were all that happened it would have changed me. Can you please go and get Evelie?"

"Who is he?" Ivan jerked his chin toward Trevon.

Mila felt a slight flush creep up her cheeks, one born of frustration. "His name is Trevon, and he's my...friend."

Trevon smiled a slow, warm smile that transformed her blush from anger to something else entirely and put a flutter in her stomach.

"Mila's never brought a boy home before," Olen teased from behind them all as he rooted through the shelves of his shop.

The heat in her cheeks grew hotter, creeping up toward her ears. "Father, please."

It's bad enough Ivan's jealous, let's not add fuel to the fire.

Too late. Ivan's expression darkened, and he shot Trevon a poisonous look. He rounded on the scout, hands balled into fists. "You—"

Mila braced herself to stop a brawl, stepping forward on instinct, her fury back so hot she thought she steamed.

"Ivan," Olen interrupted, heading everything off. "I believe we need your mother here. Go to the flower shop. Right now."

Trevon's brows rose. Mila could guess why. Ivan looked nothing like a florist ought to, with broad shoulders and lots of muscle. He resembled a soldier more than a shopkeep and carried himself with the heavy grace of a bull.

"What am I even supposed to tell her? Mother, you'll never guess what happened. Mila came back from the dead, come and see!" He threw his hands up, his tone mocking. "I hardly believe it myself and I've seen her. I've held her."

The longing look Ivan gave her made a shudder run down Mila's spine. She huffed, pressing her fingers to the bridge of her nose. How could he still hold on to some faint hope that she might change her mind? She couldn't say 'no' any clearer. *I'll have to figure out what to say to convince him that courtship will never, ever be on my mind.*

"Just tell her to come for lunch," Olen suggested, crossing the shop to open the door.

Mila ducked to the side, pressing herself against the wall to ensure she stayed out of sight.

"In fact, why don't you insist on it?" Olen planted a hand firmly on Ivan's back, steering him out the door and latching it shut. He ignored the florist's petulant gaze. "Mila, you and your friend can head upstairs. I'll clean up down here and set a few things aside before we join you."

Mila pushed down her frustration, closing her eyes for a moment and taking a deep breath. This was a happy occasion. This was the reunion she longed for.

It looked different than she imagined.

"Thanks, Father." She smiled at him, crossing the store to sweep up the steps.

This was the first time she could pause to admire the place she grew up, and the first time she got to say her goodbyes. The rafters, festooned with dried and drying herbs that perfumed the air with the musty but sharp scent of plants. The shelves with their paper packets, jars, and bottles that neatly lined the front half of the modest space, covered with a fine layer of dust without her there to tend to it. As she passed to the back half of the shop, she ran her fingers over the worn wooden counter. It had been scrubbed clean so many times she could feel the grain as ridges beneath her hands.

The back half was crowded with worktables, their surfaces littered with empty bottles and jars, wooden bowls, mortars and pestles, bundles of string, wax for sealing, scales and weights, and more. There was a door there, too, that opened onto the hothouse they'd converted their tiny garden into. It was practically glowing green and gold with the sunlight through the leaves, and water pooled between the cobbles on the floor. Olen had already watered them for the day.

The steps leading upstairs were tucked into the back of the shop beside that door, hidden from view. Mila gestured for Trevon to follow her, then walked up. The wood creaked beneath them, just like it always had.

I will never come back here again, she realized, her heart aching. If only they could hide the shop away until...

Until what? Even if they broke the curse, there was no guarantee that Soren would leave her be. What if she were never free of him?

She fanned the thought away as though she were clearing a cobweb. *Enough time to worry about all that later. One thing at a time. This time, Thislen needs help. Not me.*

The second floor was bright and open, lit by two windows on the front wall lined with lace curtains yellowed with age. Dappled light filtered in through the little holes of the fabric, offering illumination and privacy at the same time.

Beneath each window was a bed. They were rarely used for sleeping, though the odd patient had been tucked into them. Sometimes, Mila napped in hers during the daylight hours, but mostly she remembered long afternoons curled up with one of the books her father owned, pouring over the pages.

Olen hadn't touched it since she left. It was still there, still neatly made. Embroidered cushions decorated with flowers lined three sides of it, all laid over a quilt her mother had made many years ago. Her father's bed had a simpler quilt and only two pillows. Mila couldn't remember the last time Olen used it for himself.

A hearth sat on the wall between the two beds, a small fire crackling and a kettle hanging on a swinging iron hook on one side, ready to be boiled at a moment's notice. They'd used it more than once to help wash out wounds or sterilize bandages. *She* used it more than once.

The wall opposite the beds held no windows. A long table sat lined it from end to end. Shelves were hung above it, laden with plates and bowls and jars of foodstuffs. In the corner stood the pump and basin—a luxury they'd found very necessary in their line of work.

A knotted cloth rug that Mila had made herself lay across the center of the room, pinned in place by a dining table and two benches. Mila sat on one. To her surprise, Trevon sat beside her.

"Anything you want to bring with you?"

Mila smiled. "If we can send someone back up for most of it, yes. I'd love to take some pillows, and my quilt."

"I'd take this rug, too, and some dishes. We can give your family a cavern, if you'd like. You can stay with them again."

Mila hesitated. *If we stay together, will that make it easier or more difficult for them? They'll have to come to terms very quickly with who I am.*

"Think on it," Trevon offered. "You know, you don't look as happy as I'd like."

She glanced toward the stairs, glad that the scout captain was keeping his voice low. "I love my father, I do, but the vision he has for my life isn't one I want to live. I like who I am now, what I *do* now. He'd have me be just like him. He and Evelie would love for Ivan and I to end up together with a whole herd of children, too." She sighed.

"Not interested in an entire herd?"

"Not interested in any. I've never felt that way toward Ivan, and I don't know if he actually feels that way toward me or if he's just following their plan. Honestly, Trevon, I..."

Trevon waited, watching her as she sorted through her feelings.

"I don't know if I even know what love looks like, or *feels* like. I just know when it isn't real. I know when it isn't what I want. Soren wanted me to marry him, and the life he offered was my worst nightmare. He didn't care that I didn't want it. Ivan wants me to marry him, and I just don't see him that way. I know I never will.

"Truth be told, I think I can love, but I never want to marry. I'm...afraid of it. Afraid of what's expected after you're married." She dropped her head into her hands, mortified now that she'd admitted it all.

Trevon was quiet for a long moment, his fingers drumming on the table. "Are you afraid of...the wedding night?"

Mila tipped her head back, tracing the heavy beams of the ceiling with her eyes. "Not so much afraid, but not at all interested. It sounds unpleasant at best. I'm afraid that if I fall in love, my husband will never understand that. I don't want to bed anyone, and no one seems to be able to wrap their head around it."

There, there it was. The secret was out. Mila knew others her age felt differently. Several of her former friends boasted about sneaking off to try this or that somewhere, or whispered delightful stories of the scandalous positions someone else had been found in. Mila'd stopped talking to most of them when every conversation became about boys and marriage. She never once wanted to explore such things in stolen moments.

If I ever fall in love, I don't think I could stand anything more than holding hands and kisses. I couldn't bear more than that. Maybe there's something wrong with me after all.

"I think," Trevon said carefully, "if you fall in love with the right person, they won't pressure you for such things. Not everyone wants that. It's normal, it happens. I think when you find the right person for you, you'll trust them. You'll know they mean it when they look you in the eye and say they don't need sex to be with you." Trevon met her eyes. "Sex and love are two different things, Mila, and you only need one to have some sort of a relationship."

She felt a bloom of warmth in her chest, like something unfurled deep within her, a muscle she hadn't noticed was tensed. Her throat was tight. She folded her arms on the table with a sigh. "I've always worried that if I told anyone, they'd think I was...defective."

Trevon's hand covered hers, warm and rough with callouses. He leaned forward to catch her gaze. "You are not broken, Mila Ominir. You're just...you."

Mila's eyes stung. She blinked quickly, tipping her head back to make sure no tears would fall. Her chest was tight, but perhaps that was because it felt as if her heart was swelling to ten times its size. She never realized how much she wanted—no, *needed* to hear those words.

Trevon didn't press her to speak, nor did he pull away. He just waited.

I needed someone to tell me that everything we've been through just because I never wanted to be married...was worth it. A knot of guilt she never even realized she carried began to unwind. Her shoulders relaxed. Slowly, she fought her tears back. Her choices saved her and changed the lives of so many people. Sometimes she thought it wasn't fair. Other times, she'd never change a thing.

And it isn't because I'm damaged somehow, it's because the people around me love me enough to give me this choice.

Her hand turned over, fingers lacing with Trevon's. He smiled.

The bells jangled over the door below.

"Why is there a crate in the middle of the—Olen Ominir, why is there a crate in the middle of your floor?" Evelie's voice floated up the stairs, tinged with exasperation. "For Ancestor's sake! What is going on? Ivan won't tell me a thing, but you're both dreadful at surprises."

Trevon pulled his hand away. The warmth of his skin still lingered on Mila's.

With him beside her, Mila felt braver already. She straightened her back, lifted her chin, and braced herself.

It was time to explain everything.

9

*T*hislen knew it was a dream. He knew it, but he couldn't wake himself up. The spires of Perilee loomed on the horizon, growing closer and closer as he stood in the middle of a featureless plain.

He couldn't look away from the growing shadow of the castle, even as he felt eyes on his back. The space between his shoulders prickled. The faintest whispers reached his ears, too indistinct to make out. The Vaim whispered that way. Fingers he couldn't see brushed over his arms and along his back and shoulders. Mounting fear made a cold pit in his stomach.

"Leave me alone!" Thislen roared, his voice echoing. It took every ounce of effort he had to tear his gaze from Perilee and turn toward the faceless dead—

Only they weren't faceless. They were still the Vaim, misshapen and contorted, but where he was used to flat faces with hollowed red eyes, there were now the impressions of noses and mouths. Their lips moved, their claws stretched out toward him entreatingly.

Percivan's ghost stepped out of the crowd, his hands tucked behind his back as he looked the spirits over like one might look over the vegetables at a market stall. "It seems they're waiting for you to do something about all this, Thislen."

"I'm not the one in charge. Mila is."

"That didn't work out very well for you before."

"I don't care. I'm not a leader. I haven't done it once, not successfully." Thislen shied away from a Vaim whose fingers curled loosely around his wrist. "Stop that!"

"You'll do it when it counts," Vern said. The Vaim parted to show the sailor's waterlogged specter staring up at something behind Thislen.

The castle. He knew it was the castle. The weight of the shadow that fell across them all was titanic, pressing down on his shoulders until his knees buckled.

"Try, Thislen. Go back. Go back to Perilee and try." Percivan took his shoulders, turning him on the spot.

Thislen's eyes were fixed on the many gleaming spires of the keep. Slowly, his eyes dropped further and further down, tracing the windows and the carvings until he saw the massive double doors. Silently, they swung open. Percivan and Vern urged him to step forward, and he did—one reluctant step.

"If you want to go through this door, you're going to have to answer some questions first."

Thislen felt as if he'd fallen through ice into a rushing river, knocked sideways and chilled through in the span of a single heartbeat. He knew that voice.

Garridan Artaith stepped out of the darkness inside the castle, holding a hammer in one hand, and a cherry red iron rod in the other. "Really, Thislen, I thought we talked about this."

"No. I'm free of you," Thislen protested, voice cracking. His hands shook. He balled them into fists so the spirits wouldn't notice.

"Are you?" Garridan stalked forward, eyes boring into Thislen's. The Vaim drew back with a chorus of hissing, their whispers doubling in volume.

Thislen's heart raced. "You can't hurt me now."

"What I want to know," Garridan said, as if Thislen hadn't spoken at all, "is what you plan to do once you get to Perilee."

"I'm not going to the castle."

"What are you going to say when you get there?"

"I told you, I'm not—"

"Who in their right mind would trust you? How will you get them to believe a word you say?"

"Go, Thislen. Someone has to go," Percivan whispered.

"No! This isn't me, this can't be me," Thislen cried, whirling to face the dead nobleman.

The Vaim and Percivan were gone. Instead of a wide plain, there was only a wooden wall. Thislen was in a small room—a small room with a table, a barrel, and...

His stomach churned as he turned slowly to face the chair in the center of the room, with its leather straps and mottled red and brown wood. Garridan stood behind it, smiling his kind, affable smile.

"Take a seat, Thislen."

He shook his head, backing up until he bumped into the wall. Garridan advanced, dropping the hammer on the table.

"Let's try this again, shall we? I'm running out of patience, you know."

Thislen shouted hoarsely, hands flying up as the torturer lunged forward. He grabbed a fistful of Thislen's hair, and then—

Thislen jerked awake with a gasp to find that the hand on his head was very, very real. Instinctively, he grabbed the wrist of his unseen assailant and twisted it, practically throwing himself against the back of his bunk in his haste to put distance between himself and...Olen.

"Ow, ow, it's me! Thislen, it's me," The healer pulled back as soon as Thislen let go, holding both hands up placatingly. "Really, we have to stop meeting like this."

That was not a voice he expected to be paired with the faint echoes of the Nattfolk caverns. It took him a moment to wake up enough to remember that Mila and Rendyn argued over—

She brought Olen underground? Ancestors—for me?

Thislen trembled, passing a hand over his eyes. Part of it was from pain. Moving so quickly rekindled hot agony in his hip, his knee, and down his side. Now that he was awake and moving, he was well aware of how injured he still was and how weak he felt. More painful than that, however, was the knowledge that Mila risked banishment on his behalf.

"You aren't supposed to be here," Thislen murmured.

"It's too late, as has been pointed out a time or two before." Olen smiled, a broad grin that crinkled the corners of his eyes. "Why don't you let me take a look at you?"

More voices were echoing off the stone. Thislen thought at first it was the Nattfolk preparing for their evening, but he was wrong. It was only two voices reverberating off the stone and crossing over one another until they were a muddled din.

"—exactly what I told you not to do, you little viper. You think you're special enough to do whatever you want anyway? I have given you far too many chances already, Mila Ominir."

"I did what I had to do to help Thislen, and more people! Your people."

"What about before that, when you broke our laws?" Rendyn snapped.

"To save your children from being tortured? I didn't think I would have to remind you of that. Besides, what's done is done. My family is down here now, so the rules apply to them the same as they do to everyone, right? Once they know, they make the choice."

"The choice to stay or be sent off the island—and I get the final vote," The councilman roared. "I can send you all off this island on the next damn ship if I want to."

"I told you I'd go with her if you tried," Tamsa said firmly.

"Not just her, either. A lot of us. You're going to lose both your children, sir, and an entire scouting group at least." Trevon pushed off the wall near the foot of Thislen's bunk.

"Trevon." Rendyn said the scout captain's name like a curse. "I never took you as someone who would go along with such schemes. What in Ancestor's names were you thinking?"

"Gone along? Councilman, I was involved in planning both of these. It was well worth it for the Nattfolk. She was ready to *do* something, and she's got a good head on her shoulders. That's why I agreed, why I helped. Mila is the hero of the hour, and everyone knows it."

"Except you," Aften said, irritation clear.

Rendyn scoffed. "I didn't take you for one so easily swayed, Scout Captain. I should have known better when you brought her back down here at all."

"Yes, because leaving me tied to a pole to be executed would keep the Nattfolk secret so well!" Mila snapped, planting her feet and squaring up as if she intended to start brawling with the man.

Mila was nearly abandoned? I didn't know that. Not that they'd had much time to talk since he was brought down here. All he really remembered was sleeping off and on.

Thislen slowly leaned out of the stone bunk. Olen moved away to one of several small crates to start pulling out jars of dried herbs, clearing the view.

Rendyn Sivivan faced off a miniature army all on his own. A few Nattfolk drifted in and out of the Barracks, clearly watching what was happening and taking it in turns to report to their fellows, but the councilman couldn't see them.

Mila stood at the forefront of the group, dressed in the black and gray leathers of a full scout. She'd changed, Thislen noticed, and not just her clothes. He liked seeing her this new way, with her shoulders back and the start of a dangerous grace to her movements.

Trevon stood behind her, his arms folded over his chest. Darran, Aften, and Tamsa were a cluster on Mila's other side, though once she caught sight of Thislen, Tamsa abandoned the pair to come to the edge of his bunk.

Every single one of them seemed poised to leap into the fray. The argument was one wrong word away from turning physical.

I should do something, say something. He didn't.

Jars clinked as Olen dug through the box. Evelie, the plump matronly florist, appeared at his elbow.

"Tell me what to do, Olen."

"Take these and grind them for me. We need to lower that fever, so I want this mixed in a broth."

"I can go get some from Kellan." Tamsa gave Thislen a worried look before she circled wide around the ongoing battle of wills. She vanished into the tunnel to the Commons.

"How much of these?" Evelie tipped her stone bowl toward Olen.

"Pinch more. There, that's perfect."

All of them kept their voices low, trying not to attract the attention of Rendyn or the others.

"You look awful."

Thislen gaze snapped to the owner of the voice. Ivan propped one arm against the top of his bunk, leaning in to study him.

"Wish I could say the same about you," Thislen said dryly. Ivan, apart from being a bit rumpled, still looked as handsome as ever with his broad shoulders and bright eyes. Thislen eased back onto the stuffed wool and straw pallet of his bed, propping himself up on the pillows.

Ivan smiled at the compliment, though he sobered quickly. "I never got the chance to thank you, you know."

Thislen's brow furrowed in a silent question.

Ivan smiled faintly. "When you and Mila were making a break for it, you stopped me from doing something stupid. So...thank you."

Thislen's jaw worked as he wracked his mind to find something to say. He hadn't done it for Ivan, after all. He did it for Mila.

"Ivan, can you find the meadowsweet and get me a few of its leaves?" Olen asked over his shoulder, saving Thislen from having to say anything.

Ivan turned away, going to one of four trays of small potted plants or cuttings in water and sorting through them. Beyond those were two more crates of jars, and three large packs all leaning against one another. Mila's family was moving in.

How did they get all of that down here in the first place? Industrious to say the least, to move so much in such a short amount of time. At least, he hoped it was a short amount of time. There was always the chance that he slept for days, not hours.

"Let me take a look at the rest of you, Thislen. I need to see any injuries you might have. Mila didn't tell me much of what happened." Olen sat on the edge of the bunk. "Judging by your appearance, though, none of it was good."

Thislen plucked at the ragged remnants of a beautiful linen shirt, ruffled at the collar and the ends of the sleeves. It was white once, but was now stained brown and gray and rust. Ninian Ominir gave him the shirt when the Vaim had dragged him into Perilee. His pants were once soft and supple hide but were now ruined from salt water and blood.

"I'm worried about my leg, and my hip. I can't bend my leg." He stalled for time, shifting with a wince of pain. Thislen still hadn't decided if he wanted to take his shirt off. He didn't want anyone to know what he'd been through.

Why? Am I worried they'll look at me with pity, or disgust? Do I think they'll think less of me—or worse, think more?

The last thing he needed was to be hailed as some kind of hero for what he went through. It felt wrong to be praised for surviving endless torment.

"I'll take a look at everything. Shirt off, please. Ivan, do you have scissors or a knife?" Olen held out a hand expectantly.

It wasn't Ivan who set a knife in Olen's hand, however. It was Trevon. He turned away from the argument, which started back up again at the beginning it seemed.

"Who are they, really? What do the Nattfolk know about them?" Rendyn folded his arms over his chest.

"What do we know of every other new arrival when we bring them down here?" Aften countered.

Olen leaned in. The knife's edge caught the light and Thislen's stomach clenched. A shudder ran down his spine, though he tried to hide it. The apothecary wasn't fooled. He moved slowly as he set it down and pulled off first one boot, then the other.

The second gave a rattle and a thunk. Thislen's heart began to race again as Olen's brows rose and he tipped the shoe upside down. The gleaming gold signet ring Thislen hid away, the same signet ring he once showed Olen in his shop, fell into Olen's hand. A gray and fraying piece of cloth was tied over the crest, hiding it from view. The leather cord it was once strung on was long gone.

Thislen held his hand out, his eyes sweeping over the others. They stood just feet away on the other side of Olen's things, forming a living barricade. "Quick, before they see."

"You try and hold everyone in line with fear. The problem with fear is that once we aren't afraid anymore, it stops working." Mila planted her hands on her hips.

Olen gave the ring back without question, folding Thislen's fingers over it.

Thislen tucked it beneath the far edge of his pallet for now, disguising the motion by shrugging his shirt off.

Olen wasn't looking. His head was bent as he cut Thislen's pants away.

"I am the leader of a people who would be wiped out down to the last child if we were discovered. It is my job to enforce the…" Rendyn trailed off, the first to see Thislen's injuries. The councilman stood only a few yards away. The extent of what Thislen endured for the Nattfolk was laid bare.

The others stared at Rendyn, confused by his silence—until they turned to see what he was looking at. Aften paled. Mila swayed where she stood, her eyes wide. Trevon and Darran looked grim.

The bruises that littered Thislen's ribs in various shades of purple, blue, green, and yellow would have been bad enough on their own, but they spoke to broken ribs underneath. Ribs that were showing clearly enough to be counted, because he had been half starved.

Thislen hardly felt those anymore. Everything else hurt worse. The perfectly straight cut down his chest was a mess of a scab that cracked every time he moved. Pearls of bright red blood welled from it, adding new color to his already battered body.

The burns down his side, all in a row and too perfect to have been made by anything but a hot iron, were swollen. The edges had turned yellow and the skin over the top was white and dead. Puss oozed out of the wounds, and they were red and inflamed. He'd have scars when everything healed.

Olen finished cutting up the side of Thislen's pants and pulled the fabric apart without compromising his modesty. It was only then Thislen realized the extent of the hammer's blows. First he saw the knee, swollen almost twice its size. It was a dark purple, mottled with the red of tenderized meat. Stabbing agony ran through him at the slightest touch or twitch of movement. His hip above that was the same, swollen and discolored.

Olen's eyes drifted from the hip up his chest, eyes dancing from wound to wound. The blood drained from his face.

"Torture? Who did this?" Olen turned to look at the rest, a deep frown settling onto his features.

Tamsa returned, a large clay mug in her hands, curls of steam coming off the top. She stopped dead when she saw Thislen.

"I must look worse than I thought," Thislen said, forcing levity he didn't feel into his voice.

Tamsa passed the mug to Evelie before she perched on the edge of his bunk, wringing her hands. She couldn't tear her eyes from his battered body. "You never told us what they were doing. I didn't know it was this bad."

"If I had, you would have done something stupid. Don't try to deny it."

Tamsa's mouth shut with a click of teeth. She sighed. "You're right. You did more than anyone should have to do in order to protect Aften and I—and the Nattfolk."

Great. They chose the heroic route. Thislen couldn't decide if that was better than pity.

Trevon rubbed the back of his neck. "You really went through a month of...well, of *that* and you didn't tell them anything?"

"Not about this place. Not about any of you."

Rendyn's lips parted, his scowl still in place—but then closed. His shoulders relaxed. His arms dropped to his sides. He stared at the burns for quite some time, expression easing. His lips twisted. His shoulders hunched as guilt crept across his features.

And not every torture they subjected me to can be seen, Thislen thought, sagging back against his pillows.

The Nattfolk hadn't cared much about Thislen. Mila told him once that they didn't want to send a rescue when Ninian took him. No doubt they hadn't wanted to this time, either. He didn't know more than five Nattfolk by name, yet he'd held his tongue for twenty-seven days through torment after torment.

Rendyn swallowed, then cleared his throat. His anger guttered, then went out. "Well, what's done is done. It isn't productive to be cross about it now," he said gruffly. "Someone get warm water and a cloth for the healer, and a fresh set of clothes for Thislen. And food! You can count his ribs. See to it. I expect a full report."

Without another word or any chance for someone to contradict him, Rendyn retreated. Thislen snorted softly. *I guess that's as close to an apology as I'm going to get.*

As he left, Rendyn caught sight of one of the eavesdropping Nattfolk, paralyzing them with his gaze like a mouse beneath a serpent. "You—go clear out a family cavern and get this mess out of the Barracks. Someone's going to trip and break their neck."

"Yes, Councilman, right away!"

"Aften and I can get the water and cloths," Darran said, towing the scout along behind him.

"I'll go with you. I can get Thislen a proper meal on the way." Tamsa joined them, ignoring the dismay on Aften's features and the disappointment on Darran's. The three of them left the cavern.

Trevon turned toward the storeroom at the far end of the Barracks where they kept spare clothing and bedding. Presumably, he'd gone to get Thislen something clean to wear.

Mila nibbled at her thumb, brow furrowed as Olen set to work. "Why didn't you tell us about your leg when we came for you?" she burst out at last.

"I wasn't about to get us all killed because of me. I barely made it to the rowboat. I couldn't do it again. I don't think I could even stand on it right now." Thislen draped an arm over his eyes, letting Olen prod at the inflamed tissue around Thislen's burns.

"Infected," Olen murmured. Suddenly he paused, leaning forward and putting his ear to Thislen's chest. "There's a rasp in your breathing that I don't like."

"They drowned me a time or two, and...brought me back."

Evelie gasped, covering her mouth with her hand. Her eyes gleamed and she blinked quickly to stop any tears from falling. She sat the doctored broth full of herbs on the bunk's stone shelf, above his head. "Who would...what sort of..."

Mila was pale as she turned to take Evelie by the arm. "Let's take some of this stuff to the Commons, that's probably where our new home will be. Come on. Leave my father to his work."

The two of them each took one large pack and staggered off under the weight of it toward the exit. Thislen didn't blame them for needing time with what happened. He knew he'd need a decade, at least, to come to terms with it on his own.

"Ivan, hold this leg for me while I look it over. Right here at the ankle. Thislen, don't move."

Ivan did as he was bid, expression grim, even as Thislen writhed. Olen's prodding pulled several curses from his lips. His head spun and spots danced before his eyes. It hurt enough to make his stomach roil and bile coat the back of his throat.

"Whoever did this to you knew what they were doing. Nothing is completely broken, though you might wish it were. I'll bind them for a few days with a poultice and the swelling should go down."

Olen turned back to his work on the floor, rummaging through boxes and trays of plants.

Ivan sat on the edge of Thislen's bunk. "They didn't feed you?"

"Not enough," Thislen admitted. "Aften and Tamsa saved scraps sometimes, but they weren't being fed much either."

"In a few days, Thislen, the worst of all this will be over," Olen assured him, the sound of stone grinding against stone in the air as he crushed a few herbs into a fine powder. He worked quickly, efficiently—no surprise with how long he'd been a healer, but still impressive.

"You two must be glad to have Mila back."

If he hadn't been looking at Ivan, he would have missed it. A flash of hurt, another of resignation, and then a crooked smile crossed his face all in a split second.

What in Ancestor's name is that about? Did he —Oh, no. Ivan must have confessed. Thislen knew from the first time they met that the florist loved her. *Did she finally lay it out for him?* She must have.

"I missed her something awful. I think we need to have a talk, but...having her back in my life is more important to me than anything else." The florist leaned back against the stone edge of the bunk, facing Thislen.

"I, of course, am beside myself. This wasn't anything like what I expected our lives to look like, but here we are, *living* those lives. Even Mila." Olen sat back on his heels. "I need water before I can do much else."

"Evelie and I didn't question it when she said we had to come with her. I'm a little worried my mother didn't know what she was getting into, though." Ivan grimaced.

Thislen snorted softly. Was anyone truly prepared to find a city beneath their city?

"Really, our arrival could have gone much worse," Olen said with a booming laugh that echoed off the walls.

Ivan snorted. "If it weren't for Thislen's timing, it might have been. They were at each other's throats."

"The Nattfolk need a healer, so it's a good thing I am one. I'll get Rendyn on our side soon enough." Olen sorted through his things, setting a bottle, two paper packets, and a jar of small yellow flowers to one side.

"I'm glad to be staying, but I don't know what I'm going to do with myself. It's going to be hard to grow flowers underground." Ivan sighed.

"I always thought you looked like a fighter. Join the scouts. Mila and I did."

Ivan brightened at that idea.

Tamsa came back, carrying a bright red apple in one hand and a single roll in the other. "Kellan said this is what you, me, and Aften need to eat for the next few days, and he'll add more for us later," she announced, reaching over his head. She pressed the cup of hot broth into Thislen's hands. "Drink."

"As you command," Thislen muttered with a faint smile.

Tamsa rolled her eyes and shooed Ivan off the foot of the bunk.

With his hands raised and a grin on his face, Ivan retreated. "I'm going to see if I can find someone who can direct me to the scouts. See you lot later."

Thislen watched him stride into the mouth of the tunnel. *At least he's got some direction.*

Movement flickered in the corner of his eye. Instinct took over, screaming that whatever was coming toward him would hurt. Thislen jerked away, broth spilling over his hands and chest. It took him several seconds to breathe again and realize it was Tamsa, her hand frozen in the air where his head had been.

"I'm so sorry, I didn't even think—"

"It's fine," he said quickly, cleaning off what he could of the broth with the cloth Olen silently pressed into his hand.

What else could I even say? This is what I am now. A frightened little mouse hiding in the hole to avoid the cat. His eyes flicked up to the stone roof of the cavern. Garridan Artaith and Soren Bestant were up there, probably hoping that he'd turn up so they could finish him off.

Tamsa took the cloth and nudged the mug gently toward his lips. Obediently, he began to sip at what was left of the broth. The delicious taste of salt and chicken ran over his tongue. Before he knew it, the mug was empty and he was relaxing against the pillows with a pit of warmth in his stomach. Tamsa passed him the roll. He picked it into little pieces and ate them, reveling in the crisp crust, soft inside, and the slightly bitter taste of the sourdough. The apple that followed was sweet and refreshing, and gone long before he was ready for it to be. It was a feast.

Exhaustion washed over him as he finished, promising the deep sleep only being full and safe could offer. Tamsa took the mug from his hand with a small smile.

"Better?"

"Yeah, thanks."

Olen stood. "Tamsa, was it? Can you help me find the two that were getting the water? I need more for the medicines."

"Of course. Get some rest, Thislen. We'll be back." She moved slowly as she reached out to pat his good knee to avoid startling him again.

Thislen nodded, watching her walk away. Whatever passed between them on the ship seemed to still be there. *That's good, isn't it? Unless she's expecting something from me.*

For a moment, Thislen understood Mila better than he ever had before. He closed his eyes, every limb too heavy to move, and let his mind wander down toward slumber.

I don't want people to expect anything from me, either. If they knew...

If they knew...

Garridan Artaith stood at the doors of Perilee, his arms folded over his chest. "There you are. I was wondering when you'd show up for a little chat. Let's go over these questions again, shall we?

Who are you?"

10

Moving house, it turned out, was difficult. It wore at patience, strained muscles, and lit tempers like wildfires. Mila was glad the hardest part—getting everything underground and into her family's new cavern—was over. They were far from finished unpacking or setting up, with crates, bags, and heaps of odds and ends in the way. Mila refused to move in until the worst of it was over.

Evelie was fussing over the perfect spot for everything and insisted on doing most of the work herself. She was intolerable, shifting everything around again and again. The vase looked fine on the mantle over the hearth, but what if it were on this shelf? What if it were by the lamp? What if it were...?

Olen had been assigned a cavern to serve as an infirmary, and was off setting that up. Things vanished from the living cavern to find new residence there, at least. Ivan was avoiding his mother as much as Mila was, but kept showing up among the scouts. He wanted an assignment. What was he thinking?

But there were no more trips to the surface to fetch things from the Ominir Apothecary or the flower shop. That was a relief.

Mila was excused from her patrols for a week to help her family settle in and adjust. It had been two days, and already she was eager to get back to the rooftops and ghosts above. She closed her eyes, shutting out the noise of the Commons to picture instead the silence of the night, the moon and stars overhead. She could feel the breeze off the sea, taste the salt it carried. She flexed her legs, ready to run, to leap across to the next roof over, then—

"Mila, what do you think of this for a new quilt?" Evelie asked, elbowing her gently.

Mila's eyes snapped open. She was still in the Commons, hovering near the cloth stand, and far away from the open air.

Dutifully, she turned to study the fabric. It was a rust-colored red. "Looks good to me."

"Not for your bed, though, not with that lovely quilt your mother made. I think Ivan will love it, don't you?"

Mila nodded, distracted by her thoughts. If she couldn't go up into Astera, there might be another way to escape, even if only for an hour or two. Her eyes swept over the crowds, trying to pick out the people she knew. Maybe she could get away for a sparring match if she could find another scout.

"I'll come back for it later," Evelie decided, turning and looping her arm through Mila's.

The two walked through the stalls of the Nattfolk side by side. Mila didn't know what to say to the woman who helped raise her. There was a gulf between them that made her stomach clench. She knew it would only widen before it closed.

I spent so much time away, and then I turned her entire life upside down. And she doesn't even know how much I've changed, not really. This can't end well.

"So this is what you wear these days, is it?" Evelie asked, her voice light and cheery as she plucked at Mila's dark sleeve.

Speak, and it shall appear.

"Yes. It fits well, don't you think?"

Evelie pursed her lips. "Mm, I would think it might be better for you to wear something prettier. You're a lovely girl. You always looked so nice in a full skirt."

Heat prickled up Mila's neck. "A skirt would look pretty strange when I'm running over the rooftops," she said, forcing a smile.

Is it really going to start this soon? We only lasted two days.

"Running over the rooftops," Evelie said with a soft scoff. "If that's what you want to do for a bit, I can't blame you. Young folk always want a bit of adventure before they settle down."

Mila clenched her jaw.

"Speaking of settling down, these family caverns are pretty nice, aren't they? You'd think the stone would be cold and unforgiving, but no. They quite warm it up with those nice big hearths, hm? One of those might be nice for you and one of these boys." Evelie's tone took on a coy, slightly teasing tone. "I've met them all, now, you know."

"I know, Evelie," Mila said slowly, though her mind was racing.

I don't know what to say. I don't want to be rude, but if she starts in on—

"So what about that Aften, hm? Handsome, if a little skinny."

The flush that raced over Mila's cheeks must have been visible, because Evelie beamed at her.

"I knew it. He's a nice boy, yes?"

"He is," Mila agreed. "But I think he has his eye on someone else."

And that someone else is Darran, not me. Aften doesn't seem to be interested in women.

"Well, if not him, what about that nice tall friend of his? Darran. In line to be a scout captain again, by all the rumors."

"No, I don't think so."

"You and Thislen seem close. Poor dear. You could spend some time nursing him back to health if you want to win his favor. It works every time."

"Evelie," Mila said, stopping dead in her tracks and pulling her arm free of the florist's. "Stop. Please."

Evelie adjusted the basket over her arm. "Stop what? I'm just trying to get to know your new friends."

No, you're trying to marry me off. If you can't have me with Ivan, you want a reason why.

And Evelie made no mention of Trevon, who she brought up to the surface with her in the first place. Trevon checked in every night before he went to the surface. If Ivan couldn't have her, it seemed Evelie didn't want Trevon to, either. Not that Mila was interested.

Was she?

Mila held her tongue, taking a deep, deep breath. "I'm not looking at boys right now, Evelie. There's a lot going on."

"Even secret societies have weddings, you know. I heard it from Rachelle, someone got married two moons ago. It was a lovely party."

"I'm not saying people can't get married down here, I'm saying I'm not interested," Mila said, fighting the urge to throw her hands up or raise her voice.

Evelie sniffed, turning to walk again. "We need to see the smith, I want a new kettle. What do you want to talk about, then, if you won't talk to me about your friends?"

About boys, you mean.

"We can talk about the past moon or so, when I was away."

"Away," Evelie said with a scoff. "That's one word for it. We were grieving, of course. It was miserable for all of us, Olen most of all. And there I was, trying to keep everything together. Didn't matter what I felt, someone had to feed Olen and Ivan. Someone had to make sure we all left for the ships on time. Someone had to be the glue, and of course it fell to me. Nevermind the fact that I lost a girl I consider my daughter."

Guilt swelled in Mila's chest and throat, threatening to burst out in the words she knew Evelie wanted to hear. *I'm sorry, I didn't realize, of course we can talk about whatever you want.* It would work, too.

Which was exactly why she couldn't do it.

"I'm here now," Mila said instead, stepping forward to walk beside the plump woman, taking her hand. "You don't have to do all that. I can help. Do you want to hear about the ghosts, or the first few days that I was down here? I know exactly how you feel, you know, trying to settle in."

Evelie looked around the huge stone room, crowded with people and full of laughter, chatter, and warmth. "It's a nice enough place, and nice enough people. I don't mind sleeping in a still bed, either," she said slowly.

"There's a sewing circle, you know. Our cavern could use some of those tapestries and wall quilts the others make."

"A sewing circle?" Evelie tried not to look interested. She couldn't quite keep the gleam out of her eye.

"Oh, yes. And there's a baking group, and a group that teaches the little ones to read and write. All things I think you'd be wonderful at. It's a good way to make friends down here."

"Oh, Mila," Evelie sighed, smiling as she gave her hand a squeeze. "Don't you worry about me. I didn't have all that many friends in Astera, and I don't need that many down here. I have Ivan, and you, and your father. I'm sure you lot will keep me plenty busy."

I don't want to be your project. I'm fine on my own. Another reason not to move in with her family, not yet. Mila cleared her throat and forced another smile. "Just something to consider."

An awkward silence fell between them as they crossed the Commons, threading their way between Nattfolk. The *clang, clang, tink,* of the smithy drew them on.

"Mila!" Olen called, lifting his hand. As he passed through the crowd, he was stopped often by people offering him a hello, calling out his name, stopping him for a word. Evelie and Mila stopped where they were, waiting for him to catch up.

She couldn't help but smile at her father's popularity. He was a good man. His kindness radiated out of him like beams from the sun, and he cared deeply for every person he met. The Nattfolk knew he was their healer. Word spread like wildfire. The Commons gossips saw to that.

At last, Olen broke free of his new friends, coming to a stop beside them. "Ah, Evelie! Looking lovely as always. Did you find—"

"—a kettle? Not yet. I'm on my way there now."

"Perfect. Can you ask for two? I'd like one for my infirmary. You don't mind if I steal Mila for a bit, do you?"

"Not at all. I have some things I'd like to ask around about. Did you know they have a sewing circle?"

Mila smiled. "Good luck."

"Thank you, but I won't need it," Evelie said with a wink. She left, each step purposeful. She was on the hunt for things to do, and she would find them.

Mila kept her sigh of relief quiet. When she turned to Olen, his sharp eye was on her face, and a brow was raised.

"Please don't lecture me, too."

"I wasn't planning on it. Is there something I ought to be lecturing you for?"

"Skirts or boys, apparently," Mila muttered.

"She's missed you. It might take her some time to realize that you've changed." Olen put an arm around her shoulders, steering her through the crowd.

"You see it, don't you, Father?"

"I do. You seem much stronger than the girl I saw at the Justica. You also want to go running around at night. That's new." He laughed, a deep belly laugh that drew smiles from the Nattfolk around them.

Mila rolled her eyes, but she was smiling, too. "As long as you don't expect me to turn around and start making a wedding gown."

"Me? Never. Now, helping me with some salves..." He arched a brow. "Different matter, hm?"

"I told you, I can't." She lowered her voice. "If the Night Council finds out I know how to mend, they won't let me go above-ground again. I can't do that. I need the sky. I need to move."

Olen nodded slowly. "I'm wrapping my head around it. I'm a little surprised. You spent your entire life learning our—*my* trade, and now you want nothing to do with it! But," he said, lifting a hand just as Mila opened her mouth. "But. You want it, and that's going to have to be enough for me for now, yes?"

Mila smiled. "Can it be?"

"I think so. You might have to tell me all about it for a bit. I don't know anything about Nattfolk scouts, after all." He grinned.

"It's so beautiful at night, Father. And the whole city looks different from a rooftop. The Vaim in the streets below, they're...odd, but they don't frighten me anymore. And the freedom of it all, the running, climbing, leaping, and exploring. I've seen more of Astera in a moon than I have in my entire life before this."

"My goodness. It sounds...dangerous, I admit. You jump off rooftops?"

"No! I jump across them. It's different."

"Not to the gray in my hair," Olen chuckled. "You need food to do all that, yes? Have you had your...do they still call it luncheon when it's midnight?"

Mila laughed. "Yes, they do. And no, I haven't. Come on." She turned toward the tavern.

"You'll be back out with them in a day or so, yes?"

"Tomorrow."

Olen glanced at her. "Can't wait?"

She sighed. "You aren't mad, are you? Or disappointed? Evelie seems..."

Olen nodded slowly. "She'll come around. This is what you want, and I...well, I may not understand it, but what sort of parent would I be if I didn't encourage it?"

Mila's relief was a weight off her shoulders. Yes, Olen was struggling with her new appearance, her new duties and hobbies, her proficiency with weapons and picking locks, and her sense of adventure. But at least he let her have them.

I was afraid it would be harder with my father, but I should have known better. He listens. Once I find the words, he hears me.

"When you were little," he said slowly, wrapping his large, rough hand around hers, "and your mother was still alive, we talked about what we wanted for your future. I had a list a thousand miles long. I wanted so much for you. Your mother wanted only one thing."

Mila arched a brow. Olen rarely spoke of her mother, a woman he loved so dearly that part of him died with her. He'd never once been interested in someone else after she passed. What little she knew stemmed from stories of their courtship, before she was born. She was just a year old when her mother passed, after all.

"She said all she wanted was for you to be happy."

A lump grew in Mila's throat. "That's all?"

"That's all," Olen said, a sad, wistful smile on his lips. "She told me nothing else mattered, so long as *you* loved your life. And we decided then and there that whatever you wanted to do, you should do.

"Now, I admit, I've struggled with it. I hated seeing you leave. I hated seeing you *want* to leave. But now that I see you here... The *confidence* you have, Mila! It's like steel. And the grace you carry was formed under pressure, hardened into a diamond. You like what you do. You like who you've got around you. I would say you're happy. Are you?"

Mila snorted softly. *There's still a family curse to break, and two councils to fight, and a vial to find, and Thislen isn't healed, but...*

"I think I am, or at least on my way there."

Olen smiled, swinging their hands like he used to when she was little. "There. See?"

She swallowed the lump in her throat, blinking the sting of unshed tears from her eyes. She smiled back at him.

"My goodness, is that a gravy stew I smell?" Olen asked as they reached the scattered tables of Kellan's domain. His shaggy head turned, nose in the air, and he inhaled deeply.

"And fresh bread," Mila assured.

Olen's deep, loud laugh filled the cavern. "Then what are we waiting for? Come on, my love. Let's put some happy in a bowl."

After lunch, Mila usually joined her patrol and went to the surface. Trevon was running with a different group while she was away. Darran was spending a few days with Aften, since Aften wasn't allowed to rejoin the scouts yet, either—not until he was cleared by Olen. Nearly a moon in captivity weakened his and Tamsa's muscles. They had to eat, stretch, and lift things.

Which meant they would be in the training cavern. Eager to join them, she moved around the Commons by the wall to avoid the crowd. She'd walked Olen to his assigned cavern. He and two Nattfolk were busy unpacking and arranging things. She wouldn't be missed.

Mila wanted to stretch her muscles. She wanted to spar, or shoot her bow, or practice on the pells. Anything, so long as it was physical.

A figure stepped out of the training cavern's tunnel, stopping and waiting beyond the lantern's light for her to draw near. Her heart sank.

Oh no, not Ivan.

Her brother in all but name looked sullen, his brows drawn down and his jaw set. His shoulders were hunched, as if he might make himself look smaller, impossible as it was. He was practically a giant.

"Mila. You've been avoiding me."

She stopped in front of him with a sigh. "I have."

"Because of what you said in the shop."

"Yes, that's part of it."

"What's the other part?" he demanded.

Mila ran her tongue over her lips. The honest answer would cut. Experience told her that lying or cushioning her feelings with Ivan would lead to misunderstandings. Her choices were limited at best. Neither was good.

"Honestly, I dread the conversation we have to have. Come on." Mila turned away from the training cavern toward the mouth of Trevon's favorite exit tunnel. She knelt to strike flint to her dagger and light a lantern, then led the way toward one of the few places she knew they wouldn't be overheard.

The smooth surface of the underground lake was black as obsidian. Mila had to be as hard as that stone herself.

"What are we doing here?" Ivan asked, his voice hushed. The cavern did that; inspired people to speak quietly and reverently, even when they came to haul water back to the Commons with splashes and grunts of effort.

"We're talking," Mila said firmly, planting the lantern atop a stone.

Ivan scowled, his fair features twisting with the motion. The shadows turned those creases in his face into jagged chasms. "I don't want to talk if you're just going to tell me that you don't love me again. Not when I love you."

Mila sighed, sitting at the edge of the water. She wrapped her arms around her legs. "*Do* you love me, Ivan? Or am I just...convenient?"

Ivan was still for so long Mila turned to see if he was still there. As if her gaze reminded him to breathe, the florist moved. He sat beside her and crossed his legs, leaning back on his palms and studying what little he could see of the cavern ceiling.

"I'm trying to decide what you mean," he said at last.

"I mean we grew up together, and we both knew almost all our lives that our parents wanted us to fall in love. Do you love me because you love *me*, or do you love me because it's what's expected of us?"

Ivan's brow furrowed, but his irritation had eased. "I haven't really thought about it."

"I know. That's why I'm asking now."

When he didn't speak again, Mila stole another glance. His gaze was never still. It swept over the water, the ceiling, the pebbles by his fingers. His lips pressed together, but he looked more curious than anything else.

"Expectation is a weight," Mila said slowly, gently. "I felt it crushing me. I had to be a healer and inherit the shop. I had to marry you or Soren. I had to live my life the way my father and Evelie would want it, the perfect picture. I was uncomfortable with it before I left home, but since coming down here I've learned it was because I was fighting who I *am*."

"I don't...know who I am," Ivan admitted softly. "I like flowers, I do. But I never asked myself if I wanted anything more. I guess I can't be a florist in a cave."

Mila laughed, and it echoed over the water and back. "Probably not, they're already struggling to get my father's plants enough light down here."

Ivan turned toward her, catching her hand in his own. "It does make me certain of one thing, though, Mila. You're the only constant. You're the only person I'm drawn to. I do love you. I love you, and I want you to love me, too."

Each word was firm as a hammer blow driving another nail into a coffin. Mila drew back and wrapped her arms tight around her knees. Her brow furrowed. *All I want is my family, not this. Why does he have to ruin it?*

"Mila. Please. Please love me."

"I told you before that I won't love you as anything more than a brother. You're family. I'm not interested in anything romantic with you. I'm not going to pretend, either."

"Why?"

Mila was silent.

"Why?" Ivan repeated, the word harsh with simmering frustration.

"Do I need a reason not to be attracted to you that way?"

Ivan frowned. "I'd like one."

"Well, I haven't got one," Mila snapped, pushing to her feet. "I don't feel any draw to you, not like that."

"Plenty of people fall in love after they get married. It happens all the time," Ivan said, standing as well.

"No, Ivan! I'm not going to marry you on the off chance that it will get better some day. Look at me. Look at me!" She stamped her foot.

Ivan stood with his shoulders hunched, the dark sullen look of a looming stormcloud on his face. He reluctantly met her steady gaze.

"We will never be like that. Ever. You can't convince me or force me. Asking me a hundred times doesn't make me change my mind."

The silence was heavy, broken only by the distant drip of water somewhere on the lake. Mila's hands were balled into fists. She trembled from the effort of biting back harsher words, words she knew would cut him to the quick. She didn't want to lose him entirely, but if she had to...

If I have to, I'll make sure I never see him again.

"It's that Trevon's fault, isn't it?"

Mila jerked, startled by his leap in logic. "What?" Her cheeks grew warm.

"That Trevon person, the one from the shop. The scout captain. You like him," Ivan accused.

"That has nothing to do with you and I."

"If he weren't here, would I have a chance?"

"No!" Mila said, throwing her arms up. "You didn't have a chance *before* I met Trevon. He has nothing to do with this!"

Her hand smacked into the lantern. It tumbled from its perch on the stone. Lightning fast, she twisted and caught it before more than a few drops of oil spilled on the ground, but the flame went out.

Mila and Ivan were plunged into darkness. She swore softly, kneeling and feeling in her pocket for her flint.

Ivan's breathing was loud in the darkness. He hadn't moved, but she felt his presence at her back, looming over her.

"Are you saying I *never* had a chance?"

She found her flint. Pulling her dagger, she struck against the stone. The sparks flared to life, then faded. The darkness crept back in. She felt the bulk of the man behind her and a chill ran through her.

"Mila," Ivan said, his foot scuffing on stone as he stepped closer. "Are you saying I *never* had a chance?"

"Yes, that's what I'm saying," she said bitterly.

"That isn't fair. I've been here longer than any of these others. Thislen, Trevon, all of them."

She struck her flint again. The sparks didn't catch. Her hands were shaking, and that warm, boiling feeling started roiling in her stomach. "What kind of argument is that? By that logic, I should love the first man besides my father I ever met."

"I was that man. I *am* that man."

"And I don't love you. Not the way you want."

"But you haven't even tried," he said loudly with another scuffed step toward her.

Mila felt the heat bloom from her chest and down her arms, tingling as it got to her hands. "I don't need to try, Ivan."

"This just isn't fair."

"Feelings don't care about *fair*," Mila shouted, the heat bursting out of her. She smacked her dagger and flint on the ground.

The lantern wick burst into flame, the sudden bloom of yellow light pushing back the shadows surrounding them.

Mila was still. *The flint must have sparked when I put it down.*

But she hadn't seen any sparks.

Ivan's hand fell on her shoulder, interrupting her thoughts. He turned her around and drew her to her feet in a single motion. "Mila."

She folded her arms over her chest. "Ivan, I swear to the heavens and the Ancestors, if you push this any further, I will never speak to you again. I deserve better than this."

Ivan's eyes widened. His teeth clicked as he closed his mouth, biting back whatever words he'd nearly spoken.

Mila picked up the lantern and pressed it into Ivan's hands. "I don't want to lose you. You're still my family, after all. But I won't be bullied or guilted into a decision that will affect the rest of my life. The next time you talk to me, you had better think about that. Do you want me around, or do you want to drive me away? Forever."

The lantern dangled from Ivan's hand. His mouth opened, then closed, shock, anger, and misery crossing his face one after the other.

"You have a lot to think about. Go." She pointed down the tunnel toward the Commons.

"You can't just send me away like a child to his room," Ivan snapped.

Mila leveled her gaze on him, brows drawn down, jaw set. She didn't lower her arm or say a single word.

Ivan stepped back. A scowl crossed his face. He turned on his heel, storming down the passage, taking the light with him.

Mila was used to the dark. When her eyes adjusted, she could go back to the cavern. She sighed softly, turning to crouch beside the water. *That didn't go the way I wanted it to, but at least he got the message. I think. I hope.*

A pebble clacked and clattered across the ground behind her. She stood, turning on her heel, scooping her dagger off the floor.

"Who's there?"

"That didn't sound like a fun conversation. Are you alright?" Trevon asked, voice soft. He unshuttered the lantern he carried, the flame turned down until there was barely any light at all.

Mila groaned, burying her head in her hands. "Don't tell me you heard all that."

"Not all of it, but some."

She groaned again.

Trevon gently set his hand on her shoulder, the handle of his lantern squeaking softly. He smelled faintly of salt and earth.

He was above-ground, she realized with a pang. Of course he was. It was past midnight. He ought to have been above ground still.

"Why are you down here?" she asked.

"We only need a half patrol to run our route at the moment. I wasn't needed. And...you and I hadn't talked much in a couple days. I wanted to check on you."

She scowled. "I don't need watched like I'm a child."

"I never said you did." Trevon settled on the ground, his head bent. A lock of his hair hung down over his eyes.

Mila's fingers itched. She wanted to tuck it back into place. She looked away with a soft huff and plopped down beside him.

"I wanted to check on you because of what you said in the shop. How you were worried about your family and how they'd take all this. Adjusting is hard at the best of times, and this...this isn't the best of times."

"You can say that again," she sighed.

He grinned, a twinkle in his eye. "This isn't the best of—"

"Trevon!" She laughed.

He grinned, though it faded slowly. "It sounds like Ivan, at least, is still trying to adjust."

Her own smile vanished, and she sighed heavily. "I needed to lay it out for him, but that doesn't mean it was pleasant. I hated that. I hated hurting him. But he wouldn't *listen.*"

Trevon nodded, studying the faint flame of the lantern, watching it dance. Mila couldn't stop looking at him out of the corner of her eye.

"You always find a way to be heard. It's hard right now, but it won't be hard forever, Mila."

She stared out over the water with a thoughtful hum. Silence fell throughout the cavern. She savored it, letting it sit unbroken while the knot in her chest full of anger, resentment, and guilt eased. *He's right. This can't last forever. If I hold my ground, in a little while...*

"You know what cheers me up?" Trevon asked suddenly.

"No."

She didn't, she realized, but she wanted to.

"Hitting things with swords." He grinned.

She couldn't help another smile. He always knew what to say. "That's exactly what I wanted to do before this whole spat with Ivan. You don't happen to have time for a spar, do you?"

"With you? I'll clear my schedule." He stood, offering her his hand.

She accepted it, grinning as he pulled her to her feet. They stood close for a moment, faces nearer than they'd ever been. Mila's smile faltered and she stepped back. She watched his features, but the disappointment she expected to see on Trevon's face never came. He just kept smiling.

Mila's heart was racing, though she stood still. She felt that flutter in her stomach again. She faltered, uncertain what to say, what to do. Her hands felt suddenly awkward. She clasped them together, then tucked them behind her back.

Trevon held up the lantern, starting toward the Commons and the training cavern beyond. "Coming?" he called over his shoulder.

There's something about him, she mused.

Like a moth to a flame, she followed Trevon and his lantern's fading light.

11

"It's time for us to break the curse."

Mila stood with her hands on her hips, facing all of her friends. It took her days to herd them all into the Barracks at the same time. To say they were busy was an understatement. The day after her and Trevon's sparring match, she requested to go back on patrols. Darran was working with Aften and Tamsa to get their strength up every night. Thislen had slept through a fever for the better part of a week. Trevon had a list of scout captain duties as long as his arm.

Tonight was her scouting group's night off, which meant there was time to present her latest plan. Well, plans, really.

Thislen lay in his bunk, carefully bending his knee, testing it. His fever had broken, he'd bathed, and he was more alert, all of which was good news as far as Mila was concerned. Tamsa and Aften were also on the mend, both of them eating as much as they could stomach for every meal.

Darran glued himself to Aften's side ever since the rescue, and tonight was no exception. The scouts stood with their shoulders almost brushing, each of them studiously avoiding looking at one another. Tamsa perched on the edge of Thislen's bunk, her hand on the blanket beside his leg. Thislen didn't mind at all. Trevon leaned against the stone wall. Mila invited Ivan along as well, though things were still strained between them. He stood nearby, shoulders hunched to make himself appear a little smaller, as if he didn't believe he belonged there.

He isn't the only one.

"I still can't believe there's a curse at all," he said.

"Which is part of the problem." Mila spread her arms wide. "Who knows? Outside of us here, there's Olen, Evelie, and the Night Council—and the Ruling Council, though they don't know the extent of it."

Ivan cast a glance at Thislen.

Thislen shrugged. "We're pretty certain they don't know that the curse affects their bloodlines, however diluted they are, otherwise they never would have given ships to the rest of Astera."

"Oh."

Mila cleared her throat. "Which brings me to one of our biggest problems. Rendyn."

Aften grimaced, and Tamsa sighed.

"Rendyn," Mila continued, "is going to stop us from doing anything if he catches wind of a plan. We need to distract him. I think we can kill two birds with one stone if we widen the circle of those who know the truth about the Vaim."

"What are you proposing?" Trevon asked slowly, a smile tugging at one corner of his lips.

He guesses, and he...approves? Mila's cheeks turned pink. She cleared her throat. "I think we get overheard. Specifically, I think you two do." She pointed at Aften and Tamsa.

Tamsa's eyes widened, then she relaxed, head tipping to one side. "Because we're Sivivans. We're credible sources for information from the Night Council. But we can't just march into the Commons, stand on a tavern table, and announce it like we would a festival."

"Well, half of the Nattfolk think I'm a fool thanks to him," Aften mused, fiddling with the hilt of the dagger on his belt. "What if we use that to our advantage? I think I have an idea. Leave that one to me, Mila."

Mila shrugged. If her plan was to work, she needed to delegate. She couldn't control every aspect of this, no matter how much she wanted to—and she really, *really* wanted to. *If only the whole world was a Hunters and Hounds board, and I could move all the pieces myself.*

"How does that break the curse?" Trevon asked.

"It buys us time for the other plan. I figured out how to steal the vial."

Thislen sat up, gaze intent.

"Well, don't leave us in suspense." Darran grinned.

"The rescue gave me the idea. We steal another ferryboat. We go in the middle of the day and there won't be anyone on the ship. We'll have all the time in the world to crack the safe on the *Bestant Belle*. If we're lucky, Soren won't even know we've been there until long after we're gone."

"We don't know if the vial is in the safe," Thislen countered. He grimaced as he moved, swinging his good leg to the ground.

Mila frowned. A tingle of hot frustration ran up her spine. "Well, it will give us a chance to check at least, as safely as we can. We won't get caught again."

Thislen paled at the thought, and Mila's anger faded in a heartbeat. *Too soon.*

Darran cleared his throat. "It's true, though. We never did open the safe. What if there's just money inside or something? There must be a way we can figure out where the vial is. What if they keep it inside of Perilee, or—"

"Wouldn't Ninian be able to find it if the vial were in the castle or on land?" Aften plucked at the bandage wrapped around one of his wrists. It covered the sores from the manacles he wore in captivity. "The Vaim would sense it."

"Alright, then what if it's on another ship? The *Bestant Belle* is one ship, but then there's *Ship Artaith*, too. What about that other one, the judge? Doesn't he have a ship?" Darran folded his arms over his chest.

Mila looked up at the ceiling, taking a deep and calming breath. *Darran is just worried about Aften, about being separated again. He might even have a point.*

"How do you propose we figure it out?" She dropped her gaze to the scout.

"We've been watching him," Trevon said casually.

"What? What do you mean?"

"We've had at least two Solwalkers following him and his friends around to figure it out. We're also working on getting someone into the Bestant household."

"Who is we?" Mila's voice rose in pitch, much to her dismay. *I had no part in it. I should have been included!* It stung, knowing Trevon didn't trust her. She thought he did, considering all his help with her schemes.

Then again, Trevon had a habit of only sharing what someone needed to know *when* they needed to know it.

"Me, mostly. After word came back that you all rushed into a trap—" Trevon started.

"It wasn't rushed!"

"—and got captured, I put a watch on the people who held you captive. I was trying to find a way to rescue Aften and Tamsa at first, but I haven't told the Solwalkers to stop their spying yet."

"We have eyes on the three in question. Good." Tamsa folded her arms. "I don't see a problem in that. Some of us aren't in good shape right now anyway, and Ivan needs training before we can send him into the field."

Ivan grimaced. "A lot of it."

"And the best person to crack the safe is Thislen, and he's not even walking yet," Aften pointed out.

Mila's hands balled into fists, and she fought the urge to stomp her foot. "You're proposing we wait."

"For more information," Trevon said soothingly, coming to her side. "We can run everything through you."

Mila's frown only deepened.

"What is it, Mila?" Thislen asked, fixing her with his dark eyes.

He's always been able to see right through me. Even if he's changed, it's nice to know that hasn't.

"This curse was started by my family. No one else's. Every person who died at the hands of the Vaim died because of *my* grandfather. I feel responsible. How many people are going to die because of him, because of us, because we waited?"

A flicker of something passed over Thislen's face and he dropped his gaze. She couldn't tell what it was, it came and went too quickly for her to read.

"You aren't responsible. You know that, right? You're doing what you can to end this mess." Trevon put his hand on her shoulder. The warmth of his words and his touch sank into her like sunlight, and she basked in it.

"I want the curse broken as soon as possible, so no one else dies. So the Nattfolk have the choice to rejoin the Solfolk if they want, so the Solfolk don't have to crowd onto ships every night, and we can all live our lives without being afraid of the dark." Mila put her hand over the scout captain's.

Ivan stared at the distant, shadowed ceiling above them. "I can't even imagine a life like that."

"Neither can I," Aften admitted, a wistful look on his face. He didn't look up from the frayed edge of the bandage he was steadily destroying.

"There's so much we've been told our entire lives about protecting our secret, to protect ourselves and the Solfolk," Tamsa said slowly. "If we slip, then Solfolk will try to stay on the island, and many will die. If we slip, then the Ruling Council will hunt for us during the day and we'll be trapped if they find us. If we slip, the history we're protecting down here, the notebooks my father has and other archives besides, they'll be lost. No one will know the truth anymore. No one will know it's a spell."

"I know I didn't cast this curse, but more than anything I want to be part of ending it. I *have* to be part of ending it. I can feel it, like a knot all tied up in my stomach. I don't quite know how to explain it, but..." Mila trailed off.

To her surprise, it was Thislen who nodded his agreement. "I know that feeling, the feeling of something hanging over your head, something you should be doing that you aren't. There's an invisible chorus of people inside you, and all of them are clamoring for you to move. It's impossible to get rid of them." His gaze slid to the side.

Mila glanced over her shoulder. There was nothing there. A cold tingle spread across her chest and down her spine. *I wonder if he's really alright.*

"Unless you do something. Let's get going, then." Aften pushed to his feet. "Tamsa, I need you for my plan to work. Ivan, since you have to stay here for now, I want you to help too. We'll give you a sword lesson after we finish."

Ivan shrugged. "Works for me."

The three of them headed toward the Commons, and Mila let them go.

"Trevon," Thislen said, looking up at the man. "You said you have people watching Bestant. What did my cousin do when he found out we were gone?"

Trevon grinned. "He was livid. He threw a lovely chair off a balcony, and the Solwalkers could hear him shouting for bells. Stormed to *Ship Artaith* and laid into the guards all night, too, from the sailors' accounts."

Good, Mila thought fiercely. It was about time Lord Soren Bestant was taken down a peg or two. The best part? He wouldn't know who stole his prizes away. Mila and Darran were supposed to be dead. They'd never cross his mind as the culprits.

Does he think it's spirits, or some enemy of the Ruling Council we don't know about? Or something else entirely, perhaps. Whatever he thinks, it no doubt plagues his mind.

A tight, vicious smile crossed her lips.

Oh, how the tides have changed.

Aften caught Tamsa's wrist, pulling her behind Rachelle's fabric stall. "Wait, you can't just leave it at that. Tamsa, stop! What does he mean the Vaim are a curse?"

Tamsa turned with a hiss, covering his mouth. "Are you an idiot? We can't talk about that here. Father trusted us with this, so you keep your trap shut."

When she uncovered his mouth and stepped away, he followed her to the corner of the booth. "If the Vaim are a curse, doesn't that mean we can break it?"

"Aften, I swear—"

"Alright, alright." He held his hands up placatingly and followed Tamsa a few booths away and around a corner. Once they were out of sight, he grinned. "That was kind of fun."

Tamsa gave a helpless little smile, rolling her eyes. "Was I really that bad, before?"

"Worse, actually. You'd have dragged me to the Council Chamber and turned me over." Aften grimaced. *And Rendyn would have locked me in our family cavern for days, so he knew I couldn't get out.*

Ivan rounded the corner. "She heard," he reported. "She leaned back and her eyes got big as tea saucers."

"Perfect. That's half the gossips in the Commons, so far. Think we need a few more?" Aften stretched. They'd played through their little act, dropping tidbits about the ghost in Perilee, the journals the Council kept hidden, and the Vaim being a curse. Aften checked off the list in his head. *Rachelle, she'll tell her entire sewing circle. Kellan will drop hints about it to the regulars. No one down here can resist a puzzle. Polly will tell her family, and her uncle's got the biggest gob in the caverns. Toman can't resist bragging that he knows something other people don't, he'll drop it like tidbits to hawks for all of his friends over the next few days.*

"I don't think so, I think they'll get the news to the rest." Tamsa leaned around the edge of the wooden stall's back, scanning the crowd.

Aften watched her, a painful hope aching in his chest. Working with her felt *good*, but part of him still didn't trust this newfound camaraderie. *She went along with my plan, though. She didn't even question it. No one did.*

He paused. No one questioned him. No one belittled him, put him down, or made him defend his idea. Aften felt the first stir of something deep inside his chest. He didn't know if it was nerves or elation.

Still, his plan was working. Quick as he'd thought it up, it was *working*. He helped.

"Ah, hello you three."

They turned to face Olen, who was carrying a basket over his arm with some jars, bottles, and clean cloth inside.

Aften didn't know the giant bearded man very well, and fathers in general made him nervous, so he didn't say anything while Tamsa greeted him.

"What are you up to, Olen?" Ivan asked.

"I could ask you the same thing." He grinned. "I'm taking a few things around to people who said they need them. I could use someone to help carry this basket, though."

"We were about to take Ivan to the training cavern for his first sword lesson," Tamsa hedged.

"Oh, by all means then—you two go on ahead." Olen's smile was a bit strained, but he turned to Aften and held out the basket. "Aften, was it?"

Tamsa and Ivan hurried away, casting apologetic looks over their shoulders as they went. Aften frowned after them. He heaved a sigh as they disappeared from view. Tamsa *was* the better swordsman. He took the basket. It was as heavy as it looked.

"Yes, sir. Aften Sivivan."

"You were with Thislen on that ship."

Aften moved stiffly a few steps away. "Can we go?"

"I'm just wondering if you need anything."

"No, I'm fine."

"Have you ever helped a healer before?" Olen asked, catching up in a few long strides. He walked beside Aften, indicating direction with nods of his head or gestures of his hand.

"No, I haven't."

"Well, I'll need you to pass me things. So let me explain, this one here is for inflammation, it's made of witch hazel and garlic, distilled with some rosemary. There's a few other things, but how it works, basically, is..."

As Olen went on, Aften began to pick up what each bottle was for, much to his surprise. He followed the apothecary around the cavern and passed out paper packets of tea or rolled pills, bottles of tinctures, and jars of salves. He watched curiously as Olen showed a few people how their medicines were to be used and lectured them on how things were to be taken. As they worked, the basket got lighter and lighter, until there was hardly anything left.

"Well, thank you for all your help, Aften." Olen took the basket back. There was a knowing twinkle in his eye. "There's no chance I can convince you to come help me again for a few days, is there?"

Aften hesitated, chewing the inside of his cheek for a moment. "I mean, if I'm not busy, I guess," he hedged.

Olen smiled, patting Aften on the shoulder before he walked away. Most of the night was gone now, but he didn't mind. That small swell in his chest was much larger now.

I...liked that. Learning, helping, carrying. Strange. He'd never pictured himself as a mender before, especially not with how much he ached for open air. Now, though, he was reconsidering everything he thought he wanted before his capture, weighing the options against one other.

It might be useful to have someone with basic healing skills in the scouts. No one is saying I can't do both. Well, as long I don't tell Rendyn.

He grinned, threading his way through the crowds of Nattfolk on his way to the training cavern to see if Tamsa and Ivan were still there. He should get in some training while he could.

He'd be busy soon.

It was late, or early if you were a Solfolk. Dawn had come and gone. Mila couldn't sleep. Her mind was full of plans, of counter plans, of arguments to convince the others. She lay in her bunk in the Barracks fully clothed, turning over her worries like familiar little stones in her hands. How many more would die? How much longer could this go on? Was Astera ready for the curse to end? The scuff of a boot on the stone drew her attention. It seemed Trevon couldn't sleep either. Without a word between them, the two left the Barracks and made their way to the training cavern. They picked up practice swords and circled one another slowly.

"Something on your mind?" Trevon asked.

"A lot."

She stepped in with a feint and he sidestepped, not falling for the trick.

"Anything you want to talk about?"

"I hate how you keep fixing all my plans." That wasn't what she meant to say.

Trevon stepped in, and their swords met with the sharp clang of metal on metal. They swung, parried, and blocked in rapid succession. When they broke apart again, Mila's breath had quickened. Trevon's hadn't.

"Why?" he asked, circling slowly again.

He wasn't upset or angry. Good. "Because I want my plans to be good to begin with. Every time you or someone else pokes holes in them, I feel like I'm going to lead us right into Soren's hands again."

Trevon rushed in, and Mila was hard pressed to keep him away from her, backpedaling several feet before he leapt back again. Her arms were getting tired.

"There's that chance, yes. Are you going to stop leading because of it?"

She frowned, lowering her sword. "I don't give up very easily."

He grinned, his arm dropping too. "I know. What do you need from me?"

Mila shifted her weight from foot to foot. "Teach me. Teach me how to be a better leader," she blurted. "You've been one for years, and I want to learn. I want to know."

"Done." He held out his hand.

Mila stepped forward, and they shook on it. He didn't let go right away. She didn't either. His fingers were warm, wrapped around her wrist. His grip wasn't too tight. She could pull away if she wanted. His eyes met hers, a silent question on his face.

"Trevon!"

Mila jerked her hand away and turned, startled, toward the young man running toward them. He was dressed in the bright clothes of a Solfolk and he was drenched in sweat. He could hardly breathe, gulping in great lungfuls of air as he skidded to a stop.

Well, our sparring match is over.

Darran and Aften, both half asleep, followed a moment later. They were pulling on their leathers as they moved.

"He woke us up looking for you," Darran started to explain.

"What's going on?" Aften interjected.

Mila felt a mounting sense of dread.

"It's Illi, she showed up for the interview but some guards cornered her, and she was fighting them off, but—"

Trevon didn't wait for him to finish, and neither did Mila. Both of them dropped the practice swords with a clatter. She was right on his heels, pulling her cowled hood up to hide her face as they tore through the quiet Commons, dodging stalls and leaping crates as they went. Mila could hear footsteps behind her. She feared if she looked back to see who it was, she'd lose Trevon. He was moving fast.

The scout captain skidded into a tunnel entrance Mila hadn't been in before, one that ran flat, with the sound of dripping water somewhere above. They tore through the near-dark. Someone behind them had grabbed a torch or a lantern, and though the light was dim and swung wildly, it was bright enough they wouldn't run into any walls.

If the Solwalker talks, the Nattfolk will be hunted like mice by those...those bastards!

A stitch began to form in her side, small and high, beneath her ribs.

We're under the canal, we're going to come up in the Grand Quarter. She wondered briefly which noble house or wealthy merchant had ties to the Nattfolk before pushing it from her mind. Mila didn't know Illi personally, which wasn't surprising knowing she was a Solwalker, but Trevon seemed to.

Her heart pounded as his broad back vanished. He was running faster than whoever had the light. She plunged after him, the shadows swallowing her whole. In the dark, she could hear her breathing sawing raggedly in her ears. She could feel the burning ache in her legs and her arms. She followed the steady sound of Trevon's feet ahead of her, hoping against hope that the path stayed straight and flat.

He turned; she heard it. He slowed, and then the sound moved off to her left. She held out her hands, slowing down as quick as she could. The breath was driven from her lungs anyway as she collided with the stone. Mila pushed off in the direction he'd gone and heard the muffled curses behind her as the others veered too. The light was catching up to them, and not a moment too soon. In the vague gloom ahead, she saw a set of steep stairs.

Before she'd gone up ten of them, her legs were burning and the stitch in her side had become a hundred needles in her lungs. There was precious little time, if there was any at all. *What if she's been hauled away? What if she's already dead? This could be a trap, an ambush!*

Her mind raced along with her feet, but until she could talk to Illi and Trevon, she'd never know the answers.

Out of the gloom loomed a shadowed figure. Mila gasped, but she couldn't stop in time. She crashed into Trevon's back, driving him into the stone.

"Ow, damn it!"

"Trevon," she gasped.

"I'm opening it. Hold on, hold on."

Another body slammed into Mila from behind, and she yelped. The three of them went tumbling out of the darkness into the early morning light streaming through a window—her, Trevon, and Darran. After the darkness of the caverns, it was blinding. She shielded her eyes.

They stood panting in a small shed with the door hidden in the wood paneling of the wall. Darran looked back over his shoulder, catching the Solwalker who brought them the message. "Stay here, watch the door. Wait for us to knock to let us back in."

The Solwalker looked exhausted. He didn't protest at all as he stepped back inside and hauled the heavy door—stone on one side, wood on the other—closed again. Apart from the window, there was a single worn door on the other side, and scattered gardening equipment.

Trevon waited for the wall to stop moving before he bolted into the open air. Mila followed him onto a long swath of green grass, shock slowing her steps for a single second. They weren't just in the Grand Quarter, they were on the grounds of an old noble estate. No one else had hedgerows laid out in a fanciful maze, or a fish pond with delicate lilypads on the surface, or a massive three story mansion with carved scrollwork all over.

How did they—who lives here?

She got no answer. Darran passed her, and she picked up her pace once more. The shed they'd emerged from was tucked into a back corner, against a large stone that had been carved into a little grotto to hide its true purpose. A stone and iron fence flew past on one side, the hedges on the other, until they suddenly reached an open gate. A pair of startled lady's maids scattered out of their way like little chicks, eyes wide.

Whoever's estate it was, it faced the sea and a few piers on the opposite side of a modest park.

The Bestant Estate can't be far!

It too, sat on the sea. They passed only one more house before the massive miniature palace came into view. It was a great carved monstrosity of gilt work and paint. Not a single inch had been left plain, it seemed. A high stone wall surrounded the grounds, and for once this gate too stood open.

A small cluster of guards held the arms of a young woman in a plain but serviceable skirt and shirt, her apron crooked from their manhandling. Her hair was braided back in a simple plait. Though she was held fast, she hadn't stopped struggling. It took them no small amount of work to hold her still. Mila felt a fierce pride for the unknown Illi.

The guards weren't the only people present, however. Lord Soren Bestant, Lord Judge Avasten Barnweir, and Master Garridan Artaith stood at the gate, conferring in a little knot. Soren was furious, a hand cutting through the air to emphasize whatever point he was making.

Mila pulled up the front of her cowl like a mask as they ran, covering her face. She was chilled through even as sweat stuck a loose coil of hair to her cheek. She hadn't seen Soren since she'd been left for dead.

I'd hoped I would never see him again.

Trevon didn't slow. He didn't signal or shout any commands. Mila's mouth went dry as she realized he must not have a plan. They hadn't had time to make one.

Oh no.

He lowered his shoulder and charged the City Guard. Darran was on his heels, and he did the same, aiming for the second. Mila sucked in a deep breath. *They'll handle the guards, I'll get Illi and run.*

Wild shouting broke out as first one, then the other of the Nattfolk ran into their assigned guards. Both men lost their grip. Wrenched free of their grasp, Illi looked down at her hands, stunned.

Mila darted past, grabbing her wrist as she did and pulling with all her strength. Thankfully, Illi took the hint and staggered into a run. There was still shouting behind her, and she could hear Soren loud and clear.

"What is—will you inept oafs just grab that one already? Flatten him, if you must!"

Mila let go of Illi's wrist. Illi kept running, and Trevon ran past hot on her heels. He had a split lip. As he passed Mila, his head jerked around.

"Come on, keep running!" he urged.

Mila slid to a stop, reversing and running back toward the guards. Trevon froze at the corner, anxious eyes boring a hole into her back.

Darran flailed at the guards, all of whom were still tangled in a heap with one another. He kicked free. He twisted—

—and he came face to face with a wide-eyed Soren Bestant.

The shock of recognition was clear as day from both of them. Darran's eyes widened, and Soren recoiled, pale.

"You?" The nobleman barked. "I left you—"

Mila dropped her shoulder the way she'd seen the others do. It was supremely satisfying to ram into Soren's side and send him crashing to the cobblestones of his own front path. The nobleman let out an undignified yelp. She grabbed Darran's wrist and yanked. "Run, run, Darran!"

"Get them," Soren bawled at the top of his lungs. "Stop them, catch that man, I demand you catch that man!"

Mila glanced back. Two guards climbed to their feet, setting off halfheartedly in their wake. Their heavy chain shirts would hinder them in a flat-out chase. The Nattfolk would escape.

But the glittering eye of Avasten Barnweir followed her and Darran, reminding her as always of a spider waiting in the center of its web. A single touch of his hand drew Soren's attention. Soren, nearly frothing at the mouth, glared at the judge. Garridan stood open-mouthed in the middle of the street, watching them flee.

"Soren, they're never going to catch up," Avasten said, loud and clear.

Mila shuddered. Was that for her benefit?

"I don't care. Chase them, damn it, don't stop. You idiots. You laggards! I recognized that man, Avasten, I'm telling you—I killed him."

They reached the corner. Mila glanced back one last time, her heart skipping a beat. Avasten wasn't looking at anyone else. Had he heard her speak?

Trevon fell into step beside her and Darran, and Illi when they reached the next corner. As they wove quickly through the streets to the shed, its door, and the dark safety of their warren of caves, Mila's heart beat a different refrain.

He knows, he knows, he knows.

Soren or Avasten would figure it out, she was certain. One or the other of them would piece together that Darran, at least, could survive on the island at night. They would wonder who else could. They might even recognize her voice, though her face had been hidden. The Nattfolk might be exposed once and for all. Their lives, their secrets, the history they protected—all of it was in danger.

He knows.

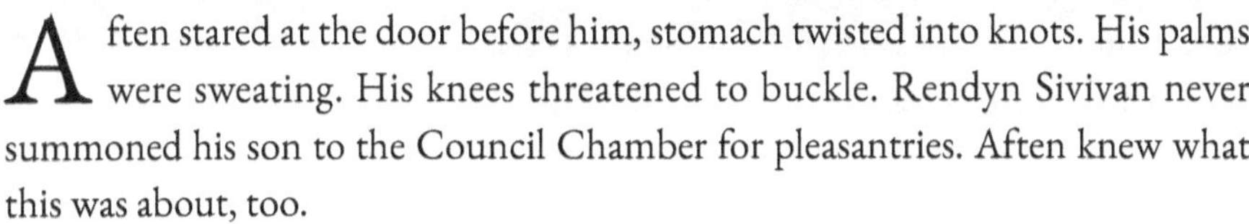

12

A ften stared at the door before him, stomach twisted into knots. His palms were sweating. His knees threatened to buckle. Rendyn Sivivan never summoned his son to the Council Chamber for pleasantries. Aften knew what this was about, too.

The Commons was abuzz with information, and the Night Council finally caught on. Rumors of the Vaim being a curse were the loudest. There were a thousand questions on everyone's lips. Who, why, how?

But I know the gossips. They wouldn't sell out their sources.

So why had Rendyn ordered Aften to report at the Sunset Bell?

He balled his hands into fists.

There was still time to turn around. He could walk away. It would be a statement.

It would make Rendyn much more angry.

Better to handle it now, before it festered into something worse. Besides, he had something he needed to say. He braced himself.

Footsteps echoed off the smooth walls of the carved tunnel behind him. "Aften," Tamsa gasped as she ran up.

"What are you doing here?" he asked, voice low. "Did he call for you, too?"

"No, Darran told me where you went. You don't have to go in there."

Aften swallowed, frowning at his feet. He didn't want to, but he *did* have to.

Would she understand if I tried to explain? I've been trying so hard to avoid disappointing him, so hard to prove *myself to him—but now it's time to prove myself* for *me.*

"I do have to."

"Then I'll come with you. With me there, he can't—"

"Tamsa," Aften interrupted, smiling and grasping her shoulders. "Thank you for wanting to help me. Thank you for trying to do better. But I need to go in there alone."

It was time to sort a few things out with Rendyn Sivivan.

Tamsa hesitated, then sighed. "Alright. But if you don't come out in a bell, I'm sending in a small army."

Aften grinned. "Deal."

She smiled at him. He could hardly remember the last time she'd done that. This was the first time in their lives that he felt like he had a sister instead of a rival. He'd grown up watching other families interact, never understanding why his was so different behind closed doors.

Now, he was learning what it felt like to have a real family, and it had nothing to do with the man waiting in the Council Chamber.

Tamsa left, going back the way she came. Aften watched her retreating back for several heartbeats, then turned and knocked firmly on the door.

"Come in," Rendyn called, his voice flat.

Aften stepped inside. The door closed behind him with a *clunk* that reverberated off the smooth walls. The room was dominated by an ornate table, polished to a mirror shine. Lanterns of all shapes and sizes hung from dozens of chains of different lengths overhead, flooding the space with light. Mismatched chairs, stools, and a bench lined the sides of the table.

And at the head, in the tall-backed wooden chair that looked like a throne, sat Rendyn. He had stacks of parchment before him, all untouched. The inkwell wasn't open. His quill lay beside it. Instead, he was leaned back in his seat, a hand splayed on the table, fingers tapping all in a row. *Tadadada, tadadada.* He didn't look up.

"You called?" Aften said, proud that his voice didn't shake.

"Sit down."

"No, thanks. I can't stay long. I have to get back to the training cavern if I want to rejoin the patrols."

Rendyn scowled, gaze dropping onto Aften like a hammer blow. His eyes, hazel like his son's, were hard as agates. "I said sit down."

"And I said no. What is this about?"

Rendyn's hand clenched around the arm of his chair until the knuckles were white. Instinct screamed inside Aften, telling him to apologize, to sit, to bow his head. He fought his thoughts, standing firm. Over and over, he reminded himself of what it felt like in the bottom of that ship, in the cell. The chains were heavy on his arms. They hurt. He'd decided his only value to his people was *dead*.

He wasn't ever going to let that happen again. Being trapped, wrapped in chains of his own making, of Rendyn's, wasn't an option.

"Fine. I should have known you'd resort to being rude. Worse, however, you have betrayed this family." Rendyn relaxed all at once, his demeanor turning icy.

Aften's stomach twisted into such a tangle that he felt nauseated. He folded his arms over his chest to hide the tremble in his hands. His palms were still sticky with sweat. "And how did I do that?"

"Have you heard the rumors circulating in the Commons?"

"About Grace and Kellan? I think it'll be a good match," Aften said lightly.

Rendyn's face twisted into a scowl. "No!" As quickly as his fury came, it left, and his features were smooth once more. "No, I meant the rumors about the Vaim being a curse. The rumors about how we can break it. The ones where our people seem to know all about the Sivivan journals, and half the secrets they contain."

Aften lifted his brows. Bile coated the back of his throat. *If he had any proof it was me, I'd already be locked up,* he assured himself. He wasn't certain it was *true,* but it helped steel his spine.

"I hadn't heard all that, no."

"You told them."

"I didn't," Aften said firmly.

Rendyn pushed to his feet, stalking closer. "You told them. It must have been you."

"Because I'm the only person who knew? Didn't the entire Night Council? And Tamsa, Darran, Trevon, Mila, and Thislen? Olen, Evelie, Ivan. Am I forgetting anyone, or is that about twenty different possible sources for your little leak?"

Rendyn stopped three steps away from his son, scowling darkly down at him. "You are loose lipped and irresponsible. It was you, and I know it. Admit it."

Aften forced his shoulders to stay square, his chin to stay up. His mouth was dry. He met Rendyn's gaze. "No, because it wasn't me." *Not just me, anyway.* "Why are you always determined to see the worst in me?"

He hadn't meant to say it. He bit his lip as soon as the words were out. A chill slipped down his spine. Did he really want to hear the answer?

Rendyn snorted. He didn't answer, and Aften hated the relief that flooded him when he didn't. "If you won't admit it, I'll have to put you under house arrest until you're ready to talk."

Aften snorted right back, rolling his eyes. "You can't. I don't live here anymore, and I'm not staying."

"You don't have a choice!" Rendyn roared, throwing his hands up. "You're stubborn as a damn mule, and just as stupid. You're *my* son, and you will do as I say! A few weeks on a boat is no excuse for behavior like this. Your little rebellion is *over*. Over!"

Aften's face was hot, his cheeks flushed. He dropped his hands by his sides, glaring. "You have no idea what we went through on that ship," he said, every word clipped and hard. His voice was barely above a whisper. "You have no idea what Tamsa and I went through. You have no idea who I even *am*. My little rebellion? You have no right to speak to me this way."

"You will show me the respect I am owed."

Aften's laugh was shrill, a wild edge to it. "Who do you think you are?"

"Your father," Rendyn said, jaw taut.

"Some father."

The sharp report of Rendyn's hand across Aften's cheek echoed off the stone walls. Aften's head jerked to the side. The sting came a moment later, blooming into heat. He turned a stunned look up at Rendyn.

Rendyn was just as shocked, staring at his hand. "I..."

Aften backed up a step, eyes stinging as realization sank in. The man who was supposed to be his father *hit* him.

"Aften, wait."

He didn't. Aften turned, yanking the door open. It slammed behind him with a satisfying sound that echoed ahead of him down the hall. His breath came fast and hard as he slid between cold misery and white hot anger.

Before he knew it, the distant hum of the Commons had grown to a cacophony, and he was threading his way around other people, head low. He didn't know where he was going. He didn't know what he would say when he got there. All he knew was his chest was tight, his eyes stung, and he needed to get away.

I won't cry. Not over him.

"Aften? Aften, wait a moment!"

Aften stopped belatedly, wrestling his features into something neutral—or as close to it as possible. He took a deep breath.

Olen Ominir appeared at his elbow, beaming. "I was hoping to run into you. I wanted to speak to you about...about..." He trailed off, studying the angry red skin of Aften's cheek. "What happened?"

"Nothing," Aften said automatically. He knew the rules. Rendyn was a cruel, strict, uncaring parent—and he wasn't supposed to talk about it.

"Come with me," Olen said. He hand closed around Aften's shoulder and steered him toward one of the ramps that led to the gallery level of the Commons.

They wove across the cavern using the rope bridges strung between the carved stone pillars, until they stood before a set of heavy curtains. Olen drew one back, gesturing Aften inside.

Aften had yet to see Olen Ominir's new infirmary. It was a modest cavern. A hearth and three alcoves were carved into the walls. Two of them had beds tucked inside with crisp, clean linens and curtains that could be closed to offer patients privacy. The last alcove held—

That's...that's mine!

Hanging from the ceiling in a woven rope sling was his glowing orb. The enchanted object was a Sivivan heirloom, with a light that never faded. It could be rubbed to brighten it, or held tight to dim. And now, there it was, hanging in Olen's infirmary like a miniature sun.

Because beneath it was a riot of plants.

"Interesting, isn't it? Councilman Rendyn gave it to me. Apparently the enchantment will keep my plants alive. Good thing, too. Some medicines require fresh picked leaves, roots, or berries."

The surge of fury, that his father would give something of his away, something he thought he lost forever, faded with the realization of how important it had become. He wrestled a scowl off his face, hands clenched. It still didn't seem fair.

Olen crossed to the worktable in the center of the room. It was mostly clear, as the apothecary kept all his odds and ends, tools, tinctures, and salves on the shelves carved into the walls or spread on the stone counter that encircled the room. He moved a few books aside, then dragged two stools to it.

"Now. Sit."

"I'm fine."

"That's wonderful. Sit." Olen arched a brow.

Aften sighed heavily, but he perched on the edge of the stool. He folded his arms over his chest, studying the shelves.

"You haven't come to help me yet," Olen said, gently turning Aften's cheek toward the light from the fire and the large glass lantern overhead.

"I've been busy."

"Busy with your own healing, no doubt. Eating. Stretching, too, yes?" Olen stepped back, pulling a cloth off a shelf and dipping it into a bucket of water. He wrung it out before taking his own stool beside Aften and pressing the cool cloth to his cheek.

Aften hissed softly. It helped, but it stung for a moment, too.

"Who hit you?" Olen asked softly.

"It doesn't matter."

"Your father, then."

Aften scowled. "He's not my...not anymore."

The sting returned to his eyes, accompanied by a lump in his throat he couldn't quite swallow. He would never call Rendyn his father again. He met Olen's gaze, and he saw nothing but pain and understanding in the man's bright eyes.

"I know that feeling. Too well, perhaps."

For a moment, they said nothing. Aften took the cloth from Olen's hand, holding it to his cheek on his own and scooting his stool back.

"Let me make us some tea, hm?" Olen fetched a polished kettle from a shelf and hung it over the fire. "What was the argument about?"

"Telling the truth, and how I shouldn't do it, I guess. Funny thing is, he always told us lying was bad."

Olen sat two of Kellan's thick clay mugs on the table, ready for water. He groaned as he sat again. "I creak more than an old ship these days. The truth is very important. You seem like a very honest young man, and if you felt you had to say something...well, I believe it had to be said."

A pang of guilt twinged beneath his ribs. He *had* lied to Rendyn, saying it wasn't him who started the rumors. It had been his plan, even if Tamsa helped. He sighed. "It doesn't matter. I can't seem to do anything right. I'm sick of trying to guess what I'm supposed to do."

"You did a good job helping me. As I said, I'd like to show you more. Why, we could start right now, if you'd like."

Aften grimaced. "I've been thinking about that, actually, and...when I go back to scouting, I won't have much time."

"A few hours a day, perhaps?" Olen poured hot water over sachets of herbs. The earthy scent of chamomile filled the room.

"I...guess I could manage that. After weapons work, but before patrol." He, like all the others, was being put on the second patrol to keep them out of trouble.

"And you can read after your patrols, yes? I have a few books you might like to go through."

"I'm not taking this seriously," Aften warned. "I'm a scout."

Rendyn Sivivan spent years trying to trap Aften below ground to make him miserable. If he sensed any interest in a craft, Aften would never see the moon again. No more prisons. No more chains.

Olen nursed his mug, elbows resting on the worktable. He studied the shelves of his infirmary. "I don't think I need someone serious about all this, yet. There's plenty of time for us to make up our minds. What I need is someone with talent. You learned those herbs and medicines faster than just about anybody I've ever met. Even Mila!" He laughed.

Aften flushed. "Are you saying I...have talent?"

"You do. I understand you want to stay with Mila and your friends, running around out there. We'll keep this between us, and you just sneak over for a few bells a day, hm? We'll do what we can."

Aften picked up his mug, taking a sip to buy himself time to think. He grimaced as it scalded his tongue, swallowing quickly.

I don't want to be trapped again. But if I choose this...if I choose this, it isn't a trap, is it?

"All right," he said, slowly. "We can try."

"Good." Olen took the mostly-full mug out of Aften's hands. "Let's get started."

"Now?" Aften stood, following Olen to the corner with the plants.

"Why not? When something ends, the best thing to do is start something new."

Aften froze, his gaze drifting toward the curtain. The chatter of the Commons was a dull hum, and somewhere beyond that was Rendyn Sivivan in the Council Chamber, undoubtedly fuming.

When something ends...

Aften took a deep breath. Olen was right.

It was time for something new.

13

Thislen adjusted the straps on his new knee brace with a grunt. Olen designed it with the help of the Nattfolk's smith and leatherworker. Metal bars with hinges at the sides allowed his knee to bend. A thick leather square with a circle cut in the center laid over his knee to keep it where it ought to be, and four thick straps with heavy buckles held all the pieces in place.

It pinched. He plucked and tugged at his pants underneath the contraption until it was more comfortable, then sat back to study the brace critically.

At least the leather is finished and the metal is polished. It was noticeable and made him feel too self-aware, but he needed it.

It had been a moon since his rescue. He ate and stretched and took medicines as he'd been told. His burns were now pink scars, his bruises faded and ribs healed, his hip stiff and yet in full working order. All that remained was his knee. Every time he stood, it buckled, a sharp stab of pain lancing through him. It might never recover entirely, Olen warned him. The brace, all those straps and leather, was meant to help. Tonight was the first night he put it on, because tonight was the first night he was given a clean bill of health. He was cleared for duty.

Tonight, Thislen rejoined the Nattfolk scouts.

Not a moment too soon, if the reports are to be believed.

Thislen got his news in fragments, in rumor, one piece at a time.

"It's weird," Aften said from the bunk above. "Usually the Vaim don't dash around unless someone's come ashore, but that's usually the first shift's problem. Not ours."

"So they're alerting after midnight?" Thislen frowned, an arm behind his head as he stared at the stone overhead.

"Yeah. Weird, right?"

"Very."

A few days later, Tamsa toyed with her stew at the table in the Tavern where she and Thislen were eating dinner before the dawn bell.

"Copper for your thoughts?" Thislen asked as he mopped up gravy with his bread. His crutch rested against the table beside him.

"It's nothing."

"You're thinking awfully hard about nothing."

"No, I mean it's nothing. *When the Vaim alert, we follow them. We either find bodies or blood or someone who needs help. Every time they alert these days, we find nothing. Literally nothing. Not a drop of blood or a scrap of flesh. I'm trying to figure out why."*

Mila paced back and forth while Thislen stretched in the training cavern, keeping an eye on him. He stopped stretching and raised a brow, staring at her until she slowed down.

"Don't look at me like that."

"Then say it already."

She bit her lower lip, then resumed pacing. "What if the Vaim are acting up because Ninian is mad we haven't gone for the vial?"

Thislen felt a pang in his chest. "We decided to wait until I was healed, because I'm the best person we've got to crack that safe. We decided as a group."

"Yes, but what if it was the wrong decision?"

He dropped his gaze, jaw clenched. He refused to begrudge himself the time he took to heal. "Why do you think it was?"

"Because the Vaim—"

"Have you found any bodies?"

"Well, no, but—"

"And have they gone after any of the Nattfolk?"

"No, but..."

Thislen waited, then sighed, sitting back and watching her more closely as she walked back and forth, back and forth. "But what?"

"I can't shake the feeling that this has something to do with the Ruling Council. With Soren and his toads and that stupid vial."

"Why would you think that?"

Mila's hands balled into fists. "Nevermind. I have to go, it's almost midnight." She left without another word, leaving Thislen frowning after her.

Thislen mulled over the information, fighting the feeling that he was standing under an ax. The pieces added up little by little, and he knew something was going to happen...but it never did. It never came. All the while he was here, among people he hardly knew anymore—including Mila.

Did I change, or did they?

Aften groaned above him, pushing the curtains aside and poking his head out of his bunk. "What time is it?"

"Almost sunset. We're going to be late for training."

"That's right, you're back with us today," Aften said enthusiastically, tugging the curtains closed so he could change. Aften and Tamsa rejoined the scouts a fortnight ago, after being cleared by Olen.

Thislen stood, testing his knee. It wasn't painful, but it was uncomfortable. The brace was tight, as it was meant to be. Despite the discomfort, it offered stability. His leg didn't buckle, and he wouldn't need a crutch anymore. He paced while Aften changed, adjusting to the feeling and testing it.

"Where's Tamsa?" Aften asked. He climbed down and the pair headed toward breakfast.

"In the Commons already. She woke me up on her way out."

Aften wrinkled his nose in distaste. "I could never get up that early."

"We know," Darran said with a grin, meeting them at the tunnel entrance. "I was just coming to wake you myself."

The scout fell in beside them. His eyes drifted down to Thislen's new brace, then away. A flush of heat crept up the back of Thislen's neck, and he walked faster. *It doesn't matter that I have a limp. I'll be able to run the rooftops, just see if I can't.* He'd be damned if he let Soren or Garridan put an end to his life as he knew it.

"There's no need to push it, Thislen. We'll go at your pace for a bit," Darran said, clasping him on the shoulder.

Thislen frowned. "I can keep up. If I can't, I'll let you know."

"You swear?"

"I...swear." A cold prickle settled between his shoulderblades. He didn't take his eyes off Darran to look at the indistinct forms of Percivan and Vern in the shadows between torches, but he knew they were there. They knew he saw them, listening as he made another promise, swore another vow. The pair of them stepped into the light, joining the group as they entered the Commons. Thislen shuddered as people walked right through the apparitions.

His dreams tied the pair to the Vaim. Maybe there was a connection there. If that were the case...

No, these two have been with me since the ship, since the torture. The Vaim didn't start acting odd until after I was rescued. There can't be a connection.

He hoped.

"Hey!" Mila waved from the table she'd claimed in the Commons.

Trevon sat beside her, as did Tamsa. Thislen took a seat quickly. His knee already ached, a dull and steady pain that threatened to get worse. He didn't say anything. They already treated him like he might shatter at a touch. What if they made him stay?

Once everyone was seated, a server set down a platter of food. They divvied it up onto their plates. Thislen noticed they left some of the choice bits for him. Was it kindness or pity?

"Your brace looks like it fits well," Tamsa said as she heaped her plate with warm flatbread and soft cheese.

"It'll do." Thislen was thinking of ways he could improve the contraption. Olen had described his plans to the Nattfolk's leatherworker, and the woman assembled it in record time off the description alone. The smith finished it off with his metal bars and oiled hinges the next day. The best way to improve the experience of it now was to wear it and take notes.

Like about how it pinched.

"We're all going up together, aren't we? Trevon, did you get Harron, Ophelia, and Penni re-assigned?" Aften crammed a huge bite of muffin into his mouth.

"For now. Councilman Rendyn is no doubt going to have us split up, given our histories and what's happening above." Trevon's words cast a hush over the table.

"About that," Thislen said slowly. "What exactly is happening up there?"

Mila's lips parted, but Trevon cut her off. "Nothing. We find nothing, so it's nothing."

Thislen arched a brow.

The scout captain sighed. "I know what you're all thinking. We're not going to Perilee without proof. We don't know enough about Ninian's ghost or his spells to know what he'll do if we try to show up without the vial."

"Well, I think we should—"

"I know, Mila. I know you think we should get on the ship and see if it's there. We haven't been able to get anyone close enough to find out since Illi almost got captured."

Thislen nodded. Illi, a Solwalker, was Trevon's cousin. Trevon grew up with his aunt and uncle—he and Illi were as close as siblings. The scout captain wouldn't risk anyone else if he could help it. No one was sent to infiltrate the Bestant Estate.

Tamsa pushed her plate away. Her chair scraped the stone as she stood. "Thislen, do you want to go warm up before weapons practice?"

A rush of gratitude washed over Thislen at the offer, though none of it reached his face. He nodded. "Sure, I'm full anyway." He glanced at Mila, then gave her a slow nod. *We'll sort it,* he tried to say with only his eyes.

He hardly knew her anymore, but he knew she trusted him. He knew the two of them still had a bond no one else had broken. He was the first to free her from the life she'd been living, the first to tell her to take the risks. He wondered sometimes if that was the right thing to do. Mila was harder now, stubborn and insistent. She expected everyone to fight with her and often started an argument first just to get it over with. Thislen hoped she wouldn't do anything rash until he knew he could keep up with her. This time, and every time hereafter, he didn't want to be separated again. Not like last time, when he thought she was dead.

As he walked away with Tamsa on one side and the ghosts haunting him on the other, he hoped he and Mila would be alright.

We'll sort it.

Mila sighed, watching Thislen disappear into the crowd. His limp was slight, but noticeable—or maybe her upbringing as a healer made it obvious to her. More worrying than that was the gulf between him and everyone else, a chasm that no one seemed able to breach. Not even her. Not even Tamsa, who was arguably growing closer to Thislen than she was.

It took every ounce of her patience to interact with him, sometimes. She reminded herself constantly that he'd been tortured and deserved time to heal. The toll it took on him was evident in the way he sometimes stared at nothing, how he jumped if someone touched him with no warning, and the new scars he bore. At the same time, she wished she had her friend back. She wished she could pour her heart out to him like she used to. Thislen always saw right through her, always understood that she was wilder, freer than her family gave her credit for. She could hardly talk to Ivan at all right now, and Darran and Aften were still dancing around one another, neither making the move they wanted to. She could talk to Trevon, but not *about* Trevon and her confusing tangle of thoughts and emotions surrounding the scout captain. Her family certainly hadn't helped anything, expecting her to be more like she was before, and less like she was now.

In short, everything was stuck. Everything.

It felt as though everyone around her were holding their breath, waiting for something to give. They expected her to snap and go after the vial herself, or change into a skirt and start healing, or run off to Perilee, or, or, or... All their expectations circled around her like a flock of birds. Sometimes the wings of what they wanted battered at her, but most of the time they fluttered at the edge of every conversation she had.

Trevon frustrated her the most. Illi's near-capture rattled her so badly that she'd retired from the Solwalkers and joined a scout patrol on first shift. He was so protective of his cousin that he'd become insufferably cautious. He insisted on going through every door first. If a gap between rooftops looked bigger than usual, he took them on a longer, safe route. He fought differently when they sparred, pulling his hits. Mila's patience was a frayed thread, ready to snap at any moment.

Why not now?

Aften finished his food and went off into the Commons, a book tucked under his arm. Darran finished his and headed toward the training cavern. Once she and Trevon were alone, Mila took a deep breath.

"You're going to give me a piece of your mind first, and then come in with a plan you've concocted and convince me to go along with it, right?" Trevon leaned on the table, his eyes on hers.

"How did you—"

"Mila, you always look like you're plotting when you're plotting. You have this nefarious little brow furrow you do." He mimicked a concentrated scowl.

"I do not!" Still, she was fighting a smile as she pushed at his shoulder.

He laughed softly, resting his cheek on his hand. "I can't say I blame you for wanting to move. I've been dragging my feet, taking my time. The truth is...I don't know what to do next. You asked me how I made plans that worked, and sometimes they don't. Like with Illi. That rattled me. Now I'm afraid I won't see the holes in your plan, and we'll end up in another mess."

Her heart pounded, her own fears echoed in his words. *What if I get someone hurt, or worse—killed? On the other hand, how many will die if we do nothing? How long will we all be trapped in this web the Ruling Council wove, all unaware that we're the flies to be consumed?*

She closed her eyes.

Trevon nudged her shoulder with his. "Tell me what's rolling around inside your head. Let's see if we can get through this together."

Together. She liked that.

After scanning the tables surrounding them to ensure they wouldn't be overheard, Mila leaned in. "I think we're out of time to make a choice. We have to look on that ship, to make sure it isn't there. The Vaim are getting restless, whatever else is happening, and that gives us two options. Ask Ninian what is happening, or get the vial. I agree with you that talking to Ninian is...dangerous, at best."

"At best," Trevon agreed.

"We take a small group. Thislen to open the safe, you and Darran because you're our best fighters. Aften to stay with the rowboat. Me, because if you try to leave me behind, I'll scream."

Trevon laughed. "I wouldn't doubt that."

"We'll ask Tamsa to help hide what we're doing or distract her father."

"Think she'll do it?"

Mila lifted her chin, a frown on her face. "She better."

Trevon stood with a sigh. "Breaking the rules is getting to be a habit with us." Then, he grinned. His hand covered hers, the warmth of his rough fingers spreading all the way to her chest. Without another word, he left for the training cavern.

Mila watched him go, heart sinking. It wasn't just rules they were breaking, it was Nattfolk *law*. *It's for the good of Astera, for the good of the Nattfolk and Solfolk both.*

Who was she to make that decision? Her only claim to any of this was one of birth, of luck, and little else. She sighed heavily, stacked the dishes on the end of the table, and headed for the training cavern herself. Today they'd be sparring hand-to-hand, but she had a new bow and wanted to practice a bit before their lesson.

Everyone was there before her, even Aften. Thislen and Tamsa stretched in one corner, faint smiles on their faces. They spoke low. She couldn't make out what they were saying. They were lost in their own little world.

I'm not jealous, Mila told the pang in her chest. *I just miss my friend. I don't know why he's there for her, and not for me.* Maybe she and Thislen hadn't been as close as she believed.

At least Tamsa could get the ghost of a smile out of him.

Darran and Aften hefted practice swords, running through the racks of dulled weapons for ones they liked best. Trevon...

Trevon was nowhere in sight.

"Boo."

Mila jumped, whirling. Trevon stood against the wall beside the tunnel entrance, smiling.

"Don't do that!" Exasperation raised the pitch her voice to a squeal. She flushed as heads turned toward them, other scouts who were already practicing. Mila and Thislen were already a favorite subject of the rumor mill. This wouldn't help.

"Sorry. I didn't mean to scare you. I just wanted to give you something. A gift." Trevon stepped forward, hiding something behind his back.

Mila's mind filled with visions of flowers, ribbons, and sweets; things Ivan or Soren would give her. *I don't really want those things, but if it were from Trevon... Would she mind as much?* Her blush deepened. *From Trevon, I might treasure a piece of charcoal.*

When had she grown to like him so much? Should she say something? Would that ruin whatever they had? She took a deep breath.

"Oh?" She kept her voice light.

Trevon grinned. He saw right through her act. He produced a narrow bundle wrapped in plain canvas from behind his back. Mila held her breath. That didn't look anything like flowers. It looked more like...

Trevon untied the knot of string holding the bundle closed and flipped the fabric back, revealing a beautiful pommel engraved with the image of a Vaim, of all things. Sleek black leather gleamed around the handle, and the guard was adorned with decorative scrollwork in delicate whorls.

Mila's breath caught. She reached for it without thinking, drawing the short sword free. It was the perfect size for her, and the weight was flawlessly balanced. It felt as if the hilt had been fashioned for her hand. Her heart raced. Mila laughed breathlessly, her smile stretching ear to ear. The blade was polished to a mirror shine. She could see her own reflection in the metal.

Trevon finished unwrapping the scabbard made of tooled black leather to match the hilt, adorned with another engraving of a Vaim on a ring of metal near the top.

"Why the Vaim?" Mila asked. She stepped away to give the weapon an experimental swing.

"Because one day you're going to get rid of them all, and we'll need some way to remember the woman who broke the curse. What better way than a sword of legend?" Trevon grinned. "Of course, you still have to make the legend."

Mila laughed. "I can do that." She swung her way through her sword exercises, admiring the soft whistle of the blade through the air, the glint of torches in the metal as it spun. It felt like a piece of her arm in a way the practice weapons and her borrowed sword never had. It was hers, only hers.

It was the best gift she'd ever gotten.

She stopped, turning to Trevon. "I've never been given something like this before, something that makes me feel so understood. Trevon, this...this is exactly what I wanted, and I didn't even know it." Her feelings for him sat on the tip of her tongue, threatening to pour free like water from a broken dam. All she had to do was open her mouth again, and...

But what if he wants more from me than I can give?

Trevon offered her the scabbard. "I know your family has been..."

Mila slid the blade home, her smile faltering. Moving back in with her family presented every problem she'd worried about and more. Olen busied himself with tending to all the Nattfolk who hadn't had access to a healer in years. When he wasn't doing that, he absent-mindedly asked her to help him mix this or that, just this once. Only 'just this once' turned into half a dozen times before Mila put her foot down. She struggled with him over remaining in the scouts, though he never once asked her to quit. Olen didn't like the amount of danger it put her in. There was a constant refrain of 'don't fall and break your neck.' She heard it every time she leapt from one roof to another. Or 'watch out for the Vaim,' which made her notice them all the more as they lurched through the streets.

Ivan joined a scouting group, also on the second shift. He was picking up weapons work nearly as fast as she had. While they'd made up and agreed to be friends, she could tell he wasn't over her. She caught him studying her when he thought she wasn't watching. She couldn't even begin to guess what he was thinking, but at least he didn't make it her problem.

Evelie was most difficult of all. Her entire life had been uprooted in a day. The florist was used to having her shop to run, blooms to arrange, customers to chat with, and now they were gone.

She didn't resent Mila for the sudden change, but she hadn't adjusted well. First, she'd fussed over their family cavern, trading for furniture and stitching up embroidered pictures to decorate the walls. She threw herself into making dinners and insisted everyone sit together to eat them, even though Mila and Ivan returned from their patrols minutes before. She'd joined the sewing group, the knitting group, and the baking group, throwing herself into them with something nearing frenzy. Worst of all, she picked and picked at Mila.

It was out of the goodness of her heart, Mila knew. It was how she was raised and how she expected things to go. The matronly ex-florist constantly commented on the black and gray and how it didn't suit her complexion, or about how trousers weren't very ladylike and wouldn't Mila like a skirt to wear *outside* of work? And what about boys? Boys, boys, boys. After Mila explained for the hundredth time that she was happy as she was, Evelie would purse her lips, tilt her head, and start in again.

"You know, you can't be alone forever. That'd be so lonely. What about that Darran boy, then? He's very handsome."

Mila sighed heavily. "Everything is expectation, and I thought if I lived with them, they'd see how I changed. Instead, they keep trying to cram me back into who I was."

"I know between them, what's happening with the Vaim, and your worrying about Thislen, you've felt misunderstood. I know you've felt like the ground is constantly shifting under your feet. I thought you needed someone to see you. Just you, exactly as you are. I...I see you, Mila." Trevon's eyes fixed on hers, holding her spellbound.

Before she thought about it, she'd taken his hand. Their fingers interlocked. Warmth spread up her arm and into her chest, until she felt as bright as the sun. She beamed. Trevon smiled back.

"What does this mean?" Mila whispered.

"What do you want it to mean? For me, it means...we see how things go. We don't have to do anything different or tell anyone anything. Not until you're ready."

"If we get to courtship, if we eventually get married, I won't want to—"

"I know. And I don't care. I don't like you for that. I like you for your reckless spirit and stubborn plotting." He grinned.

A laugh bubbled up from Mila's chest. She felt a little light-headed, holding her new sword in one hand and Trevon's in the other. "I don't know what's happening."

"We can talk about it later, there will be plenty of time. After we get the vial."

Her joy was cut in half as she fixed on those words. "You mean..."

"Go. Tell everyone your plan. I'm in—for all of it."

Mila pulled away, fastening the scabbard to her hip. The woman who would vanquish the Vaim, armed for battle. She squared her shoulders, hand resting on the pommel. "Right. We have work to do."

14

Wool, Thislen reflected, was the strangest fabric ever invented. In the steady fall of late autumn rain, the cloth of his cloak was sodden and heavy—and yet it remained warm. At least it stopped itching when it was soaked through.

He was one of several cloak-wrapped shapes huddled in the stolen rowboat. This time, they didn't wear Ravan cloaks. The soggy gray weather made regular cloaks common enough to avoid attracting any notice. That, and the near-empty streets. Very few people were out in the downpour, and the ones that were didn't linger. Water pooled in the bottom of their vessel, with Aften bailing out a bucketful of water every few minutes to keep them afloat.

This weather is perfect.

He looked at Astera with grim satisfaction as they drifted past the city. Rain dripped off the front of his hood and onto his nose. Buildings loomed out of thick mist or huddled as indistinct shadows in the distance. Perilee was invisible.

This was how he preferred to see his home: as shrouded in secrecy and isolated as he felt.

Not that he felt that way anymore.

Mila shifted, her elbow bumping against his arm. "At least this rain will make it harder to spot us."

Despite it being the middle of the day, she spoke in hushed tones, the gravity of their task hovering over all their heads.

Thislen nodded, sending more water cascading down his face. "It'll mask sound, too. We might be able to get aboard without being noticed."

"Glad we chose today, then?" Darran asked, taking the bucket from Aften's hands. Water splashed and gurgled as it met the choppy gray surf.

"Not entirely." Thislen frowned at the gray lumps of buildings along the shore. They'd passed the Justica, and that was the last landmark he'd recognized. With the estates of the Grand Quarter set back from the ocean, they all looked the same. Tall and square.

Ships slid past, moored for the day and swaying back and forth, their dripping masts undulating like upside down pendulums. Their names were hard to read beneath the gleam of moisture on every hull.

Thislen leaned forward in his seat on the prow, straining to read one as they passed. *The Lively Lily.* He sat back with a frown. His position put him in the perfect spot to find the *Bestant Belle*—if only he could see.

"Where are we?" Aften asked.

"The Grand Quarter?" Trevon hauled on the oars with a grunt. "Does anybody else want to take over for a bit?"

The rowboat rocked and bobbed in the water as Darran changed places with the scout captain. Thislen held onto the side, his gaze dropping to the water.

Vern the sailor stared back at him, his blue face rippling beneath the waves. Bloated lips stretched into an easy smile. Thislen felt a chill that had nothing to do with the weather. *What do you want?*

"Easy, boss." Vern broke the surface. He didn't tread water, he just floated in it. "I'm here to help."

"How can you help me?" Thislen murmured under his breath.

"What was that?" Mila asked.

"Nothing."

The rowboat lurched into motion again. Vern drifted along beside them.

"You're looking for my ship."

Thislen's eyes widened. He'd nearly forgotten that Vern belonged to *The Bestant Belle* and its master. All he remembered was the man was dead because of him.

Can he really help me find it?

"Do you want me to?"

He didn't know what his connection with these ghosts was. He wanted them to go away, signs as they were of his pain, of his failures, of his torture. With freedom should have come peace and time to mend the cracks of his heart and mind. Instead…

Instead he was plagued by ghosts and nightmares. Every night, his dreams were filled with Percivan and Vern before the gates of Perilee. His days were the same. Ghostly faces watched him wherever he turned. Fear settled in his gut like a cold stone, slowing him with its weight.

Have I lost my mind? Did I break on that ship, in that cell, without realizing it? Why won't they go away?

"You want us to? We can. Just takes—"

No.

Vern pursed his lips, he stopped following the boat and sank beneath the water, sinking until he vanished into the black depths of the sea.

Not for the first time, Thislen wondered if he should tell Mila or Tamsa what he saw. If only they didn't look at him like he already shattered into a thousand fragments, he would. When he turned to Mila, he caught her watching him with a worried crease in her brow, chewing the end of her thumbnail. She looked away quickly, playing nonchalant.

Either she'll believe me, or she won't—and then she'll drag me to her father for healing.

Thislen scowled as he turned back to the water.

"Are you mad at me?" Mila whispered.

Before he could answer, a spired shadow formed in the distance, its towers ghostly lines thin as reeds. They grew thicker the closer they floated. Thislen sucked in a breath. Even through the fog, he recognized it, thank the Ancestors.

"Look, it's the Bestant estate." He pointed.

"That means the ship is—" Mila craned around him, distracted by the mission at hand.

"There, first one at the dock behind it."

Darran leaned into the oars, guiding them toward the vessel. Its distinctive carved prow loomed overhead as they passed the bow, paddling toward the shore. The closer they got to land, the choppier the water. It slapped at the hull and sent up little gouts of spray that were only noticeable because they came from a different direction than the rain. The midafternoon sun was hidden behind the clouds, so the gilt on the boat's carvings didn't shine. It glistened as the drizzle turned into a deluge and washed over every surface like a dozen tiny waterfalls.

"Pull up here," Thislen whispered as they drew even with the stern.

Above, the curved glass windows of the *Bestant Belle*'s greatroom rippled. No light shone within. No one was home. Darran pulled hard on the oars to keep them from bumping against the larger boat's keel, then passed them to Aften.

Thislen's heart pounded. Now everything relied on him, on skills he hadn't used in moons. He stood, shedding the heavy cloak with the soggy slap of fabric on wood. He took hold of the nearest carving, slick and precarious beneath his fingertips. Suddenly, the weather wasn't as perfect anymore. He pulled himself up, one finger and toe hold at a time. His hip and knee protested the strange contortions of the climb, unfamiliar movements after all this time. He adjusted a foothold more than once, working awkwardly around his brace. A twinge of discomfort promised to become pain.

He ignored it. Though it was a short climb from the water to the windows, his fingers ached from holding on tight enough he wouldn't slip, and his knee was burning. He perched carefully on a familiar set of carvings. This was the third time he sat beneath this very window, the third time he'd clung to the side of this ship, and he vowed it would be the last.

We'll succeed. We have to. Then I am never coming back here. I hope it sinks, and the fish use its bones for their homes.

With that he slipped a thin knife from his belt and wedged it under the sash. He probed with the tip until he could feel the lock. A push and a deft twist and the window lifted with a *schlick*.

Breaking into something helped Thislen feel more like himself than he had in ages. For just a moment, he indulged the triumphant roar of blood in his ears. He closed his eyes. *This is what I am. Not a bastard, not a noble. I'm a thief.*

He pushed the window open the rest of the way. It slid up silently, though it stuck once, the wood swollen with the moisture in the air. He stuck his head inside.

Water dripped from his curls to land on the thick rugs of the floor with a dull patter. There were no lanterns lit. The occupant of this den would be up at Perilee, running a council meeting, dividing funds between groups, counting taxes, or some other official duty. Lord Soren Bestant wouldn't be back for another two or three bells. There was time.

The desk sat like a monolith before the windows opposite Thislen, the chair facing in toward the cabin's door. Half of the greatroom was made of windows, the other half of shelves with low guards in the front to keep the many books from tumbling off in a storm. A gaming table with an empty Hunters and Hounds board stood between two chairs, all of them fastened to the floor. A comfortable cushioned seat filled a corner near the door.

Everything was as it had been before. Thislen's heart pounded, the hair on the back of his neck standing up. The past flashed before his eyes. Finding the safe behind the painting, Tamsa shouting, the guards bursting through the door. He felt cold from head to toe, the chill going all the way through to his bones. Slowly, silently, Thislen eased one boot to the ground, then the other.

Nothing happened.

He didn't relax. On either side of the door were two unlit lanterns dangling from elegant golden hooks. Beneath each of them was a modestly sized painting.

One depicted a young woman and a young man beneath a tree. The other was of the Bestant Estate itself. The safe lay behind the second.

Thislen turned away, though it raised every hair on his neck. A rope sailed out of the mist and through the air. It was heavy, and smacked against the side of the ship with a slap. Still, he caught it. It was easy enough to pull the rope over to one of the bolted chairs and tie it around a leg. He gave it a tug.

The rope pulled taut, and a moment later Trevon appeared in the window. "The others are going to wait below," he said softly.

"Suits me just fine. I don't need an audience to open the safe."

Thislen pulled his new set of lockpicks from his pocket. He sighed. The old ones fit in his hands like extensions of his fingers. These felt strange. The handles were thicker. Still, he pulled free the tools he needed as he crossed the room, swung the painting out of the way, and worked the first piece gently into the lock of the modest safe behind. It was narrow, hardly big enough for the lock on its surface. It wouldn't hold much, but Mila had a point.

This is just large enough for a vial.

His heart began to race, anticipation and elation mingling. This was it, this would solve so many problems, and all he had to do was—

He took a deep breath. *Slowly. You'll break the pick,* he urged himself. *No one knows we're here. We have time.*

Trevon, behind him, kept an eye on the hazy line of the dock out the window, and watched over the rowboat below, head cocked. "Did you hear...?"

Thislen froze, glancing over his shoulder.

"No, nevermind, it was the waves." Trevon laughed nervously.

Thislen swore under his breath, brow furrowed as he turned back to the task at hand. A little wiggle to the left, a small tug, and—

Click.

It was faint, almost inaudible, but it was there. With a heavy exhale, he held both picks in place and twisted.

The door to the safe swung open on silent, well-oiled hinges.

Thislen stared at the empty space within. His heart sank. He grasped the edges of the compartment, willing what he saw, or didn't see, to change.

"Damn. *Damn.*"

"What is it?" Trevon turned from the window.

"It's...It's empty."

The cabin door flew open, hitting the wall with a bang like a thunderclap. Thislen recoiled, shoulder catching the edge of the bookshelf. He stumbled. His brace creaked, making it impossible to steady himself until his back hit the shelves, books tumbling to the floor around him. That was all the time the two guards needed to rush into the room, their weapons out and trained on him and Trevon. They both froze, raising their hands in surrender.

No, not again. Thislen's mouth was dry. Blood roared in his ears.

Lord Soren Bestant paced into the room, rolling a glass bottle between his fingers. He was dressed in his noble best, in sage and forest greens accented with gold that matched his perfect curls. The bottle, as he held it up, winked in the light. It was crimson, the same shade as the eyes of the Vaim, and decorated with gold filigree. The stopper was sealed with black wax.

Thislen knew it was *the* vial, the one that held Ninian's concoction from centuries ago.

"You've gone through so much trouble, cousin. For this?" Soren held it up, shaking it so the dark liquid inside sloshed back and forth. It was half full. The nobleman's lips curled into a smug, knowing smile. "How *did* you learn about this, I wonder?"

Thislen's eyes flicked from Soren to the sword the guard had leveled at his throat.

A ripple of anger washed over Soren's face. "Oh, come now, you don't really believe that I'll ask him to lower his sword to get my answers? And here I thought you weren't as stupid as you seemed. Answer me. How did you learn about this vial? Do you even know what it is?"

"It's a poison. A plague," Thislen snapped, his gaze going to the guard that held him pinned in the corner.

The guard's expression wavered, and his eyes darted to the side, then back.

The seed of an idea grew in Thislen's mind. "Why do you have it, Soren? Why hold on to something that dangerous?"

Soren scoffed. "I ask the questions here." He walked over to his desk, reclining comfortably in his cushioned chair. "Who told you about this?"

Thislen scowled, about to answer when—

The ghost of Percivan stepped out of the shadows behind Soren's chair, looking down at his murderer. Slowly, the nobleman's dark eyes lifted to Thislen's own.

"Percivan Coppermund," he found himself saying softly.

"Impossible. He didn't know."

"I did, my father told me," Percivan said sadly, perching on the desk as he studied Soren's face. "Me and my little brother, when we each turned fifteen. Our family has tried to make things better from the inside for generations. I must have slipped somehow. I must have shown them my intentions."

"Who told you, really?" Soren drawled, a foot hooked up over the arm of his seat and swinging idly back and forth. He studied the vial in the meager light.

"Does it matter?"

"I suppose not. For now, anyway. That fisherman friend of yours, the one I killed..."

Darran. Thislen's breath caught. "What about him," he grit out through clenched teeth.

"Why is he alive?"

Trevon cleared his throat, easing away from the window. "What exactly is—"

"Silence, peasant." Soren's eyes flashed and his gaze snapped to the scout captain. "You will speak when you are spoken to."

Trevon ducked his head, lifting his hands a bit further and falling silent.

Thislen's eyes fixed on the window. With Trevon out of the way, it would only take him a few steps to cross the room and dive out. The scout captain would be left behind—

Which meant it wasn't an option. *Damn my bleeding heart. When did other people start to matter this much?* How could both of them escape?

"Well, I owe you twenty gold."

Thislen stopped breathing, his entire body going numb. He could feel the percussive thud of his heart beneath his ribs, bolting like a startled horse.

Garridan Artaith stepped into the room. Thislen's knees buckled. Shame twisted his stomach in a knot as he turned toward the window. Trevon would have to find his own way out. Thislen would never fall into Garridan's clutches again. He bolted like a hare for its burrow.

Only for Mila to roll over the windowsill and land dripping on the rug with her sword drawn. She straightened, squaring her shoulders as she faced down the nearest guard. "That's enough."

"Mila?" Soren asked numbly.

"So Avasten was right." Garridan folded his arms over his chest, leaning against the open door.

"About many things, it seems." Soren stood, using the barricade of the guardsman holding Trevon at swordpoint to move closer to the exit.

When the guard glanced back at his boss nervously, Trevon brought his arm up and knocked the blade wide, drawing his sword and dirk in a fluid motion.

Though his heart was still racing for the window, Thislen turned and drew the two long knives from his belt and braced himself. He knew how to fight with them. He'd grown up fighting with knives in seedy dive bars or using them to cut purse strings. Armed, he did feel better, but his knees were still weak.

Outside the window, a voice came. "Hey! Who's down there?"

The rowboat was discovered. There'd be more guards soon.

I am not going to die here. Thislen tightened his grip on the handles as everyone waited, the air still. The only things moving were everyone's eyes. The tension built like a thread pulled taut.

"Well, it looks like the only way we're getting answers is to ask all of them, hm?" Soren raised his voice. "Get them, idiots!"

The thread snapped.

Ropes hissed from the deck above toward the water, and there was a soft shout of alarm from below. Thislen couldn't tell if it was Darran or Aften, and he wasn't given time to find out. The guards charged Trevon and Mila—and Garridan Artaith charged him.

Soren disappeared into the gloom of the corridor, the bottle in his hand winking faintly in the dim light before shadows swallowed both.

Garridan closed in with a knife of his own in one hand, and a familiar hammer in the other. Thislen's hip and knee ached at the mere sight of it. With a sudden lunge, the torturer swung.

Thislen twisted to one side, scoring a hit down Garridan's extended arm in the same moment the glass of the window shattered. The hammer crashed through the space where Thislen stood only a moment ago. An outraged shout came from the corridor.

Two shadows dropped down the ropes outside, and the shouting below doubled. Aften and Darran fought to protect their escape. Metal on metal clashed and screeched as Mila and her guard clashed, as Trevon held his at bay. Everything came in confused flashes, glimpses between Garridan's movements before Thislen had to duck and dodge. He caught a swing of the nobleman's knife against the hilt of his own, his arm quivering as he held it off. Sweat rolled down the side of his cheek as he strained, teeth gritted. The knife was moving toward his neck. Garridan's weight and strength far outmatched his own.

With a shout, Thislen twisted to the side and dropped his arm, and Garridan stumbled into the bookshelves. Tomes fell with dull thuds and the sound of splintering wood as the thin rail that held them in place broke against Garridan's face. Blood flowed freely from a cut on the man's forehead as he turned.

Hurting him was a mistake. His eyes gleamed with a mad fury, his affable smile replaced with cold, cruel madness that had always lurked beneath the surface. Thislen thought the smile would haunt his nightmares for the rest of his life, all calm, peaceful, and reasonable. Now he knew he was wrong. This one, this was the expression he would never forget.

"When you and I are alone again, Thislen, I think we're going to have a nice long talk. I'll break every one of your bones and let them heal, and break them again until you tell me every thought inside your head whenever you see my face." His grin stretched toward his ears, blood gleaming on his lips as he laughed madly. "I'll drown you and bring you back a thousand times. I'll burn my name into your flesh."

Thislen's breath came short and sharp, hands trembling. His mouth was dry, and no amount of swallowing could fix it. Fear made him feel like a house of cards. He'd crumble with just one breath in the right spot.

But I am not tied to a chair. I can fight. I can fight, *damn it!*

Thislen lunged. Garridan lurched forward to meet him, hammer upraised. Thislen twisted under the torturer's arm and slashed at his side. The knife bit, though barely. It cut the fabric of Garridan's fine linen shirt, however, leaving a blooming red stain behind.

Garridan looked down at the mark, at his own blood, and laughed. Thislen felt his knees buckle again.

"Good hit. How many do you think you can land, Thislen? How many will I return to you tenfold when we're together again?"

Their dance was interrupted for a moment by the crash of a body into the shelves as Trevon finished his assailant off with a slash to the throat that sent him spinning, a spray of crimson staining the spines of a dozen books. That guard was clearly handled. Trevon spun, but a desperate shout from below decided him. He dove out the window, and a moment later the rope yanked taut hard enough that the chair's leg made a splintering sound. It held, barely.

Mila's guard was bleeding from a dozen small wounds, standing between her and the door. His face was pale, and hers was twisted in determination. She wanted to pursue Soren, and they both knew she'd get to. It was just a matter of time.

The rush of air was the only warning Thislen got. He ducked instinctively, the hammer swinging through the space where his head had been. It struck the shelves with a massive crash, sending books tumbling over Thislen's head. A lance of pain shot up his knee as it bent strangely, as his brace dug into his skin. He pitched to the side. One of his knives skittered across the floor, the blade vanishing beneath the books as he caught himself.

Thislen flung his other hand into the air. Garridan's knife met his with a screech and a shower of sparks, hard enough that the impact made his arm go numb. They weren't playing anymore. Garridan was determined to maim him, if not kill him. With a grimace, Thislen scrambled to the side as the hammer came down again. There was a crash as it met the floor and wood splintered, the head passing through to the room below. Garridan paused to yank it free—which gave Thislen his best, and perhaps only, opportunity.

Thislen switched his knife to his left hand and drove himself upward, using his legs for every bit of momentum he could get.

The knife drove home, the sudden resistance shuddering up Thislen's entire arm—but then it gave. It slid into the torturer's body. Garridan inhaled a sharp, startled breath. He turned to face Thislen, brows raised, lips parted.

"What? No...No, I can't. I can't lose. I can't die." Garridan breathed.

Thislen's face was carved from stone as he pulled the dagger free from the nobleman's armpit. Blood, warm and sticky and smelling sharply of metal, coated his hand and made the handle of the blade slick. His heart hadn't slowed. If anything, it pulsed faster and louder than before.

The light faded from Garridan's brown eyes, turning them black as he sank to his knees. One hand clung to the shelves as if he could hold himself up, keep himself alive, through sheer willpower. Then, like a puppet with cut strings, he toppled slowly to the side.

He did not rise again.

Everything went silent. Thislen felt the vibrations of moving feet through the floor, the tickle and shiver in the air as blades swung and bodies shifted. He felt the pressure on his ears of distant, dreamlike echos of shouting voices, none of which actually got through. He sank to his knees.

Thislen couldn't tear his gaze away from the slack jawed face of the first man he ever murdered, on purpose, with his own hand. His own hand, which was covered in bright red blood, quickly congealing into a dark crimson stain.

Percivan's ghost knelt by his side, putting his hand on Thislen's wrist. Vern stood over the body, water dripping off his nose.

"This time you actually did it. How does it feel?" The sailor crouched, ducking his head to catch Thislen's gaze with his own.

Thislen recoiled. He could hear again, hear the rasp of his own ragged breathing in his ears. His head was spinning. *What have I done? What am I turning into?*

It was kill or be killed, part of him argued.

Was it?

"—slen! Thislen!" A hand yanked on his arm, hauling him to his feet. He stared blankly into Mila's face.

"Mila?"

"Come on, let's go. Go, go, go." She shoved him unceremoniously toward the window and the rope, casting a longing glance back toward the shadowed corridor.

Thislen dropped his knife into the choppy gray sea below, not even waiting to watch it sink quickly out of sight. Two guardsmen's bodies floated in the water, and Aften and Darran each held an oar. Trevon held the boat steady, looking up at them expectantly.

Thislen swung out and climbed quickly down, fighting a rising tide of nausea and exhaustion. Before his boots touched wood once more, his dark hair was plastered to his head by the rain, and his clothes were soaked through. Trevon pressed a bucket into his hands, and Thislen bailed out of the bottom of their vessel.

The rope slid free, falling into the sea with hardly a ripple. Mila, cursing like a sailor, jumped. The heads of three more guards popped out of the window as she hit the water. One vanished quickly.

Reinforcements. They're going to get more guards. It was time to go. Thislen leaned over the side, thrusting his hand toward the waves. Mila surfaced, and her cold fingers closed tight around his wrist. Trevon grabbed her other side, and the two of them hauled her aboard with a rush of water.

Thislen slumped, panting, in the prow. Darran and Aften leaned hard into the oars, and the rowboat leapt away across the rising surf.

Mila wiped her sword off on the hem of her shirt before shoving it forcefully back into its scabbard. "I nearly had him. He was right there, Trevon, *right* there."

"We didn't have a choice," Thislen snapped. "We just killed a nobleman's son, and almost a half dozen more. If we stayed any longer, there wouldn't have been any escape at all."

"He's right. They went for reinforcements before they opened the door." Trevon mopped rainwater from his face with his hand.

They raced for the open sea, where they could follow the shore from a distance and be lost in the mist. Darran paused his rowing. "What about the safe, the vial?"

"Did you get it?" Aften leaned forward eagerly.

"No," Trevon sighed. "Bestant had it."

Thislen, numb and cold, turned away from the argument. The rain cut through the blood staining his hand and arm, painting tracks through the red and dripping pink from his fingertips. Slowly, he lifted his gaze to the receding *Bestant Belle.*

Lord Soren Bestant stood on the deck, watching them from beneath an awning carried between two sodden servants. His chin was lifted as he watched his prey escape. When he caught Thislen's gaze, he smiled and held the vial aloft, shaking it again. The smile turned cruel and bitter, twisting into a leer.

"This one is for Garridan," he shouted.

Then he flung it at the deck with all his strength.

Thislen didn't need to hear it shatter. He felt it all the way through. He jerked to his feet, setting the boat rocking, a hoarse shout tearing from his throat. Mist swallowed the ship.

The vial was gone.

One of the three ways to break the curse was *gone.* Now only two remained—one impossible, and one unthinkable.

They'd lost.

15

Mila sat in the neat, comfortable little cavern that her family now lived in, head buried in her hands, elbows resting on the table that dominated the space in front of the hearth. Its surface was littered with papers, maps, and three of the Night Council's long-hidden journals. Tamsa stole them from her father's rooms. Rendyn and the Sivivans long before him hid the truth away, but now they needed it more than ever.

I told everyone we were going to break the curse. We spread the rumors too soon, thinking everything would be fine. I can't *let them down. I can't fail at this, it's my fault, our fault!*

Mila struggled to see how she could possibly uphold her end of the bargain. Her great-great-many-times-great grandfather, Ninian, gave them three ways to break the curse. The first, to return the vial of the deadly alchemical he made centuries ago, could never happen now. The vial was gone. Thislen swore that Soren smashed it to pieces, and she believed him. The pallor of his face and the haunted look in his eyes convinced her, though she sensed there was something more he hadn't said. Regardless, Mila doubted that explaining it was destroyed would be enough to stop her ancestor's spirit.

That left two other ways to free Astera. They could allow him to take his revenge upon the bloodlines of his enemies. The curse was meant to target the Ruling Council, the ones who staged a coup and murdered the Royal Family because King Barleyn wanted to expand their borders. A war would have strained the kingdom's coffers. The Ruling Council wanted to retain their power, not spend it.

The only problem? Over the past three hundred years, those men and women had children, got married, and sired bastards. And those children and bastards got married and had broods of their own. So on and so forth for generations, until it was impossible to tell who had blood ties to which family. Astera was not a large kingdom. Who knew how many would die? No, that wasn't an option, even if it was what Ninian wanted most.

Mila leaned back, sighing heavily. Their only choice was to find the lost heir to the throne, King Barleyn's descendent. Prince Yewen, heir apparent at the time of the coup, escaped underground with the first of the Nattfolk. It said so right there in her great-grandmother's journals. The eldest son of the king vanished not long after the Commons were established and before Willa Ominir left the island. By the time Willa returned, the trail had gone cold.

Mila hunted through every scrap of paper Tamsa smuggled to her, copying over every bit of information on Yewen. Centuries ago, he was a teenager who lost his family and set off on his own—but he couldn't have just vanished. Not a single page made mention of him or his lineage after that, though they did say he took what few treasures the Nattfolk managed to save from the castle.

Mila picked up the worn journal again. This one was in a different hand, not Willa's. It was written while she was away, in the hand of some long ago Sivivan ancestor. It was one of four such journals that chronicled the founding of the Commons and the creation of Nattfolk society. Here, in the spidery script on yellowed pages, was her only clue.

Yewen came down to us today for a few supplies. I can tell that he means this to be the last time. Grief and time have changed him. He is quiet and solemn, and determined to keep an eye on his people even still. He cannot be seen, so he takes pains to disguise himself. He asked for woad to darken his hair. His clothing was that of the poorest of Asterans, well patched and mended. He told me something happened above, on the surface. Something he never expected.

Then he asked me for nappies. Yewen is to be a father. I asked him about his wife, about where they lived and what we could do to help. He refused to tell me anything. The fewer who know, said he, the fewer who are in danger. Yewen plans to keep his family a secret, to let only himself and his heir know until such time as the throne can be claimed again. He has not even told his new bride!

If only we Nattfolk were strong enough to aid him. With our struggles to find food and the constant clangor of hammers as we carve out the place where we will live, we are useless to him. I vowed to him that when we were strong, we would follow him and his heir without question.

Yewen thanked me. He pointed out what I have been avoiding these past few years. Our recovery will take a generation, perhaps two. The work I have begun will not finish in my lifetime. Our strength will be a long time in coming. All I can do is pass the tale along, and hope that the leaders of the Nattfolk remember the promise I have made.

I let him leave with all of the supplies he asked for, and extras besides. He has never had children before, there is much he doesn't know. Before he vanished, I stopped him with a question. How will we know you when you come again?

The answer was as obvious as it was clever. Yewen carried with him the small things we stole from the palace as we fled. Each one we took bore the royal crest. The pendant has it on the back, stamped into the metal. The tobacco case, on the lid. All of them were small enough to put in a pocket, to hide away. Trinkets, jewelry, someone took a hairbrush. Yewen has them all. He said he would give them to his heirs, pass them down. They'd be kept as secret as the heir themself, and if that line should come to an end, his heir must ensure that they were buried with them or thrown into the sea. Both would put it far beyond the reach of ordinary men who might stumble upon it. We'd know them by what they carried, he said. I believed him.

I was the last person to bow to Prince Yewen Asteran, heir to the throne. I doubt we shall see him again.

True enough, Yewen was never mentioned again. Tamsa checked at Mila's insistence. Twice. She let out a frustrated sigh, pushing the journal away.

"We'll know them by what they carry. Right, because I can just go ask everyone in Astera if they're carrying a royal hairbrush in their pocket!" Whatever those trinkets and jewelry pieces were, they weren't listed anywhere.

"Still at it?" Trevon ducked under the heavy curtain hung across the entrance of the cavern, his arms laden with food.

She didn't deign to answer him, fixing him instead with a sullen glare. He grinned as he cleared space for his miniature feast and laid it out. "The others are on their way. Stop and eat something, will you?"

"Where's my father?" Mila asked, closing the journals and setting them aside. She took the food Trevon offered—bread, soft white cheese, and sliced hard sausage.

"Olen? He's seeing to the Hayfews. Tilli is pregnant again, and she can't keep anything down." Trevon pulled an apple from his pocket and rolled it across the table.

Mila caught it. "Evelie is with him?"

"Yeah, and Ivan is on his patrol, last I heard."

"He is," Darran confirmed, coming in with Aften on his heels. Both of them had damp hair and smelled strongly of soap, fresh from the bathing caves after their weapons training.

"He took out one of the dummies. Cut it right in half," Aften offered brightly. He seemed to be getting some of his old spark back, though it never seemed to last.

"He did?" Mila hid her grin behind a bite of food. It gave her no small amount of pleasure to find that Ivan had an aptitude for weapons—and a great deal of pleasure to know she was still better than he was. He had the build for fighting, and she was slimmer and shorter. Winning against him in a sparring match was their new favorite way to say good morning.

I'm so glad we made up. I missed him, I missed us.

They were back to ribbing one another like siblings, to teasing one another mercilessly, and to talking about any and everything. They even covered the subject of the spurned kiss in the apothecary.

Ivan sighed, reclined on Mila's bed with his back propped against the stone wall, looking up at the unremarkable ceiling. "I wasn't really thinking, I admit. I guess it was that I didn't know any other girls I got along with, and I knew I could get along with you. That's what it boils down to."

"So I was just convenient?" Mila wrinkled her nose.

"No! You were important, and it was love. It just wasn't actually romantic, and I kept pushing for it, hoping that it might be someday."

"I love you too, Ivan, but not that way."

"Yeah. I see how you look at Trevon." Ivan grinned and waggled his eyebrows.

Mila flushed bright red, swinging her pillow at his head.

She looked away, hoping the blush would fade from her cheeks before Trevon noticed it.

She was glad she and Ivan were on speaking terms again, especially as things were still strained between her and—

Thislen ducked into the cavern with Tamsa on his heels. Tamsa lifted her hand in a little wave and sat on the bench beside Mila, snagging a piece of bread and some of the cheese. Thislen took himself to the cushioned chair the Nattfolk had gifted Olen to read in.

In fact, half of their cavern was made of such gifts. So glad were their new neighbors to have a healer on hand, they ensured there was no comfort missing from the space. The chamber was mostly one large circle with four small nooks carved off the sides. Each one was just large enough to hold a narrow bed and a clothes chest. Curtains provided the illusion of privacy, should one want it. The Nattfolk sent scouts to the apothecary and spirited all of their blankets, quilts, cushions, and dishes down to the Commons in the night.

Between their own belongings and the basics, there was the chair and a bookshelf, crammed full of Olen's books and scrolls on healing. The table sat before the hearth, with three vases of fresh flowers on top, though where and how Evelie had gotten ahold of them, Mila couldn't guess. A set of shelves held their dishes and some food.

Anything they hadn't already owned found its way quickly in. There was a nice knotted rug beneath the chair, a sewing kit, a basket of yarn with two knitting needles sticking out of it, a few spare blankets, some simple painted art of the city above through a window in the daylight, and a large hope chest topped with cushions that doubled as a sofa when they had guests.

Mila was glad for the separate cavern assigned to Olen for his herbs and unguents. If they had all his healing goods in here, there wouldn't be room to move.

It was a far warmer welcome than her family expected, and was both less and more than they were used to having. None of them complained, though Evelie still seemed to be finding her feet. Some days she looked like a stormcloud, scudding from place to place with a bleak, gloomy expression on her brow. Mila hoped she'd be alright.

Ivan is looking after her.

As if the thought summoned him, the slightly breathless giant ducked inside. "Sorry, patrol almost went long. The Vaim went tearing off again."

"Was there anything there?" Mila asked quickly, pushing to her feet.

Ivan shook his head, sitting heavily on the chest.

She sighed, shaking her hair back. It wasn't bound in its usual scarf, and she sincerely regretted not taking the time to tie it up earlier. "Right, well we can't do anything about that now. I'm glad you all came, though. I need your help."

All eyes were on her, and she lifted her chin. *Don't let them down.*

"Let's get down to what we know. The heir to the throne carries at least one item that will identify them, but the journals don't mention anything specific except a hairbrush, a pendant, and a tobacco case." Mila pulled all three journals over, passing them around. The relevant pages were marked with thin ribbons.

"We haven't learned anything new, then?" Darran sighed, taking one of the offered tomes and opening it. "I hoped Tamsa might have found another passage."

"No luck," Tamsa said with a shrug.

Mila sat. "We don't know where Yewen went, we don't know all of the items he has, and we don't know if his lineage even survived. That makes this all ten times harder."

"Ten times? Try a hundred thousand times," Aften groaned.

Thislen's lips pressed into a thin line, his eyes wandering around the room. Mila felt a flash of irritation heat her chest. *This is our only hope! Why doesn't he care?*

He'd been a thorn in her side the past weeks, dragging his feet or outright neglecting any tasks she asked him to do in their hunt for the heir. The irritation turned to anger that flashed across her face quick as lightning, and she took a deep breath. The coal in her stomach rolled and sparked.

Yelling at him won't help anything.

"Does anyone have any ideas?" Mila asked, pinching the bridge of her nose.

Silence filled the cavern. The journals were slowly passed from hand to hand, the pages read, and then on to the next person they went. Mila watched Thislen take one of the journals and pass it to Ivan without opening it. Her brows rose when he did it again. When he did it with the last of the journals, her patience snapped.

Mila slammed her hands onto the table. "Are we *boring* you, Thislen? Is there some reason you don't want to help us with this? I thought you wanted to help me break the curse!"

Thislen grimaced. "Think about it, Mila. You might as well be looking for a needle in a field of haystacks. How are you going to find one person among the thousands on this island, operating only at night, in a kingdom slowly filling up with people who want to kill you? The heir isn't going to just stand up and tell you who they are because you ask, either. The journal said they've been told to keep it a secret from everyone. *Everyone*, Mila."

Her hands balled into fists until her nails dug tiny crescents into her palms. "Do you have any better ideas?"

"We should go to Ninian."

Mila threw her hands up with a scoff.

"We should!" Thislen said firmly. "If we explain that the vial can't be used again, he might break the curse anyway. We can at least ask him if there's anything else he'll accept."

"Or we tell him, he doesn't believe us, and things get worse. We don't know exactly how his curse works, Thislen," Mila snapped.

I don't want to tell Ninian I failed. I said I'd bring the vial back, not see that it was destroyed. We don't even have the fragments of the bottle to prove it. He'll never believe me. A chill slid down her spine, as if someone put snow down the back of her shirt. No one knew how magic worked, because Astera's magic dried up long ago. Mila worried he would add her to his list to seek vengeance upon, and Olen.

She showed no outward sign of her racing heart, however, planting her hands on her hips. "If the terms for breaking a spell are woven into it and the caster is now a ghost, it stands to reason that there is no chance at all of him adding some sort of an exception or simply turning it off."

She hadn't meant to sound like she was explaining something to a child, but even she could hear the condescension in her voice.

Tamsa's brows lifted. "How would you know?"

Darran and Aften exchanged looks, their brows raised. Both of them prudently moved over to Ivan, out of the line of fire.

Thislen leaned forward, planting his elbows on his knees and steepling his fingers. He fixed Mila with his intent dark eyes, his thoughts hidden from her while she felt like hers were laid uncomfortably bare.

"Tamsa has a point. How exactly did you come to know so much about magic, Mila? No one has been able to use it in hundreds of years, not since Ninian sucked it all up for the curse. Do you know who does know about magic? The court magician, who is very conveniently a ghost trapped in the castle at this very moment."

A flush rushed across her cheeks and down her neck, and she squeezed her fists tighter as the coal inside of her expanded, threatening to explode. *She* was threatening to explode.

"If you won't come up with any helpful ideas, Thislen, then maybe you should leave." Each word was clipped and cold and fell from her lips like lead.

The two of them stared at one another, the tension so thick it seemed to keep everyone else in the room from breathing. At length, Thislen sat back, stretching out his brace-clad leg and folding his arms over his chest. He didn't get up, though. He didn't leave.

He was being so damn contrary between one moment and the next. It was driving her mad!

I don't have time for this. Thislen is being a stubborn oaf, but he's right, too. This search is going to take ages. We have to get to work.

"What if we search the houses?" Ivan offered, shattering the silence.

"What?" Mila asked, her thoughts still following Thislen.

"We can search the houses. We'll mark them all down on a map, then search them for the items. We look for loose floorboards or safes or whatever, and if we find one of the items, we wait for the heir to show up."

Mila's eyes widened. "That would...that might actually work."

Unless the heir was dead or had left Astera entirely. Then they would turn up nothing at all. She pushed that thought out of her head. *I know the heir will be in Astera, in the city even. They wouldn't leave their people.*

Would they?

"That sounds like as good a place as any to start," Darran said, stretching. "We can split off one or two of us from our patrols easily enough to poke about."

"There's so many houses just in the city. What about Barred Town, or the farms and villages?" Aften's eyes were wide as he slumped against the wall.

"We'll search the city first," Mila said decisively. "If we don't turn up anything here, then we worry about everything outside of the walls."

Ivan drew up one of his knees, looping an arm around it. "When did you turn into a miniature general, Mila? It's only been a few months since..."

Mila cleared her throat. "Since my first execution?" she asked dryly.

Ivan flushed, shrugging his shoulders. "Guess that was a bad question."

Thislen leaned forward suddenly, eyes fixed on Mila. "Oh, I see."

For the thousandth time, Mila felt as if he was gazing right through her, into her very soul. "See what?"

"Nothing, it's just...you were afraid until you learned you could do something about the Vaim. That's why you want to break the curse, isn't it?"

She remembered the way her entire body felt like ice when the rowboat approached the shore at twilight, the way her heart raced and she couldn't catch her breath. Some nights she still dreamed of the frantic race through the streets of Astera, the shadows boiling to life around her. She ran her tongue over her lips, belatedly realizing she was gazing into the fire.

"That fear is felt by every citizen of this kingdom except the few hundred down here or the ones who want to keep us all under their thumb. There's nothing out there for Asterans but darkness and death. We don't have to be afraid of the dark anymore, not like this." She spread her hands on the table. "So please, Thislen. Please help me."

They stared at one another. Mila tried to read the thief's steady gaze, but his eyes were shuttered. She could see nothing in them.

At last, he nodded. "I'll help you, Mila. As much as I can."

Relief washed over her, and that feeling gave her pause. *Why does it matter that he's helping with this? He hasn't got any better chance of finding Yewen's heir than me or any of the others.* She smacked her hands on the table—gently this time.

"Right, then let's get started. This might take us some time, after all. Tamsa, can you get a map?"

"Of the city? I'm sure we can find one up there if not down here."

"Good. Aften, Darran, and Thislen—you three will start searching houses. We'll cover for you on our patrols."

"You're going to patrol instead of looking?" Aften asked, brows raised.

"I'm not good with a lockpick and we all know it." Mila frowned. "I'll stick with Trevon and Tamsa and we'll run our patrols. Ivan, you can listen for us. If any of the other scouts notice our three running around, I want to know about it so we can come up with an excuse."

Ivan shrugged. "Easy enough."

"Alright. Let's get started."

Everyone stood but Thislen. Trevon hovered near the door, looking between the pair. Mila waved him off. "Don't worry, Trevon. I didn't forget my promise. We can spar after this."

He nodded, and as he ducked out of the cavern he twitched the heavy curtain into place so it would muffle their voices.

Warmth crept through Mila from her core outward, as if she'd swallowed a big gulp of soothing tea. *At least Trevon understands me, and he's the only person I can tolerate worrying about me these days.*

His worrying didn't feel smothering or expectant. He genuinely seemed to care.

With a sigh, she turned back to Thislen. "How are you feeling?"

His hand went to his side, where she knew the scars from his burns were. "Fine."

"Not physically. Mentally. You killed someone on that ship."

"So did you."

"I didn't know mine by name, and mine didn't torture me."

Thislen inhaled slowly. "I don't think I want to talk about this."

"Yet, right?" Mila frowned. "You don't have to talk to me, but you need to talk to someone, alright?"

Why would he choose anyone else, though? I'm his closest... Was she? Had Tamsa stepped into that role while they were aboard that ship?

Mila's eyes widened for a moment. Was she jealous?

"Sometimes the healer in you leaks out," Thislen said softly.

Mila frowned. She wasn't the same girl anymore, naive and restless. She tempered herself into something stronger every day. "I hate that."

"Don't." Thislen stood, walking toward the door. "I like that part of you just as much as I like the part that's good with a sword." He flashed her a small smile, however brief, and for a moment everything felt like it had before they were separated.

"Thislen," she said, catching his wrist.

He stopped, looking down at her hand in surprise.

Mila let go quickly. "Thislen, I just want you to know that I like you, too. Even this new you that's somehow quieter before. Which I didn't think was possible, by the way."

The smile returned to his face for a moment, and she smiled back.

"Thanks." The curtain rustled, and Thislen was gone.

It was only then Mila realized she hadn't asked Thislen what his real intentions were in refusing the journals. There was something more to it all, she sensed, and she had been determined to lead the conversation back around to that.

He always throws me off balance. Damn it!

No one else did. Not in the same way. Since they first met, he could take her smallest reaction and deduce an entire story. He was the witness and the watcher as her life was upended, the guardian as she found her feet again, and now...

Now he was like the carvings on the walls of the Justica, distant and made of stone. She couldn't tell what *he* was thinking, but he always knew what *she* was. He steered all their conversations around exactly the way he wanted. She never pried a word out of his lips that he wasn't willing to give.

But I'm not the fragile little girl I was before. He could at least trust me.

Did he not trust her?

Did *she* trust *him*?

Did it matter? Whether she wanted to or not, she was drawn to him. They were tethered to one another, by experience if nothing else. They braved the island together. They met the Nattfolk together. They would break the curse. Together.

I'll just have to corner him and pry it all out, whether he wants to talk or not. He's my friend, she thought firmly. *We need each other.*

With an irritated sigh, she tidied all the papers and journals away, then pushed through the curtain into the corridor beyond. The short tunnel let out onto the second level of the Commons, bustling like a hive of busy bees as the evening neared midnight. Mila walked to the railing that wrapped around the gallery-style walkway, watching people move from stall to table or table to stall, clustering here and there and then bursting apart again.

A hand clasped her shoulder. Instinctively she twisted and batted it away, only to come face to face with—

"Trevon." Relief colored the word.

Trevon gave her a small, crooked smile as he held up both hands. "I'm unarmed, I come in peace," he teased.

She rolled her eyes, smiling. "You just surprised me is all. You ought to be proud, those are instincts *you* taught me, after all."

"Proud as I can be. I figured you might want someone to talk to after all that." He gestured toward the tunnel behind them. "And we still have that sparring match."

A physical fight instead of an emotional one? That sounded like bliss. She could feel the tension in every line of her body. It held tight in her shoulders, her neck, and her arms and she itched to work it all out.

"That sounds amazing," she breathed, leaning heavily on the rail. "Ancestors, Trevon, sometimes I feel like you're the only person who really understands me."

"You mean because of who you were before you came down here."

She nodded.

He started toward the ramp that would lead them to the ground level and the training cavern beyond. "You forget, Mila. I met you after the fire was kindled."

She smiled. "That's true. There's no before to measure me against." Sometimes starting over was so much easier. Was that why she liked him so much?

Her cheeks heated again, and the warmth in her chest had spread until her fingertips tickled. They walked so close to one another that their hands and shoulders brushed with every step.

No, she decided. *I like Trevon because when I walk next to him, I can feel him. He's like sunlight. I've never felt like this about someone before.*

He was a balm when she felt out of control, a balance to her plotting, an ear she knew she could rely on. After everything, after everyone, she knew that she could find him and he would understand—or at least try to. He was no Soren who wanted her to be a trophy bride, or an Ivan who only wanted to be with her because there was no one else.

Trevon wouldn't push her to be anything besides herself, a thought that made her head light and her heart swell. This was what she wanted, *he* was what she wanted.

The words might still be beyond her reach, but there was something else she could do.

Silently, as they walked, Mila took Trevon's hand.

His fingers laced with hers.

16

Thislen took a deep breath, crossing the training cavern to clasp Aften and Darran on the shoulders. Darran lowered his bow and turned, but Aften yelped. His arrow clattered to the stone floor, drawing a few stares.

"Sorry, sorry," Aften said to them, picking the arrow up again. "Ancestors, Thislen, you nearly gave me a heart attack."

He released both of them, glancing around the cavern before lowering his voice. "Look, I need a favor."

"You want us to go to Perilee with you," Darran said. It wasn't a question.

Thislen's eyes widened. *Perceptive. I don't give Darran nearly enough credit.*

"Yes," he admitted.

"I thought we were going to help Mila look for the heir." Aften's brow furrowed slowly.

"Thislen was right, earlier. We should at least ask if there's anything else Ninian will accept. You want us to go with you so he can't put you to sleep again?" Darran arched a brow.

"A good guess," Thislen muttered, eyeing Darran curiously. Had he always been like this? If so, it was no wonder he'd been made a scout captain. Suddenly Thislen found himself wishing he'd met Darran earlier. *Maybe I would have turned out differently, more open, if I knew someone like him.*

"I don't know about that," Vern's spirit said behind him, setting every hair on the back of his neck to rise. "You don't talk to us, and we know everything you're thinking."

Ignoring the phantom, he gestured. The two Nattfolk fell in behind him. They put up their weapons and slipped through the Commons toward the long stone staircase that would bring them out in the graveyard. From there, it was only a few streets to Perilee.

Darran lit a lantern at the bottom of the steps. As soon as they began to climb, darkness enveloped them, stretching the staircase out like something from a nightmare. Percivan's ghost climbed the steps ahead of Thislen.

Why won't they just go away? I'm fine, I feel fine.

"Liar." Percivan didn't bother to look back as he said it.

"You trust us, then?" Darran asked.

"I trust you enough. I'm not so foolish as to go to Perilee alone."

"Why did Ninian take you in the first place?" Aften asked.

The light from the lantern swung, casting wild shadows on Percivan's face above them as the spirit glanced back. Thislen looked down at his boots. "When I was injured by the Vaim, they burned the Bestant blood from my veins. He hadn't seen someone from the lineage of the Ruling Council survive before."

Vern's gaze bored into his back. He could feel it, could tell exactly who it was. The disappointment radiated from both ghosts at his lie.

For a few minutes, they trudged up the steps in silence.

"You know, I owe you," Aften said softly. "You protected me and Tamsa on that ship. I don't think I'll ever stop owing you."

"I didn't do it so you'd be in debt to me." That was the last thing he wanted. *I did it to make up for my mistakes.*

Mila made the first plan, the one that got them caught, but she couldn't have gotten as close to the vial as she had without Thislen. He shouldn't have gone along with it so quickly, without thought. *Did I do it because she's my friend?*

Was she his friend still? It was hard to tell. Both of them had changed. Mila was running toward something, and Thislen...

Thislen had always been, and would always be, running away.

"Well, either way. I'm in." Aften flashed Thislen a grin.

"I think he might have guessed that, considering we're sneaking out of the Commons with him," Darran said dryly.

They fell silent. The flickering, dancing light of the lantern played across the rough hewn walls. The steps, won into dips and hollows by hundreds of years of footsteps, ran up into the darkness as if they would never end.

And then they did. The ceiling flattened, the stairs ending at a small door. It was one of the walls of a stone casket, standing in the heart of the long abandoned Sivivan mausoleum. Darran left the lantern at the top of the steps, turning the flame down to the barest blue whisper before pushing the entrance closed behind him.

Thislen took a deep breath as they stepped out into the thin moonlight. Tonight, the weather was clear and cold. His breath curled away on the barest hint of a breeze. The moon was a thin crescent above their heads, barely painting the island in a silver glow.

Perilee loomed above them. It sat sedately mere streets away, a beautiful building. The bulk of the castle was built against—and in some cases into—a sheer cliff face. The dark twisted shadows of climbing vines played across the walls. Only the soaring spires of the castle stood above that cliff, their windows gleaming even in the night.

To Thislen, it felt like he was headed for the gallows.

How does anyone get anything done with that huddled over them like a gargoyle?

Set in the castle's outwall was a familiar side gate, though in the pale light of the moon it was little more than a dark shadow sunk into the stone. That gate, Thislen mused, was what set all of this into motion. If Aften hadn't touched Mila's hand to the wood, it never would have opened. They never would have gone to Perilee. Would they have learned about the curse?

Aften lifted his hand to the wood and pushed. The door didn't budge. He sighed.

"I thought it opened to the old noble bloodlines. Sivivan is one of those, isn't it?" Thislen folded his arms over his chest.

Darran shrugged, putting his hand on the door. "Coppermund doesn't work either, I guess. If it's magic tied into the Vaim and all that, I don't know that any of us will be able to open it."

"We got lucky with Mila," Aften said, craning to look further along the wall for another way in.

Percivan's ghost walked up to the door. "Go on. You know he's waiting for you."

Perilee was tucked behind tall, thick walls. Thislen knew there wasn't another entrance that was open. The Royal Guard, a relic of an age long since past that served more as ornamental decoration than soldiers, sealed the grounds every evening before they left for their ship.

There was no point in wasting time, not with the moon beginning to set. Thislen stepped forward and pressed his hand to the cool, rough surface.

Clunk.

He pushed. The door swung open.

"Huh. Thislen opened it. He's full of Bestant blood, isn't he?" Aften stepped through the gate.

Darran cast a look at Thislen, a brow arched. "Yeah. Old spells work in strange ways. Who knows what the original intent behind this locking spell even was?"

Thislen's heart raced in his chest. "It might be no blood at all. When the Vaim touched me, they burned the Bestant out of me. At least, that's what Ninian told me."

"No noble blood at all. Huh, I could see it. The Vaim didn't want to attack you when we first found you. I never considered the possibility." Darran passed into the courtyard with the crunch of gravel beneath his boots.

Thislen closed the gate behind them, and the lock fell into place. The three of them strode toward the castle, weaving through hedges and flower beds and around a decorative pond on their way to Perilee.

"How did the Vaim burn an entire bloodline from your body?" Darran asked.

"I don't know. All I know is that it hurt, it almost killed me, and I was feverish for days. It's how I met Mila, actually. Olen healed me, and Mila helped."

"You never told us that." Aften trotted a few steps to walk beside Thislen.

"You never asked."

"We didn't ask now, either," Darran pointed out.

Thislen didn't justify that with a response, though it did give him pause. *Why did I tell them that?*

"Because you're starting to trust them. As you should," Vern said. He and Percivan walked without a sound over the loose stone alongside the Nattfolk and Thislen.

He ignored them as best he could.

Perilee's grounds weren't particularly expansive, as the keep was pressed against the cliff face. It didn't take them much time to cross the gardens and come to a stop in front of the massive double doors. The carvings were difficult to make out in the dark, cast in shades of gray and black.

Thislen slapped his hand against the wood. This time, he didn't push—but the doors opened anyway without so much as a sound. He froze as a tickle of cold air came from the darkness beyond the doors. Every hair on his body stood on end.

Magic lit the candles on either side of the door, bursting to life with dancing flames. Garridan's ghost met Thislen's eyes, his arms folded over his chest and a brow raised. "It took you long enough."

I'm dreaming. I have to be. This is just another nightmare.

"No, it isn't." Garridan's shirt was still cut in two places, still stained with red. His face was pale, his lips almost blue. "Look at all this. Magic. People on the island at night. The sorcerer up in his little rooms. If the Ruling Council knew about all this…"

There'd be war.

Garridan smiled. "Precisely. The Nattfolk would be eradicated. Imagine the power someone could have, if they were able to stay on the island at night when no one else could. They would control everything."

"Thislen?" Darran asked, touching his shoulder.

Thislen jerked away with a sharp gasp, his heart racing in his chest. His ghosts walked into the foyer, sizing one another up with quiet resignation. None of them could avoid the others, after all. He tried not to look at them.

"Is it the candles? Those always freak me out, too." Aften shuddered.

"Yeah. The candles," he muttered, stepping inside. It felt as if Perilee sighed around him, its centuries-old bones settling in relief.

The Nattfolk followed. As soon as all three of them were clear of the doors, they swung shut and the massive bar slid into place, locking them in with a thud that echoed in the empty marble hall.

Thislen felt a roll of nausea, looking around. The light of the candles couldn't reach the vaulted ceiling. They barely lit the walls. The massive entryway had doors off either side, but it also bore two grand curving staircases. Between them sat another pair of carved doors, though these were smaller than the ones that trapped them.

He looked quickly away from those. Percivan was gesturing for him from the base of the steps. Garridan and Vern were already halfway up.

Thislen turned to his companions—his living, breathing ones. "This is where I need you both to trust me."

Darran folded his arms over his chest. "You want to go alone," he accused.

Thislen nodded.

"What? But why?" Aften asked, voice echoing faintly off the walls.

"I think I can get through to Ninian. I think I can convince him." It was partially true. He knew he would be able to ask the spirit things no one else but Mila could. He neglected to tell them that he wanted to ask about his ghosts as well.

"But—"

"Aften," Darran interrupted, putting a hand on the scout's shoulder. "Go ahead, Thislen. We'll catch up in a bit."

Thislen nodded, turning away. The candles at the foot of the steps caught fire, their light painting the plush rug in pools of gold. He balled his hands into fists and marched up them to his waiting retinue of the dead.

Time to get some answers.

Aften sighed. "Sure, fine. We'll just wander through the creepy castle, waiting for you to finish. Thanks, Thislen. That sounds really fun."

The candles at the bottom of the stairs flickered out. Aften sighed again, louder than before.

"What's wrong with the big empty castle?" Darran asked, flashing him a grin.

That grin sent a flutter through Aften's stomach, and he quickly looked away. For months, he'd pushed down his feelings, wrestling them into a place where they wouldn't do anything stupid.

I can't lose my best friend. What if I was imagining all that happened in the cell, reading more into it than there was? After all, he never did it again.

He'd never put his forehead to Aften's, cupped his cheek, said his name with that much relief and worry...

Darran's hands dropped to his side and Aften couldn't help but look at them. The tops were a rich, dark brown and the palms were lighter, a burnished gold. He knew they were calloused and warm, and he wanted to hold one.

His hand lifted, almost of its own accord, and—

He forced it back down by his side with a shrug and a small smile. "What are we even supposed to do? Stand here?"

Aften yelped as candles sprang to life nearby, at the foot of the *wrong* set of stairs, the set that led away from Ninian's hidden rooms. Darran pressed a hand to his chest, letting out an explosive sigh.

"I wish he wouldn't do that. You think he wants us to go that way?"

"Um," Aften answered numbly.

Darran brushed past him, accompanied by the smell of soap and leather. Aften swallowed.

What if he really does like me, too? What if he's not making any moves because I haven't? He bit his lip, trailing after Darran. "I think we should consider not listening to a ghost," he muttered.

They both paused at the bottom of the steps.

Aften wished he could go back an hour in time and tell Thislen to go to the castle on his own. It was one thing to wander around the dark in numbers, and another to be trapped with the person he loved, following the whims of a mad sorcerer.

"Come on. Together." Darran planted a hand at the small of Aften's back and gently propelled him up the first few steps.

Aften felt like lightning arced through his body from the place that he'd touched, his skin tingling from head to toe.

This was going to be impossible. If he opened his mouth at all, he'd confess, and he knew it. In the Commons, he'd been able to distract himself with helping Olen, or training, or any number of chores and errands. He firmly reminded himself of all he had to lose and clenched his jaw. Not a word would get past his lips, he vowed.

Another set of candles lit at the top of the steps.

"What if, for once, we didn't follow the magic candles into the dark?"

Damn it. Aften couldn't keep his mouth closed for twenty seconds.

"What do you think Ninian is doing? Letting us take a moonlit stroll, or leading us to something?" Darran flashed another grin.

Magic made him uncomfortable. Imagining that Ninian Ominir was playing matchmaker with it only made it worse. No one else used magic in Astera. No one else *could*. It didn't exist anywhere outside of Perilee's stone walls. Well, except for the magic that had long ago been tied into objects, like the Nattfolk pendants or the Sivivan's glowing orb. Aften would have been very content to keep it that way forever.

He stopped short, catching Darran's wrist. "What if we really don't follow the candles? Let's go this way."

The corridor branched, and the candles lit up on the left. Ahead of them, it was dark.

"We can always try it." Darran slid his hand into Aften's and towed him along, footsteps muffled by the plush rug that ran the length of the passage.

This was a mistake. Never in his life had Aften regretted a decision so quickly. The dark was full of looming shadows that wouldn't quite resolve into actual shapes. The figures on tapestries turned into ghostly shades. Vases huddled on tables like hunchbacked monsters. Stands of armor sent shivers down his spine. He swore they moved slightly whenever they passed, as if they were filled with Vaim. Even the thrill of Darran's fingers around his wasn't enough to put him at ease, even though it felt as warm and rough as he remembered.

"Maybe we should go back," he whispered. Even that sounded too loud in the almost unnatural hush of the castle.

The candles behind them flared and Aften twisted, stumbling into Darran in his hasty retreat. Darran put his arm around his shoulders. Aften found his balance and quickly pulled away, lips pressed tight together. He couldn't look at his face. He'd say something.

I need him. I don't understand Tamsa, I don't know Thislen well enough. Darran's been my best friend for years. I can't ruin this.

When they didn't turn back, the magical lights faded and then blew out, coils of smoke making pale white ribbons in the air. Darran took both of Aften's hands in his, smiling encouragingly. The dark didn't seem as foreboding this way, standing mere inches away from the man he was infatuated with. That was all it was. Infatuation. Even if it started years ago.

His gaze dropped to their joined hands. His heart and stomach both fluttered, as if he'd swallowed an entire flock of hummingbirds.

"I was so afraid," he blurted.

"Of the dark?" Darran asked, his voice low and soothing.

"The day they took you away. When I thought you died. They pulled you out of the room, and the sun was setting, and you didn't have your pendant. I was…" Heartbroken. The word stuck in his throat. He closed his eyes and swallowed.

Here in the dark, in front of a window painted a soft silver by the feeble light of the moon, it was easier to speak. Darran's face was hidden in the shadows. Aften couldn't see his expression.

"It was terrible," he continued. "All I wanted was…was this. To know you were okay, to be able to prove it to myself."

"Aften, you can say it, you know."

He laughed, high pitched and uneasy. "Say what? I have nothing to—that was all I wanted to say. I was afraid. I was sad. Now I'm not."

"You are, just for different reasons. You aren't afraid for my life or sad because I died. You're afraid I'll push you away, you're sad that you can't tell me you love me."

Aften froze. His breath caught in his chest and blood roared in his ears. *Was I that obvious?*

Darran tipped his head to one side. "You can say it," he whispered.

"Y-Yes," he stammered. "Darran, I love you. I didn't tell you before, and I wasn't planning to tell you now, I don't want to lose you. It's just…"

It was the first real opportunity he'd had to say something, where the two of them were truly alone, with no risk of interruption.

"Is that alright?" Aften's voice cracked.

The smile on his face was clear when Darran spoke. "I nearly blurted it out when we came to rescue you, and I saw you alive in that damn cell. I thought you might need some time to heal before I made any moves."

His mind was filled with static, his eyes wide. *Is he saying...no, he can't be. Can he?*

"You wanted to make moves?" Aften echoed numbly.

Instead of answering, Darran drew Aften close. His arm slid around his waist, and he leaned in. He moved slowly, his hold loose. If Aften wanted to, he could step away. He could stop this.

Aften didn't want to. He leaned in, closing the distance between them. Their lips met in a crush far sooner than Aften thought they would, but Darran didn't seem to mind. His arms tightened, and he guided the kiss to something deeper, something softer. Aften's arms lifted, wrapping around Darran's neck and waist.

He couldn't help but marvel at this turn of fate. *He likes me, too. Maybe even loves me. I'm such an idiot.*

With a soft *whoosh* of air, candelabra burst to life on either side of a polished wooden door mere steps away. Aften broke the kiss with a yelp, Darran with a shout. Both of them, still tangled in one another's arms and panting softly, stared.

Irritation swept through Aften like grassfire. He glared up at the ceiling. "Really, Ninian?" he shouted. *Next time I see that ghost, I'm going to give him a piece of my mind.*

"I don't think he's planning to leave us alone."

"Why not? He's talking to Thislen by now, isn't he?"

Darran shrugged. "Should be."

Aften eyed the door across the way with distaste. Their last visit to the castle, he'd *wanted* to open a door. Now that Ninian was giving him permission, it suddenly felt like a terrible idea. With a heavy sigh, he walked over and pushed. It swung open without a sound.

A fire burst into life in the fireplace directly across from the door, casting a warm russet glow over the walls. The glimmering lettering on the covers of countless book spines of all sizes winked in the light. They stood at perfect attention on the floor-to-ceiling shelves, made of dark polished wood. A massive wooden desk was set at an angle to face the door. Two large plush armchairs sat on the other side, for reading or conversation.

"It's a study," Aften realized.

"Whose?" Darran asked, brushing past Aften to examine the space. He ran his fingers over the carved shield with the Spine's mountain and Perilee on the front of the desk. "This is the Asteran crest. The Royal family's?"

"If it was theirs, it would be sealed off. Someone else is using it." Aften picked up a stack of papers from where they sat on the corner of the heavy wooden piece, behind a small stone bust of King Aldan, founder of Astera. He shuffled through them idly, skimming the first few lines of each.

A report on crops. A report on prices of common goods, a report on...

I, Lord Soren Bestant, do suggest to the Ruling Council—

Aften's eyes widened. He flipped to the next.

Soren—I have some information about our mutual friends that I wish to pass on to you at your earliest convenience. It will change the instructions I gave you, and I—

And the next?

Lord Bestant, I would be most honored if you would grace my home with your presence for luncheon on the—

"It's Soren's office! Soren Bestant."

"What?" Darran turned away from the books, hand dropping back to his side.

Aften passed Darran the papers, frowning at the shelves that marched all the way up to the ceiling. *A library on his boat and one on the shore. Some of these have to be duplicates. If we knew which ones he kept in both places, we might learn something about our enemy, something we could use.* That was the problem they were facing now. Either Mila was correct and Soren knew about the Vaim. He would eventually try to find a way onto the island at night. Or she was wrong and their foe was beyond their reach.

Aften wasn't deluded enough to believe, like Rendyn did, that Soren Bestant was no longer a threat.

"We should make a list of the books and a list of the people he's talking to. It might be easier to get into their—" Aften turned, his elbow catching the bust perched on the corner of the desk. With a gasp, he bent to catch it—

But it was gone.

Aften crouched down, feeling around beneath the desk with his hand. Where had it...?

"Aften."

"Hang on, I knocked this—"

"Aften!"

"What?" He looked up—right into the placid stone face of the bust, which hadn't fallen off the table at all. It sat tipped at an angle, frozen.

"It's a latch," Darran said, pulling Aften around to point at the sliver of old iron beneath the figure.

"Then it has to open something!" Aften ran his fingers over the desk, feeling for anything out of place.

"It opens a secret door."

"There's no door in the desk, Darran."

The scout pulled Aften to his feet, turning him to face the fireplace.

The marble mantle above the crackling fire was decorated with beautifully carved whorls of leafy vines and impossibly delicate flowers of fine white stone. Set in the dead center of that mantle was a large square piece that bore the Royal crest of Astera. Aften hadn't paid much attention to the hearth when they'd come in, but he was paying attention now.

That crest was a cleverly hidden door. A marble facade had been fixed to a wood panel hung on invisible hinges. Aften pulled it open. It hid a small cabinet full of paper.

Darran pulled a sheaf of them out. "Some of these are old."

Each page on the top of the pile was pristine, pale white with black ink. The further down the stack one went, the more yellowed and aged the sheets became. The bottom pieces seemed impossibly delicate, but they didn't crumble as Darran touched them. He frowned as he scanned them.

"Percivan Coppermund, considered a threat. Eradicate. Julia Hartsmettle, will settle. Arrange marriage. Corbin Raithcliff, considered a threat. Eradicate. Look, right here—there's check marks next to most of these names. This is..." Darran flipped through the pages one by one.

"It's their kill list, to keep their secret." Aften's stomach churned. "The names, are they all on the Ruling Council?"

Darran nodded. "On the Council or supposed to be. A lot of them were killed to clear the way for second or third sons and daughters." He shook his head, brow furrowed.

Aften turned back to the cabinet, pulling the last of the papers, crackling like dry leaves, from its depths. Something caught his eye, though barely. He passed Darran the stack, then stuck his hand into the dark.

Smooth leather met his fingertips. He pulled out the journal, its pages bloated with added papers. It looked like letters, recent letters, all written in different hands, all glued into the pages of the tome, and all addressed to Lord Soren Bestant.

Darran held papers in both hands, examining them. "There's two families that got wiped out entirely. They've been keeping records of who they think can't keep their mouths shut. Every one of these people was someone with a conscience, and they keep killing them."

Aften was only half listening, his eyes moving faster and faster across the letters. His heart raced even as he went cold. Phrase after phrase jumped out at him.

—since we have lost the reagent, alternative methods must be devised to cull the population—

—something so obvious as closing the gates and sweeping the City Guard through the streets will only cause outrage and make the populace difficult to control—

—food stores are not unlimited and the farms we have are struggling to maintain the populace. Something must be done, and the sooner the better, for our sake and theirs alike—

—there's no reason to spare the poor—

—investigate ways to transfer a true plague successfully. Perhaps we put a person so afflicted on one of the Gate Quarter ships at night, then quarantine it. We can repeat the measure a few days later with another, and so on and so forth. Keeping the ships out at sea will solve the problem of what to do with the bodies as well. Ships are easily scuttled, after all, and fish make quick work of—

Aften felt bile rise in the back of his throat. He slammed the book shut, closing his eyes as the world spun.

"Aften? Are you alright?"

Helplessly, he looked up at Darran as the scout put his arm around him.

"Darran," he breathed. "They're going to do it again."

17

"There *has* to be something, Ninian." Thislen paced, every step carving a path through the thick layers of dust draped over everything. It coated chairs, the rotted bed, the heap of rags that were once clothes, the wardrobe, the worktables with their bottles and beakers and papers—even the chandeliers above, their light flickering, were covered in cobwebs that drifted gently back and forth. The only sign of passage was Thislen's track, and the half-faded marks from when he and his friends had been here last.

Friends. The thought stopped him in his tracks. A few moons ago, he was alone. He planned to leave the island. *How quickly things change.* He frowned.

Inevitably, his gaze was drawn to rippling light against the back wall, carved into the cliff itself.. A waterfall ran over a large, seamless pane of glass to fill a small pool with a patter like distant rain. Behind that window, lit by a grand chandelier, was a chamber untouched by the ravages of time. It held a massive canopied bed with heavy curtains. Paneled walls with gilded detailing encircled the sides. There was nothing else, but where Ninian's bed was a heap of tangled and rotting cloth and dust, the bed there was covered in rich dark blues and piled high with cushions. There was no dust, no decay, nothing.

Thislen slept in that bed, after he was taken from his friends. Ninian insisted, eager to speak with him more. Only Mila could have freed him, and she did.

Twice now, technically. Once from *Ship Artaith*, and once from here.

"I don't like the options you've given me. I want something else," Thislen continued, turning to the spirit.

Floating in the air was the figure of a man. His features were sharp and angular, formed and reformed by a cloud of dust and cobwebs, held together by the flickering candlelight from the wall sconces and chandeliers. The edge of his shell, apart from his hands and face, was hazy and indistinct. The impression of a sweeping robe came and went, as though he hadn't finished forming. It was in an ancient style long since gone out of fashion, with a broad belt and decorative trim made of spiderwebs. The dust-cloud of fabric around his legs covered whatever might have existed once as feet. Golden eyes glowed bright in the long-dead magus's face, tracking Thislen as he moved.

Every inch of him swayed and rippled in an invisible breeze, hair and clothes alike, giving the floating ghost the illusion of being underwater.

The spirit of Ninian Ominir laughed softly. A strange echo filled the room, coming from everywhere at once and not from the spirit himself.

"If you truly wish for other options, I can give them to you. I am very willing to accommodate."

Thislen felt as if he'd swallowed ice. Something in the way he said it, something in the set of his shoulders and the tilt of his head, told Thislen this was a very, very bad idea. All this time arguing, and he was giving in now?

Still...

I have to hear it.

"Do you?" The ghost of Percivan whispered anxiously. "Thislen, I don't think this is a good idea."

Ninian's eyes snapped to the other ghost, a frown on his face. "Be quiet."

The chill settled deeper, and Thislen felt a prickle between his shoulderblades. "You can see him?"

"Of course I can see him. And the other two."

His quest was forgotten in an instant. "How? What are they? Are they real?"

"As real as I am, and yet of something different. Something deeper." Ninian floated across the room to study the spirit of Garridan Artaith, the robe billowing as if he walked—yet every step took him too far, too quickly.

"Deeper?" Vern asked, a smirk on his face. "Is that what we're calling it?"

"Older, then," Ninian said with a shrug.

"Older how? Just tell me!" Thislen's hands balled into fists.

"Is that an order? A command?" Garridan grinned.

"No," Thislen said quickly.

Ninian turned to him, the shadowy hollow of his mouth opening—

The stone door hidden in the wall ground open, cutting the conversation off. Thislen swore silently as he whirled to face it. *They couldn't have waited like I asked?*

"Thislen! Oh, Ninian." After skidded to a stop, then coughed as dust clouded around him. In his haste, he'd dropped a piece of paper from the stack in his hands.

Darran followed, scooping the paper up and holding a bound leather tome tucked under his arm. He looked up at the last second, narrowly avoiding a collision with Aften. The urgency bled out of both of them as they stared at the mage.

Thislen crossed the room, taking the stack of documents from Aften's hands. "What? What is this?" He scanned the pages. "A list?"

"Not a list. *The* list," Ninian said calmly, drifting languidly toward him, like a cloud scudding across the sky in a light breeze.

Thislen's brows drew down. He scanned the names, flipping through a few sheets, eyes skimming quickly over the words. Slowly, his forehead smoothed. His brows changed direction, climbing further and further up.

These names—I recognize them, nearly all of them! His father long ago forced him to memorize every name of the Ruling Council, if not every individual within those esteemed houses. Now, here they were, laid out in a list that went back further than even Linden could have ever remembered.

Near the very top of the list was a painfully familiar name.

Percivan Coppermund.

"Oh," Percivan's spirit sighed sadly.

"This is the list of those they've killed or managed?" Thislen looked up.

"We think so," Darran said.

"I know so," Ninian corrected. "I have been watching them put this list together for centuries."

"Why didn't you tell us the last time we were here?" Aften folded his arms over his chest.

"Before, you didn't need to know. You were going to break the curse. Now, as I understand it, you have little choice. And you need to know that." The mage stared steadily at Thislen.

Thislen frowned. "How? How did you watch them?"

"The Vaim may vanish during the day, but I do not. I cannot form, but I can see and hear, and I am not bound solely to this room as they once believed. It amuses me to wander, to watch."

"You lit the candles to guide us to all this, right?" Aften asked.

"Yes."

"Do you have to make them so sudden?"

"No." Ninian grinned.

Aften scowled at him.

"You are correct in guessing that I led you there to find these things. It was knowledge necessary to you, to allow you to make an informed decision." Again, Ninian's gaze drifted to Thislen.

It had been some time since Thislen felt like a noose of connection, of obligation, of responsibility was threatening to tangle around his neck—but now it was back in force. He grimaced, turning away to set the papers on a worktable.

I am not the person who is going to break this curse, Mila is. She wants *to.*

Not that Thislen didn't want the curse to end. He wanted to see the streets safe at night, empty of spirits, but not because of him. He didn't want to be the hero. What sort of hero came so...broken? He rubbed his leg above his brace. It wasn't the only wound he still carried, just the most visible. How could he help?

"You two certainly took your time getting there," Ninian continued, turning back to Aften.

Pink crept across Aften's cheeks, and Darran grinned.

"We were busy," the former scout captain said brightly. He slipped his hand into Aften's.

Thislen arched a brow. "You two finally talked?"

"Thislen!" Aften's flush deepened.

"It's about time. You spent the entire time on *Ship Artaith* grieving him like you'd lost half your body."

Darran's grin faltered, then softened. "I'm glad none of us is in that situation anymore."

Garridan's ghost scoffed. "It wasn't bad for me."

Thislen's hand closed around a beaker on the table, but he fought the urge to turn and throw it at the spirit. It wouldn't do anything.

"Here, Thislen, this is the rest of it." Darran set the leather-bound tome beside Thislen.

Its pages were rippled and stiff with glue. Letters lined every one, written in different hands. His eyes widened as he read over note after note. A chill in his stomach grew, spreading throughout his body until he felt like he was encased in ice.

"They're planning to kill Asterans again," Aften said grimly.

"And that isn't all. We found a few letters of names that the Ruling Council plans to add to the List." Darran passed over only one letter. "This was on Soren Bestant's desk."

Thislen scanned it. There was no name at the top or bottom, but inside?

We must take a look at the next round of heirs. Lord Artaith is old and ailing, Garridan Artaith is trustworthy. Lady Junmarke is with child, and at her age is not expected to survive the birth. If she does, such the better. If she does not, her eldest daughter may be tested. If she is found unsatisfactory, we'll marry her to Artaith. We must encourage the Coppermunds to sire more heirs. Arman Coppermund is too kind, much like his brother, and will also require elimination. Soft hearted fools. Lord—

Thislen stopped reading, his jaw clenched. *Not another one. Not another Coppermund.*

"You can't let them hurt Arman, Thislen, please," Percivan's ghost begged.

I know.

He lifted his eyes from the letter, meeting Darran's. Darran was also a Coppermund, a cousin. His expression was grim.

"I may not have met this family of mine, but I don't want to see anyone killed just for being kind-hearted."

"Then we're on the same page." Thislen offered Darran his hand.

The Nattfolk grasped his wrist. An unspoken agreement passed between them. Thislen made a note to pull him aside later.

"Is there truly an issue if this Arman should pass?" Ninian said airily, reading over Thislen's shoulder. "You are a Coppermund, Nattfolk, are you not? If their line were to pass, you would have claim to their land and holdings. Is that not something you wish for? Wealth, power, recognition?"

Despite the light taunting tone in his words, Thislen could see the manic glint in those golden, pupiless gaze. His eyes narrowed. *He's testing Darran, but Darran isn't that sort of person.*

Darran laughed. "I hope I never, ever have to become the head of the Coppermund family. I wouldn't know what to do with a title. I think I'd miss the rooftops, too."

Thislen lifted his chin. He knew it. A tension bled out of the room at the answer, one Thislen hadn't realized was building up like the pressure of an oncoming storm. Ninian's robes and hair slowed their undulating movements.

Was he about to use magic on Darran? His heart beat faster. He didn't know how to fight a ghost, but he had been moments from trying.

Aften and Darran took the papers and the journal, clearing space on a dusty worktable to spread them out. Ninian drifted after them. The two of them were talking, discussing the families and heirs that were named and their histories dating back to the coup itself. Ninian watched them the entire time.

Thislen tuned them out, studying the Nattfolk, his arms folded over his chest. He was protective of both of them, a feeling he thought he'd reserved for Mila and perhaps Tamsa, but no one else. More and more, he was learning he would throw himself into the fray for those he cared about. More and more, he learned he cared at all. The more he came to know Ivan, Olen, Evelie, Trevon, the other scouts, the Nattfolk craftsmen, the Night Council—the more he came to know them, the more he found himself wanting to help, wanting to see them safe and happy. He'd taken a liking to every one of them. Vern and Percivan were no exception, though they haunted him. Thislen had yet to meet an Asteran he didn't like, apart from those on the Ruling Council.

I can't claim that I want nothing to do with them or this island anymore. I'm involved. I should ask Ninian what he meant. Not just about the deeper magic, but about our options. He said he might be able to change the terms, to break the curse another way.

There had to be another way. He couldn't help them find the heir. The secret his father long ago made him swear to keep sat on the tip of his tongue, but it wouldn't help anyone. It might make everything worse. What he knew...

No, what he knew wouldn't help anyone.

A sudden prickle between his shoulderblades made Thislen turn on his heel. He'd felt eyes on his back and—

And he was right. There, the ghosts of Vern the sailor, Percivan Coppermund, and Garridan Artaith stood just behind him. All three of them stared, their eyes unblinking. Did the dead need to blink? Need to breath?

Thislen's heart pounded, his own breath coming in short, quick bursts. He could feel the weight of their stares bearing down on him, the unspoken expectation swelling like a wave that had yet to crest.

They knew.

There has to be another way. The people of Astera don't deserve this, and there must be another way. I don't want the Ruling Council to continue to harm them, but I don't think I can do anything to stop it. I don't think I'm the man for the job.

"Why not?" Vern asked in a whisper.

The question was a stone in Thislen's gut. He didn't answer, turning back to the three at the table. Ninian's golden eyes were fixed on him, the spirit's expression thoughtful.

Thislen couldn't help but wonder if Ninian's alternative would put him in some sort of debt to the spirit. What if it led to a fee he couldn't pay?

He straightened his shoulders and set his jaw. He'd have to ask. *This isn't just about me. This isn't about Mila, either. It's about our future. Everyone's future. The Nattfolk, the Solfolk—I want to help them.*

I want to help them all.

18

“**I** can't *believe* you went behind my back!”

Mila whirled on Aften, Darran, and Thislen, hands quivering, balled into fists at her sides. The three of them sat along one side of the long polished table in the Night Council's chamber. Lantern light reflected in the gleaming surface from the multitude of lanterns hung on chains above. The table was surrounded with mismatched chairs, stools, and a bench.

It made the best place to yell at someone, lending her an air of authority. Mila paced the far side of the table, the hot coal sparking inside of her and spreading until she felt like fire was running through her veins, just beneath her skin.

“You said that,” Aften pointed out.

Mila shot a glare at the scout. The flames of the lanterns leapt higher, then faded. She paused, gaze flicking up to them, a sense of foreboding rolling down her spine.

“There are rules about going to Perilee at all,” Rendyn interjected. “No one should be going to the castle, even if there are rumors that we can destroy the Vaim. I still wonder where those came from.” He stared steadily at Aften from his massive wooden seat, carved all over and draped with fur and cushions. His throne, really.

Mila tore her gaze from the ceiling to glare at the Councilman. *You're losing your grasp on these people, Rendyn Sivivan.* She would fill the gap. After all, someone had to, didn't they?

She rounded on the three men again, planting her hands on the surface of the table. “We agreed to wait. We agreed we weren't going to go to Ninian until we found the heir, or at least proof that the heir exists. What were you thinking? You could have made him angry. You could have made everything worse!”

“We didn't,” Thislen said flatly. Again. He folded his arms over his chest, slumping back in his seat like a sulking child. “We told you as much, twice.”

"What you haven't told me is what in the heavens made you think this was a good idea."

"No, what we haven't told you is what we found." Aften leaned forward, nervously fiddling with the end of a sleeve and casting sidelong glances at his father. "The Ruling Council is planning to cull the population again."

The fire inside her died as abruptly as if she'd been doused with water. Her hands went clammy, and a hollow pit opened in her chest. She wiped her palms carefully on her trousers. "I'm sorry, what?"

"Ninian showed us their papers and letters. They were discussing ways to kill off hundreds, if not thousands, of people."

Darran nodded, studying the lanterns overhead. "They kept saying they didn't want to reach a point where resources were scarce, where they'd have to tighten their belts. I think they worried it would be suspicious if Astera reached that point and then half the Gate Quarter died."

Rendyn stood, the loud echo of his chair scraping against stone echoing off the carved walls. "Show me."

"We can't!" Aften stood as well. "We had to put the papers back so they wouldn't know we found them, and if we go back to Perilee—Ninian is dangerous at the best of times."

And this isn't the best of times. Mila frowned. Aften had a point. Her great-grandfather's patience would run out eventually, and it was best not to test it. *Especially not by traipsing into his castle and pestering him about the curse over and over again!*

Her anger threatened to spark to life again. "Exactly what I was saying before. Now you've made it impossible to go back, not just risky."

Aften scowled.

"We're already raising suspicion among the Solfolk," Darran said as he pulled Aften gently down into his seat once more. "If the Vaim haven't stolen those papers before, it would stand out all the more if we did it now."

Thislen's head dropped back against the top of his chair. He sighed.

Mila's teeth ground together. *Is he* bored? *I'm going to strangle him. Why won't he take any of this seriously?* Her nails dug into her palms.

"We decided to leave them behind. All of us, together." Darran turned to stare Rendyn down, whose irritated gaze had never left his son.

"Walk me through everything you did, everything you found. From the beginning." Rendyn circled the table slowly, pacing like a hunting cat to stand at Mila's side.

That was a good idea, though it raised a sour taste in her mouth. She should have thought of it. She was at risk of losing control over this situation if she gave Rendyn half a chance. They couldn't go back to his strangling rules and edicts.

"We went to Perilee, through the side gate," Aften began. "Thislen went to talk to Ninian, and Darran and I—"

"Thislen went alone?" Mila interrupted, her gaze snapping to the thief. "Why?"

Thislen shrugged, not even bothering to lift his head. "I thought I might have a better chance of convincing him. I was alone with him before, after all."

Mila felt a pang of guilt. Thislen had been taken the first time because she couldn't leave well enough alone. Surely he saw how similar these two situations were. He could learn a thing or two from her mistakes!

"What did you talk about?" she pressed.

Now he looked at her, sitting up and meeting her gaze with his own. Once again, his dark eyes were closed to her, offering nothing but a wall she couldn't get past. "That's between Ninian and I."

"We tried to get him to tell us, too, but all we know is that they agreed to meet again in a few days." Aften shrugged, as if it didn't matter.

That was the last straw. Something inside her snapped, and she slammed her hands onto the table. "I am sick of this, Thislen. You have Aften and Darran wrapped around your finger, you have Tamsa mooning after you, but I'm not falling for it! I have been patient. I haven't pried, I haven't forced you to talk to me, I haven't pushed for any answers—until now. This could be important, and you want to keep it a secret? Why? That's all it ever is with you, secrets. Every time I turn around, I stumble over something else you won't talk about."

Thislen's eyes widened with every word. He sat frozen, stunned, as if she'd hit him over the head. Aften, beside him, had his mouth hanging open.

Darran's brows were raised. "I don't think that's very fair, Mila, he told us—"

"I don't care what he told you," she snapped, pointing at the scout. She rounded on Thislen. "I have been your friend through thick and thin, without even knowing a thing about you. I climbed aboard a prison ship to rescue you from people who have already tried to kill me more than once! I have done everything I could to be supportive while you were recovering. Now this? This is too far, Thislen. You said you were going to find us a solution. Either you found one and you won't share it with me, or you didn't and you won't and you're giving us false hope. Which is it?"

"Neither," he insisted, shock turning to a frown.

"Tell me what you and Ninian talked about the first time, then."

"No."

"You're being a horrible friend. After all this, you still don't trust me?"

"It isn't that. I—"

"Maybe you don't know how to be a good friend because you've never had any before, but this isn't how this works." She regretted the acid in her words as soon as she finished saying them.

Thislen looked stunned and hurt. He'd have made the same face if she punched him in the nose. Her stomach twisted. An apology sat right behind her teeth, but...

It's too late. The words are said. I can't take them back, can I?

What was she doing? The frustration with their impossible quest, with each dead end they hit every time they turned around, with her helplessness—all of it boiled out of her at once. She couldn't rein it in, even if she'd wanted to.

Everyone sat perfectly still for one second. Two. Ten. Even Rendyn didn't break the silence. He wasn't at all surprised, just unamused. His gaze slid over all of them, assessing.

No, I haven't lost control. It was a temporary outburst. She could fix this. Her lips parted and—

The sound of Thislen's chair scraping across the floor was impossibly loud in the hush. The firm sound of the door closing behind him reverberated around the chamber as Thislen simply...left.

Mila's heart sank in her chest. *What have I done? I should go after him. I need to find him and...*

And what? What would she say? Thislen wouldn't want to hear an apology, if she could even find him. Her mind raced, trying to puzzle it all out. Only one thought kept surfacing. *I don't want to lose him. He's my friend.*

"Further discussion on these matters can wait, I think," Rendyn said at last, returning to his chair at the head of the table. "You're all late for a patrol, aren't you?"

How can anyone expect me to go on patrol right now?

She took a deep breath. Responsibilities didn't disappear because of a childish spat. Yes, that's what this was. Thislen was being childish. *I'm not entirely wrong. Thislen and his secrets have put us at risk more than once. He's going to have to get over himself and talk to me, or I won't be able to help him the next time he needs me.*

That settled it. Thislen could wait. She started toward the door, beckoning at Darran and Aften. "Come on. Let's go before Trevon comes looking for all of us."

Trevon would be a balm after this disaster. There was no doubt that he was waiting above for them to appear at their usual entrance. Mila didn't hesitate as she led the way into the sloping tunnel and past the lake. A stone fell into the water somewhere, the plop echoing and the ripples creating wavering lights on the ceiling.

When they reached the surface, she nearly crashed into Trevon's back. He certainly was waiting for them.

"Hey, there you are. You're late. What happened?"

Fresh air was exactly what Mila needed. She took a deep breath, looking up at the setting moon overhead. "A lot. I'll tell you everything later."

Darran and Aften emerged as well, closing the hidden door behind them. Aften looked sheepish. Darran didn't seem concerned at all.

Though there was hardly more than a sliver of moon to speak of, she could still see the streets clear enough. She watched the dark shape of Trevon scale a drainpipe. She followed. Movement bled the anger out of her better than anything else could have. The way her arms and legs tensed and relaxed, perching on precarious little ledges as she pulled herself up, took most of her attention.

Cresting the rooftop at last, crouched on the edge, she paused and leaned out.

Red eyes turned toward her, studying her. The streets were left to the wandering Vaim, their irregular movements and jerking steps carrying them through the pantomime of their lives before they died. They were uncanny, their faces twisted in anger Mila wasn't sure they felt.

She shuddered. After so many years of being raised on stories of the murderous spirits, of hearing tales about someone else killed in the night, it was difficult to adjust to being this close even still. *I don't know if I really believe I'm safe, even if I have a blood tie.*

It was easier to navigate Astera from the tiled rooftops. The Vaim had bodies, smokey and indistinct as they were. They couldn't be walked through. Some Nattfolk pushed them to one side or the other like unruly sheep. Mila couldn't imagine touching one.

"We're going toward the water, alright? I want to sweep the shoreline." Trevon rolled his shoulders, waiting for the others to be on their feet before loping down one side of the roof and leaping easily to the one below.

Down the terraced levels of the Goods Quarter they went, until the buildings evened out again at the start of the Guild Quarter. Their group managed both. Two other patrols were assigned to the Grand Quarter and Gate Quarter respectively, both of which were larger and took longer to sweep. The Grand Quarter's crew had to thread their way through the Vaim. The estates of the wealthy and powerful weren't close enough to one another to run the rooftops. The Gate Quarter's scouts traversed the wall that separated it from the rest of Astera in addition to the rooftops, circling their territory twice.

Mila was right where she wanted to be. She liked watching over the Goods Quarter where she'd grown up and traversing the familiar streets that led down through the Guild Quarter. She'd walked those same paths a thousand times as she and her family made their way down to the ships, to spend their nights safely anchored off shore where the Vaim couldn't reach them.

That thought inevitably led her back to her self-appointed task. *I have to break the curse. We should be able to live in our homes, we shouldn't have to go down to the sea every night. What more could we do with our lives if we didn't have to spend all that time traveling?*

Mila leapt across a gap, landing easily on the other side. Slowly, she straightened, her eyes sweeping the sea and the distant twinkling gold of lanterns. She would make the shore safe for the Solfolk, and soon.

Even if it feels hopeless. Doubts crept up the back of her head with a tingle, their poisonous voices whispering in her ears. How would she find one person with hidden relics on an island this size? How long would it take her? Would she succeed, or would someone else have to take up her quest when she was old and bent? Mila had no idea what to do anymore. *This is why whatever Thislen and Ninian spoke of is so important. If he's talking to my grandfather, then maybe he knows something. Maybe he knows where the heir is, or at least where to start looking. That's why he should just* tell *me already!*

Aften ran past her, Darran on his heels. Trevon was already two buildings away. Shaking the thoughts from her head, she took off after them.

They reached the shore moments later. Mila stood on the last rooftop before the water, her eyes trailing over the many docks and piers that stretched out into the water like so many fingers. They were too long and dark, like the Vaim's, and it was easy to imagine that they wanted to grasp the distant ships and drag them back to land.

Somewhere out there was her own neighborhood's ship, now with two empty cabins. What did the tailor and the potter think of her family's mysteriously abandoned shops? What rumors were whispered at the inn?

Did anyone care at all?

"Hey, look!" Aften flung out his hand, shattering the near silence entirely.

The Vaim were reacting. Their heads turned one by one, every glowing red eye fixing on something to the east. Several took off suddenly, hunched over to run on their hands and feet, scurrying at a terrifying pace into the night. Twitching, lurching monoliths turned into darting shadows, quick as arrows loosed from a bow, scuttling like spiders toward the water.

"It's too late for a new arrival," Mila said numbly. *Why does this keep happening?*

The Vaim were already gone. There was a good chance that whatever it was, *who*ever, they would be too late to save them. She was the first to break into a run. Trevon followed hot on her heels. Mila leapt a gap between two rooftops, rolling back to her feet as she landed. Clay clattered beneath her. Her soft-soled boots allowed her to feel the tiles beneath her toes, keeping her from falling as she raced the spirits.

The specters came to a sudden stop, and Mila skidded to a halt above them. A tile slid from the roof, shattering on the cobbles below. Her heart pounded. The Vaim gathered in a crowd, encircling something near the shoreline. As they always did when gathered, the faint hiss of whispers rippled through the shadows like leaves rustling in a breeze.

A soft splash drew Mila's attention. In the water, barely visible, a rowboat full of huddled shapes was making its way back out to sea. They bore no lanterns. She couldn't make out anything distinctive, not even general build—just silhouetted heads on a mass of shoulders, a black blot against the gleam on the surface of the water.

It's Soren. She knew it.

The boat was beyond their reach, but the Vaim were still fixated on something at the edge of the water. Mila was the first of the scouts to ease off the rooftop. *The Vaim will never hurt me. I'm an Ominir.* She held that thought in the forefront of her mind, ignoring her last close encounter with the ghosts, when she was chained to a post and the Nattfolk were going to leave her to their mercy. *I'm one of their masters, now. I am an Ominir.*

That had to mean something.

She reached out to touch them, fighting the urge to recoil. They were solid, their smoke-filled shells giving slightly with each push, like she was touching skin. Cold, cold skin with a faint pulse beneath it. One by one, Mila ushered the Vaim to one side or the other, pushing her way through them.

The sound of a soft boot scuffed the ground behind her. Someone, at least, was following. That helped her nerves.

Mila stepped into the semi-circle the Vaim had formed, standing right on the edge of the shore. The water lapped at the lip of a stone seawall, smacking against it just out of sight below a wooden walkway. The walkway was built above the water, standing on great round posts that were overgrown with barnacles and algae. There was no railing at the edge, nothing separating it from the sea.

Why would Soren row so many people to shore? Everyone knew it was dangerous. Soren should know that most of all. The Ruling Council used the Vaim to eliminate their enemies regularly. The retreating rowboat was indistinct. She kept losing sight of it among the waves. The ocean was a ripple of deep blue and black, glinting white only at the topmost edges. Whoever rowed the boat, though she still felt it was Soren, they'd made a clean escape.

But not all of them.

Mila dropped her gaze. A dark heap lay on the pier before her, surrounded by its audience of ghosts. Their faces were twisted with naked hatred, their baleful eyes fixed on that lump. They watched. They waited, as if they expected the corpse—no, corpses, she realized—to rise again.

She knelt, gently turning over one of the two bodies that fell tangled together.

Mila recoiled, her eyes wide, blood rushing through her ears in a dull roar.

"Hellfires," Trevon breathed beside her, before spitting out a few more choice curses.

"What is it?" Aften called from the rooftop.

Mila's eyes ran over the familiar crest embroidered in the dark tabard. It was too dark to tell the color clearly, but there was no mistaking the marking, even stained as it was with gleaming black spatters of blood. The glassy eyes that stared sightlessly up at the stars belonged to a member of the City Guard.

"Why would they even try to come ashore, especially at this hour?" Trevon asked, echoing Mila's racing thoughts.

She shook her head slowly, stomach sinking. The sudden weight of something truly massive loomed behind her. She whirled, half expecting to see Death itself, waiting with the scales of judgment.

There was nothing there, and the weight still bore down on her shoulders until she felt she would be crushed. Mila didn't have an answer for Trevon, and part of her hoped that her guess—that it was Soren Bestant—was wrong. Still, whoever it was, they were testing the island. They had been for weeks.

They were testing the Vaim.

"We have to tell the Nattfolk about the bodies, all of them, not just the Council," she said, her voice wavering. "I have a bad feeling about this."

"You, too?" Trevon used his foot to push the bodies off the dock and into the sea.

Within moments, dark hands from the Vaim beneath the waves rose from the depths, breaking the surface with their long fingers. They tugged and turned the bodies this way and that before closing around their arms and dragging them down into the dark, cold water.

"I don't know what's going on, but I don't like it." Trevon studied the ships out at sea with a frown.

"I don't either." Mila did know one thing, however. Whatever this was, *who*ever it was?

The Nattfolk were in danger.

19

Water dripped, soft and steady. Not an echo of sound bounced off the undulating natural rock. Thislen had circled the edge of the lake to a small lip. He sat on a stone perch, the cold leeching the heat from his body. He hardly settled in when the flicker of a lantern glowed in the tunnel that led to the Commons. He held his breath, hoping that whoever it was wouldn't see him in the dark. He didn't want to explain himself, and he certainly didn't want company.

From around a column, he saw Mila holding a lantern to guide herself, Darran, and Aften. She scowled, clearly still cross. He leaned back quickly, foot scuffing the ground. A pebble fell into the water. The surface of the lake, crystalline clear, rippled as it sank to the bottom. Mila paused, looking at the surface of the water, then up at the ceiling.

The reflection created by the lantern made dancing lights over the shadowed crevasses above. Thislen held his breath. Mila turned, and the silence was broken by the sound of footsteps. Within one heartbeat, two, the light faded. They were gone.

Thislen hadn't brought a lantern with him. He found out weeks ago that he didn't need to. When there was no light in the cavern at all, a moss on the stones that Olen called 'goblin gold' would begin to glow, painting the walls with mottled sprays of gold and green. It was enough to see. It was enough to reflect off the water of the lake and cast dancing ripples over every surface.

It was a safe retreat. No one bothered to come this far around the edge of the lake, not when they could fetch their water along the path. This was how Thislen preferred it, with the shadows pressing in all around him, alone but for his ghosts. He drew his legs up, wrapping his arms around them and staring at the water as the spirits paced, circling like sharks in the water.

"Well?" whispered a voice beside him.

Percivan's ghost drifted to a stop beside the stone. The blood at his throat still gleamed, though it looked black in the gloom.

"Well what?" The words were heavy, laced with exhaustion. They echoed softly off the walls.

"Do you want to talk about it?"

"He isn't asking the right questions." Garridan's spirit sat at the edge of the lake. When he stuck his legs in, the water didn't even move.

"What questions am I supposed to be asking?"

"Who are we?" Vern stayed in the dark, his voice burbling and damp.

"Where did we come from?" Garridan asked.

"Why are we here?"

Thislen turned to Percivan's ghost at the question, his brow furrowed. "Ninian said it was magic."

"Old magic. Deep magic," Percivan confirmed.

"It bound you here, so you can't go on to the Ancestors. It bound you because of my guilt."

"Did it?" Garridan leaned back on his palms, staring up at the mossy ceiling. His blue-white skin seemed even paler in the thin light. The huge red stain beneath his arm gleamed wetly with his lifeblood, now spilled. "Do you truly feel guilty for killing me?"

No. The thought came before Thislen could answer, and the torturer's ghost turned a knowing look on him.

"If it isn't guilt, then why?"

"Who are we?" Vern asked again, stepping out of the shadow of the column. Water dripped off of his body, keeping time with the distant drip somewhere deeper in the cavern.

Is this a trick question?

"Who are we to you?"

Thislen frowned. "You are people I knew once and can't know any longer. You're strangers, or you used to be. You're figments of my imagination. I've gone mad."

"Ninian saw us. He knows we aren't." Percivan leaned a hip against the stone. "I told you. We're old magic. Deep magic. Magic placed in the earth of the island at its founding, so far down that even Ninian couldn't pull on it for his curse."

"Why are you telling me this?" Thislen hugged his knees tighter.

"You know why."

"I can't help her."

The last echo of his words faded, and still none of the ghosts spoke. None of them moved. Thislen stared at the rippling water.

"Mila thinks the best of everyone. She thinks I'm strong. Infallible. She and all the others think that I can always come in and help, or at least hold my own. Even after the torture, I was left...to pick up the pieces alone. If she finds out that I could help her find the heir, she'd hate me for not saying so sooner. I'm not allowed to make mistakes like that."

"Why?" Garridan asked.

"She'll want me to help, and I'll just fail again. Every time I've tried to help, I failed. I failed when we tried to leave Astera, I failed when I tried to save her from the Vaim, I failed to help her get the vial—twice." Thislen picked up a pebble, throwing it into the water with a *plip*. Ripples ran wild over the ceiling.

"You haven't always failed. You protected Aften and Tamsa from me."

Thislen scoffed. "I did, but barely. I wouldn't have lasted another night."

"But you didn't fail before they came for you. Mila is strong, but so are you. It's just different." Percivan's ghost put his hand over Thislen's, though he couldn't feel it, not even a touch of cool air. "Think of what the two of you could do together."

"I'm not strong, I'm lucky. Everything's been sheer dumb luck."

Vern gave a sodden laugh. "Has it? Or has it been something else guiding your hand? Astera wants her throne filled."

"I'm not going to be able to help Astera with that," Thislen said flatly, turning to stare across the water. In the gloom, the other side wasn't visible. It wasn't difficult to imagine it going on forever, an underground ocean instead of a lake.

I'd sail away from here. I meant to, before I met Mila. Now I'm trapped.

"*You're* trapped?" Vern's ghost laughed again, louder than before.

Garridan shrugged. "I'm tired of being here, and none of us can leave."

"Why?"

None of them answered. They just stared at him, unblinking.

Because of me? Am I keeping them from their Ancestors?

Guilt rose up in a cold wave and sent a shiver down Thislen's spine. He rested his chin on his knees. "I don't want to keep you here."

"Then let us go."

"Percivan, he's not going to." Vern folded his arms over his broad chest.

"He will."

"He doesn't know how."

Thislen turned with a frown, meeting Vern's bloated face. His eyes were red around the iris, his lips blue, his hair stuck clinging to his forehead. He didn't shy away from Thislen's stare.

Garridan's ghost rose from shore, coming to stand before Thislen. His skin was too pale, bloodless and cold. A fountain of red flowed down his side, but never seemed to reach the ground.

"Own up. Tell them. That's how you do it," he said.

His arguments were wearing thin, and he knew it. Still, Thislen didn't want to face the future the specters wanted. "None of them will understand why I didn't say anything."

"And? What, you don't think you're strong enough to handle their anger? They're already mad at you, Thislen." Garridan leaned down until his nose was inches away.

"Garridan tortured you for weeks," Percivan said, gently pulling Garridan away. "You never broke. What's an argument compared to actual, physical torture?"

I'm not ready. How do I know I can really trust my friends?

If he said it, everything would change. The world as they all knew it would be irrevocably different, no matter what happened next. Would they forgive him for keeping the heir secret all this time? *I only know who it is by chance. It could have happened to anyone.*

"But it didn't. It happened to you." Vern's impatience was growing.

"Things are coming to a head," Percivan said. He folded his arms on the stone beside Thislen, pillowing his head on them. The gold thread on his doublet glittered as he moved. "We're getting stronger with every passing day."

It was true. He saw them all the time now. They were there every time he turned around. He could feel their eyes on his back if he ignored them. "This really isn't a side effect of Ninian's curse?"

"Do we look like Vaim?" Garridan spread his arms, turning slowly on the spot.

Thislen rolled his eyes. "No. What are you, then?"

Percivan touched the black stain at his neck, thoughtfully studying his two companions. "We're an unanticipated side effect, I think. This was coming from the start, from the moment you met Mila."

He remembered her turning, the golden light of morning pouring through the door behind her. The light haloed her. She glowed. His shoulder burned and his head swam. The moment their eyes met, he fell.

Was that because of the Vaim and their poison, or was it something stronger?

She was his first connection on the island, the first person he ever wanted to help. One by one, he built others around her. Some he sought, like Tamsa. Some he dreaded. Despite his best efforts, the tangled threads of a community built around him anyway. He couldn't lie to himself any longer and pretend they didn't exist. He *did* want to help the Nattfolk. He wanted to help Astera. As much as he said it was only for Mila, it wasn't true. Without thinking, he'd stepped up to defend Tamsa and her brother in the belly of *Ship Artaith*.

To think all of this began with accepting a single nobleman's request to share a rowboat.

Percivan gave a soft smile.

"And it led to you murdering me in cold blood." Garridan folded his arms across his chest.

Thislen hoped talking to Ninian about that would offer some solace, some ancient wisdom, but the spirit hadn't been any comfort. The Artaith family was on his list for revenge, and Ninian had been giddy with delight knowing Thislen killed one.

All I wanted was for someone to tell me it wasn't the end of who I wanted to be. Now here I am, looking at myself, and wondering why I don't recognize my own face.

He leaned forward to study his dim reflection in the water. Dark wavy hair, dark eyes, a strong nose. The hint of a beard darkened his jaw, though he shaved a few days ago. He frowned.

"I never wanted to kill you, you know. I never wanted to kill anyone."

Vern scoffed. Garridan barked out a roaring laugh. The sound echoed off the cavern walls.

"We were fighting. It was my life or yours," Thislen said.

The laughter stopped abruptly.

"For all of you, it was my life or yours."

Percivan's smile turned sad, the light going out of his eyes. "You needed to make it this far. Now you're Astera's only hope."

"I don't want that."

"You don't want this, you don't want that," Vern mocked. "Haven't you realized that what you want doesn't matter if you *want* to save this kingdom?"

Thislen let out a frustrated sound that reverberated through the chamber, pushing off the rock to pace along the water's edge. "That's part of the problem. What if I fail again? What if, in the end, the heir isn't what they want?"

"Failure is part of life, my mother always said," Vern murmured.

"That's not good enough."

"Neither, it seems, are you." Garridan grinned as he circled Thislen, looking him up and down.

"Tell me how to make you go away."

"We have," Vern said sharply.

"Tell me plain!"

"You have to tell them. You know you do," Percivan said softly. "One will lead to two. Two to three, and three to many."

Vern stepped close, his hand resting on Thislen's shoulder. He could feel the weight of it, but nothing else. Not hot or cold or wet, though his skin glistened with sea water.

"You've met these people. You avoided it for as long as you could, but now you know them. Every day, you come to know them more. Don't you want to help them?"

Yes.

The sailor leaned in, whispering in Thislen's ear. "Then do something about it."

He had to tell Mila, plain and simple. She'd be furious, but perhaps he could soften the blow. "I need to find Olen, Evelie, or Ivan."

"You won't find them here," Garridan said flatly.

Thislen set off around the edge of the lake as quick as he could with the dim light hiding any number of hazards, picking his way back to the path with the heavy feeling of his ghosts behind him.

It took only moments to get from the lake cavern to the Commons. The brilliant torchlight blinded him. His eyes watered as he threaded his way through the crowds toward the cavern Mila shared with her family. Dawn would arrive sooner than Thislen would like.

I'm going to tell her before sunset tomorrow.

He paused outside the thick, heavy drapes that covered the cave entrance, lifting his hand to the metal ring beside the door.

"Thislen," Percivan said, interrupting him.

Thislen froze, glancing over his shoulder.

"I don't know how long this magic will last after you tell. Before I go, I need to ask a favor."

If you ask me to find Soren again—

"No! No, I want you to take care of Arman. I want you to save my brother."

Thislen's eyes widened. He'd nearly forgotten about the youngest—and now only—Coppermund son. The List flashed in his mind, a neat hand condemning a young man he'd never met. "Can you see him, like Ninian can see inside Perilee?"

"No." Percivan dropped his gaze. "But I can feel him running out of time. I can feel my entire family running out of time."

"You can...sense death?" Thislen asked falteringly.

"We all can," Vern said.

Questions rose in his mind, but Thislen pushed them down again. "I'll help him, if I can. I'll help Arman."

Percivan smiled, putting his hand over his heart. "Thank you," he said, bowing.

It was little more than a slight bend at the waist, but Thislen had never been bowed to before. It felt strange.

"Don't do that," Thislen murmured. "Please don't ever do that again. I'm not nobility. I'm just some street thief."

"Hello? Someone there?"

Thislen turned away from the ghosts as the curtain in front of him was pushed aside. Ivan stared at him for a moment before his face broke out in a tired smile.

"Thislen. I thought you might be my scout captain. Have you met Amelie? She's terrifying. She's been after me all week to practice my swordwork more."

"I haven't met her. Ivan, I need to talk to you. I need your help."

The urgency in Thislen's voice gave Ivan pause. He looked up and down the corridor, eyes lingering on a few Nattfolk down the way. "Why don't you come inside?"

Thislen slipped into the cavern. He didn't hesitate. As soon as they were safely behind the heavy drape, Thislen pulled Ivan down and whispered into his ear.

Ivan's eyes widened. "You...you knew this entire time," he said numbly.

"I did."

"You didn't say anything. Ancestors, Mila's going to be furious. Why didn't you say you knew where everything was? The hairbrush, the pendant, the—"

"Yes, all that and more. I've seen it. I know exactly where it is. Help me tell her."

"She's still going to yell at you, you know." Ivan grimaced.

Thislen scowled, pulling the curtain aside. "Just help me soften the blow, will you?"

With a shrug, Ivan stepped into the corridor. A girl ran past him, no more than eight or nine, calling down the corridor to what must have been her older siblings.

"Wait for me!"

They weren't the only people hurrying toward the Commons, either. Urgency filled the air, carried in tense expressions and low murmurs.

Thislen pushed past Ivan. He walked quickly, on the brink of running. The murmurs grew louder, then louder still. When he and the florist-turned-scout burst into the Commons, it was to find the massive chamber was full. Far more full than it ought to be, this close to dawn. People crowded shoulder to shoulder, and the whole place was packed tight as fish in a barrel.

"This must be every Nattfolk there is!" Ivan looked around the room at the press of bodies. "Why are they here?"

Thislen caught sight of a familiar fall of curls among the crowd and dove in, threading between bodies where he could, and using elbows where he couldn't.

He caught Tamsa's wrist. "What's going on?"

Her expression was tense, her lips pursed thin.

Something's wrong. Very wrong.

"What is it?" he asked breathlessly.

"No one else can know," she said, stepping close to whisper in his ear.

His heart began to pound.

Tamsa led him to the long, low corridor that housed the Night Council. Though the crowd was gathered thickest at the mouth of the tunnel, none of the Nattfolk went any further. Eyes turned toward them as Tamsa broke free of the throng, and the murmurs rose in volume.

Thislen's knee ached as he hurried after her, brace creaking. He was nearly holding his breath. He waited until the murmurs faded behind them before speaking. "Tamsa, tell me what happened."

"Trevon's patrol came back. Mila and Trevon came down and started spouting orders, sending scouts to gather the Night Council right away. Someone said they saw blood, but I couldn't get more than that out of them."

"Someone was hurt?" Thislen pulled her to a stop. "Who?"

"I don't know. I don't even know if they were hurt or someone else was. Come on, they've already gathered. I had to change."

Thislen glanced over his shoulder as he followed Tamsa again, a momentary pang of realization passing through him. His ghosts weren't there anymore. He couldn't feel them, not since he told Ivan what he knew.

Ivan, he thought with a grimace. He'd left him behind in the Commons. *Well, he'll have to wait.*

Thislen frowned as they neared the wooden wall that divided the stone passage into the Night Council Chamber. He was meant to be with Trevon's patrol, with

Mila, Darran, Aften, and the scout captain. Whatever happened, was it because he wasn't there?

They reached the door. He didn't bother to knock. Instead, he cracked it open and slid through, hoping to go unnoticed. Tamsa was right on his heels. They made hardly a stir. Aften and one of the council members noticed them, but they said nothing and quickly turned their attention back to the chaos around the table.

Aften, Darran, and every scout captain available stood in a cluster near the door, shielding Thislen and Tamsa from view as they entered. Rendyn Sivivan sat in his throne-like wooden seat, head resting on his hand and brow furrowed. Trevon and Mila stood at the opposite end. Mila planted her hands on the polished surface, her jaw set as she leaned forward. The Night Council itself was arrayed on either side of the massive wooden table, every one of them talking over one another. The air was full of barely contained panic.

Tamsa shot Thislen a tight, worried look.

"I am *telling* you, there's no way I could have made a mistake." Mila's voice cut through the din like the crack of a whip. She stared Rendyn down. "Believe me, I know what I saw. I grew up with the Solfolk, I saw their tabards every day."

Tabards? What tabards do you see every—

Thislen's eyes widened. The City Guard? Why was Mila talking about the City Guard? He went cold all over. The small, 'x' shaped scar beneath his collarbone ached, the mark of a thief caught twice over. He and the City Guard were far from friendly, especially after the past few moons.

"I saw it, too. There was a crest embroidered on the fabric, they wore chainmail shirts, they had weapons on their belts. There were two of them, dead and still warm."

"And the rowboat?" Rendyn asked calmly.

Thislen shuddered. It was clear that the head of the council believed the tale, even if the rest of them didn't. Yet. That did not bode well.

"It was there, and full of people. I don't know how many exactly, and I don't know who." Mila straightened, folding her arms over her chest.

Soren Bestant. It had to be. He'd seen Darran when they saved the Solwalker from him. There'd been no shock on his face at all when Mila climbed aboard the *Bestant Belle* to help Thislen and Trevon when they failed to get the vial. Soren knew, or guessed, and began to experiment with people he no doubt saw as disposable, replaceable, and unimportant. *Those poor guards.*

Thislen frowned at the floor as he listened to the Council questioning Mila and Trevon at length, to the scout captains asking questions, to the plans being laid. Soren Bestant was testing the defenses of the Vaim, of the Nattfolk. Soren guessed, or maybe already knew, that some people could remain on Astera's shore at night.

There would be a fight.

His heart sank in his chest. *If I tell her what I know now, it will leave the Nattfolk without one of their most important defenses. If anyone at all can set foot on the island, they'll be overwhelmed. I can't tell her. Not until this is over.*

The Nattfolk's very existence was protected by the Solfolk belief that the monstrous Vaim left no one alive. Without that, Soren Bestant would attack to test their strength or lack of it. With the Vaim as a deterrent, there'd be few volunteers and fewer soldiers who could stay on shore—another secret lost to the nobleman's experiments, even if he didn't know exactly how the Vaim chose who to kill.

No, if he told Mila about the heir now, she would be too tempted to do something about the curse. He knew she would be needed for the upcoming battle. She was a general in all but name. His secrets could wait a bit longer. Still, he wanted to speak to her. He owed her that much.

While the Night Council hotly debated what to do, who needed to go where, and what preparations were most important, Thislen slipped past Darran and clasped Mila's shoulder. She glanced back at him. He wasn't sure if he'd imagined the faint relief in her face or not.

"Thislen, there you are. I found—"

"I heard. Mila, if there's anything I can do to help, anything you need..." He poured every ounce of sincerity he had into the words, hoping she would read his resolve to do better by her. He'd give her a proper apology later, when they weren't standing in the middle of a crowd.

The relief this time was real and clear. Mila smiled. "Thanks, Thislen. After this whole mess is settled, let's find a time to talk, alright?"

He nodded. He couldn't tell if Mila forgave him or not, but at least she was willing to talk. Hopefully she would listen, too. That was a start.

Thislen drew away, returning to his spot at Tamsa's side. She gave him a small, taut smile, her fingers brushing against his. He slipped his hand into hers and gave it a small squeeze. His eyes drifted over the chattering crowd.

These are my people, all of them. I need to protect them—and when they're safe, I'll tell Mila what she needs to know. One thing at a time.

For now, his focus would have to be on the start of this war.

Aften leaned against Darran, curled up in his bunk in the Barracks with the curtain drawn. It was nearly noon, but Aften couldn't sleep.

"Talk to me," Darran murmured, pressing his lips softly to his temple.

"What? What do you mean?"

"I know you well enough to see when you're tying yourself up in knots. Your mind is a thousand miles away. Bring me with you."

Aften sighed, lacing his fingers with Darran's. "I've never met Solfolk soldiers. I've never met any proper soldiers in my life."

"Neither have I." Darran's voice had gone grim.

"Scouts are the closest we have, and Darran...*we're* scouts."

The former scout captain said nothing, laying his head back against the cushions.

"We weren't trained to kill. We're not actually fighters, not the way they are. When they come..."

When, not if. Everyone agreed on that much. When they came, they would come with as large a force as they could muster. They'd been testing for weeks, seeing who could and couldn't survive the Vaim. All of the ghosts' strange behavior was suddenly explained in the worst way possible. Who knew how many soldiers would land on Astera's shore?

No one is talking about what comes next, though. What comes after the fight. If we survive, what do we do with the bodies? Will there be another fight after that? Why can't we just hide?

He knew the answer to that one. They could very easily lock themselves below in the Commons and last a few weeks, but eventually they would need supplies. Food, mostly. The farms on the outskirts of Astera might be safe for a while, but eventually the soldiers would spread out. It would get too dangerous to go up. They'd have to fight anyway, only then they would be hungry, weak, and outnumbered.

Aften buried his face in his hands. "I don't want to fight."

It was just like on the ship. He knew he would break. He knew he wouldn't be able to take someone else's life. If he couldn't do that, he'd be killed.

Darran kissed the side of his head again, lips lingering as he murmured. "Your heart is too soft, you care too much. I don't want to see you lose that, either. What do you want to do?"

"What *can* I do?" A frustrated, disgusted noise escaped him. "We need every eye we've got, so I'll be out there patrolling with the rest of you. I just...don't know what I'll do when the fighting starts. If I run away..."

He could picture Rendyn's reaction to that, to finding out his son was a coward. As strained as things between them were before, they would only get worse.

"I don't think you will. You're stronger than you give yourself credit for, Aften. You're braver. I can see it in everything you do. You're gentle, but you're not a coward. Anyone who can't tell the difference between those things is blind."

Aften gave a helpless laugh, rolling over to rest his head on Darran's chest. Darran's arm encircled him, warmth sinking through his shirt. "You'll be careful, won't you? When it starts."

"I promise I will."

"I don't like this."

"I don't think we're supposed to like it, Aften." Darran shifted until he was flat, pulling the blanket up over them both. "We need to try and sleep. Tomorrow night is going to be..."

Aften sighed. Darran didn't need to finish that sentence. Even if nothing happened at all, they would be making preparations.

"Our entire lives," Aften whispered, "we've been the greatest secret on the island. Now someone knows. I thought it would have been louder."

"What do you mean?"

"I never thought the realization that we've been discovered would creep up on us like this. We almost didn't know at all."

The covers rustled, but Darran didn't speak. The silence stretched on. Aften closed his eyes with a sigh. *Everyone is at a loss. None of us expected this, not in our lifetime. Not in the next. I'm afraid, but I'm not the only one.*

It was everywhere, on every face, in every word, even filling the very air. The Night Council explained to the Nattfolk they thought their presence was discovered. The news didn't go over well. Dozens of people cried. Children wailed and needed soothed. Elder scouts grimly offered to pick up their weapons again. Some people demanded weapons training. Some begged to retreat to the forest at the feet of the Spine. No decisions were made before Rendyn sent everyone to sleep with promises to speak more in the morning.

He won't be sleeping either. For all that Aften and Rendyn were at odds, the man did care about the Nattfolk.

Darran's arm slowly went slack. His breathing grew deep and even. Still, Aften lay awake, pondering the same questions as the Night Council, wanting only to spare his people, to save the only life he'd ever known. No longer was his head full of fantasies of the sun. There was a chance he'd never see the sun rise again. There was a chance that dozens, if not hundreds, of Nattfolk would die.

None of us are fighters.
What are we going to do?
I'm not a soldier.
What am I going to do?

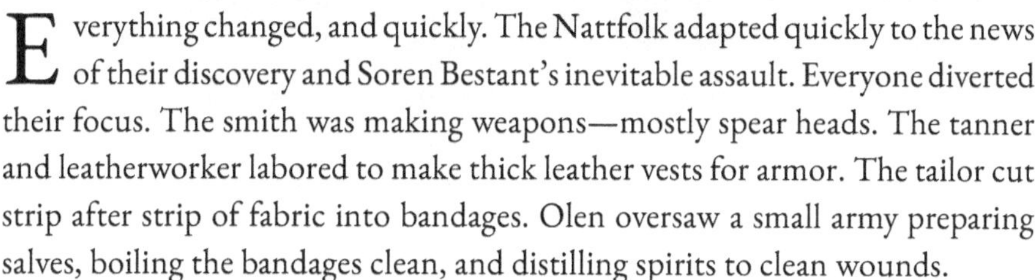

20

Everything changed, and quickly. The Nattfolk adapted quickly to the news of their discovery and Soren Bestant's inevitable assault. Everyone diverted their focus. The smith was making weapons—mostly spear heads. The tanner and leatherworker labored to make thick leather vests for armor. The tailor cut strip after strip of fabric into bandages. Olen oversaw a small army preparing salves, boiling the bandages clean, and distilling spirits to clean wounds.

Thislen tried to pull Mila aside any number of times, but she was at the center of everything. Most of her time was spent surveying preparations, planning the patrol routes alongside the scout captains, and in training. The Night Council had her in meetings with them half the night, telling them everything she could remember of the City Guard and the nobility she'd encountered.

Thislen thought about telling them what he knew, too, but he didn't want to be treated like a general, like Mila was. He let her take the brunt of their demands.

The scouting patrols were the first thing to change. Groups of six were reconfigured into groups of four and positioned along the shoreline only to keep watch. There were no more early or late patrols. Every scout stayed out all night without a single complaint. No one wanted to be caught unawares, so they roved back and forth, their eyes constantly on the Vaim below.

More than once, the scouts reported that Vaim had darted to the shore. Twice, more bodies were found. Rowboats were spotted, but their assailants remained unseen. They bore no lanterns. Ever.

Thislen knew it was Soren. He could feel it in his veins, rushing through him with every pulse of his heart. He knew, he *knew*, but he never got the chance to find out.

Thislen had been pulled from Trevon's unit when the groups were split. He had been placed with Ivan, Amelie, and Penni instead. They ran the portion of the Gate Quarter near the shipyard, and it was quiet as a grave.

Amelie was a strong older woman with a handsome face and a hawk-like nose. Streaks of gray colored her hair and wrinkles adorned her skin, but despite her age she was limber and strong. She rarely spoke unless she had to, usually to correct her charges on techniques. It chafed Thislen when she picked at how he ran the rooftops or corrected his stance. His brace, his knee, forced him to change how he moved. He couldn't help that.

Ivan was an unexpected saving grace. As night after night crept by, Ivan and Thislen grew closer to one another. Ivan didn't press Thislen to tell Mila the identity of the heir, nor bring the subject up again. Instead, the pair of them took turns leaping rooftops under Amelie's gaze or training with their weapons on the flat top of a tenement. Thislen instructed Ivan in better ways to wear his weapons and gave him pointers on how to hide a blade or two on his person. Ivan gave Thislen advice on interacting with people, a skill he'd long neglected in his efforts to stay hidden.

Within a week, Thislen had become Penni and Ivan's trainer, and the three of them sparred each night. When they weren't beating at one another with swords, they spoke of whetstones, oils, mending leather, and strength exercises. Anything to fill the air and pass the time.

After the second week passed with nothing happening, Thislen began to offer suggestions to his scout captain. To his surprise, Amelie took every one.

By the end of the moon, the power in the squadron shifted. Thislen was in charge in all but name. And still, his patrol had very little to do. Their stretch was silent, and all they heard were the reports of the other scouts at dawn.

A month after the discovery of the first guard, Thislen sat on the edge of a rooftop, legs dangling. Behind him, Ivan and Penni were flirting through a debate on which mineral oil was better for keeping leather supple. They'd grown closer every night. He guessed they'd be courting within a fortnight.

Damn it all. Something is coming, something more than this. The silence pressed around him, sitting heavy on his shoulders like a stone yoke. *It feels like seeing a heap of wood before it turns into a bonfire. Where is the spark?*

Thislen couldn't help his relief at the fact that Mila was running with Aften and Trevon. Darran had been given back his title of scout captain and ran a different group. Tamsa had been given a command as well. They were all spread out and he found it soothing. Only a few of them would be in danger at a time.

Look at me, sitting here and fretting over them. Not just them, either. I know the name of every scout, now. He sighed. This was what giving in looked like, what helping looked like. He wished it didn't feel so...*right.*

"Thislen," Ivan called softly, interrupting his thoughts. "Help us settle a debate. I told Penni your twist of the wrist trick could be used with any size weapon, if you can get in close enough."

"And I told Ivan that can't be true." Penni folded her arms over her chest, a mischievous twinkle in her eye.

"Show us?" Ivan grinned.

Thislen rolled his eyes, his mood lightening. He glanced at the full moon as he stood and dusted himself off. It sat high in the sky, marking the midnight hour by bathing the streets in silver.

Amelie sat cross-legged nearby, going over her arrows and keeping an eye on all three of them. As Thislen stretched, easing the stiffness out of his knee and adjusting his brace, she spoke up. "Remember to save some of your energy. We've bells to go yet."

"He needs to work on his knife grip before I can show him anything, that's half the problem," Thislen pointed out, gesturing for Ivan to stand.

"I thought I was getting better."

"You're never done learning. Now, go slow to start." Thislen rolled his shoulders and drew a dagger from his belt.

Penni retreated to sit by Amelie with a grin. "You can do it, Ivan. This time for sure!"

Thislen stepped forward with exaggerated movements, stabbing his knife toward Ivan's gut at a snail's pace. Ivan watched, then grabbed his wrist, stepped to the side, and pinned Thislen's arm beneath his, trapping it. A twist of the wrist and—the moment it began to hurt, Thislen dropped the knife. Ivan let go, scooping it up and raising it to defend himself.

Thislen didn't even bother to do the entire maneuver. He simply stepped forward and struck just beneath Ivan's wrist. The scout's fingers jumped. He fumbled, struggling to regain his grip on the knife.

Thislen plucked it from the tangle of fingers and hands, flipping it easily in his hand and dropping back into the starting position. "This is what I meant when I said your grip isn't right. You need to loosen up."

Ivan nodded, a determined look on his face.

Penni clapped quietly, laughing. "Thousandth time is the charm!"

Ivan stuck his tongue out at her, and Thislen began the movement again. Ivan twisted, pinning his arm and taking the knife. He turned back with a triumphant look on his face, raising it once more. "We should do it with a sword next."

Thislen didn't move. His eyes were fixed on a burst of yellow light beyond Ivan's shoulder.

"Is this part of the training, too? Patience or something?" Ivan asked.

Amelie looked up from her arrows. She inhaled sharply, shoving them back into the quiver.

Penni ran over to Ivan, spinning him around just as another bloom of torchlight grew below. Another two were lit in almost no time at all, little bobbing specks like fireflies, lighting one of the great stone berths of the shipyard so their bearers could see.

Thislen couldn't count how many there were, but it was certainly larger than a token force. *Seventy? One hundred?* His heart pounded in his chest.

Amelie swore softly. "This is too many for us to handle alone."

"Run," Thislen said, turning to them. "All of you, run. Amelie, go underground and get as much help as you can. Penni, you're fastest, so you go to the Grand Quarter and then circle back. Ivan, go along the shore from here and send everyone you find."

"But what about you?" Ivan asked softly.

Thislen found himself saying words he never thought would come from his lips. "I can't run far or fast, not with this knee. Someone has to buy time, right? Might as well be me."

What am I doing? When did I become the sort to martyr myself for others? Ancestors, please, don't let me die a fool.

His mouth was dry, his blood rushing in his ears. For the others, however, he maintained a mask of calm, taking his dagger out of Ivan's hand and sheathing it with a *snick*.

Amelie clasped his shoulder before she turned to leap off the roof, rolling as she landed and coming up at a dead run. Ivan turned to run along the shore's rooftops, and Penni, though she hesitated and cast a glance over her shoulder, set off quick as a hare for the Grand Quarter on the other side of the island.

Right. I can't let them leave the shipyard. They'll be too hard to find and too hard to fight in the streets.

As soon as the thought left his head, he was moving. He didn't look back for any last glimpse of his friends. The Solfolk on the shore were setting their torches up in a perimeter. Thislen was running out of time. They'd form up after their base of operations was established. The Nattfolk had to strike now, before the soldiers were organized.

Thislen dropped from the rooftops to the ground two streets away from the shipyard. His knee throbbed. He ignored it. The Vaim were all lurching toward the invaders, creating a river of shadows that Thislen threaded his way through. Every one of the specters had their ember red eyes fixed in the direction of the torches, drawn forward like moths to the flames.

Thislen pressed himself up against the tar-and-plaster side of a building to catch his breath. Around the corner was only a short stretch of dark street, and then the wooden walkway that encircled the stone berth. The torches were tied to the railings, forming a horseshoe shape of protective light.

Protective, because the Vaim wouldn't step out of the shadows into the ruddy glow. They hissed softly around him, like waves on the shore. Thislen pulled up the mask of his mottled black and gray leathers and stood among them, just one more blot of shadow in the night.

It was the City Guard, though none of them bore their tabards. Mail shirts shone bare in the torch glow. Dozens of them. Thislen's guess hadn't been far off. *This is why it took Soren so long. He wanted to come in force.*

If that was his goal, he succeeded. Every soldier was armed and armored. Thislen saw bows, swords, maces, and a handful of axes. The way their chainmail shirts gleamed with every movement reminded Thislen of a fish just beneath the surface of the water, its scales flashing in waves. He took grim satisfaction in watching them glance at the sea of red eyes ringing them in on three sides, their unease thick enough he could almost taste it.

They'd been convinced they wouldn't be torn apart instantly, but they were clearly still terrified of the taloned specters. *How much gold did Soren offer to get them to do this?* He hoped their conviction would break quickly and they would retreat. Their rowboats were all drawn up on the stone surface, waiting.

One of the Vaim lifted its hand, reaching into the circle of light. Nothing happened but that its pitch black form turned smoky and gray. Others lifted their arms, fingers drifting through the air as if brushing through cobwebs. The light didn't hurt them. No, it was more like when Thislen and Mila had first come ashore. The Vaim weren't afraid, they were *curious.*

None of the soldiers, many of whom were pulling their weapons as they watched the Vaim experiment with the torchlight, had the blood of the Ruling Council in their veins. Every single one must have had to set foot on Astera at night and wait to see if they would die. Some lucky few may have been saved before the Vaim got to them, considering how few bodies the Nattfolk found. Some may have fallen to the spirits in the water.

At least Soren can't come ashore. Whoever is giving the orders here, it isn't him or his cronies.

"Alright, you lot. Form up. We're to sweep the city, ignore the ghosts, and dispatch any living person you see who isn't in armor." The captain who spoke had a plume on his open-faced helmet and carried himself with a puffed chest.

Mutters rose from those gathered as they shifted their feet. Several adjusted their hold on their weapons, gripping them close. Others set out the last of the supplies, glancing constantly at the ghosts looming nearby. One pair of soldiers stood near the mouth of the street where Thislen hid, tucked safely within the torchlit circle. Their eyes ran back and forth over the creatures, but they never saw him, a shadow amongst the dead.

"I still don't see how anyone *can* live on Astera at night," one soldier muttered.

"We are. Right now, even. Look at us."

"We lost two dozen people testing all those units! Who can tell for sure if the monsters will leave us alone once we start walking the streets? This is madness. We shouldn't be here."

A third soldier stepped up beside them. "Orders are orders."

"How can you say that?" The first soldier paused for a long moment. "Who are these people we're supposed to kill anyway?"

"They say they're the ones controlling the spirits. If we kill every one of them, the Vaim will disappear." The second soldier scanned the dark windows of the buildings around them.

Thislen clenched his teeth, fighting down a rising tide of anger. *A bald-faced lie buried in hope, just to get these people to kill us. They don't even know—*

They didn't. They *didn't* know who the Nattfolk were, many of them innocents who had never seen the sun in their lives. Children would be found. The elderly would be slaughtered. There were so many who couldn't defend themselves. The Commons might not get discovered tonight, but the soldiers would come again tomorrow, and the next night, and the next. If they didn't stop them here, it was only a matter of time. How many would lose their lives?

Still...

These soldiers don't deserve to die in this fight. Why? Why is it like this? The rich and powerful didn't care what happened to these men and women, didn't care what lies they had to tell to get them to fight and die for their cause. The City Guard thought they were saving Astera.

The Nattfolk *knew* they were.

Does that make us better? Does that make it easier? Solfolk or Nattfolk, we're still Asteran.

The captain gave a sharp whistle. "That's enough dawdling. Come on, all of you. We know what's at stake here. Line up, let's get our patrols assigned and get started."

Thislen's eyes narrowed. If they formed up, they'd be harder to fight. If they split into groups, there was no promise that the Nattfolk would be able to find all the soldiers in the streets. He didn't like either option.

Time had run out. There was no sign of help, no stir amongst the Vaim that might have been a Nattfolk. It was up to Thislen and Thislen alone to do something. Before he could think about it too much, he forced his feet to move. He pulled his hood down as he went, stepping out of the Vaim and into the light of the torches.

A startled shout erupted from the Guard nearest him, causing others to jump, to recoil, to whirl with their weapons drawn.

Thislen drew himself up. "Stop. You can't go any further than this. Get back in your boats and leave, this city isn't yours at night."

"Ancestors," A guardswoman breathed. "There really are people living on the island at night." She was pale, her hands trembling.

Thislen drew his sword slowly, letting the blade catch the light. He watched the City Guard pull back, every eye fixed on him.

"Do not come any closer. Turn away. This is your last warning. Leave, or I'll set the Vaim on you."

It was a desperate bluff, playing on their fears that the Nattfolk controlled the spirits, but it would do what he needed it to do. It would buy time, for him and for the scouts alike. Thislen prayed that the soldiers wouldn't want to press their luck.

"You don't control the Vaim. No one can control the Vaim!" A guard shouted dismissively, shouldering his way to the front. "You can't make them come any closer any more than you could send them away entirely. There's no magic!"

"Is there not? Can I not?" Thislen raised his arms to either side, his words loud and firm.

The hair on every part of Thislen's body stood on end as the Vaim, all at once, took a single step forward. Their whispers grew into a hiss, the mutter of words he couldn't make out pressing in on every side. His heart hammered away in his chest. He fought to keep the shock off his face.

Can I...control the Vaim? Or is this Ninian?

It would be just like the mage to play along, to find this amusing. Somehow, he was tied to the ghosts through his curse. Somehow, he kept an eye on everything that was happening. Help was not something Thislen thought to negotiate for when he visited the long-dead mage, but now he was very seriously considering it. No matter what debt the spirit laid on his shoulders, in this moment it was worth it.

The guards retreated three steps for the Vaim's one, shouting and stumbling into one another. Two slipped, landing dangerously near the edge of the water. They were quick to scramble to their feet again and press forward against their fellows.

"It's just him. Kill him, and the ghosts will leave us be," the captain barked.

They began to move, drawing their weapons and keeping a cautious eye on the spirits.

"There are many more Vaim and many more Nattfolk than there are soldiers on this shore," Thislen shouted, stopping the advancing soldiers in their tracks. "I am your only warning. I am your last chance."

He swept his sword up, the tip pointed directly at the rowboats.

"Leave!"

The captain began to laugh, a harsh sound edged with unease. A few soldiers joined in, the entire group balancing on the edge of a knife. One push and they would fall. One last blow and some of them, at least, might leave.

"He's bluffing. Where are they then, these others? There's no one here but you, and you've made the mistake of coming right to us. I swear to you," the captain shouted, turning to his soldiers, "if we kill him, we kill the Vaim. For Astera!"

The captain lifted his sword, roaring as he charged the wooden steps at Thislen's feet. Thislen adjusted his stance, lifting his sword and waiting for his first foe to come closer.

This is it. How many can I stop before I die?

He took a deep breath, a strange calm settling over him with a tingle like snowflakes on his skin.

Thwump. The captain's shoulder jerked back only a few steps shy of the walkway. His wide eyes slid from Thislen's face to the arrow sticking out of his chest. He breathed out in a sigh, his sword falling from numb fingers, and fell to his knees. The soldier's eyes closed, and he crumpled sideways onto the stone.

Thislen barely resisted the urge to look back over his shoulder. That arrow could belong to anyone, but part of him hoped it was Tamsa's, that she'd been close enough to reach him first. She was a damn good shot.

That doesn't matter, damn it. He pushed the thoughts from his head. What mattered was that the Nattfolk made it. They were here. He wasn't alone.

The guardsmen were in an uproar as their leader died. Some retreated, but only a few. The rest surged forward as one with a roar. Thislen braced himself, mind racing.

What if only one patrol has arrived? What if all they have are bows? What if it's just me, a lone swordsman, trying to hold off the tide alone? Four, at most. Four bows, and however many arrows they have, and me on my own in the melee.

The guardsman drew up short one after the other, their eyes drawn to movement amongst the Vaim.

Leather-clad figures were stepping into the torchlight one by one, their weapons raised. Not all of the leathers were the mottled uniform of the scouts, either. Browns and greens were scattered here and there – some of the others had come from the Commons to protect their home. Every single Nattfolk bore a grim, determined expression on their faces.

Amelie made it.

The enemy milled reluctantly in the center of the smooth stone. With their captain dead, there was no one to spur them on. Three more peeled away and ran for the single rowboat that was loaded with retreating soldiers.

Someone shouted from within the armored throng. "None of them are in armor. None of them are true soldiers! Mow them down, damn it. For Astera!"

"For Astera!"

The roar went up as their weapons did and the soldiers scattered like birds from the bushes, spreading out to attack every Nattfolk they could see.

"Wait," Thislen shouted, throwing up a hand and arresting several Nattfolk as they stepped forward. "Wait for it."

His heart was racing, his blood singing in his veins. He still felt calm all the way through his core, his eyes fixed on the oncoming charge.

The first pair of boots hit the wooden steps below.

"Now!"

Arrows whistled through the night air, picking off guardsmen at the back of the charge or those climbing the steps on either side of the stone berth instead of the center. Nattfolk surged forward like charging horses, their silence an eerie counterpoint to the guardsmen's shouts.

Thislen himself led the charge, throwing himself toward the first man up the steps. The sound of metal on metal screeched in his ears, the force of impact shuddering up his arms and making his teeth rattle.

The battle was on.

21

C haos.

Thislen's world narrowed to what was directly in front of him. Everything moved as fast as flickering lightning and as slow as if it were underwater at the same time. Metal gleamed in the torchlight, orange and red flashing off sword and chainmail, off darting arrowhead and dagger. Sprays of blood flew through the air, falling across faces and hands alike in a spatter or hanging in the air like a mist. Every time he licked his lips, he tasted copper and the brine of the sea.

Horrible sounds pressed in on every side, making him feel like he could hardly breathe. Thislen could hear the squealing crunch of metal as weapons bit through mail, the clash and screech as blade met blade. Somewhere nearby was the sickening snap of bone and the squelch of flesh and a desperate, agonized shout.

The battle played out before an audience of dark monsters, their glowing red eyes tracking every movement as if watching a mummer's play. Every time Thislen turned, he saw them standing stone still in the corner of his eye.

It was chaos.

With every new threat, every soldier that rose before him, he turned to face it. That calm still held him, shielding his heart from the horrors around him. A man with a dagger and a sword appeared from nowhere, as if by magic. Thislen jerked his own sword up to block, arm vibrating all the way up to his aching shoulder. He twisted to the side as the dagger came in. He felt it score, a thin line of fire that cut through his leathers, merely a graze on his side.

The move he'd taught Ivan floated to the surface of his mind. He stepped in, completing his turn, and clamped his arm down over his foe's, then brought it sharply down to his knee. A sickening crack rent the air at the same time as the man's choked shout. The dagger skittered off to disappear among the clusters of boots around them. Thislen turned back, thrusting his sword forward. The soldier's hoarse cry died off in a gurgle, shock on his face. He touched Thislen's hand, wrapped around the hilt, and then it fell away. The tip gleamed silver and red on the other side of the man. He was dying.

He was dead.

Thislen's stomach churned as the light faded from the stranger's eyes. He pulled back, letting the guard's weight drag him free of the blade.

Breathe. This is not the time to fall apart, a small voice said inside him.

He lifted his head, gaze sweeping over the tumult—and ducked. An arrow whizzed past his ear, close enough he felt the wind of its passage. He lifted his blade, charging the armored markswoman who fired at him.

Someone else in Nattfolk leathers got to her first, leaping on her from behind and carrying them both to the ground in a tangle. Thislen stopped short, turning again, boot slipping in a deep red stain on the stone.

For a moment, his heart skipped a beat. His brace rattled, the metal digging into his skin. A knife of agony slid up his leg to his hip and down again. Then, he was on his feet. Standing. Fine. He crouched, testing his knee again. It throbbed, but it would hold.

He tried not to think about what that stain on the stone was. Every thought felt a thousand miles away, as if he floated along behind himself on a tether, there but not there, watching the entire battle from on high. He could feel his heart racing. He could tell his stomach was in knots and bile coated the back of his throat. He knew his side burned, and he could feel the slick, sticky trickle of his own blood. His clothes stuck to his skin with sweat and peeled away when he twisted. The cut pulled and stretched. His knee throbbed.

None of it felt immediate. None of it felt like it was his. It was as if he held everything at arm's length but control of his arms, his weapon, and his feet.

Caught in an eddy in the midst of the battle, surrounded by a small pocket of peace, he watched from that detached, distant place. Nattfolk charged, leaping off the wooden walkways to fall on guards below. The guards were being driven back step by reluctant step, toward the rowboats and the black and silver surface of the sea. Bodies littered the ground. Some were moving, but others were not.

The taste of bile grew stronger. Not every corpse on the ground was a soldier. Thislen recognized Grayson's body splayed on the ground, the Night Councilman's eyes gone dim and staring up at the stars, his stomach a mess of red blood and torn fabric. He'd died to protect his people.

They're my people, too.

A roar came from behind him and Thislen whirled, shattering the moment of calm. He brought his blade up, and not a moment too soon. The beast of a soldier was twice his weight and a full head taller. As their blades met with a crash like thunder, Thislen flew backward. He fell. His head hit the stone so hard he saw spots, but even as he gasped in pain, he brought his blade up again. He was feeling something, now—terror held him in an icy grip. Being on the ground was his death sentence. This was how he joined the Ancestors. This was how he died.

But not without a fight.

He shoved his sword upward, blinded. A heavy impact drove the hilt into his gut, forcing the air from his lungs with a wheeze. The guardsman's sword sparked on the stone beside his head and a massive weight forced him to release his weapon. The body of the guard fell sideways enough not to smother him, but the man was heavy. His blood soaked Thislen's leathers at the hip.

Thislen didn't know how the man managed to impale himself on his blade, and he wasn't about to ask. There wasn't time for that, and the dead couldn't answer anyway. Trying not to think about who the man once was or what he left behind, Thislen writhed out from under him and hauled his blade free of the corpse.

His head hurt. He realized it belatedly, probing the back of his skull with his fingertips. His hair was matted with something thick and sticky. When he pulled his hand away, his fingers gleamed dark red.

Oh. That's...not good.

A ragged cheer went up. Thislen jerked, twisting again to look. The world lurched and spun around him as he did. The ocean glittered with every foam-capped wave that washed up on the stone, swirling around the back ends of the rowboats. Rowboats the guardsmen were leaping into. In their haste, one guard stepped into the water.

No. Thislen's stomach clenched, but he could only watch.

Three black hands shot out of the water, closing fast around the soldier's ankle. The Vaim yanked, and the soldier went down in a splash with a strangled, horrified shout. They lashed out at the water with their sword, but it did nothing. Slowly, inexorably, the monsters dragged the soldier down. No one tried to help them. The shouting stopped when their head vanished below the water. A dark cloud billowed up from the depths, along with a rush of bubbles.

Blood, he realized.

For a moment, the horror of it all froze everyone, Nattfolk and Solfolk alike. Silence was broken only by lapping waves, until a guard levered herself into a rowboat with the thud of boots on wood. The guards burst into life again. They were all far more careful as they made their retreat, now.

Several Nattfolk surged forward, their weapons drawn, ready to pursue the soldiers to the last.

"Stop! Hold your ground."

It was only when heads swiveled toward him that Thislen realized the shouted command came from his lips. The Nattfolk slowed, then stopped. The air now was only full of the groans and cries of the dying and injured, and the panting breath of the combatants.

Thislen inhaled deeply. This was not glorious like the wars in tales and stories. This battle, even small as it was, was a nightmare painted in flickering torchlight and smears of red. *No more bodies. No more Asterans dead. I don't care what side they're on, this has to be the last of it. It has to.*

The spot between his shoulderblades prickled as he gestured at the rowboats drifting away on the water, little more than dark shadows, now. "They're retreating. Leave them be."

Another weak, half-hearted cheer went up, though it died as quickly as it started. While they were glad to be alive, none of the Nattfolk wanted this. Thislen tore his gaze from the sea, sweeping over the bodies of the fallen. He stared at the faces of two guards at his feet, caught on the slack-jawed, fearful looks frozen on their features. Blood pooled on the stone surrounding them.

"Gather the injured," Thislen called, sheathing his sword. "Carry them to the Commons. *All* of the injured. Any soldiers who still live are Nattfolk now. Take the bodies of our fallen, too. Leave the enemy's dead."

The Solfolk would need bodies in the morning to explain away the torchlight. Thislen bent to check the pulse of one of the guards at his feet, unsurprised to find still, cooling skin instead.

"Thislen, look out," a familiar voice shouted behind him.

Thislen whirled. An arrow flew past his cheek, the cold metal head raising fire in its wake as it grazed his skin. Tamsa perched on the edge of a rooftop nearby, outlined in moonlight. Her warning shout had saved him, but she was no longer paying attention. Over and over she fired arrows from her bow, aiming straight down. Her hands were a blur. Other Nattfolk archers came to her side. Three, then five fired at the street below. The Vaim stirred and sighed, parting around pale-faced soldiers.

Nearly double the number of retreating guardsmen poured out of the storehouses that ringed the shipyard. This time, the ragged cheer was from the retreating guardsmen, none of whom stopped rowing for open water.

Thislen's stomach fell away, his hands gone cold and clammy. They were trapped. There were no boats to carry them out to sea, just the Vaim and the promise of a watery grave.

"Charge!" Thislen roared, drawing his sword again. He was exhausted, but it was fight—or die.

The Nattfolk rushed to meet the enemy. The archers fired away, out of reach on their rooftop perches—but for how long before some soldier took it into his head to climb up? How long before they ran out of arrows? Thislen was fighting among a knot of no more than two dozen Nattfolk, the only ones left to face double that number and more.

We're going to die.

"Get ready," Thislen shouted hoarsely, planting himself at the base of the wooden steps that led to Astera. "Hold!" His throat was scraped raw from being loud enough to reach every ear. "Hold, let them come!"

The guards bellowed like bears and plunged into the Nattfolk line. The blows drove nearly everyone back. Thislen held firm, barely. There wasn't enough *room* to retreat. Thislen shouted his defiance into the helmed face of the attacker he was sword to sword with.

The deadly dance of battle began again. Partners came together with a clash, a twist, a turn. One always fell. The other always turned to someone else. Thislen dispatched the soldier before him with a sidestep and a stab, his arms aching and his sword feeling heavier by the moment.

"Stay together, protect your people," Thislen called, running a guardsman through from behind and offering his hand to the Nattfolk on the ground.

It was Kellan, the tavern keep, far away from his kitchen and counter and spattered with blood. He gave Thislen a grateful look as he found his feet and fell in beside him. Slowly, they gathered the Nattfolk to them, even as they were forced back step by step.

The Nattfolk were his people, he now knew that beyond any doubt. He'd die to protect Kellan, if he must. These guardsmen, these foolish, stupid soldiers didn't know they were slaughtering untrained Nattfolk. They didn't realize their orders were just more of the Ruling Council's lies. The Nattfolk were simple people who did their best to exist in a world that didn't want them, and they deserved the chance.

So these soldiers can't have another one of their lives.

Thislen dove back into the fray with renewed vigor. The world was made of the feeling of shoulders on either side and the sight of blades and faces before him, flashing into view and then out of it again. The Nattfolk fought like cornered badgers. Desperation twisted their faces when he glanced to either side.

His neighbor—not Kellan—buckled beside him and Thislen whirled to fend off what would have been a killing blow, stumbling. He lurched back, turning then to Kellan's aid. There were faces near him that he didn't recognize, names he didn't know. It didn't matter. He didn't want to lose them.

The water lapped against the stone behind them, louder than ever. There was nowhere left to go.

"Don't retreat, don't step back!" His shout was echoed down the line on either side, tinged with the same desperation. This was it, the last stand. They would die here at the water's edge and take as many soldiers with them as they could. The archers could escape. The Commons wouldn't be completely helpless. Thislen tried to take solace in that.

Ancestors, are you ready for me?

Guards at the back of the throng fell, feathered shafts sprouting from their backs and necks. Would it be enough to turn this tide, to save them all? What if there were more reserves threading their way through Astera's streets even now?

Why didn't I check the warehouses? Boats must have landed two or three times in absolute darkness, allowing their passengers to hide before bringing in the bait at the end. They would have been invisible without the torchlight. They couldn't have stayed on the island as the sun set, the residents of the Gate Quarter would have noticed.

There could be even more of them that landed on other boats, at other berths, already ranging through the streets to slaughter others. None of them would know until it was too late.

If he died here, Thislen would never know at all.

A furious cry on his left caught Thislen by surprise, tearing him from his thoughts. The soldier's face was twisted in fury as she lunged with her shortsword held low. Thislen's eyes widened. He knew he would be too slow, even as he forced numb arms to lift his sword to parry. He wasn't moving as fast as before.

Ivan darted around Thislen, grabbing the guard's arm beneath his own, dropping his blade with a clatter and twisting her wrist. She ran into his broad back with a yelp and instinctively dropped her blade. Ivan stepped aside.

In one fluid movement, Thislen stepped forward and ran her through. She looked at him, stunned, her hands pressed over the wound as he drew his blade free. Then she crumpled.

"Thanks," Thislen panted, giving Ivan a smile despite all the energy it cost him.

Ivan flashed a brief grin, scooping his sword up. Another guard, big as a horse, raced toward them, swinging overhand toward Ivan's head. Just as Thislen taught him, he brought his sword up and braced himself for the blow—

—by stepping back.

No one would have been able to hear the splash over the fighting, but Thislen didn't need to. Ivan's face paled and his gaze dropped to his feet even as he held off that screeching blow. Thislen ran the attacker through, leaving his sword in the man's side as he turned quickly.

His fingers closed around Ivan's wrist at the same time the Vaim appeared. Dark hands burst up from the sea, soaking Ivan's pants as they clutched at his leg and ankle.

The yank nearly wrenched Thislen's arm from its socket, threatening to drag him into the waves as well. He braced himself with all his weight, holding onto Ivan with both hands, straining. The battle raged around him, and he ignored it.

I won't lose this one.

"Don't let go," Ivan gasped, eyes bulging. He clutched Thislen's wrist with his other hand, kicking at the shadowy fingers wrapped around his other leg.

Thislen couldn't spare the breath to answer, his features twisted with fear. His grip was slipping. *Please, not again,* he begged silently, hoping that someone would hear. *Please don't let me fail again.*

One of his hands was slick with blood. He shouted as he pulled with all his might. "Let go of him!"

More dark hands shot from the water as Ivan inched further into the sea, joining their fellows.

Thislen met Ivan's gaze, eyes wide. "Hold on, Ivan. Hold on!"

"Take care of them," Ivan said, an eerie calm settling over him.

"No!"

The Vaim hauled on Ivan as one, and the florist-turned-scout let go. Thislen fell backwards, a hair's breadth away from the waterline. He flung his hand out, shouting until his throat burned from the force of it.

Ivan was gone. The Vaim dragged him below the surface so quickly there was nothing left but rippling water.

A clash and a roar came from behind him, filled with battle lust. Instinct took over, letting his mind retreat to that place somewhere outside of himself as he turned his back on the sea. His fingers closed around the hilt of Ivan's sword and he surged to his feet, throwing himself into the fray again. He stopped a guardsman from driving a Nattfolk woman into the water, grabbing her wrist just in time and yanking her a few paces forward.

"Drive them back!" He bellowed. Thislen flung himself toward a cluster of soldiers, laying into them for all he was worth.

Later. Later he would mourn. There was no time now.

The chaos continued.

22

Mila's fingers throbbed and burned in turns. Her arms ached. From her perch on a rooftop, tucked in the lee of a crumbling chimney, she fired her bow over and over, not daring to stop. The stiff feathers passed through her hands, the rough string pressed against her fingertips. Every shot reverberated through the bow, through her other arm and up to her shoulder. She longed more than anything to set it down.

She didn't dare. She loosed arrow after arrow at the swarming silver carapaces of the soldiers below. Her accuracy was starting to fall, but she was still hitting soldiers in shoulders or legs, so she wouldn't stop. Not yet.

When Ivan met their patrol on the rooftops, when he told her that Thislen was facing a small army alone, she and Trevon bolted for the shipyard at once, leaving the others behind. She didn't know where anyone else was—but Trevon knelt beside her, his bow drawn up to his cheek, his brow furrowed. He fired. The arrow whistled toward the surging throng below.

When his hand dipped into the quiver on his back for another arrow, the last few of them rattled. Mila was in the same spot, feeling only five more shafts to fire. They were running out of ammunition.

She took a deep breath, fighting down the rising unease at the idea of having to go down into the mob of crashing bodies and flashing swords. The sword on her hip felt heavier with every passing moment, as if it knew she'd draw it soon.

I'm ready for this. If I have to fight, I will.

Men and women fought in knots and tangles before the shore. It was impossible to count how many, now. Worse, Mila couldn't tell who was winning. Enough bodies littered the stone that maybe no one was.

She nocked another arrow, sighting down the length of the shaft—and froze.

Is that—

Her heart pounded in her throat, the string going slack in her hands. She couldn't breathe.

A soldier charged Thislen, a barely distinguishable bit of dark hair and dark leathers by the water's edge. Ivan, having just felled an enemy between the pair of them, raced forward to his side.

It took only a moment. Ivan and Thislen dispatched the soldier together—and then dark shadows boiled up out of the sea. Helpless, too far to make any difference at all, Mila watched Thislen grasp Ivan's hands and fight against the underwater Vaim. She could tell he was pulling with every ounce of his strength. Even from here she could see the muscles at his neck straining. She stood, bow dangling from one hand, arrow in the other, praying to the Ancestors.

Help him. Help them, both of them. Please, please don't do this.

Mila watched as Thislen lost his grip and Ivan vanished beneath the water in the span of a single heartbeat, horror dousing her like ice water.

He was gone. Her childhood friend, the man she thought of as a brother, dead.

I'm never going to see him again. But I just got him back. The chill spread deeper, toward her bones, toward her heart. *I'm going to have to tell Evelie that her son, her only son, is dead. Will she ever forgive me for bringing them to the Nattfolk?*

But it wasn't her fault. If they hadn't been attacked, Ivan would never have gone anywhere near the water at night.

The encroaching cold vanished as the coal deep inside her roared, growing into a bonfire that warmed her all the way to her fingertips. With a frustrated screech, she drew her bow again. She loosed the arrow into the back of a guard, and was surprised to see flame licking at the shaft. She must have fired it closer to the torch between her and the soldier than she thought.

Mila grit her teeth and fired again. She knew who to kill. If she were being honest with herself, she *knew* who ordered all of this. Only one person would want to attack the Nattfolk, to slaughter them on the shores of their home.

She would kill Soren Bestant herself, without remorse, this very instant. If only she could *find* him.

For now, she vented her frustrations on the attackers below. The last of her arrows flew true, every one. She hardly felt her body's protests anymore. With a growl she threw her bow down onto the roof and drew her sword. Any unease about having to plunge into the fight below was gone, replaced with the terrible desire to kill them all for Ivan, for Evelie, for the Nattfolk...and for herself.

As she turned, a tile slid free from the roof on the other side of the chimney. Mila and Trevon, his last arrow vanishing into the soldiers below, turned at the noise.

"Are you alright?" Trevon called out, before glancing at Mila. "Who else is up here with us?"

She didn't know. Silently, she crept across the roof. She swung around the side of the chimney, coming face to face with a startled guardsman—and not the only one. Two more crept across the rooftop toward the Nattfolk archers.

"Look out," Mila shouted, lifting her blade just in time to deflect the soldier's lunge. "They're on the roof!"

Trevon shouted the warning along to the next archer even as he threw his bow at their enemies. A guardsman flattened himself, the weapon flying over his head.

Trevon pulled a dagger from his belt and started to draw his sword, but the other two soldiers charged him with a shout.

Mila deflected an overhead blow, her wrist threatening to buckle beneath the weight of it. "Trevon?" She called, the word taut with worry.

A clatter of tiles answered her, and mingled shouts. She glanced back in time to watch a tangle of arms, legs, and glittering silver topple over the edge of the roof and out of sight. Wood splintered somewhere below.

"Trevon?" This time, desperation tinged the word.

The soldier before her kicked. Her leg buckled and she stumbled to one side, bringing her sword up to slide another blow harmlessly aside. She fell to one knee and twisted, bringing the blade around in a vicious swing with all her strength. She felt it bite through flesh, heard the sickening crunch as it met bone. She'd nearly cut the man in half at the waist. He looked just as stunned as she did, staggering back.

The motion yanked the sword out of her hands. It was stuck in the bone. Scrambling to her feet, Mila reached for the hilt—and the soldier fell backward, taking her weapon with him as he plummeted to the street below.

The blade could wait. Mila turned away from the battle and scrambled to the lip of the roof and the alleyway beneath it. "Trevon? Answer me, please."

A groan came from below. She couldn't tell who it was.

"Trevon, damn it," she spat, turning to find a way down.

Mila came face to face with Lord Soren Bestant, his beautiful features twisted into a snarl so rabid she instinctively recoiled. Her foot slipped.

Only one thought went through her mind as her stomach dropped. *He can't be here.* The Ruling Council couldn't set foot on the island, not at night.

Before she lost her balance completely, Soren's fingers wrapped around her wrist like a vice and jerked her forward, into his arms. One wrapped around her, pinning her limbs as he leaned in with a leer.

"I knew you were alive the moment I saw that little fisher friend of yours. Only they aren't fishermen, are they, Mila?" His whisper was hot against the side of her face and her ear.

"Let go, let go of me!" Mila struggled, twisting her wrist free and punching up.

Her fist connected with the sharp jut of his chin, her knuckles flaring with pain. She was held too close to get much power behind it, but Soren spat blood onto her cheek with a high-pitched laugh. Madness glittered in his eyes and blood painted his teeth.

He leaned in. "We're going to discuss all of this at length. We want answers. *He* wants answers. And for being so clever, for surviving so much, we'll revisit your *use* to me."

Mila stomped hard on Soren's fine boot, then punched again, this time low, to his gut. He groaned as he stumbled back a pace.

"Mila?" The ragged call came from below.

Trevon! He was alive! Thank the Ancestors. She turned to the roof's edge.

Soren caught her wrist again, but this time he twisted it behind her back, pushing her balance until she teetered on the edge of losing it, facing the shadows of the alley below.

"Mila," Trevon sounded relieved as he saw the outline of her silhouetted against the moonlit sky. "Are you alright?"

Her teeth were grit with pain. She parted her lips to answer—and Soren yanked her backward. He pulled on her arm until her shoulder and elbow were screaming and her eyes watered, holding tight enough to bruise.

"I am so sick of finding you alive, Mila. You're like a little rat, and just like a rat, your kind *breeds*. It doubles every time I see you. Do you know what we do with rats?" He pushed her wrist up higher.

Mila cried out, her eyes closing as a wave of nausea came with the pain. Any further and her arm would break.

"Mila?" Trevon's shout this time was tinged with alarm.

"We exterminate them," Soren whispered, lips brushing her cheek. "Tell him you're fine, or I'll ensure he's first."

Her heart dropped inside her, even as the coal began to boil in her stomach. How *dare* he threaten Trevon?

She couldn't push the memory of finding Thislen again from her mind, though. She remembered how thin, how hurt, how changed the thief was when they found him in the cell on *Ship Artaith*. She couldn't let that happen to Trevon, not while she could do something about it.

She hesitated.

Soren wrapped his free arm around her, fingers curling around her throat. "Tell him."

The clatter of wood came from the alleyway. "Hang on, I'm coming up."

Mila could open her mouth, could form the lie and let herself be dragged away from her friends. She could protect them from Soren...but not from his soldiers. Even if she saved Trevon in this moment, there was no promise he would survive the next.

She seethed at her helplessness, at the trap she'd been so neatly cornered in. *I hate this man. I hate him, and I hate his stupid games. I'm not playing.*

"It's Soren! He's—" Mila's shout was cut off as Soren's hand flew up and pressed harshly over her mouth and nose, cutting off her air. His fingers dug into her cheeks as he dragged her back, pain flaring in her shoulder.

She threw her head back, striking him so hard she saw stars. He howled in agony, letting go of her mouth to cover his bleeding nose.

"You damnable *witch*," Soren spat. "You'll pay for that."

Once, Mila might have feared a threat like that. Before she'd found Thislen, before she'd been sentenced to die twice, before she found her place among the Nattfolk, she would have cowered. She might have begged and pleaded. She certainly would have cried.

Once.

Now, the coal began to spark within her, fury battering any hint of fear away. She tested his grip as he forced her to walk before him, but there was no give. "Let go of me, Soren!"

"Shut up, just shut up," he snarled. He pressed his bloodied hand over her mouth. She recoiled, the slick copper tang on her lips turning her stomach. She felt dizzy, unable to breathe.

She bit.

Soren cursed, jerking his hand away. Mila sucked in a deep breath of air, her head spinning at the sudden rush of oxygen. It felt like she was falling.

She *was* falling. She realized it a split second before she hit the stacked bags of grain, flat on her back. All the air was driven out of her again, leaving her reeling. Her arm tingled and throbbed. With a groan, she pushed herself up.

A hand grabbed hair and headscarf alike, yanking her backward off the sacks. She stumbled to her feet, guided by that pull, and her arm was yanked behind her once again.

Damn it!

"Mila, where are you?" Trevon's anxious call came from above, now.

Soren dragged her around the side of the storehouse and into the alleyway. The bodies of two soldiers lay in a heap of splintered wood. Mila tried to kick a piece of it, to make a noise, any noise.

"Behave yourself," Soren snapped, jerking her back. He tucked them into the shadows behind a stack of barrels, pressing her against the wall with his bulk and covering her mouth again. The rough wood of the warehouse was scarcely an inch from the front of her nose. She couldn't see anything.

The ice-cold touch of fear threatened to put out the fire coursing through her veins. She was helpless, utterly at Soren's mercy, and she didn't know his plans. His body was big, every inch of her pressed against it. She couldn't move. He could do anything to her, now. Anything. Her heart hammered in her chest.

Footsteps ran past, wood from the broken crates clattering on the cobbles.

"Mila?" Trevon called desperately. "Where are you?"

Mila sucked in a breath. As if reading her mind, Soren quickly shifted to pinch her nose closed again, worsening the dizziness that hadn't quite left her yet.

Is he going to kill me?

He twisted her arm further, until she was perfectly still, her breathing hard and fast. She twisted her wrist, fingers scrabbling for purchase against his wrist, wrapped in fine cloth and lace. Of *course* Lord Soren Bestant would wear lace to a battle.

A battle which still raged on the other side of the warehouse, the clangs and shouts sounding strangely far away the longer she went without air.

"No, no, no, no—Mila! Damn it, move, you stupid ghosts." The sounds of Trevon nearby faded away at a run.

Soren released her nose, and she sucked in a deep breath, dropping her forehead against the wall.

"How sweet. He's run off to find you. It's too bad he's going the wrong way." Soren laughed low in his throat, dragging her back out into the open and heading away from the battle. He slowed as they neared the street. The Vaim standing there turned to look at Mila, the fury in their red eyes abating—or did she imagine it?

They didn't look at Soren at all. His hand left her face, touching the front of his doublet.

Mila glared at him. "It's the pendants, isn't it? The ones you took from the Nattfolk. That's how you're here."

Soren steered her between the Vaim, avoiding contact with them. She lurched to one side, bringing them closer to one, meeting its red eyes. Could Ninian see them? *Help, help me!*

With a curse, Soren yanked her away again, his fair skin gleaming with sweat.

Savage glee surged through Mila at the sight. *He's still afraid of them. Ha!*

She didn't have much choice in going where he led, but she began to struggle as much as she could, pulling Soren into the path of the Vaim over and over again. Their red eyes always dropped to the pair, and Soren's grip tightened as he jerked her away.

With every jerking, uneven step, the sounds of fighting faded behind them. Her empty scabbard banged against her hip as they threaded their way through the dead, caught up in a silent battle. A dagger hung on Soren's belt and her fingers itched to grab it, but it was behind the wrong arm. The only good thing about her position was that Soren couldn't draw the blade either, not without letting her go.

Soren didn't speak to her again until they were several streets away, surrounded by nothing more than the eerie whispers and red eyes of the ghosts. "You and those people are a pestilence."

A flush of anger crept up Mila's cheeks. She gritted her teeth, a lance of pain shooting through her arm as Soren jerked her around a corner. The dark monolith of the Gate Quarter's wall loomed ahead of them.

The nobleman's golden curls were a sweaty tangle, no longer perfect. They stuck to his cheeks, framing the maniacal gleam in his eyes. The whites were very, very bright in the moonlight.

"The dead of long ago walk the streets, and you and those little plague rats walk among them free as birds. Because of the pendants. Magical pendants! Did you think we didn't have people who can sense magic, even if they can't use it?"

She cried out as she tripped over a crumbling cobblestone, twisting her arm uncomfortably. *I didn't know that. I didn't even* think *about it. Who? How?*

"But I'm impressed," he panted, shoving her into the dark shadows of the gate through the wall, pulling her toward the sloping ramp that led to the first terrace of the Goods Quarter. "You have managed to survive again and again, no matter what I throw at you."

They passed near a low garden wall, the top adorned with plants in colorfully painted pots. Mila's hand darted out, snatching one and swinging it awkwardly over her head. The grip on her arm loosened as Soren ducked with a curse. The whole limb tingled. She dropped the plant, pulling with all her strength.

Her arm came free. She backed up several steps, her fingers numb, her shoulder throbbing, and raised her fists. "Bastard," she spat. "I know what the Ruling Council has done. I know what you're doing next. You're going to kill people again. None of us will let you get away with it, not this time. Not a single one of us Nattfolk will see it happen again."

He laughed, a shrill cackle with a wild edge. "Who will stop me once I've killed all of your—what did you call them? Nattfolk?" He bared his teeth in a feral grin. "I have killed before, and I will kill again, and again, and again. We're killing them right now, down by the water. There won't be any of you left soon enough."

She expected the feeling of ice, not fire. It roared through her body, turning every bit of fear to fury, raw and raging, barely contained beneath her skin. "Then *you* won't survive tonight, either."

He drew his dagger, circling around her slowly. The Vaim in the street drew back, watching Mila with glittering eyes. "Careful, Mila. I don't want to damage you. Not yet."

She seethed. "I'd like to see you try. I'm not same as I was, Soren." She kept her voice even, her hands still raised, one tucked against her cheek just as Trevon taught her.

"That's precisely what will make this so. Much. Fun." He lunged.

No, it wasn't a lunge, it was a tackle. Mila brought her wrist in to deflect the knife but was met with all of Soren's weight instead. She flew into the wall, the air driven from her lungs as the nobleman's shoulder dug into her stomach. She wheezed, and the fire grew. She pushed him away.

Tendrils of steam curled up from his shirt, barely visible in the moonlight. The fabric was singed. He didn't notice. "I've made a decision, Mila Ominir. I'm going to get what I want, all of what I want, and you're not going to be able to stop me. How long can you fight me, a twig of a girl like you?"

Her skin was so hot she saw a faint shimmer of heat rising from her arms. She stared down at her hands, ignoring the aches, bruises, and pain she felt from head to toe.

"After I question you, after I get my answers, I'll take you to Perilee. Beneath the castle is a little stone room with a little stone block, an ax, and nothing else."

She curled her fingers into fists. *What is happening to me?* Distracted as she was by her hands, she still saw Soren lunge for her, twisting to the side at the last second. He was panting. His movements were slow and clumsy.

I'm stronger than he is. Confidence ran through her, steeling her spine. She could win if she wanted to. She could get away.

A spark flickered at the tip of her finger, gold as sunlight. She froze, eyes widening.

Soren grabbed her hand and twisted it, pressing her against the garden wall. A pot fell into the small yard on the other side, shattering. Mila pressed her hand against the stones with a grimace, trying to wrestle herself free.

"This time," he hissed in her ear, "I'm going to make certain you're dead. I'm going to do it myself. And after I've finished with you? I think I'll go back for your little friends. Aften, Tamsa, even my dear cousin. And who was the one you were calling out for? Trevon?"

White hot fury ran through her. The coal inside didn't just ignite, it *exploded*, bursting into a raging inferno. Threatening her was one thing, but threatening her friends? Threatening Thislen and Trevon? That was too far.

She screeched, a sound of absolute fury as sharp as a hawk's cry. She closed her eyes and let the heat she'd been holding inside of her go, let it tear through her skin and burst into the night air. She thought it would hurt. It didn't.

Sparks of energy and a massive rush of air erupted from every inch of her, in every direction. It flung Soren and the Vaim away, scattering them all like leaves before a storm. It pushed her away from the wall and into the air at the same time, so she tumbled to the cobbles in the middle of the street, stunned by her own...power.

Red-eyed spirits scattered like a herd of cats, startled by her outburst. They turned into little more than flickering shadows, retreating into every nook and cranny.

Mila's ears rang. As she shook her head to clear it, she became aware of the only other sound there was. A gurgling, wet rasp. Quickly, she turned, crouched and ready to spring away from Soren—but she didn't need to.

Slumped against the wall, a smear of blood above his head showing where he'd slid down the stones, Lord Soren Bestant sat dying. A sodden, choking laugh came from the battered heap of blond hair and embroidery, his blue eyes still bright with madness. His head lolled to the side. More blood stained his teeth and ran from the corner of his lips.

"You...surprised me...again," he said brightly, as if she'd amused him by playing a sleight of hand trick at a market faire.

The light in his eyes died, and with one last sickening rasp, air left his crushed chest. His smile went slack.

A wave of exhaustion swept over Mila and she sat heavily in the middle of the street, eyes wide. *What...just happened? What did I do?*

Soren Bestant was dead.

Is it...over?

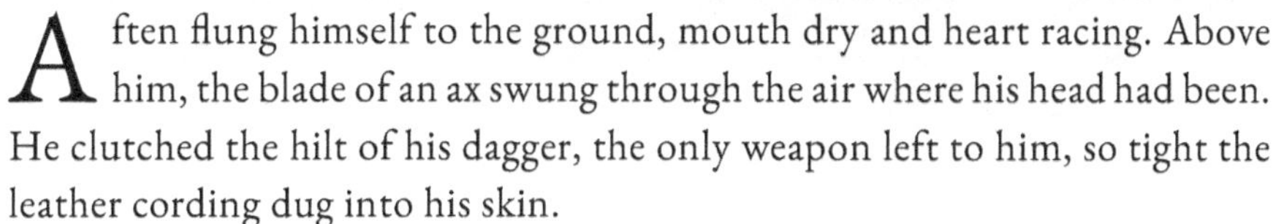

23

Aften flung himself to the ground, mouth dry and heart racing. Above him, the blade of an ax swung through the air where his head had been. He clutched the hilt of his dagger, the only weapon left to him, so tight the leather cording dug into his skin.

I'm trapped in a nightmare. Wake up. Please, wake up.

Not that he could. This was real. All around him were flashes of metal in the torchlight, shouts, curses—and screaming, so much screaming. He scrambled to his feet, stumbling as he trod on something soft and squishy. He looked back to see it was a corpse's arm, a soldier's, and his stomach heaved. The taste of bile raced up the back of his throat.

Ax and sword clashed behind him. Ophelia was fighting a Solfolk guardsman, the pair of them oblivious to how close their blows had come to ending Aften's life. He lifted his dagger and watched them struggle, hoping for an opening. He saw one, when the soldier lifted his arm to block an overhead blow.

He didn't take it. Sweat slid down the back of his shirt and he shuddered. He wasn't a fighter, just like Darran had said.

Darran.

Aften turned as Ophelia's blade slid through the soldier's ribs. He hunted through the ebb and flow of the battle for the familiar dark-skinned, dark-haired figure of Darran. Nothing. He couldn't see him.

I can't believe I lost track of him. What if he's dead for real this time?

He went cold all over. No, no, no. He shoved that thought down deep and started toward the water. His palm was sweaty. He didn't want to fight, he just wanted to find Darran, to help if he could.

A furious roar made Aften spin, bringing his knife up instinctively. Against one of the wooden pilings of the walkway that surrounded the drydock, Kellan the tavern-keep was pressed in place. He held a heavy cudgel over his head. A guard's sword bit into the wood. The two of them both had their teeth bared, locked in place.

Help him. The soldier can't see you. Stab him, stab the guard!

His arms wouldn't move. Aften back-pedaled, tripping over something. His stomach lurched as he fell and his hand flew open. His knife skittered away across the stone, vanishing behind a knot of fighters.

Kellan roared again. He wrenched the guard and his weapon to the side, letting the man's own strength carry him past. The soldier ran into the thick wooden post. Kellan knocked the dazed man out with a sharp rap to the back of the skull.

His enemy crumpled. Kellan flung himself toward a group of three soldiers harrying Amelie, the fierce scout captain.

Hands shaking and breath coming in hard pants, Aften pushed himself upright. He tore his gaze from the fighting at last to see what he'd tripped over.

Helena, a member of the Night Council, whimpered softly. She stared at Aften with eyes so wide the whites showed all around. His heart plummeted. Her hands were pressed to her side. Dark red blood glittered in the dancing torchlight.

"No," he breathed. "No, no, no—hold on, Helena, hold on." He was on his feet before he realized it, grabbing her under the arms and dragging her as steadily as he could to the edge of the fighting. Little memories he'd long forgotten surfaced in his head as they worked their way across the smooth stone. Helena gave him his first bag of marbles when he was six. She had a son of her own, around his age, and Aften and Ulan played together all the time. She made wonderful stew.

Don't die, please don't die. His eyes stung. He blinked to clear them, hunching his shoulders as they passed a tangle of fighting soldiers and Nattfolk. Silently, he prayed to the Ancestors that no one would notice them.

The bulk of the fighting was down at the water. The soldiers had knots of Nattfolk pinned against the waterline. Archers who ran out of arrows, their quivers empty on their backs, came down to attack from the rear, giving the Nattfolk half a chance. Others, like Kellan, came from the Commons to tip the scales. A few stragglers, guardsmen and Nattfolk alike, had staggered or dragged themselves to the edges of the drydock. Many of them were injured.

Aften reached the base of a set of worn wooden steps, the boards warped and uneven. Sweat rolled down his brow as he hauled, straining to pull Helena up each one. She choked back a groan of pain. A fresh trickle of blood ran over her fingertips. The stairs shuddered and creaked alarmingly beneath their weight, but Aften was too close to the top to stop.

When they reached the flat surface of the wooden walkway, Aften staggered, panting. "Are you alright?"

"Do I...look alright?" Helena asked, voice strained but a weak smile on her lips.

"Helena, Aften!" Calin, another member of the Night Council, ran toward them, his brow drenched in sweat. "Ancestors bless. You're alive. Don't set her down, Aften."

Aften, arms trembling, stared at Calin in dismay.

"We've secured a building for the injured. Come on, this way." Calin picked up Helena's legs.

Between the two of them, carrying Helena was easier, and they skirted down the side of a warehouse, threading their way through the Vaim that still lingered at the edge of the pool of golden torch light. Once they rounded the corner, they practically fell through the propped open door and into a brightly lit space. A few armed Nattfolk stood just inside the entrance, their eyes wide.

"Who is—" Ami began, lifting her head. Her sleeves were pushed up and her arms were bloodied almost up to the elbow.

"Some of ours," Calin called.

"Oh no, no, Helena! Olen, handle this," she snapped, already halfway across the room. She cupped her wife's cheek in her hand, heedless of the smear of red she left behind.

"Just a scratch," Helena joked faintly.

"Calin, set her down over here and get me some of that hot water. I need to work." Ami soon had Helena laying on a bedroll, her brow furrowed as she sorted through torn strips of fabric and needles and thread.

Olen took over working steadily at the patient—a young Solfolk soldier—Ami left behind. Evelie bustled up with a steaming bowl of hot water, setting it at Ami's side and giving Aften a tight, worried smile. Her face was pale.

Aften stood, shoulders aching, his eyes trailing over everyone there. No Darran. He wasn't sure if he should be grateful or not.

Calin pulled a sack of grain over to tuck underneath Helena's head, his face grim.

"Ulan?" Helena asked softly.

"He was fighting," Calin said.

Ami paled, but her hands never once stopped moving. Ulan was her son, too, after all.

Evelie pulled Calin up by the sleeve, guiding him away so Ami had room to work. She looked After up and down. "You two are all we have right now. Go, if there are more injured, bring them here. Take this."

She pressed a pouch into Aften's hands. Inside was a tin of needles and thread, with rolls of ripped cloth to serve as bandages.

"You know how to use it, right?" She ducked into his eyesight.

Aften felt strength running through him slow and warm, like the sun cresting the horizon. "I do."

Olen enlisted Aften to carry his supplies all over the Nattfolk caverns, quietly telling him about this herb and that ailment, how to solve this problem and when that dose was too much. He'd lent Aften his books. He told him the names of the plants and how they worked. He taught him to clean wounds, what staunched bleeding, and when to know when a wound was fatal.

Aften knew how to keep people alive long enough to be brought here, to get help.

"Good. Take one more of those three," Evelie gestured at the Nattfolk by the door. "You're in charge."

Aften turned to Calin, a determined set to his jaw. "Let's go, they need us." Soldiers and Nattfolk alike, they needed help if they were to survive.

Calin nodded. A scout named Julian stepped forward, silently volunteering to help by simply sheathing his knife. The three of them plunged back into the dark of night.

After that, the world narrowed to little more than what was right in front of him. He rolled bodies over, putting a mirror at lips to see if there was breath or feeling for a pulse. The ones that were still alive, he dragged to the edge of the fighting, to the bottom of the same worn steps he'd carried Helena up. The ones worst injured he bandaged as best he could before moving them. Calin and Julian ran back and forth, carrying whoever they found on the stone, regardless of which side of the battle they'd fought on.

A few times, Calin returned with another pack full of supplies and took the one Aften nearly emptied back with him.

Too many times, Aften rolled over a body to find a familiar face, only to take their pulse and realize the people he knew, the people he had always known, were gone. The dead he left behind. He couldn't help them now. He fought the urge to say their names. Grayson. Pollon. Ophelia. If he called for them before they'd been given their last rites, they might get lost on the way to the stars and the Ancestors.

His heart ached as much as his back, shoulders, and arms did. He was sticky with blood that stained his hands, arms, and clothes. The fabric clung uncomfortably to his chest, stomach, and legs. For every person he found alive, he found two dead. Too few of his people survived. He pulled, he strained, he bandaged, he carried, he stitched. Twice he scrambled away from soldiers that turned and saw him, that came after him with their weapons raised. Twice, Julian leapt from the wooden walkway above to save Aften's life.

After another trip to the impromptu field hospital, Calin caught Aften by the shoulder and gestured to the steps. "Take a moment. Drink some water, then go back."

Reluctantly, Aften did so. His mind was roaring with the need to help, a whisper of desire fed until it became a hurricane. He took the waterskin Julian pressed into his hand and swallowed, only to discover how thirsty he truly was. He chugged mouthful after mouthful, until his stomach was uncomfortably full.

A body slammed into his own and twisted. Aften choked, instinctively grabbing at the wrist of his unknown assailant. Adrenaline catapulted his heart into a race. Julian caught and steadied them both.

"Trevon?" Aften gasped between coughs.

"Have you seen Mila?" Trevon asked, eyes wild as he grabbed the front of Aften's shirt. Mila's sword was clutched in his other hand. "She's been taken, she's gone, she said it was Soren. Bestant has her, and I can't find them. I thought maybe he'd taken her to the water so I—"

Aften felt a chill slide down his spine. "Slow down, breathe. Here."

Unceremoniously, he shoved the half empty waterskin into the scout captain's hands. It gave him a moment, only one, to think. Soren Bestant was on the island. The man who so casually imprisoned him and his sister, even when he believed they were innocent, had now taken Mila.

He *must have ordered all this,* Aften thought, fury rising in his veins. So many lives were changed, were ended, all so Soren Bestant could have one last go at Mila Ominir? This disgusting, horrible fighting was all his fault.

"Where?" Aften asked crisply. He could ignore how tired he was, at least for a little longer.

"I don't know. Darran is looking in the Guild Quarter, and—"

Darran was alive! Better still, he was nowhere near the fighting. Aften turned to Calin and Julian.

"Don't worry about us," Julian said, holding up his hands. "We can go down there and get people. Find your friend."

Calin nodded, taking the supply pack when Aften held it out for him.

"Let's go, we'll split up on the other side of the Gate Quarter wall," Aften said as he turned toward the dark streets. "You go to Bestant's estate, and I'll go to the castle. You're faster than I am."

Trevon nodded, relief flooding his features as Aften took charge. They ran, the sounds of battle fading behind them, though they were few enough as it was. The fighting was coming to an end. Aften didn't know who was winning, not that anyone ever won in a war. The bodies proved that, speaking louder than words ever could. They raced along the streets, darting between the Vaim like minnows in a stream. The wall rose above them, then over them.

A scream of pure fury tore through the air.

Boom. They came out into the open air to the deep sound of an explosion, skidding to a stop. Sparks rose on the terrace above them, accompanied with the sound of shattered ceramics, a rush of wind, and—

And a torrent of panicked Vaim. Aften flung his arms in front of his face as the ghosts raced past him. They clipped his shoulders, they pushed him, they jostled him out of the way of the gate. Then they were gone.

His heart was racing as he slowly lowered his hands, panting. "They were..."

"Terrified," Trevon confirmed, slowly picking himself up off the cobbles. "I've never seen them frightened before."

They had to see what happened. Silently, the pair of them headed toward the nearest stone ramp. Reluctant wasn't a strong enough word for how Aften felt as they climbed to the bottom tier of the Goods Quarter. Whatever happened, whatever it was, it was powerful enough to scare the dead. He was unarmed. There were only two of them, against whatever *that* was.

No matter how he wracked his brain, Aften couldn't think of a single thing that would spark, explode, move the air, and chase off the spirits that roamed Astera.

He and Trevon rounded the corner cautiously, stepping onto a nearly empty street. Aften's hands were balled into fists, the hair on the back of his neck standing on end. Trevon lifted Mila's sword in one hand, drawing his knife with the other. A dark shape sat in the road, another huddled beside the wall.

Trevon lowered his blade, running forward. "Mila!"

Her head came up, wobbling on her neck as if it were too heavy to hold. Her eyes were unfocused. She sat alone on the cobblestones without a single Vaim in sight.

As Trevon wrapped her in his arms and she slid hers around his neck, Aften tore his gaze away. The other dark shape had blond hair and a fine doublet stained with blood. He stepped closer, heart pounding.

His eyes widened as he stared into the slack face of his enemy. "This is Soren Bestant."

"It was," Mila corrected, pulling away from Trevon and passing a hand over her eyes.

"What happened?" Aften knelt.

Trevon looked around. "One of the Vaim?"

"No," Aften reached forward, hooking his finger around the hint of a metallic glint. He pulled the fine chain until the talisman at the end came into view. "No, it couldn't have been them. He's wearing one of our pendants."

He'd all but forgotten that Garridan, Avasten, and Soren Bestant had taken their pendants when they were captured. The magical talismans were limited in number, bespelled centuries ago by Willa Ominir herself.

Bespelled...

Aften looked up at the sky, his brow furrowing. The sparks, the wind, the sound—they almost seemed...magical. It was the only thing that could explain what happened.

That's ridiculous. No one has magic anymore. No one's been able to touch it in 300 years. Ninian told us himself that he tied every bit of it into the curse.

Aften turned to look at Mila, rising certainty making his knees go weak.

"If it wasn't them, then who?" Trevon demanded.

"It was me." Mila drew her knees up, dropping her head to rest against them. "I think I used magic."

A nervous laugh bubbled out of Aften's chest as he sank to the ground.

Trevon frowned at him. "That's impossible. There's no magic left."

"Ninian tied it into his curse, which is tied into his bloodline, and I'm..."

"An Ominir," Aften finished after she trailed off, pressing a sticky hand to his forehead.

In the distance, a few dark heads eased around the corner, their glowing red eyes scanning the Nattfolk and the corpse. Aften briefly wondered what they were thinking, then pushed it aside. That wasn't nearly so important as knowing that Mila Ominir could use magic.

"It's exhausting," she mumbled.

Trevon knelt at her side. "Let's get you out of here."

"There's a warehouse where they're tending to the injured. We can take her there." Aften stood.

Another shape skidded around the corner, one that was so familiar it made Aften's heart soar.

"Darran!" He closed the distance between them in three big steps.

Darran's eyes were wide and panicked as he wrapped Aften in his arms. "You're covered in blood, are you—"

"It's not mine, I was helping the injured," Aften said quickly.

Darran pushed him out to arm's length, studying him. "I was down in the Guild Quarter when I saw all these sparks and heard this sound. What was it?"

"Mila."

"What?" Darran looked down the street.

Trevon pulled Mila's arm around his neck. It took her some time to gather enough energy to climb sluggishly to her feet. She swayed, leaning on Trevon heavily.

Aften explained as Mila and Trevon moved slowly toward the ramp and the Gate Quarter, turning to follow after them.

"Magic," Darran breathed, eyes wide. And then he stopped short. "Wait, Aften, we...we need to get the body."

"What?" Aften gave Soren's corpse a bitter look. "I don't want to. Let everyone think the Vaim killed him."

"They don't crush, and we don't want questions. We have to..."

Aften felt his stomach drop away. *Keep the secret.*

He felt as if he'd swallowed ice water. A chill spread from his chest to the tips of his fingers and toes. It hardened, freezing him. Darran's face had gone slack with the same numb dread. Both he and Darran turned toward the Gate Quarter, mostly hidden behind the encircling wall.

A red-orange glow shone in the distance, down by the shore.

Without a word, the pair abandoned Soren Bestant's body, catching up to Mila and Trevon. Aften felt nauseated, his stomach roiling. One rule, above all others, and it was shattered into so many pieces they could never hide the Nattfolk again.

Keep the secret, protect the Nattfolk way of life.

As he listened to Darran's hasty explanation to Trevon, words tumbling out one over the other, all he could hear in his head was Darran's favorite scouting rule.

We don't light lanterns, because the Solfolk will see.

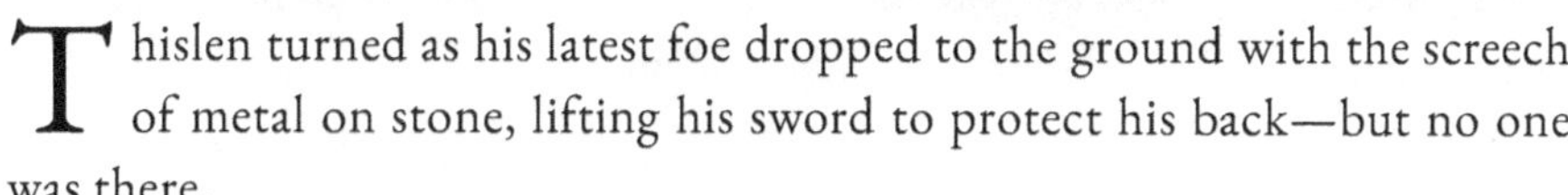

24

Thislen turned as his latest foe dropped to the ground with the screech of metal on stone, lifting his sword to protect his back—but no one was there.

An eerie quiet settled over the drydock. Not silence, no, the air was filled with groans and sobs and heavy breathing. Water lapped at the lip of the empty berth. Something clattered. The clash of weapons, the *thwunk* of arrows finding their targets, the shouts of exertion? Those were gone.

Thislen held the hilt of his sword—once Ivan's—tight, even as he lowered the blade. He pushed his hair out of his face, dark curls plastered to his skin with sweat. It tickled as they pulled away. Water splashed softly behind him and he spun, watching the guards who had escaped on their rowboats earlier paddling like mad. One boat lost an oar to the water. It bobbed toward the shore on the incoming tide, abandoned.

The battle was over.

One rowboat drew his attention. It was the only one not retreating. It bobbed in the water, far enough away to be unreachable. A lantern was lit, passed from a guard to someone else, someone wrapped in a rich cloak with embroidered trim at the edges. They stood, pushing their hood back.

The tall, slim figure was easy to recognize. Thislen grimaced across the water toward Lord Judge Avasten Barnweir.

"Thislen of the Bestants," he said in a smooth, cultured voice, a smirk on his lips. "Here we are again."

The nobleman didn't carry himself like someone who had lost a battle. He didn't seem to care at all that he'd sent dozens of men and women to fight and die on the shores of Astera, driven by a lie.

"Get me a bow," Thislen said softly. The two nearest Nattfolk turned and disappeared behind him. He didn't take his eyes off Avasten.

I knew the Ruling Council was awful, but heartless? Not a good apple in the barrel, not a single ounce of remorse or compassion? No one should live under men and women like that.

Avasten held his lantern up higher. His eyes glittered as he watched Thislen, as he waited.

"I'm here. You're out there. We've both taken losses, but one of us won, Avasten, and it wasn't you."

A grin stretched across his face, almost too wide, and he laughed deep and loud. "We'll see who won in the end. There is always a way to achieve my goals, such as they are. There is always a way to change the tide."

Thislen fought his curiosity, biting his tongue to keep from asking what he knew the Lord Judge wanted him to ask. At his silence, Avasten signaled, and the guards dipped their oars toward the water.

Anger coursed through him like lightning. *He's not getting away from here before I shoot him, damn it.*

"What goals?" Thislen kept his tone light and mocking, but he hated that he asked.

Avasten held out his hand, stopping the oars just as they touched the tops of the gentle waves. "You haven't figured them out yet?"

"You really want me to tell your little soldiers that you plan to kill half the population of the island?" Thislen made sure to raise his voice, so everyone nearby could hear.

A few of the guards in the boat shifted uncomfortably.

"Me? No, not at all. That's what *you* want. You sneaky people who lurk on the island only at night. My goal is simple. To eliminate you, and the Vaim."

Thislen drew himself upright. He knew, *knew* that Avasten meant him in particular and not the Nattfolk. He wouldn't rise to the bait. "Careful, snake. I might come and claim my inheritance at the tip of a blade. Where *is* my cousin?"

Avasten's face twisted in sour distaste.

He doesn't know, Thislen realized with a jolt. *Soren could still be on the island.*

He gestured with two fingers. Penni came up to his elbow.

"Take a small scouting party, sweep for Soren Bestant. Bring him down to the Commons."

Penni nodded, then vanished from sight with a grim smile. Thislen's heart clenched in his chest. He'd have to tell her about Ivan, later. *Later,* he told himself. *Focus for now.*

"You can have him, if you can find him. I doubt you will. It's only a few hours until dawn," Avasten drawled. "A shame I must move into the light, but the plans were always mine. I steered the ship, if you will."

Smooth wood was pressed into Thislen's hand. He raised the bow. The guards dropped their oars into the water and began to pull for all they were worth, sending the rowboat lurching. Avasten teetered, his eyes dropping to the water below. He crouched.

An arrow was offered. Thislen fit it to the string. "Get off our island, you Solfolk bastard."

He loosed. A guard stood, huddling behind her shield. The arrow slammed into the wood and stuck there. Thislen held out his hand again, but the boat drifted out of range.

The Nattfolk gave a ragged cheer behind him.

Avasten sat heavily on the rowboat's bench, his features twisted in sheer loathing. "You can't win, little rats. The next time I get ahold of you, Thislen Bestant, I'll dispose of you with my own two hands."

Thislen lifted his hand in farewell—then turned it into a rude gesture. The Nattfolk cheered again, louder this time.

The rowboats drifted into the dark, the lantern in Avasten's hands thrown over the side to plunge them into shadow once more. Thislen turned from the water, throwing the bow to the ground in disgust. It clattered across the stone to land against a heap of the fallen.

His anger faded, replaced with exhaustion and misery. Every single one of these lives—were their losses his fault?

No, I can't carry all this blame. I can't even carry blame for Ivan. They chose this. Everyone who came here tonight chose this. That doesn't mean I can't honor them, though. Their choice was brave, impossibly brave.

A gentle touch to his shoulder drew his attention. He lifted his head.

Ulan looked back at him, a scout around his age. His eye was turning a magnificent shade of purple. Behind him was a Nattfolk woman, broad shouldered, tall, and muscled. She carried a heavy hammer in her hand and wore a smith's leather apron.

"What?" Thislen asked blankly.

"I said, what do we do?" Ulan repeated.

Shock made every inch of his skin tingle. Quickly, he turned to the others. Those of the Nattfolk who could sit or stand had formed a loose half-circle around him and the water, every single eye fixed expectantly on his face. Their expressions ranged from admiration to concern, from fear to respect.

Somehow, Thislen won their favor. No, not somehow. He knew what he had done. He stepped in front of their enemy, alone, to buy them time.

I was willing to sacrifice myself for them.

Some of the younger ones, exhausted as they were, looked at him with fervent worship on their faces. He shuddered. The last thing he wanted was to be seen as a hero, especially after all he'd done—or not done. He hadn't done anything heroic, just necessary. Starting a battle, wading into a fight, a war? None of that was heroic.

The quiet stretched on as his blood rushed through his ears. Not a single expectant face turned away. He scanned every single one, steeling himself. Someone had to help, had to lead, and Mila wasn't here to bark the orders this time. There would be time to think about the consequences of what he was doing—later.

Everything had to wait for later.

He stepped forward.

"Commander Thislen," Amelie, his scout captain, stepped forward to meet him. She granted him a title that hadn't existed before, or if it had, Thislen never heard it. "What are your orders, sir?"

His heart pounded in his chest. Thislen considered never opening his mouth, stepping back, letting her take over, but something inside him had shifted. Some new part of him wouldn't let him do that, not anymore.

Besides, what came next was obvious enough.

"I know we're all tired, but there are injured, and there are bodies. Prioritize the living, and get everyone into the Commons. Dawn is coming."

The Nattfolk began to move. Thislen gave a sharp whistle, drawing their attention once more.

"That includes the injured guards. They're Nattfolk now, like the rules say. Someone run down to prepare a cavern that can hold them all."

Two people ran from the edge of the crowd. The rest began to move among the fallen.

Thislen touched the smith's arm, stopping her in her tracks. "Find someone to help you lay out the bodies of the dead soldiers with respect. Here, where the tide can't reach them. They deserve to be buried by their families."

She nodded, turning away and whistling. "Hey, Kellan, come here."

He turned to find Amelie watching him, a bitter smile on her lips.

"What?" Thislen asked.

"I'm sorry you have to wear this yoke, and proud of you at the same time. You know what you're doing."

Thislen scoffed softly, sheathing Ivan's sword. It fit in his scabbard, though it was a little too long to slide all the way home. "I know what you're doing, too. Let's get the bodies of the Nattfolk dead moved. We have to take them below."

"Leave that to me and someone else, you're going to have your hands full." Amelie clasped his shoulder.

He was too tired to argue. He waved her off. "Just ask Rendyn where he wants them, to prepare them for their last rites," he called after her.

His heart ached as he watched the grim faces of the Nattfolk set to work around him. How many of their loved ones were they carrying? How many friends?

Not now, damn it. Focus. There will be time enough to ache for every drop of blood spilled later. Later.

The smith and Kellan laid out the guards, folding their hands and straightening them as much as they could. Their faces were colored with distaste, but Thislen ignored it. He knew, even if the Nattfolk didn't, that the City Guard had been lied to, that they believed killing the Nattfolk would save Astera from the Vaim. There was no point in being cruel to people who only wanted to defend their home, especially not when the Nattfolk did the same thing.

Their bodies would be returned to their families. They would be given their last rites and tied to their Ancestors.

Thislen stopped to help here and there, clasping hands and asking what people needed, filling in where there weren't enough hands. As he worked, he waved someone over to collect every weapon they could find, and another to salvage all the arrows. It unsettled him, how every command made someone else move. His orders might be sound, but many of the Nattfolk were older than he was, and *all* of them had been Nattfolk longer.

There was a comfort, he supposed, in people knowing what to do, in relying on someone else to give the orders. It was a comfort he'd taken, once, in Mila.

"Thislen!"

He lifted his head. Through the industrious crowd, Darran, Aften, and Tamsa hurried to reach him.

"Where are—" he began.

"Mila is with the injured. She's fine, just exhausted," Tamsa said quickly. "Trevon is staying with her and helping prepare the injured to go below."

Trevon is with Mila. A knot of tension eased in his shoulders. The pair had been growing close. It was good that he was with her. *I need to go see them. I need to tell her about Ivan. I need to tell Evelie. How many others were lost to the waves? I don't remember, I don't think I saw them all.*

He pushed the thoughts down, clenching his hand into a fist. One thing at a time. They had to disappear with the dawn.

"Are all of you alright? Can you help with all this?"

"We're fine," Aften said with a weak smile. He was covered in so much blood that his entire front was stained red. "A lot of people were taken to Olen and Ami earlier, most of the injured are already gone."

"That's good." Thislen focused on Aften for a moment. Something had changed, but he couldn't put his finger on what.

I wonder if it's for the better. Can anything 'better' come out of something like this?

"That's not what's important right now," Darran said, cutting through his thoughts.

"They said Soren Bestant is dead." Tamsa shifted her weight from foot to foot.

"What?" Thislen passed a hand over his eyes. Everything was coming at him so quick it felt like he was standing on sand. "How did it happen?"

"No, let me talk," Darran said, cutting Tamsa off when she opened her mouth. "Thislen, what's important right now is the torches."

"The torches?" Tamsa echoed, a hint of her old scoff in her voice.

"Hey, look," Ulan shouted, pointing. "What are the ships doing?"

Thislen turned back to the sea, staring at the ink black shadows looming in the dark blue sky. He hoped there would be no more surprises tonight, but here was another one. The steady gleam of lanterns on the ships and in the cabins was accompanied by something new.

Flickering lights winked like so many fireflies, the glow of their light red. Every single one was a signal lantern, spelling out their questions in fire.

Who are you?
Who is there?
What is happening?
Are you alive?
Who are you?
What happened?
Friend or foe?
Where are the Vaim?

Who are you?

Thislen learned the flickering code long ago from a sailor that was a friend of his father's, each letter slowly surfacing in his mind as he read the messages, his eyes wide.

"The torches," he murmured, turning to look at the ring of golden light that lit up the shipyard like a beacon. "Someone put out the torches!"

A few empty hands scurried to start dousing the torches by simply throwing them into the sea, snuffing them with a sizzle and a cloud of steam.

As the light faded, the Nattfolk became shadows once more, but he knew it was too late. The entire battle, the Nattfolk and the soldiers were visible, shapes that moved in the light. Shapes of people, living people, on the island.

At night.

Even if they were indistinct at the distance the ships were from the shore, it would have been clear they weren't the Vaim. Some of the ship captains no doubt had spyglasses and knew more than the others.

"They know we're here?" Tamsa asked numbly, scanning the winking signal lanterns.

"All of Astera will know we're here by dawn." Thislen squared his shoulders, standing at the edge of the water.

"What do we do?" Her voice wavered. Her family had kept the secret of the Nattfolk for hundreds of years. She, herself, lied to protect it and got herself, Aften, and Thislen hurt for the trouble. Now all that effort meant nothing.

Thislen watched the messages, many of them repeating, as they shone across the water. His mind raced.

If we leave things as they are, people might try to stay on the island at night. Not all of them will die, but how many will? If we vanish into the dark, they'll look for us. If Avasten and the Ruling Council get to them first, we'll become foxes in a game of Hunters and Hounds. No matter which side wins, we will lose.

"Commander?" Amelie asked behind him.

The red lanterns began to glow on other ships, their light winking, asking what was happening. Thislen watched the story race from deck to deck.

Amelie cleared her throat. "Commander?" she repeated.

Commander. That's me. He turned to look at her, taking a deep breath. *This is my decision. I can't let the Solfolk come ashore. I can't let them get hurt. I can't let the Nattfolk lose any more.*

"Get every one of our people underground," he instructed her. "Quick as you can."

This isn't just about Solfolk and Nattfolk, not anymore. This is going to change the entire island. This is going to affect Asterans, one and all.

There are no more secrets.

Thislen pushed his shoulders back and lifted his chin. No more secrets.

"Someone bring me a signal lantern."

Acknowledgements

The process of this book was a long one. I got the rights back for the series, and this book wasn't ready to go. I got the edits done on my own and that took a long time, because I have a thing about quality control. I couldn't let it go into the world until it was up to my exacting standards. So it's been almost two years since I turned this draft in, and now here it is.

Some thanks goes to the people who have supported me from the start, including Sean Hillman, who helped me with edits and encouragement. To Venessa who cheered me on through the last few hurdles. To Joze Groselj, the most amazing cover artist, and Amphi the premier typography goddess. To Milton Brown, who was so exited to read this book he asked for it long before it was ready to read, and agreed to blurb it. And then loved it!

And to my readers, with whom this book would not be possible. But I'm not just saying that. I know you, I see you, and every time you show me you care, I remember you even more. So, to Stina, Josh, Iona, Milton, Carter, Sarah Sover, Priyah, my Nana, Kevin, Sam P., and others of course. My readers are a huge part of why I got over the hurdles and got this book ready and released. I hope you loved this one just as much as the one before.

This book has been a huge test of willpower, with a lot of political upheval in the real world reflecting a lot of political upheval in my own work. I had never written a book two before now, and I never realized how much I would need to learn about my own characters in order to show you more change, more growth, more amazing character driven story. This one doesn't have a cliff-hanger at the end! Well, not as much of one. I can't wait to write book three.

Really, though, just...thank you, from the bottom of my heart.

About the author

October K Santerelli is the imaginative author behind the Nightfall series and The Book of the Witch's Son. He has not yet been torn apart by dark spirits in the night, but hey, anything can happen. Frequently using humor to cope with writing biographies, October works on both fantasy novels and comic scripts. His other works include Storm's Eye, an Out of Time novel with David Brin, the short story Mi Jaculpo, and the novella series of Book of the Witch's Son. For more information, visit octoberksanterelli.com.

ALSO BY OCTOBER K SANTERELLI
City of Day
City of Night
City of Death (Coming Soon)

The Book of the Witch's Son
Glimmers in the Night
Under the Hill
Doors of Glass
Return to River Tor

The Fractal Heavens Series:
The Burden of Water (Coming Soon)

Primoral Descent (Coming Soon)

Storm's Eye, an Out of Time novel